822

THE RED DEATH

The Foreign Secretary cleared his throat and brushed the few remaining stray hairs back on his scalp. "As you know, we have colour-coded the various situations. Condition Black indicates that there is no information emerging from a country at all; it may therefore be assumed that all communication has broken down. Condition Red indicates that the Red Death is known to be rampant in a country, but that governmental authority is being maintained. Condition Purple means that not only is the disease rampant, but that governmental authority is breaking down, or has already done so. Condition Yellow means that cases of the disease have been reported, but it has not yet reached epidemic proportions. Condition Green means disease free. Now . . . " he indicated the huge world map which was at that moment being unrolled and pinned into place against the wall by two of his secretaries. Every head turned to see the situation.

"You will observe," the Foreign Secretary continued, "that the trend really is rather disturbing, not to say alarming."

About the author

Max Marlow is the author of HER NAME WILL
BE FAITH. His third novel, MELTDOWN, will be
published in hardback by New English Library in
1991.

The Red Death

Max Marlow

NEW ENGLISH LIBRARY
Hodder and Stoughton

Printed and bound in Great Britain
for Hodder and Stoughton Paper-
backs, a division of Hodder and
Stoughton Ltd., Mill Road, Dunton
Green, Sevenoaks, Kent, TN13 2YA.
(Editorial Office: 47 Bedford
Square, London WC1B 3DP) by
Richard Clays Ltd., St. Ives plc.
Photoset by Chippendale Type Ltd.,
Otley, West Yorkshire.

British Library C.I.P.

Marlow, Max
  The red death.
  I. Title
  823'.914[F]

ISBN 0–450–53716–1

THE RED DEATH

Contents

Characters

THE CANNINGS

Peter, Parliamentary Private Secretary to the Minister of Health
John, his father
Veronica, his mother
Claudia Briggs, his elder sister
Hartley Briggs, Claudia's husband
Sarah Lawton, Peter's younger sister
Douglas Lawton, her husband
Gladstone, Peter's cat
Anna Papagopoulos, Peter's mistress
Grant and Julia Appleton, his friends

THE RESEARCH TEAM

Margaret Calhoun (Meg), Research Doctor with the Koch Center
Graham Fitzroy, Head Research Doctor at the Center
Helen, Meg Calhoun's secretary
Hal, Fitzroy's assistant
Eddie Brent, ditto

THE MUSEUM TEAM

Tom Lintell, Professor of Palaeontology at New York Museum
Amanda Fitzroy, his secretary (Graham Fitzroy's daughter)

Charlie Oswiecki, Lintell's assistant
Al Brothers, ditto
Ira Schwartz, Director of the Museum

IN THE ANTARCTIC

Captain McGann, US Navy pilot
John Outram, Head Scientist at the Anvers Base
Colonel Burn, Military Commander, Anvers Base
Lieutenant Rodriguez, helicopter pilot at Anvers

ON ISLA HOSTE

Pepe Sanchez, fisherman
Encarna, his wife
Pedro, Miguel, Angelica, Pepito, four of his children
Señor Herrera (Abuelo), Encarna's father
Señora Herrera (Abuelita), her mother
Vicente Herrera, her brother, a policeman
Isabella, his wife
Salvador Lopez, Pepe Sanchez's friend
Maria, his wife
Father Garcia, a priest
Carlos Morena
Pablo Cardona, the mayor
Juanita, his wife
Jesus, his son

THE CABINET

The Prime Minister
The Home Secretary (Harry)
The Minister of Health, Jeremy Payne
Ann, his wife
The Chancellor, Robert Duncan
The Foreign Secretary (Charles)
The Minister of Energy (Anthony)

Characters

The Minister of Agriculture (Martin)

THE OPPOSITION

Toby Anstruther, Opposition Leader
Colin Brereton, Opposition spokesman on health
Janet, his wife
Blundell, Opposition backbencher

IN THE CAMPER

Rod, a student
Sally Ann Calhoun, ditto, Meg Calhoun's cousin and
god-daughter
Dermott, ditto
Carlie, ditto
Meryl, ditto

NEW ZEALAND HEALTH OFFICERS

Waters
Dr Musgrove
Dr Hornby
Superintendent Martell
Dr Lambert
Mr Makinson

IN CALIFORNIA

Aunt Nan, Meg Calhoun's aunt, Sally Ann's mother
Fred Rensick, California Department of Health
Joey Martinez, Meg's tennis partner
Bill and Mary Oakes, Meg's tennis opponents

IN CORNWALL

John and Betty Pengelley, Peter Canning's gardener and
housekeeper

Clive Wardle, publican
Stephanie, his wife
Fran (Frances), their daughter
Farmer Poldarren
Mr Perry, a pensioner
Mavis Tregarthen
Mr Roberts, a newsagent
Arthur Jones, Medical Officer of Health, Ridding and District
Alice Jones, his wife

IN PERU

Enrique Vita, Peruvian Health Minister
Collins, secretary at the British Embassy

CREW OF *OCEAN SECRETS*

Jim Dawson, captain
Harry Grosvenor, mate
Benetti, steward
Olsen, cook
Logan, wireless operator
McClintock, boatswain
Martinsen
Schmitt
Jonssen
De Sousa
Brown
Brent
Espinola
Harrison

IN SOUTH AFRICA

Jan Geller, a financier
Thomas, his 'boy'

Charlie
Billy
Paul

CREW OF *EASY GIRL*

Brian Munro
Tom Clarke
David Kitson

OTHERS

Captain John Plant, US Navy
Leiningen, US Assistant Secretary of State
Jennie, a call-girl
Dr Ashwari, doctor in charge at Sydney Street Hospital

'Thou shalt not be afraid for any terror by night: nor for
the arrow that flieth by day;
For the pestilence that walketh in darkness: nor for the
sickness that destroyeth in the noon-day.
A thousand shall fall beside thee, and ten thousand at
thy right hand: but it shall not come nigh thee.'

THE BOOK OF COMMON PRAYER
Psalms, xci: 5–7

PROLOGUE

Antarctic Discovery

The huge American aircraft dropped through the clouds, and the pilot pointed. "There it is, Professor."

For the approach to the station Tom Lintell had been given the co-pilot's seat. He had also been provided with a pair of snow goggles, but these he now lifted to peer through the perspex at the approaching land. If it was land. Beneath the jet the sea was a mass of ice floes; in front of them glowed nothing but unbroken ice for as far as the eye could see, slowly rising to considerable peaks in the distance.

"That's the Eternity Range," Captain McGann explained. "Antarctica is composed of names like that. The place kinda makes you think of eternity, I reckon."

"Yes," Lintell agreed. A big, bluff, normally hearty man, even he was awed by what he saw; he had never been to Antarctica before.

"Now this is high summer," McGann told him. "So there's some blue down there. Come June and it'll be sheet ice. This is the time of year the growlers break off and drift out into the oceans."

A fierce gust of wind buffeted the plane and McGann took her off autopilot.

"Do you get many storms?" Lintell asked. It might not be absolutely freezing below him, but the thought of coming down in the midst of those ice floes was paralysing.

"Not this time of year. In the winter it can be hell. You thinking about the wind, Professor? Heck, this wind never drops much below 40 knots. That's good weather. In the winter . . . we've recorded mean strengths of well over 100 knots, and when that is below freezing, you'd better look out."

"I can imagine," Lintell agreed. "Where's the base?"

"Not far now." McGann pointed down to his left. "We've just passed Bellingshausen Station. That's the Soviets. On an island called King George, would you believe? They share it with stations belonging to Chile, Brazil, Argentina, China and Poland. The archipelago is called the South Shetlands, and they lie within the British and the Argentinian claims. It's a real United Nations situation down here." He pointed ahead. "The solid piece beyond, the Antarctic Peninsula, is called Graham Land at this end, and Palmer Land further on. It all goes according to who first saw it, I guess. The Argentines say it belongs to them, and the British say it belongs to them. But we're all friends at the moment."

Lintell was relieved to hear that. The aircraft had taken off from Stanley Airport in the Falklands that morning, and down here those islands were probably known as the Malvinas.

"Where would the Larsen Ice Shelf be?" he asked, trying to keep the excitement out of his voice.

"On the other side of Graham Land, tucked in under the Eternity Range."

"Is it a long way from the base?"

"On foot. But we have choppers at the station."

Another relief. But he knew he would not really have minded if he had to hump a pack over the ice.

Tom Lintell was Professor of Palaeontology at the New York Museum of Natural History, and laid claim to being the world's leading expert on fossil remains; he was not a modest man, indeed, he was proud to have got so far so young – he was forty-five – and of the work he had put into his chosen profession, the mastery he had achieved over it. He was a Californian, had done much of his early studying on the West Coast and only moved to the New York museum three years ago.

And now he was about to set the seal on his career. Maybe. Outram's wire was burned into his brain; he had no need to refer to it: "SUGGEST MUSEUM INVESTIGATE LARGE SHADOW LOCATED EMBEDDED LARSEN ICE SHELF STOP NOT LESS THAN THIRTY FEET LONG STOP READINGS INDICATE ONCE ANIMAL STOP INSTRUCT."

He had wired back to touch nothing until he got there. And now he was there, almost.

Not less than thirty feet long. Embedded in the ice. And of animal origin. Of course he had no guarantee the thing down there would be in any recognisable condition; everything would depend on when it went into the ice. But a man could dream. Only two large prehistoric creatures had ever been recovered, intact, from the Ice Age. Both had been mammoths, and both had been in Siberia, one in 1907, the other more recently. He doubted this would be a mammoth. But it could be almost anything; he refused to let himself anticipate. He just wanted to see for himself, as rapidly as possible.

McGann pointed. "Anvers Island. You can see the Station."

Lintell went aft into the body of the plane, where his team waited. They had been assembled hastily, and were only a skeleton of the staff he would need if there was something to be taken out. Charlie Oswiecki, plump and cheerful, of course, and Al Brothers, quite the reverse: they were known as Ollie and Stan. And Amanda. Lintell went nowhere without Amanda Fitzroy. She was more than his secretary; she was also the daughter of one of his oldest friends, Graham Fitzroy of the Robert Koch Research Center in California. Fitzroy, several years the older, and the world's leading bacteriologist, had been of great help to the Museum in identifying various little-known bacteria which cropped up from time to time – some bacteria could live for centuries – and it had seemed natural for Lintell to give employment to his friend's only daughter. He had never regretted it; Amanda was a treasure. Tall and thin and somewhat angular, she was totally dedicated to her work, and possessed a memory like a computer.

"We'll be landing in a little while," he told them.

Oswiecki squinted through the window at the sun, still high in the sky. "I guess this is one of those places where the sun never sets this time of year," he remarked.

"This time of year," Lintell agreed. "That doesn't mean it isn't going to be cold."

But it was surprisingly warm, as they stepped from the aircraft on to the runway of the airstrip at Palmer Research Station on Anvers Island. Wrapped up as they were in fur-lined jackets, they looked at each other in surprise.

"Just over 50° Fahrenheit," McGann told them.

"Doesn't the ice melt?" Amanda asked.

"Some. But not enough to notice, as a rule. And it all comes back again in winter."

"Professor Lintell." John Outram was a short, stocky man. As head of the Research Station he was, in his own field, as famous a scientist as Lintell, but they had only met twice previously, and did not know each other well. "Welcome to Palmer."

"I'm glad to be here," Lintell shook hands.

"Meet Colonel Burn," Outram indicated the officer standing next to him.

Lintell introduced his staff in turn.

"You have arrived just in time for dinner," Outram said. "Come along to the mess."

"Dinner," Oswiecki remarked. "In broad daylight!"

Amanda was more interested in the little penguins, gentoos and chinstraps, which had scuttled from the runway to throw themselves into the water as the aircraft came down, but were now re-emerging with a great deal of chatter. Above them another disturbed Antarctic creature, the giant petrel, wheeled slowly in the lonely sky. Amanda shivered. The Station, much larger than she had imagined, was a small township of single-storeyed prefabricated buildings. There were more people about than she had expected, too. And the buildings were furnished most comfortably, while a huge satellite dish obviously provided television wherever it was required.

"All mod cons down here," Colonel Burn told her.

But it was still the very end of the earth.

"Dinner," Lintell said with satisfaction as they entered the mess. "I could eat a horse."

"You'll have to put up with New York strip steaks, instead," Outram told him.

"You guys really have it sorted out," Lintell laughed. "Now, when are you going to tell me about this creature?"

After the meal, Outram took Lintell and Amanda along to the laboratory, and showed them the photographs obtained by drilling through the ice and sending down a micro camera. Some small samples had also been obtained and carefully thawed out.

"We had to be careful, of course," he explained. "Because whatever it is has been frozen for a considerable time and could just break apart if we drilled in the wrong place or too vigorously. But that is definitely fur."

Lintell nodded, peering at the brown wisp. The prints were disappointing; they could well have been revealing the shadow of the aircraft which had taken them, and he was not sufficiently expert at aerial photography even to

21

determine the size of the shadow. But as Outram said, this was definitely fur. And unlike any fur he had ever seen. He did not want to speak until he had got his excitement under control.

"So what do you reckon it is?" Outram asked. "A mammoth?"

Lintell shook his head. "Not down here."

"Cave bear?"

"No cave bear ever measured thirty feet. You sure about that figure, John?"

"Nope. That's a rough estimate. It could be larger."

"Yeah," Lintell said, hopefully.

"I reckon you do have an idea," Outram said.

"Yeah," Lintell agreed again. "If I'm right, it could be the find of the century."

"So?"

Lintell peered at the fur again, and then at the photographs. "I go for a megatherium."

"That means a great beast in Greek, doesn't it? Well, I'd say you're giving yourself a lot of room to manoeuvre. Any thirty-foot long creature would have to be called a monster."

Lintell grinned without taking offence. "Megatherium means great beast, sure. But it is also the name specifically applied to the prehistoric giant sloth."

"A sloth?" Outram was incredulous.

"Sure, but this character was a real biggee. It was as big as one of our elephants, on all fours . . . and it could stand on its hind legs as well."

"Must have been some prospect. And it used to live around here?"

"That's right. The first skeleton of a megatherium was found in the pampas of Argentina, quite close to Buenos Aires, in 1789. Argentina was Spanish then, of course, and the bones were sent to Madrid for study, by Joseph Garriga. Garriga worked on them for several years, virtually reconstructed the animal, and was then robbed of all the credit. He rather stupidly lent his notes – which included a sketch of what the creature must have looked like from the bone structure – to a Frenchman, the Governor of San Domingo, and the Governor sent them to the Academy of Science in Paris. Thus Georges Cuvier got hold of them, and he published a paper on the beast, in 1795, in which he called it *Megatherium americanum*, or the great beast of America, if you like, a full year before poor old Garriga had managed to reconstruct his notes and get them published. It was coups like that got Cuvier his reputation as the father of palaeontology."

"Say, you guys were poaching even then," Outram grinned.

"And the devil take the hindmost," Lintell agreed. "The truly amazing thing, to my mind, is that all this work was being carried out right through the French Revolution. Kind of restores your faith in human nature. Anyway, the skeleton was dated something more than 60 million years ago. That was before the Ice Age, of course, and at a time when, according to the Gondwanaland theory, the continents were actually drifting apart from one great solid land mass, Antarctica and South America could well have been joined. Several more skeletons have been found in South America, and also, from a later date, in North America. That suggests they moved north as the ice cap spread."

"What kind of time span are we talking about?"

"Well, as I said, the giant sloths appeared about 65 million years ago."

"Isn't that dinosaur time?"

"Not quite. The dinosaurs became extinct about 100 million years ago. Mind you, the same kind of radiation problems that probably killed the dinosaurs could have developed the megatherium. The point is that we know the sloths were still in this part of the world when the Pleistocene began, about two and a half million years ago. It was then they began spreading north. But of course not all of them did that; the Pleistocene developed slowly. Down to quite recently, for instance – we're talking about not more than 200,000 years – Antarctica was a warm and fertile continent."

"Sure," Outram agreed. "We've been turning up evidence of that all over the place."

"Just the sort of country the sloths liked best. They weren't any quicker, at either thinking or moving, than their descendants are today. There was nothing a giant sloth liked better than to spend the day browsing, eating leaves, knocking over the occasional tree."

"But when the ice started forming they left?"

"Well, some of them did. As I said, the ice cap formed slowly. It wasn't until about 100,000 years ago that the Ice Age really began. If a group of these sloths got trapped down here when the Drake Passage opened up, they'd have had to sit it out."

"And get frozen in the ice. Wheee! I hope he's intact."

"So do I," Lintell said. "By God, so do I," he confessed to Amanda as they went to the house allotted to the visitors.

"But Tom," Amanda said. "The largest skeleton of a megatherium ever found only indicates a length of 24 feet. According to Professor Outram, that thing is at least 30 feet."

"Yeah," Lintell agreed. "Why do you suppose I'm busting a gut to get at it?"

"How the hell are we supposed to sleep in broad daylight?" Oswiecki wanted to know. "How the Prof does it bugs me."

Lintell and Brothers had retired. But Amanda was also sitting up, behind the screens on the porch – there were an amazing number of insects about. She was awake through excitement, not because of the light.

"Say, Mandy, what'd'ya think is down there, really?"

"I go along with the boss."

"A sloth, thirty feet long. Holy Jumping Jesus. Next thing we'll have rats bigger'n men. That could be nasty."

"There are no rats in Antarctica," Amanda said reassuringly.

"You mean they've never found any. And how the hell did this outsize sloth get here, anyway?"

"He never did get here, Charlie. He probably originated here, when Antarctica was joined up to all the other continents."

Oswiecki brooded for a few minutes. Then he said, "You know something, Mandy? I'm a bone surgeon, not a geologist. You reckon you could explain this Gondwanaland theory to me? The very name sounds like something out of a Japanese horror movie."

"Well," Amanda said cautiously. "Supposing you made a jigsaw of the earth, with a separate piece for each of the present-day continents, and took those pieces out, you'd find that they very nearly fit together, in one solid mass." She saw his scepticism. "Try it with pieces of paper. The Atlantic concave curve of North America fits very neatly over the bulge of north-west Africa, and New England and Nova Scotia fit in over Great Britain and Scandinavia, with Greenland filling in the wedge. Then South America, the bulge of Brazil, if you tilt it slightly to run from north-west to south-east, fits equally well into the southern half of western Africa, from the Gulf of Guinea down, with Tierra del Fuego actually curving round the Cape of Good Hope. Africa and Asia press nicely together, with Madagascar between, and the Indian peninsular tilted round to the west fitting against it. Now that the scientists have really worked out the shape of the Antarctic continent, they find that it fits just about exactly into the coastline of Africa/India. While northern Australia, tilted to the west, would fit perfectly against south-eastern Antarctica.

Once you've done that, you have a super-continent. They call it Pangaea."

"And then they just drifted apart? When was all this supposed to happen?"

"They reckon it began about three hundred million years ago. And it's still happening."

"But it's one of those things no one can ever prove. It's a woolly theory."

"Well, they do have some pretty good circumstantial evidence to offer. Just for an example, the same kind of rocks, both in age and formation, are found in eastern Brazil and West Africa, where they would have been joined. The same goes for a lot of other places. The theory would also explain several other things that we know happened. Like climate. Take Great Britain. The old theory used to be that once upon a time the British climate was tropical, and that because of the earth tilting one way or the other it gradually grew colder. According to the Gondwanaland theory, it wasn't the climate that changed so much as the island itself. Some scientists reckon that five hundred million years ago, Britain was actually situated in the southern hemisphere. Around three hundred million years ago, during what they call the Carboniferous Age, it was perched right on the Equator, hence your tropical climate. Then it moved north. It's still doing it. Right now it's centred around fifty-five degrees north latitude; in another few million years it could be in the Arctic Circle."

"Good luck to the Brits."

"The point is," Amanda went on, "that fifty million years ago, when the process of separating was in full swing, if you like, the experts consider that South America and Antarctica were still joined, right here, where Tierra del Fuego points at the Antarctic Peninsula. The giant sloths appeared some fifteen million years before that, so of course they would have roamed all over Antarctica, and some of them would have been trapped when what is now the Drake Passage became water. They would have remained here for several million years, developing in their own way, distinctly maybe, certainly, it seems, bigger than the sloths which were on the mainland, until the coming of the Ice Age wiped them out."

"It's a theory," Oswiecki said again. "I tell you something, Mandy: they'd better goddamned well leave Brooklyn where it is, because I like to go home every so often." He stood up, smothering a yawn. "I'm for bed."

The next morning a helicopter took them to the site. Even Oswiecki had eventually slept soundly, behind securely closed blinds, and this was a glorious sunny day, although there was still a brisk breeze. They had breakfasted well, and Lintell knew they were all tremendously excited, even though they kept themselves under total control.

They flew south first, over the British Research Station of Port Faraday, some fifty miles further south than Palmer, and thence on over Adelaide Island, which was of considerable size. Here they dropped in at the British Station of Rothera for lunch and to refuel, the pilot having called ahead. Now they could see the peak of Mount Stephenson on Alexander Island, over 9,000 feet high, and to its left the serrated ice-covered undulations of the Eternity Range. That afternoon the helicopter turned east before the range, however, and rose higher and higher to cross the Graham Land peninsula. Now they could see the Kenyon Peninsula to the south, and after half an hour they were descending again.

In front of them stretched a plain of ice. "The Weddell Sea," Lieutenant Rodriguez, their pilot, told them.

"Where is the Ice Shelf?" Lintell peered ahead.

"Right below us now, Professor. It makes a kind of beach, you could say." He grinned, "A hundred miles wide."

"And how far are we from Palmer?" Lintell asked, already calculating future prospects.

"Something more than two hundred miles. That's as the crow flies, of course."

The helicopter dropped lower. The mountains were to their west and south now; beneath them a colony of emperor penguins flapped their wings at the aircraft, almost as if they were waving. "Those guys never leave," Rodriguez said. "The others, the smaller ones, head north when the water starts to freeze up, but the emperors just sit it out. I guess they like to be left alone."

"Dr Outram tells me you're the one that first found the creature," Lintell remarked.

"That's right. Two years ago, almost to the day."

"Two years ago?" Lintell was astonished.

"Sure. Just a shadow. And then it froze up again during the winter. But the fact is, the shelf is diminishing every year. Not by much, maybe a couple of inches. There's that hole, see?"

Lintell nodded. He knew all about the 'hole' in the atmosphere above the south pole, through which the earth's essential carbon dioxide was pouring; there were scientists who claimed that it was caused by various man-made agencies, such as aerosol sprays, and that in time so much more of the sun's heat would penetrate that the polar ice caps might even melt.

"So last year I saw it again, and this time I noted the bearing. This summer it's more clear than ever. I reckon the shelf has gone down by several inches."

"How soon?" Lintell wanted to know.

"We're there," Rodriguez told him, and the helicopter started to hover.

Heart pounding, Lintell looked down. Beneath him the Ice Shelf stretched in every direction; it was solid, but not necessarily flat like a beach – there were hummocks and dips to be seen. He took off his dark glasses, the better to examine the unending white, and frowned. There was definitely a shadow down there. And it did not belong to the helicopter: that was being thrown much further to their west.

"Something," Amanda commented.

"Yeah," Rodriguez agreed. "Well, when I told the boss, he came out here with his people and they bored down and took some readings and photos. Seems it's animal all right."

"Yes, I saw them," Lintell said. "Can you take her round again?"

"Sure." The helicopter made a slow turn, while Lintell peered down at the ice. The adrenalin was racing through his veins. What was down there was enormous. "You wanna go down?" Rodriguez asked.

"Not right now," Lintell decided. He knew he could see better from up here. "I'd like to get back to base. I have some important calls to make."

He got on the radio telephone to Ira Schwartz, the Director. "We have something big," he said. "Could be the find of the century."

"Such as?" Ira was a cautious man.

"Well, it's been down there a long time. Since the beginning of the Ice Age."

"Hell," Ira said. "You're talking about fifty million years. You reckon it's a late dinosaur?"

"Nope," Lintell said. "That would be too much. The last dinosaur was extinct a million years before the First Ice Age. And when you say fifty million years, we know the ice cap started forming fifty million years ago, but it was a slow process. I reckon we're talking about a creature who happened to die just as the Pleistocene really got rough. Say a hundred thousand years ago. I've an idea it's a giant sloth. A megatherium. And an outsize one, bigger than anyone thinks possible right now."

"How're you gonna get at it?"

"They have steam hoses down here. I reckon that's the safest."

"It'll take time."

"It'll be worth it. It's getting the carcass out bothers me."

"What's the hassle about a bag of bones?"

"Ira, there's a chance . . . I won't put it higher than that right this minute . . . but there is a chance that the creature could be intact. If it is, I want to bring it home, intact. We can embalm it and mount it . . . it'll be the biggest attraction in the world. So I'm going to need the largest transport aircraft you can lay hands on."

"Hell, Tommy, you're talking about a fortune."

"It'll be worth it. Every last cent. I'll also need a lot more help. Amanda's standing by with a list of essential personnel and equipment. Most important, I want the sketches and measurements of Garriga's megatherium."

"Yeah," Ira said unhappily. "Okay, put the girl on. As for your plane, I'll start looking. But I'm not hiring anything until you can guarantee me that creature is intact."

"Agreed. And Ira . . . silent as the grave until I've got it up."

"You have got to be joking," Ira said. "You're digging in territory that's claimed by both Argentina and Britain."

"The operative word is claimed," Lintell reminded him. "They don't actually have sovereignty."

"I still have to square it with the State Department and see what their attitude is," Ira said. "I'll keep it as quiet as I can, Tommy. But I can't promise anything."

Lintell gave the mike to Amanda and raised his eyebrows at Outram. "John, we have to move just as fast as we can."

*   *   *

It took a week to ferry the necessary equipment from Palmer to the Ice Shelf, and then set up a camp close by the buried creature. "Say, this thing is melting, isn't it?" Oswiecki remarked, hacking at the ice with his heel; several pieces flaked off.

"It'll happen slowly," Lintell promised.

By then the rest of his team had arrived and he had some thirty scientists and technicians to work with. Outram gave all the help he could from the station as well, and the task of cutting through the ice began. The steam hoses had to be kept going round the clock, together with water pumps to carry away the melted ice – otherwise the permafrost would simply fill their gullies back in again – and the constant noise of the generators shattered the habitual silence of the frozen desert. The emperor penguins departed for quieter regions.

But by now others were interested in what was going on. A Russian helicopter appeared, and next day landed. "There is something below the ice," the pilot suggested. "We have seen it."

Oswiecki spoke Russian. "We think it's a dead whale," he said. "Who may have swallowed one of our people. We want to discover if he's still alive. You guys must've heard of Jonah."

The Russians took off.

"I don't think they believed me," Oswiecki complained.

By now they were fifteen feet below the surface of the ice, having cut a huge gully some fifty feet long by twenty wide, and only four feet from the creature.

The British arrived. "Anything we can do to help?" they asked Lintell, trying not to peer at the immense creature which was now clearly visible.

"Yeah," he said. "Just forget we're here."

The British left.

Two days later they uncovered a huge paw covered in frozen fur, equipped with gigantic claws. "Now here's

31

where we've got to move real careful," Lintell said. He was hardly sleeping now, and had stopped shaving.

The next day the entire side of the beast slowly appeared.

"It is one hell of a size," Brothers said.

Amanda was down in the hole with her tape measure and the plans of the original megatherium. "If he is one," she said, taking the dimensions of the creature's wrist, "he's going to measure forty feet from snout to tail."

"That'll cause a stir," Outram commented. He was also spending nearly all of his time at the 'dig'.

That afternoon they reached the head. "It's our boy," Lintell said, gazing at the bear-like features, the big, blunt teeth, the huge, lolling tongue, the almost indistinguishable ears of a sloth — even if it was the biggest sloth he had ever seen. "You got any champagne, Johnnie?"

"You bet," Outram said. "How are you going to get it out?"

"With difficulty," Lintell agreed.

Ira had the transport aircraft standing by, but of course to attempt to put the heavy plane down on the uneven snow and ice of the shelf would be courting disaster. Somehow the monster had to be transported from where it was embedded to where the plane could reach it.

"Where's the nearest station?" Lintell asked Outram.

"The Argentinians have one just on the other side of those hills." Outram pointed west.

"How far?"

"Oh, 175 miles, maybe."

"Holy Jesus Christ! Okay, Johnnie, can you raise me a real big chopper? Something that'll lift several tons."

Outram nodded. "I get your drift. We sure don't have any cranes down here."

"We'll also need it for transport."

Outram gazed at him. "Dangling? 175 miles, over pretty rugged and hilly country?"

"You got any better ideas?"

Outram scratched his head. "I'll go organise the flight."

"Tom, it's not gonna work," Oswiecki said. "Look at that temperature. 57° F. That critter down there may be frozen stiff right now, but he's gonna start to thaw the moment we bring him up. 175 miles, that's maybe three hours, after we get him strapped up, and before we get him unstrapped at the other end. He's liable to fall apart on you."

"Or have begun such a decomposition process we won't be able to arrest it," Amanda agreed.

"I know that," Lintell agreed. "So what's the answer?"

They gazed at him, and he grinned at them.

"We're going to do our taxidermist bit right here, the moment he comes up. Mandy, get on the radio telephone to New York, and tell Ira what we need. I'll give you a list."

An official from the Argentine Foreign Office arrived next day, in a very large helicopter, because he was accompanied by several army officers, several other officials, a couple of scientists, and half a dozen reporters.

They swarmed all over the site, taking photographs and chattering amongst themselves. The Foreign Office man, Señor Martinez, spoke English, and he, Outram and Lintell had a long talk. Much to the Americans' relief, it appeared that the Argentine Government was raising no objections to the beast being removed to New York; they recognised that they lacked the equipment and the technique to handle such an immense project themselves. But they intended to leave a scientific observer on the spot, and they required full access to all data uncovered or deduced by the American party.

"Seems fair enough," Outram said, and Lintell agreed. The secret was out now, in any event. Two days later, when the necessary gear had been flown in from New York, an enormous US navy transport helicopter had arrived, and they were ready to lift the megatherium out of its 100,000-year-old grave, there were twelve television camera crews and nearly a hundred reporters camped on the ice shelf. Outram had to bring marine guards over from Palmer to keep them at a safe distance.

Then the work of raising the carcass began. In the circumstances it was the most primitive operation with which Lintell had ever been associated, as well as the most dangerous. The possibility he most worried about was that the moment it was lifted the creature would simply break up under its own weight. Thus the channels created by the steam hoses had to be driven beneath the body in several places, and men had to crawl into the tunnels to insert the broad reinforced canvas strips which were attached to the helicopter's cables; other bands were passed round its neck and shoulders and legs, until it was trussed up like Gulliver on the beach at Lilliput.

"Say," Oswiecki remarked. "What happens if this character were to wake up? Talk about King Kong."

"He's been frozen for 100,000 years," Brothers pointed out.

"So. That don't mean he's dead."

"You been reading too much sci-fi," Brothers said.

"Is it possible?" Amanda asked Lintell.

"Theoretically, yes. Practically, no. Anyway, we're not going to hang about to find out. We operate the moment he's out."

The hoses had now cut into the ice for several feet around the creature, and everything was ready. The helicopter hovered above while the cables were attached and checked; its downdraft caused a freezing wind to blast at the technicians. But at last they signalled that everything was ready, and the helicopter started to rise. Amanda held Lintell's hand, tightly. Ice spurted as the cables took the strain, and the television cameras whirred. For several nerve-racking minutes nothing happened, while the steam hoses continued to spray the ice under the beast until the frozen monster was finally free to move upwards.

The spectators applauded, and Amanda kissed Lintell. "This," he reminded her, "is only the beginning."

The helicopter was moving the creature only a matter of a few hundred yards to the canvas-walled enclosure Lintell had had erected, over which a canvas roof would be stretched before he commenced the autopsy and the embalming process, but it was still a nerve-racking ten minutes as with the constant breeze the megatherium swayed back and forth, and controlling it was extremely difficult even for an expert. The thought of the 175-mile journey to the General San Martin Station, at considerably higher altitudes, was paralysing. Which made haste all the more imperative; it was already February, and the bad weather associated with an Antarctic autumn could be upon them at any time. Thus the moment the carcass was safely in the 'operating theatre', Lintell got to work, prepared, like his team, to continue until the task was finished. Before they could even start the sloth's fur was beginning to thaw in the unusually high temperatures, but it was necessary again to use hot water before they could open the creature up.

Then for twenty-four hours the work was simply blood and guts. Lintell had toyed with the idea of actually embalming the creature. The simplest and quickest way of doing this was to use what is called the arterial method. By this all the blood would be drawn out of the subject's veins and arteries and replaced by a solution based on formalin. Then, using a hollow needle called a tracor, the body fluids would also be drawn off and replaced by formalin, mixed with alcohol and various other embalming fluids. The body would thus remain in a state of perfect preservation for up to three months, at which time the process would have to be repeated, and again at three-monthly intervals for as long as required; Lintell reflected that this had been done to Lenin's corpse now for nearly three-quarters of a century. But long before the beast's heart and all its blood thawed sufficiently to be drawn off, the skin and outer flesh would start decomposing. That method would be impossible.

The megatherium was going to be mounted and exhibited in his museum; he was determined on that. He also wanted to get at its insides; the wealth of information which might be yielded, not only by the contents of the stomach but by analysis of the brain and circulatory systems, was almost beyond the powers of his imagination to envisage. He had thus decided to use a more primitive but hopefully successful method. Hence his need for a vast additional amount of equipment, which had now arrived.

The beast was thawed out as rapidly as possible by blowing hot air on it, while the careful opening of the stomach cavity proceeded. The team worked steadily, almost without a break, until at last Tom was able to begin the postmortem.

"This guy sure has a massive gut," Oswiecki commented some hours later. "Say, I reckon he was constipated."

"Was he really just frozen, Prof?" Brothers asked.

Having made a preliminary examination of the heart and the blood vessels around it, Lintell was working in the cavity the team had cut for him in the skull, studying the brain. "He's not going to wake up, if that's what's bothering you," he told them. "He was dead before he was frozen. He died of a stroke."

"Well, hell, I didn't know sloths got high blood pressure."

"This one did," Lintell pointed out. "It's odd, really; he certainly wasn't old; those teeth are in perfect condition. And the arterial walls look healthy enough. I mean the tissue is in good shape. Yet several arteries in the brain seem to have just collapsed."

"I guess you could say he had a rush of blood to the head," Oswiecki quipped.

"Poor old sloth," Amanda commented. "Maybe he was just terrified by something."

"Well, hell, Mandy, wouldn't you be if you saw nothing but ice coming at you?"

It took two days to complete the dissection and embalming. Lintell began as in the normal procedure and carefully drained off the melted blood; needless to say Oswiecki was soon complaining about the amount the creature had: 120 pints.

Lintell now reverted to the method used by the ancient Egyptians, amongst others, and removed all the internal organs, as well as the brain. He then filled the body cavity with plastic – the Egyptians had used a mixture of myrrh and other aromatic spices, or simply Oil of Cedar for the less well-off – while the body was arranged in such a way that it would be standing on its hind legs and reaching up into a tree when on display; the plastic would maintain it thus as it hardened, holding the bone structure in place. Every step was carefully photographed by Oswiecki and tabulated by Amanda.

While this was going on Lintell's technicians had been assembling a vast container; it resembled an inverted frame-tent, a thick plastic sack suspended within a metal frame. This was lined with fibreglass, and then filled with potassium nitrate, known as nitre, before the helicopter lifted the carcass from the enclosure and placed it in the sack – the nitre preventing any risk of decomposition of the skin and fur – and the top layer of fibreglass added before the huge bag was sealed. The seals would remain untouched for seventy days to complete the process, at the end of which time the megatherium should be preserved forever. Eventually, when it was opened up in New York, Tom would treat the fur with various chemicals to restore its original lustre.

He was able to spare the time for only a cursory examination of the various organs he had removed as by now the transport aircraft had arrived at General San Martin Base. Also, it was late February, and already the winds were becoming stronger, while the temperature was noticeably dropping. Time to get moving.

"Say, Prof, how much of this stuff you aim to take out?" Oswiecki inquired, surveying the huge mound of remains. "I have to say we don't have enough formaldehyde for everything. That goddamned small intestine is about a hundred yards long. And it's beginning to go."

Lintell considered. There was really far more viscous material than he could ever use or would need. "Choose the best bits," he decided. "All parts of the stomach with anything in them, and the heart, lungs and brain."

"And what about this blood? 120 pints."

"Bring 20."

"What about the rest? We can't just leave it here."

"I think it should have a decent burial."

"Burial?" Oswiecki thumped the ground with his boot. "Say, Dr Outram, what do you guys do with your waste?"

"It's hardly a problem in the winter," Outram said. "We just stack it. Then when the thaw comes, we dump it in the sea. If it's organic, mind. We don't want to go poisoning any fishes, or filling them up with plastics."

He frowned at Oswiecki's collection of remains – assembled in plastic bags.

"Well, I reckon you can't get more organic than this lot," Oswiecki said. "How about if I were to borrow one of your helicopters and take it out to sea, and empty it? I'll bring the bags back."

"That sounds all right to me."

"I'll bet the fishes will reckon they're having the feast of a lifetime; it can't be every day they have 100,000-year-old megatherium for breakfast." He went off to find Lieutenant Rodriguez.

Now began the most difficult part of the entire operation, transporting the creature across the hills to the Station. The helicopter hovered overhead while the cables and slings were attached to it. The audience of scientists and technicians waited, holding their breaths, as the pilot and ground crew shouted into their radios, manoeuvred controls, adjusted strapping and towed away supports. And very, very slowly the container left the ground, gradually rising higher and higher into the air, followed by a general sigh of relief.

Lintell and Amanda climbed into another large chopper with all their bottles and jars of remains; Brothers was in a smaller one flying beside the container, watching for any sign of a break in the ropes. But all went well, although Lintell thought he was going to have a stroke himself as they crossed the hills at a height of 2,000 feet, watching the huge dark shape half a mile away, swaying to and fro above the endless white wastelands.

Putting it down at San Martin was another problem, but the helicopter pilots were superb, and the sloth was lowered gently to the waiting, wheeled platform on which it could be rolled up the ramp into the transport plane. At last, amidst sighs of relief from the crews and scientists, and cheers from the eager newsmen, the slings were released.

Then Lintell could have a shave and a hot bath, and face the television cameras.

"Would you say this is an important find, Professor Lintell?"

"One of the most important scientific discoveries there has ever been," Lintell told them.

"It's going to be a great museum piece. That we can understand. For scientists, such as yourself, for anthropologists and zoologists, it must be fantastic; but does the discovery of something like this have any direct bearing on the lives of ordinary people, today, Professor? Can it? You say the creature has been dead a hundred thousand years."

"We have taken considerable samples of the sloth's internal organs, brains, and blood," Lintell explained. "And these will be subjected to careful analysis. Not only would we hope to learn a great deal about how the creatures of that period lived and ate, but what ailments they were subject to, and in particular, what kind of germs there were in the world at that time; we may be able to relate to some of the microbes which are still about today. This could have important effects on our knowledge and treatment of some of the diseases with which we are still afflicted."

"You say the creature died of apoplexy?"

"That is correct. It suffered a massive cerebral haemorrhage."

"Do animals, apart from man, usually die from this cause?"

"The human-related animals, such as gorillas and chimpanzees, certainly do so, because they are as highly strung as man. In the lower orders of animals it is rare, and in a creature as laid-back as a sloth it is surprising. But this is one of the things that we shall be looking at when we get the megatherium back to New York."

"What exactly is apoplexy, Professor? It's what the layman calls a stroke, right?"

Lintell nodded. "In most cases it is caused, as I'm sure you know, by a weakening of the cerebral blood vessels. This is a natural concomitant of age."

"So this was an old sloth."

"As a matter of fact, no," Lintell confessed. "The condition of its teeth suggests that it was a relatively young animal. A cerebral haemorrhage can also be brought about by high blood pressure, of course. What we call hypertension. As to why a creature like a sloth should have suffered from hypertension, that too will have to await our detailed analysis of its blood and internal organs. Again, what we discover may well be of inestimable value to medicine."

"One last question, Professor Lintell. Are you a happy man right this minute?"

"I," Lintell said, "have got to be the happiest man in the world, right this minute. And when I unpack that little baby in New York, let me tell you, I am going to be the proudest man in the world as well."

The helicopter droned low over the sea. There were more ice floes down there than Oswiecki remembered from when they had come down, two months before.

"When do you reckon it'll be frozen over?" he asked Lieutenant Rodriguez.

"Another few weeks."

"What happens to the fish?"

"They live underneath the ice. There are some varieties which move north looking for warmth, because they're following the plankton."

"Say, what kind of fish do you get down here, anyway?" Oswiecki was preparing his bags for emptying as they approached a relatively open area of sea. "I like to know whom I'm feeding."

"Hard to say who'll have first crack," Rodriguez said. "It's a chain, see, just like humans, you know. Cows eat grass, humans eat cows. The fish chain begins with

41

the plankton. All fishes eat plankton. But I don't reckon plankton will go for this lot. It just depends on what happens to be down there, right this minute."

Oswiecki unfastened the neck of the first bag. "Christ, it stinks. Any time."

The helicopter was hovering fifty feet above the water, waves swelling up almost seeming to touch the runners as the crewmen opened the door. Oswiecki began to empty his bags. "Let's hope something enjoys it," he said.

Pepe Sanchez fumbled at the neck of the thick woollen jersey under his coat, pulling the zip up to his chin with some difficulty – fingers numb with cold. Back turned to the icy Antarctic wind that whistled down the steep hillside into the bahía and out across the Seno Ano Nuevo, he wondered why, in the name of Santo Pedro, he had stayed in this God-forsaken place less than a hundred miles north of the Cabo de Horno. He muttered curses on the heads of Encarna's parents, in whose house they still lived, together with their children and with Encarna's brother Vicente and his family. He had desperately tried to persuade Encarna to leave Isla Hoste to live in Punta Arenas: there would be warmth in the houses and life in the town and around the port, and he would be able to give up this goddamned fishing; there would be plenty of work in the meat canneries or on the docks where Chilean mutton and bales of wool were loaded for export. He had seen it all when he journeyed up through the Cockburn Channel with his father when still a teenager, into the Estrecho Mallaganes . . . But Encarna had argued that the offer of rooms in her father's house was too good to refuse. And, anyway, she was pregnant when they married and wanted to be with her mother when the baby was born. So they stayed, and stayed. But now that the children were grown up – why, young Miguel was sixteen already – there was no need for them to remain here any longer. Of course he would not be able to discuss it with Encarna, she would only start arguing again. No, the best thing would be for him to go up to Punta Arenas alone, find a place for them and some work, then come back and tell her it was all fixed. Then she could not argue.

Pebbles crunched under his feet as he walked down to the stone jetty, heavy green nylon net over his shoulder. He threw the net into the boat and paused, looking back at the grey stone village, cowering beneath jutting rocks. It was a barren land, not a tree in sight, only a few thorny bushes and a handful of weeds showing any life at all. Yes, that was what he would do, he would go with Salvador in his supply boat when he went up to replace the drums of oil and gas cylinders.

Pepe stepped down over the net and lowered the outboard over the transom, knees flexing to the roll of the fibreglass hull. The water was rough again today, even here in the bay. That meant he would only get a few small fish. He cursed again. Small fish with hundreds of small bones. He longed for a good feed of bacalao: big chunks of succulent flesh and hardly a bone in it. He would get one to bring back from Punta Arenas; that would sweeten Encarna's temper.

Pepe was smiling as the engine coughed into life. He released the painter and pushed the boat clear of the wall.

1

A Friday in May

Friday afternoons were usually a somnolent time in the House of Commons. The majority of members had already left for their constituencies or their week-end cottages, those who remained had no intention of staying very late. The Government was not strongly represented as there could be no risk of an important division.

Yet for the very reason that guards were down, the Opposition could use these dying hours of the week's parliamentary business to score important points.

"I tabled this question over a week ago," remarked Blundell from the back bench. "The Right Honourable Minister knew of it, and promised me a full reply. And now we discover that my Right Honourable friend is not even in the House. I find such discourtesy typical of this Government, and its approach to the affairs of our country."

All eyes focused on the Government front bench. There was in fact only one Cabinet Minister present, the Home Secretary, and he clearly had no intention of getting up.

"Your baby, Peter," he muttered to the man sitting beside him.

Peter Canning sighed and rose to his feet. "It is my regrettable duty to inform the House that the Right Honourable the Minister for Health is indisposed."

"Has he got it then?" someone shouted from the other side.

Peter Canning located the heckler and gazed at him. He had a formidable gaze. He indeed presented a formidable figure. Only thirty-six, very young to be a Parliamentary Private Secretary, he was a publicity agent's dream: six feet tall, with good-looking, if somewhat aggressive, features and square jaw, straight black hair and dark brown eyes under heavy black brows. His face looked compelling on election posters and, although he could radiate considerable charm, he was also a master of the steely gaze. A certain section of his party saw him as a future Prime Minister. Many of the older hands agreed with them, supposing he would put his domestic affairs in order.

He was now using his steely gaze to good effect at the Opposition benches. "That remark was typical of the intellectual level with which this Government has to contend," he remarked, and waited for the chorus of noise to dwindle. "The Right Honourable Minister sends his apologies."

The Opposition looked upon Peter Canning as a bull might regard a red rag; he invariably had this effect on them, inspired partly by fear of how formidable an opponent he might be in ten years' time. Now they had no intention of letting him sidle away from the question. Blundell had remained on his feet. "I will then direct my question to my Honourable Friend, who, I have no doubt, is in possession of every fact known to his Minister: is it not true that the incidence of Aids in this country, and in the world, is increasing at a horrifying rate? And is it not equally true that this Government is not treating this very real crisis with sufficient urgency?"

Peter felt a note being slipped into his hand and glanced at it. The Home Secretary had scribbled: "Watch Brereton."

He understood. No one was afraid of Blundell, who was a lightweight debater. But Colin Brereton had remained behind this afternoon, seated alone on the Opposition front bench. This was unusual for Brereton's constituency, like Peter's, was in the West Country, and he usually liked to leave town early at the weekend. But not today. Brereton had been Minister of Health when last the Opposition had been in power. He was also a formidable debater. The Home Secretary was suspecting a trap.

Peter chose his words carefully. "The Honourable Member from the North Midlands has asked two questions," he stated. "With regard to the first, it is indeed unfortunate that the incidence of Aids, worldwide, continues to increase. However, due to stringent Government measures, the increase is a great deal less in this country than in many others. In addition, reports of the incidence of this disease are nearly always grossly exaggerated, and are based upon supposition rather than fact."

Once again he waited patiently while the Opposition backbenchers booed. He was interested only in Colin Brereton, who was sitting absolutely still, arms folded, gazing vacantly in front of him as if half asleep.

"With regard to the second question, may I assure my Honourable Friend, and indeed this House, that Her Majesty's Government is keenly aware of the seriousness of the position, and is doing all in its power to assist the search for an antidote and/or a cure. It is a matter of deep regret to us all that such a cure has not yet been found. However, we must be mindful of the great difficulties with which the medical profession, and the Government, are faced. Because of the very nature of the disease, it is not something that this Government can, that any government could, legislate against, as we have legislated against rabies and foot and mouth. Sexual relations are a fact of life, and that there are those

47

amongst us who indulge in those relations promiscuously, with several different partners, is also a fact of life."

He paused as a storm of protest arose from the Opposition benches, and someone called, "The pot calling the kettle black!"

Peter waited patiently, staring at his opponents. When the noise died down, he went on. "We can advise, and we can point up the dangers. We are doing that by means of advertisements and through educational channels. We can finance and encourage medical scientists in their search for a solution to the problem. But we cannot change human instincts which have obtained since the days of prehistoric man."

He sat down amidst the cheers of his own party, and the continued boos of the Opposition. The Deputy Speaker was looking at Brereton, expecting the flicker of his order paper, and was not disappointed.

"The Right Honourable Member for Haversham."

Brereton rose, slowly, regarded the Government benches with ill-concealed contempt; with his heavy jowls he looked somewhat like a bloodhound just awakened, but already scenting blood. "The Honourable Member for Trebeth Cross," he said, speaking with his invariably slow, West Country drawl, "has told us that we cannot change the basic instincts of *Homo sapiens*. I am sure he is right. I am sure no one in the House today knows that better than the Honourable Member for Trebeth Cross." He paused to allow his supporters to laugh while, this time, there were shouts of abuse from the Government benches. Peter could only sit in furious silence. That he was unmarried, and that he had a mistress, was only too well known; it was regarded as the chief stumbling block to his advancement.

"And yet," Brereton went on, "I find the complacency with which the Government, and indeed the medical profession, faces this very serious situation, disturbing.

My Honourable Friend has admitted that the incidence of Aids is serious. He claims it is not yet catastrophic. I would argue with him on that. It may not yet be catastrophic in this country, but there seems no doubt that it is reaching a catastrophic level in Africa. It is growing and spreading with every day, and it would be a bold man who would declare that it will not become catastrophic here as well, in the very near future. But this is not the point. The point is that an elected government, charged with the care and protection of the millions of people in this country, would be criminally negligent were it to await a catastrophic situation before taking the drastic measures that are clearly required, now!"

He again waited for the noise to subside. "But there are larger issues yet. Aids is a disease which has arisen, it seems, from nowhere, and for which, after several years, we have still not discovered an antidote. Does this not fill the heart of every member here this afternoon with alarm? It cannot be much more than twenty years since the medical profession was trumpeting to the world that they had got disease beaten. Who dies of tuberculosis today, or syphilis? Smallpox is almost eradicated. Even the greatest killer of them all, malaria fever, can be contained. Only twenty years ago the average man and woman was being told that the problem the next generation will have to face is not how to survive to old age, but how to die when old age is reached. It would be, we were assured, increasingly difficult."

He paused, and waited for a moment, but this time the House was silent.

"Now we have Aids," he continued. "A disease against which we cannot legislate! But can anyone here, can my Honourable Friend, assure me that we will not one day, one day soon, perhaps, in this increasingly over-crowded world, be faced with another disease which is just as deadly as Aids, or perhaps more deadly?"

"No one can say that," one of the Government back-benchers shouted.

"No one can say that," Brereton repeated. "But I would ask this House, is this not where our true concern should lie? Should not the resources of this island, this people, be concentrated upon the advancement of medicine, not only to secure a cure for Aids, but to prepare ourselves for any other 'serious situations', not to say, catastrophes, which Nature may have in store for us? Would not this be a more worthwhile, not to say greater, aim for this famous people than the maintenance of arms and armies which will never fight, or an imperial position which can no longer be supported by the facts?"

This time there was an uproar, and the Deputy Speaker had to call for order.

"I would like to ask my Honourable Friend this," Brereton eventually continued. "Can the Government say to the people of this country, you are secure in your lives? Can it say, we have disease defeated? Can it say, we will find a cure for Aids, in the immediate future, and we will find a cure for any other disease which may appear to ravage us, without hesitation? Can it guarantee that it will devote every effort, every penny, to such a cause should, God forbid, it ever arise – and as it has not done, and is not doing, in the case of Aids? Because if it cannot, then it will stand before this House, before this country, and before history, damned . . . should our serious situation ever become a catastrophe."

There was general hubbub from both sides of the floor and some voices were raised in comment above the numerous muttered discussions. The Home Secretary looked at Peter. He could give no assistance. But it was a crucial moment.

Peter uncurled his legs and slowly rose to his feet. "The Right Honourable Member for Haversham is speaking hypothetically," he said. "Of course there is no government, as there is no man, be he scientist or layman, who can categorically claim that we will not one day be threatened by a virus that is even more deadly than Aids. Although I am bound to say that I consider the prospect so unlikely that I do not propose to lose any sleep over it." He paused to allow his supporters to laugh. "Man has now been on this planet for a very long time. A very long time indeed. It may well be that Aids has been with us for far longer than is usually supposed. History is filled with examples of promising young men who suddenly sickened and died. Often they were supposed to have been poisoned. Some of them undoubtedly were. Others must have been victims to such ailments as appendicitis for which at that time there was no surgical remedy. But it is certainly possible that some of them died of a loss of the body's protective immunity. As my Right Honourable Friend has said, medicine has come to grips, eventually, with every disease that has ever been discovered. It is difficult to believe that they have overlooked one, that there is one, lying dormant in the earth, or in the sea, or in the sky, waiting to emerge with deadly effect. I may mention that, as many of the members present will be aware, the world's leading bacteriologist, Dr Graham Fitzroy of the Robert Koch Research Center in California, will be in this country next week to give a lecture on rare diseases, and especially Aids, and the means being devised to combat them. I suggest those of us who are truly alarmed by the incidence of such diseases attend his lecture; I certainly intend to. However, I can assure my Right Honourable Friend, I can assure the House, and I will assure the country as a whole, that this Government will take all the steps necessary to prevent the Aids epidemic from reaching catastrophic proportions, in this country, and that equally it will take every necessary step should any other disease, voluntary or involuntary, ever threaten the lives and happiness of the British people."

Peter stopped by the hospital on his way home. Jeremy
Payne, the Minister of Health, had actually just undergone an operation for a hernia, a fact which Peter had
withheld from the Commons knowing it was likely to
inspire the Opposition back bench to unseemly mirth.
But the patient looked fit enough, even if a little grim.
But Jeremy always looked a little grim; Peter felt he
regarded life as a far more difficult business than it
really was, an inhibiting and sometimes disturbing lack
of self-confidence.

"I saw the bastard who made that crack," he commented, glaring at his television screen. "Houghton,
wasn't it? I'll remember."

"He didn't actually speak," Peter said, regretfully.

"No, worse luck. You were good, very forceful. Perhaps a shade too forceful."

Peter waited. The Minister was a critical boss.

"I know it's easy to let people like Brereton get under
your skin, Peter, but you rather committed the Government in your reply."

"Oh, come now, Jeremy," Peter protested. "If there
were to be an epidemic of some unknown disease . . .
I'm talking about something really serious . . . we would
have to pull out all the stops."

"Oh, quite. But really, old man, in this day and age,
with the range we have of antibiotics, this seems rather
remote. What worries me is the interpretation of a
serious disease. I mean, take Legionnaires' Disease.
It's there. It does kill people. Are we, from here on,
going to be pilloried by the Opposition every time
there's an outbreak simply because you guaranteed
that we would devote our last penny to combating any
killer illness?"

"Ah," Peter said. "I wasn't actually thinking of something as selective as Legionnaires'. I was thinking of

something like the influenza outbreak of 1918."

"Not everyone is as well versed in history as you," Jeremy pointed out. "And that goes especially for those yobboes on the Opposition benches. We'll have to watch that very carefully. Now," he reached for a file on his bedside locker, "there were a couple of other points . . ."

A few minutes later the file was closed. "Anything else I can do for you, Jeremy?" Peter stood up and replaced the visitor's chair in its corner.

"Not a thing, thanks very much. Nice of you to stop by, Peter. Have a good weekend." Jeremy leaned back against his pillows with a sigh.

The bleep of the telephone could be heard the moment the lift doors opened. The pressures of the day still tensed the muscles of Peter's face as he opened the front door and he debated for a second whether or not to ignore it, but as the door slammed behind him he reluctantly crossed the hallway into the living-room to his desk.

"Canning," he snapped, irritably.

"That is no way for a Member of Parliament to greet a lady!"

Peter grinned at the mouthpiece, dropped his brief-case on to the chair and hitched half his posterior over the corner of the desk. "So, how's the most beautiful girl in the world?"

"Waiting on you. When are you proposing to turn up?"

Peter sighed, palm over the phone. He had forgotten about Anna's party; she usually liked him there well before the arrival of the first guest. He looked at his watch. "In a couple of hours?"

"Seven? That's late!"

"Sorry. I should have told the Opposition not to ask questions after four."

53

"Who's all grumpy, then?" Anna's voice was light, almost breathless.

"I'm sorry. It's been a long day. A long week, in fact. I'll be there just as soon as I can, sweetheart," he promised.

Before the phone was back on the rest Gladstone was winding himself round Peter's legs, leaving a liberal coating of long, ginger hairs on the dark, pin-striped worsted.

"Stop that, you idiot cat. Come on, I'd better feed you before you completely wreck my trousers." Together they strode into the kitchen where Gladstone purred and continued the treatment while the boss scooped Whiskas out of a tin into the cat bowl. "You're getting too fat, boy. Never happy unless your face is in the trough."

The phone bleeped again. Peter sighed and picked it up. "Canning."

"Darling," Claudia Briggs said. "I just had to ring and say how much Hartley and I enjoyed the way you put old Brereton in his place."

"Thanks." Peter often thought his elder sister should have been the politician in the family. But then, if Hartley Briggs, Chairman of the Briggs Group of drug companies, got the peerage he had always wanted, she would at least one day be a politician's wife; Hartley Briggs would certainly want to be a big noise in the House of Lords.

"You really told him." Claudia was thrilled. "I did enjoy it. Peter, why don't you come to supper tonight? I have someone I'm just dying for you to meet. Janice Ogilvy. Have you met her?"

"No," Peter said. "And I'm afraid . . . "

"She's a super person. A widow. But her first husband died several years ago. Climbing Everest or something absurd like that. She's thirty-one, has a little boy, and is ever so attractive."

"Darling," Peter said. "Are you match-making again?"

"Well . . . , Hartley and I had dinner with the PM last week, you know, Peter, and we definitely got the impression that the only thing standing between you and a Cabinet post was the fact that you're not married. Janice is awfully well connected. Her sister is married to Bobby Duncan. Well, you can't do much better than the Chancellor, can you?"

"Probably not," Peter agreed. "I'm awfully sorry, sis. I'd love to come, but I have a previous engagement."

There was a brief silence. "Not the dreaded Papagopoulos?"

"Yes, she's having a party . . . "

"Oh, Peter! You are the absolute end. I may as well tell you that in Downing Street she is regarded as the ultimate millstone around your political neck."

"I'm sure she is. But when I start choosing my friends . . . "

"Friends! You mean lovers."

"Pick a word. When I start choosing my mistresses with a view to advancement, I shall regard myself as unfit for that advancement."

"Oh . . . you are impossible. Good night!" The phone was slammed down.

Peter sighed, replaced the receiver, and headed for the bathroom, shrugging out of his jacket and loosening his tie en route. He left the pin-stripe draped over the trouser press in the bedroom and padded back to the living-room in mules and bathrobe to pour a whisky and soda, put on some background Bach and settled in his old leather chair with the *Evening Standard*. But he did not read it. His tousled head leaned back against the chair while his eyes absorbed the familiar details of his home: the shelves full of loved books, old cricketing photos, the picture his younger sister Sarah had painted for him of the old family home before she emigrated to New Zealand. It was a watercolour, full of sunshine and delphiniums, in which she had captured the warmth of mellowed bricks, and that special feeling of welcome they had always felt as children when they returned home from boarding school or university. Had it ever rained, he wondered, during their childhood? He could hardly remember an occasion, but it must have done – otherwise why would there have been a mountain of black wellies in the downstairs cloakroom? Of course, before Dad retired from the army – he had been in the Royal Army Service Corps – they had lived abroad, mostly in Germany. They had been very young then, travelling to and fro for vacations, which was possibly why they had loved their Hampshire home so much. It was sad when families broke up. Claudia had been the first to leave, when she married Hartley Briggs. Peter had not missed her too much at first. He was at Cambridge then, doing a degree in mathematics – how he had wound up as PPS to the Minister of Health was one of those inexplicable political decisions, although he had always had a deep, layman's interest in medicine – but when Sarah went off to the other side of the world Mum had been devastated. The house had seemed like a morgue without the shrieks of girlish laughter and, he had to admit, sometimes irritating bossiness. It would have been ridiculous for the old folk to remain in that huge house, rattling round like peas in a drum, but they were all sad when it was sold. The end of a happy era, and now his parents were content with their convenient three-bedroomed house in Wimbledon.

Smiling, he reached for his glass. He enjoyed this flat, and the little cottage he had bought two years ago in his Cornwall constituency, but still he hankered after a rambling old family home filled with children and love and dogs. For that one needed a wife. Mum and Claudia were forever trying to interest him in various feminine possibilities; it had become a kind of game with them – although Claudia was now starting to take it far too seriously, as he grew older – but their idea of a prospective wife did not gel with his. Not that he really had any idea what sort of wife he wanted. Certainly he thought he had known, years ago . . . blonde, curvy and sexy. Like Anna? He smiled again. Ten years ago he would have thought her the perfect answer; now he knew better. Claudia did not need to spell it out for him. Anna had all the physical attributes, was great fun to be with for limited periods, and she had money, loads of it. But as a wife, even if he had not been a politician, she would be a disaster; like so many of his girlfriends in the past. He had not been without a girl in tow since his Cambridge days; days of jeans and sweat shirts, beards and ponytails, nights of serious discussion to a background of baroque music; or rowing on the backs in evening dress, towing bottles of champagne in the water to keep them cool. Beds were often shared in those days but looking back it was incredible how often one had a girl in one's bed and never made love to her – though there were as many times when one did. He clearly remembered the ones he thought he was in love with at the time, love or lust – what matter now, only the memory of Angela still hurt.

Gladstone climbed on to the paper on his lap and Peter's fingers strayed absently over the soft fur. He closed his eyes. Angela! She was not blonde, and by film star standards she would not be classified as beautiful, apart from her eyes. They say that eyes are windows of the soul; certainly that was true for Angela Pickford, a truly beautiful person. Energetic and strong, loving and sincere, they had been so sure they were perfect for each other. Unfortunately, once his career had really taken off, she had begun to doubt. There had been so many discussions on the route their lives would take, discussions that lapsed into arguments as their dream of a big country home full of dogs and children dwindled to a weekend cottage, under the weight of his increasing political involvement.

"I am seeing so little of you, nowadays, and when I do I am cleaning your flat, cooking your meals or typing your letters," she had complained bitterly the day he suggested they make plans to announce their engagement. "You use me as a partner in bed if you happen to be randy and happen to have the time, and as a social partner at official functions. As far as I can see, marriage would only make the situation worse. I'm me! I have an identity, a personality of my own. I would be willing, God knows, to adapt, come towards you, if you would come towards me, but you don't. All you want in a wife is an appendage to your own id. You are married to your career. You can't handle two wives."

They had both been in tears when she walked out of his life. But could he blame her? Perhaps he was just a male chauvinist?

So now he had Anna, and a secretary, and a cleaning lady who sometimes left a casserole in the microwave. Anna had married once, almost by accident. Her maiden name was Smith, and she had begun life as Annie. She still occasionally slipped into a Cockney twang. Yet some Greek tycoon had fallen head over heels in love with her. That was understandable – she was a very beautiful woman. She had been swept off her feet, become very fond of him, but she had certainly not expected marriage. He had taught her to live the high life, despite his advanced years, and when he died leaving her a millionairess, she had been in a state of total bemusement, which Peter felt had never ended. She had been sure of one thing, though: she did not want to marry again. Perhaps Papagopoulos had sometimes been difficult to live with. Perhaps she did not wish to commit herself again to someone else's way of life. But in that aspect the feeling was mutual. They were both very fond of each other, but he could never love her: they simply did not have sufficient in common. The idea of spending an hour listening to

Bach would appal her, as much as continuous rounds
of parties bored him to distraction. But there was more
to their differences than mere tastes. Anna was really
a rather sweet and gentle person, and certainly confused, despite her unceasing efforts to act the 'widow
Papagopoulos'; she was also lazy and self-indulgent,
faults he could see perfectly clearly, all of which ruled
her out as the wife of a rising politician. She had filled
a gap in his life for the past six years but . . . He opened
his eyes to look at Sarah's painting again. Would it be
possible to combine that sort of home with the political
involvement he aimed at? Mum and Claudia were right,
he should find a wife. A suitable wife . . . But even if he
did make the supreme effort it was too late to get Angela
back; she had married four years ago and already had
two children.

He looked at his watch. "Hell," he said aloud, lifted
Gladstone off the unopened paper to deposit him on the
hearthrug and headed for the bathroom.

"Where did you get that thing you're nearly wearing?"
Peter examined the multi-coloured, sequinned creation.
"Turn around."

Anna pirouetted, showing off the back, cut so low as
almost to reach the nether cleavage. "I've had it simply
ages! Surely you've seen it before. I got it in Rio before
Christmas."

"There is no way I could have forgotten it. Aren't you
afraid your bottom will freeze?"

She poked a red, carefully manicured nail at his
shirt front, "Watch it, Canning, you're beginning to
sound like a husband". Green eyes teased up at him
from under long lashes and beautifully arched brows,
"When, or rather, I should say if, I ever feel the
urgent need of a husband, I will let you know. By
the way, I'm told you silenced that old idiot Brereton
this afternoon."

"Who told you that?" Peter grinned.

"A little bird." She took his glass from him and handed it to a waiter. "You up-ended that one pretty quickly!"

"Now you're sounding like a wife. Watch it, Papagopoulos!"

Anna laughed. "Come and be sociable. I've got the French Minister of Health here, he's the one talking to Marina Koltova, the ballerina. And Freddie Fortuna was able to come, too."

"Who?"

"Freddie . . . oh come on, you know, the singer."

"Never heard of him."

"Well, for God's sake pretend you have."

"What does he sing?"

"Soft, croony sentimental ballads. He's very popular at the moment," she explained, leading him into the throng.

Anna's London house was palatial. Overlooking the gardens in Markham Square, it had been gutted by her late husband and filled with marble: floors, pillars, arches and stairways gleaming pale pink under crystal chandeliers. The carpets had been designed especially for each area, a hollow circle of flowering vines lay around the fountain in the foyer, a vast white square edged with a Grecian symmetrical pattern in pink and blue, leading to the main drawing-room where settees and chairs were upholstered in pink and blue suede. Walls were panelled with classic scenes from Greek mythology or with huge mirrors which added to the already overwhelming impression of size, and every corner was occupied by marble and bronze statues or planters full of tall greenery. Peter thought the decor would have been almost obscene as a home for anyone but a Greek millionaire; it certainly did not suit Anna's personality, however much she acted up to it. But it was part of her life now, and he sometimes suspected she was attempting to mould her character to fit that life. He could not imagine her in an English country house setting amidst faded chintzes, old prints and family portraits. And he knew she had never taken a dog for a walk in her life, especially in muddy wellies. She loathed domestic pets. He had never seen her apartment in Rio – she said it was entirely black and white, which sounded ghastly – but he had spent a couple of weeks in her California home which was built into a cliff-face. Each room had only three walls, leaving it open to the west to the series of swimming pools at each level, and marbled terraces overlooking the Pacific. The house was filled with bright Mexican colours and tequila, and they lived off chilli con carne, tortillas and fresh fruits. Great for a brief holiday, but he could not have stood it for long.

"Hello, Peter, old man. Wondered when you were going to turn up."

"Grant!" Peter took the proffered hand to shake it warmly. "Didn't realise you were back. How did your kids enjoy the scuba holiday?"

Anna smiled a greeting and moved on.

"Fantastic. Only trouble is they can't wait to get back to the Bahamas."

"Did Julia dive, too?"

"A couple of times, but unfortunately she went out with a 'Jaws' complex, terrified of coming face-to-face with a shark!"

Grant and Julia Appleton were Peter's greatest friends. The two men had been at Cambridge together and Peter had actually introduced Grant to Julia in their first year. They married as soon as Grant joined his family's stock-broking firm in the City.

"Peter!" Julia took his arm and stood on tiptoe to kiss his cheek.

"Wow, are you sunburnt! In fact you're both looking disgustingly healthy." Peter kissed her back. "Grant tells

61

me you've been terrifying all the Bahamian sharks."

Julia giggled. "The mere thought of them scared me out of my wits." She was slight and fragile-looking with mousy blonde curls and huge blue eyes. "Andrew was the bravest. He actually saw several sharks on one dive and vowed he wasn't the least nervous." Andrew was their twelve-year-old son.

"What about Penny? She's only seven, isn't she?"

"No, eight now. She was just another little fish."

They chatted on for a while before splitting up to mingle with the other guests. There seemed to be hundreds, though the huge rooms were far from full.

Plied with champagne and canapés by the army of waiters and waitresses, the guests relaxed and the noise level grew. Peter had hoped that by 10.30 the crowd would start to thin out: far from it, more people seemed to arrive by the minute. A gong was pounded at 11.30 by a majordomo, and Anna waited for the hubbub to subside before announcing that supper was served. She led the way to the dining-room where an enormous cold buffet was laid out, with staff waiting, silver servers in hand, to pile the individual plates.

Peter found himself eating with a fun crowd, laughing, joking, not caring that he was consuming far more food and liquor than was good for him . . . until too late. And too late was after 2 am.

"Anna, my darling, why do you do this to me?" he yawned, stretching out on a settee.

Anna collapsed beside him and kicked off her shoes. "Good party, huh?" She rested her head on his shoulder.

"As always. You have the knack, and the bloody money, of course!" His arm slid round behind her.

"You just hit the button, sweetheart. You know what that cost me?"

"I shudder to think. Thousands."

"You can say that again."

"Why do you do it?"

"I love surrounding myself with exciting, vibrant people."

"But it's not necessary to spend thousands when you can have me for nothing."

She sat up and looked at him. "You don't look awfully vibrant to me, but I never refuse an offer." She stumbled to her feet. "Come on. Let's go up and recharge your batteries."

He stared up at her in mock horror. "You have to be joking! Not tonight, Josephine! I couldn't even raise a smile."

"Wanna bet?" she teased, tugging him to his feet.

"Doesn't your energy ever run out?" he moaned. But he followed her up the marble staircase without any apparent reluctance.

On a circular dais in the centre of the room was a huge, round bed. Peter had slept in it many times before and knew its multiple electronic secrets. There was no backrest . . . until you operated the remote control monitor and a third of the mattress tilted to the angle you required. Silken drapes were suspended from the centre of the ceiling, suffusing the lights above it, again controlled from the monitor. Another touch would produce music, or open a wall panel to reveal a large television screen a few yards away across the three-inch deep aquamarine carpet. Overcoming his urge, as always, to remove his shoes before stepping on it, Peter crossed the carpet to a series of glass panels on the wall. He knew one of them was a door, but could never remember which until he had pressed them all. Beyond was a bathroom. Anna had disappeared into the opposite wall.

She was between the satin sheets, blonde hair spread out over the lace-edged pillows, when he stepped, naked, on to the dais.

"I see I've some hard work ahead of me, tonight," she remarked, eyeing the Member of Parliament's member.

"I did warn you." He slid in beside her, closed his eyes and stretched. In moments he was asleep.

Anna smiled affectionately and kissed the tip of his nose before turning over. She could wait.

"You needn't think that because your eyes are shut you are not required to reply," Blundell was saying . . . But of course he would have to reply as the Minister was in hospital. Peter raised weary lids, but the lights in the House seemed awfully dim. A strange, rather pleasant sensation was creeping up his thigh . . .

"You decided to wake up then, at last," Anna's voice remarked.

He sat bolt upright and stared around him. "Oh hell! It's you!"

"Right first time. But what's so hellish about me. Who's the other woman?" Anna had promptly removed her hand, waiting for an answer.

"I thought you were Blundell . . . "

"Funny sort of relationship you have with him, then."

Peter looked down at her tousled head, smiling at her serious expression and raised eyebrows. "I dreamt I was sitting in the House . . . " he yawned and lay down again, burying his face between her breasts. "Unfortunately, you are the only woman in my life. About time I started looking round for a more conventional partner."

"Just think what you'd be missing." Her fingers traced up and down his spine, the long, red nails scratching gently, while a dainty heel massaged his calf.

"That's what worries me. I don't think I could live without this." He felt the skin on his back tingling, and the other response against her thigh.

"You're going to have to for a couple of weeks. I'm leaving for Rio tomorrow." She rolled him on to his back, thrust a leg across his body and lowered herself on to him, taking him into her all in one movement.

Peter gave a deep sigh of pleasure. "Why?" he murmured.

Her hair hung down to the pillows, enveloping them both in a golden cloud while her body moved sensuously, causing her nipples to brush to and fro over his chest. "Fiesta," she replied. "Coming?"

"In what context?"

"You know better than to come yet. Rio, I mean."

"No to Rio, and yes, any minute if you don't get off."

Anna quickly rolled away frowning, almost in physical pain, as the ecstasy was withdrawn.

Peter's mouth found hers, drew back while he removed the blonde strands, then their tongues circled. His lips left her mouth and slowly moved from her neck to her breasts, caressing each in turn, sucking gently, before moving on down over her stomach to the blonde vee. Her fingers combed through his hair, her body writhed, lifting towards him, pleading for more.

When he lowered himself into her she groaned with joy, wrapped arms and legs round him, thrusting passionately . . . They climaxed together, as always.

Peter staggered towards the bathroom, thumping on all the glass panels again till he found the right one. He felt weak, drained and his head hurt like hell. The shower helped a bit.

Anna strolled in and handed him a towel. "You coming back to bed?"

"If you'll feed me. What's the time?"

"Does it matter?"

"Yes. I've promised to have lunch with Mum and Dad."

"Tons of time. It'll only take half an hour from here."

"Through all the Saturday morning traffic? More like an hour." He towelled his aching head and groaned. "Anyway, we don't normally lunch in black tie. I've got to get home and change and feed Gladstone."

"That idiot cat," she pouted. "I can't think why you don't get rid of him."

He wrapped himself in a bathrobe. "Because I love him dearly."

Anna lifted the bathroom phone and ordered breakfast, but the mention of bacon and eggs made Peter feel quite queasy.

He took the shaver out of its holder. "Mind if I shave in bed?"

"Not if it doesn't interfere with the TV reception."

Anna sat on the bed holding the monitor. The back rest came up, the curtains opened and a panel in the wall slid open to allow the TV to move out a few inches. "Let's have a movie," she suggested. "How about *Passage to India* again?"

"Great," Peter replied, trying to sound enthusiastic. He wondered why the hell he did it. Why did he keep coming here to her parties? He invariably woke with a hangover. It was 9.30 already and he should be at his desk, working on a report for Jeremy. He had several people to telephone, arrangements to make regarding Tuesday's meeting. But Anna was fun and fantastic in bed. What a woman. He managed an inward smile; but she would make an impossible wife.

2

Medical Problems

"Viruses have of course been with us for many hundreds of years, many thousands of years," Dr Graham Fitzroy said, peering at his audience from above his half-lens. He was a small, rather jolly looking man in early middle age, prematurely bald save for a fringe of greying hair. He spoke with only an occasional reference to the notes which were placed in front of him by his colleague, whom the hand-out named as Dr Margaret Calhoun, an equally small, dark woman considerably younger than Fitzroy.

"We know, for instance," Fitzroy went on, "that the Chinese were suffering from a disease very akin to smallpox in the tenth century before Christ, and smallpox is most definitely caused by a virus. I would estimate that there have been viruses in the world from almost the first life . . . possibly they were the first life. Some of those may still be with us. There can be no doubt that several cancers are actually caused by a virus, for instance. Our trouble is that we do not know enough about them."

Peter Canning glanced at Colin Brereton, who was sitting beside him in the front row. Brereton had greeted him warmly, as he always did outside the Chamber, and he was now wearing that vacant expression he had so carefully cultivated over the years, but there could be no doubt that he was listening very carefully, and liking what he was hearing; the damned American was giving him ammunition with every word.

On the other hand, Peter reflected, he had got in ahead of his rival and invited both Fitzroy and his assistant out to lunch after the lecture; he had no doubt he would be able to undo much of the damage, and collect some information Brereton would not know about.

"It is important, however," Fitzroy was saying, "to understand just what a virus is, because there is some confusion about viruses and bacteria. Viruses can be said to have the same relationship with bacteria that we have with the atmosphere. We need the atmosphere in which to live; a virus needs bacteria, or indeed any living cell, in which to live. Too many people immediately associate the word bacteria with disease and illness. Some, a very few, bacteria, can cause illness. By far the greater number are benign, and are very necessary for the maintenance of life; without them there would be no fertilisation of the soil, no plant life at all. On the other hand, by far the greater number of viruses are malignant.

"Bacteria are very small. There are, for example, millions of bacteria in a single drop of saliva. A virus is only a fraction the size of a bacterium. And most viruses are infectious. They are also a comparatively recent phenomena in medicine. Because of their extremely small size it was not until microscopic science began to approach its present stage of development that they were even known to exist. It was Frederick Twort, in 1915, and Felix d'Herelle in 1917, working independently, who first truly demonstrated what many scientists and doctors had suspected for some time, that nearly all diseases are caused, not by bacteria, but by something living inside the bacterial cell, something which can also live inside the human cell or the animal cell, carrying out its work of destruction."

He paused to take a sip of water, and Peter studied Dr Calhoun. She obviously worshipped her boss. Well,

Peter reflected, he obviously knows his job; but he wished he would get on to Aids.

Fitzroy continued his lecture, now using slides to illustrate the various identified viruses. "I don't want you to go away with the idea that viruses are wholly evil," he told them. "They actually provide much that is of value, in several directions. For example, it is the presence of nucleic acid inside a virus, what we call either DNA or RNA for short, that has enabled us to work out that remarkable 'fingerprinting', if you like, of each human being. It is the study of viruses that has enabled us to understand far more about the structure of molecules than would have been thought possible a few years ago. But I am here today to talk to you about the evil.

"Now, viral invasion of susceptible cells can take any one of four forms. It can have what we call an inapparent effect, that is to say the virus becomes endosymbiontic: it lives dormantly in the host cell. Or it can have a cytopathic effect, in which the cell simply dies. Or it can have a hyperplastic effect, in which the cells divide before dying, although both then die. Or, by far the most dangerous, it can cause cell transformation, in which the cells divide but do not die; instead they assume abnormal growth patterns, and become, in a word, cancerous.

"Now, human and animal bodies, in general, naturally endeavour to resist these unpleasant effects, where they can, by immunological reactions, and of course in the vast majority of cases these reactions are successful. Until along comes the virus which destroys the immunological process. The virus of Aids."

The audience stirred restlessly; Peter wondered just how many people seated behind him suspected they might be suffering from the dread disease.

Fitzroy then went on to describe the symptoms of Aids, and the course of the disease. He was perfectly frank in his statements that a cure, whether by means of vaccination or normally preventive medicine, was not just around the corner, and he endorsed Peter's comments in the House that while Aids could be contained by a sensible level of sexual hygiene, and sexual caution, it was quite impossible, given humanity's needs, to legislate for it. "Our weaker brethren, who require the use of drugs, often illegally and surreptitiously, and share such things as hypodermic needles, which in their anxiety may not be properly sterilised, will always be dreadfully at risk."

On the other hand, he maintained a determinedly optimistic view. "Aids is a disease which has rather sneaked up on us," he told his audience in conclusion. "You open an encyclopaedia published only ten years ago and you won't find it mentioned. We need time. I know that's a horrendous thing to say when people are dying, but I can assure you we are working as hard as we can. It took something like four hundred years between the identification of the syphilis bacterium and the appearance of Dr Erhart's 'magic bullet'. I can promise you that it won't take that long to find the solution to the Aids problem. Thank you."

Brereton looked at Peter. "All rather inconclusive. And horrifying, don't you think? Especially his suggestion that there may be viruses around which have been with us since the dawn of time, and which we have not even discovered yet."

Peter grinned at him. "You intend to put down a question on that, Colin?"

Brereton grinned back. "I may, old boy. When I've investigated it a bit further."

Peter nodded. "I shall be investigating it, too."

Peter had already booked a table at the Caprice. "Do you know it?" he asked.

"No, but you're the expert, you live here." Fitzroy picked up his briefcase. "Just lead the way."

"We'll take a cab." He suddenly realised he was addressing the professor to the exclusion of his assistant. "Er . . . does that suit you, Dr Calhoun?"

Meg Calhoun suppressed a smile and nodded. London was apparently still very male oriented, compared with California. "Sounds fine, but I'd prefer it if you'd call me Meg . . . Peter." Who ever uses titles now, anyway?

"Will you have a drink at the bar, Mr Canning? I'll bring the menus," the maître d' asked.

"I think that's a brilliant idea. What will you have, Meg?"

"A glass of white wine, please."

"And you, Doctor?" He turned to Fitzroy.

"A Bloody Mary, I think. And the name's Graham, though my friends call me Gray."

"Good idea, I'll join you." He turned to the barman. "A white wine and two Bloody Marys."

While they sipped Gray commented on the traffic snarl-up in Trafalgar Square. Meg admired the use of so much black in the decor. Conversation did not return to medical topics until they were settled at their table and had begun their first course.

"That was an impressive lecture," Peter commented.

"Thank you. I hope you didn't find it too depressing."

"It's a depressing subject. But you put it across very well. May I ask a couple of off-the-cuff questions?"

"Sure."

"Well, firstly, do you think Aids is caused by a virus which has been with us for a long time, but has only just surfaced, so to speak?"

"I wish I could answer that for sure," Fitzroy confessed. "It's an evocative subject, you know, about which there are all manner of theories. If it has been with us a long time, how come it has only just surfaced? Or has it been around, and killing, for some time, and just not been identified until now? And only really exploded on to the scene with the total relaxation of morals over the past few years? It is, as you know, rife in Africa, where moral values have always been different from ours. But did it originate there?"

"One has to come back to syphilis," Meg Calhoun said. "No one is absolutely certain where syphilis originated. It was first identified in 1494 during the siege of Naples by Charles VIII of France. So a lot of people think that it must have been brought back from the New World by Columbus two years before. But that's never been proved. And the fact is that before 1500 what was called leprosy was rife in Europe, but the symptoms of certain forms of leprosy bear a remarkable resemblance to those of syphilis. So the disease could have been present in Europe for a considerable time before 1494, only confused with leprosy."

"That's absolutely true," Fitzroy agreed. "And the same could be true of Aids. After all, no one dies of Aids. People die of illnesses which the body cannot resist, because it is infected with Aids. Certainly before this century, when medicine was really groping with totally inadequate tools, it is possible that a lot of people died through a lack of immunity, and were merely regarded as having died of a specific disease."

"That's exactly what I told the House," Peter said, and asked what he really wanted to know. "So you feel, therefore, that there is no possibility of an entirely new virus suddenly appearing to attack humanity? Whatever we have we have always had, even if we haven't been able to recognise it?"

Fitzroy frowned. "I'm not sure I can go as far as that," he said. "I would say it is unlikely that an entirely new virus will appear, although we are of course still discovering viruses that are new to us. It is, I'm afraid, a constant battle. One which, on the whole, the human body is well equipped to resist. The Aids virus is a total maverick."

"Aids is, as we agree, preventable by proper hygiene,

or even proper conduct," Peter said, a sinking feeling in his stomach. "For that reason it is perhaps not being taken seriously enough . . . " he grinned. "Forgive me, Gray, I meant by lay people, and even more important, governments. I didn't mean by the medical profession."

"Sure," Fitzroy said. "We'd all like to see a lot more money spent on research."

"If that money were made available, how soon do you think a cure could be found?"

"Sorry, Pete. I couldn't possibly hazard a guess. It could happen tomorrow, but . . . "

"All right. Let's put the question another way. Supposing a new virus were to crop up, one which was as deadly and as virulent as Aids, but one which was not sexually communicated. Which was merely very contagious, like the common cold. Would we be able to cope?"

Fitzroy gazed at him for several seconds. "On the evidence of Aids, or the great influenza epidemic of 1918, or of the Black Death in the fourteenth century, I would say no."

"But . . . medicine has advanced one hell of a long way since the fourteenth century."

"So have the methods of travel," Meg reminded him. "And the number of people using them."

"I'm not saying it can never happen," Fitzroy said. "But were a totally unknown killer disease, which was also highly contagious, suddenly to appear in the world, it would be a nightmare beyond anything any of us have ever had. I don't mean to be depressing, but let's face facts: the way people move around nowadays, the way they are crammed into highrises and conurbations, half the population of the world could die before we even worked out what was causing it."

"Cheer me up," Peter said.

Fitzroy grinned at him. "It may never happen."

"Do you genuinely believe that?"

"Let's say, I'm prepared genuinely to pray that it never happens."

Their waiter returned with dessert menus.

"Peter, do you mind very much if I skip the sweet?" Gray looked anxiously at his watch. "I have a meeting at Guy's Hospital at 3.30."

Peter pushed back his chair. "I'm sorry. I've been monopolising so much of your time . . ."

Gray held up his hand. "No, no. I've been enjoying myself. But I don't want to break up the party. Meg, I can handle this afternoon okay by myself if you'd like to stay on with Peter and finish your meal. Those strawberries look real good."

Meg felt it was an order rather than a suggestion, though she was happy to comply. "Thanks, Gray. I would be sorry to miss them. Do you mind," she asked Peter, "or do you need to hurry too?"

"I'd be enchanted for us to finish the meal à deux," he smiled warmly. He spoke sincerely; he found this woman strangely interesting. She had not spoken a great deal during the meal but when she had, the extent of her knowledge of research medicine was obvious. Previously he had always thought of American women as rather forceful, pushy creatures; he would have imagined one with this woman's knowledge wanting to display it, dominating the table talk.

"Have you always lived in California?" he asked when Fitzroy had left.

"No. I went there to work over ten years ago. I was born in Hartford, Connecticut."

"I have friends in New England. In Newport," he told her.

"Sailing enthusiasts, I guess."

"Right. Very much so. Do you sail?"

"No. Never could afford it before I qualified. Then I was lucky enough to get this appointment almost immediately. Much to Mom and Pop's disgust. Tennis is my sport," she added.

"Mine too, when I get time. But tell me, why were your parents disgusted? The work you're doing is so important."

"I'm their only child. They don't go for the idea of me being the other side of the States," Meg explained. "And as for the work, well, a doctor who doesn't tend the sick is wasting his or her ability, as they see it."

"I took a degree in mathematics and my father nearly hit the roof when I said I was going into politics. I think he wanted me to go on into the big world of finance and make the family fortune. So I can sympathise with you." They had finished their strawberries and he signalled the waiter. "Coffee?" he asked her.

"Sure. Mind if I smoke?"

Peter passed the ashtray. "Go ahead. But I hope you won't think me rude if I say I find it surprising in a medical scientist," he commented.

"A girl has to have some vices." She smiled, almost to herself, a shy, half smile.

Peter watched her light up and inhale. She was a small, neat person. Her dark hair was cut very short, the slight waves swept back from her forehead and over her ears. Her dark blue suit was neatly tailored, worn over a white blouse, and there was a white silk flower in her lapel.

Meg was aware of his gaze. "My blue Irish eyes come from my father, along with the wavy hair and freckles," she informed him.

"I'm sorry, was I staring?"

"Not more than's flattering."

He presumed the small, retroussé nose, full, soft lips and almost too determined chin was inherited from her mother. "Is your father a doctor?" he asked.

"No. He has worked for a building supplies corporation ever since I can remember. Mom is secretary to an attorney." Meg sighed. "That's part of the problem. She took a job to fund me through college. I'm afraid she really feels I let her down."

"That's not fair," Peter frowned. He noticed she wore only a large lapis lazuli ring on her right hand. "Are you married?"

"No."

Her abrupt answer indicated she had nothing more to say on that matter.

"What do you think of London?" he asked, changing the subject.

"I've only seen a few traffic snarls, so far. But the weather is better than I expected."

"Then you haven't seen any of the parks?"

"No. I am hoping to visit Hyde Park while I'm over. A pal back home said there's a pretty lake . . . "

"The Serpentine?"

"That's the one."

"I haven't any appointments this afternoon. Why don't I take you there?" he volunteered. He could not imagine what prompted him.

"It would be a dreadful imposition. I couldn't let you do that." She shook her head, but not so vigorously as she might.

"I'm going anyway. I need the fresh air," he lied.

"Well," she hesitated. "If you're sure . . . "

"Splendid." He turned to look for the waiter, caught his eye and feigned a scribble on his hand.

Meg went downstairs to the Ladies while he signed the Amex slip and a cab was waiting when she returned.

It was an exceptionally warm day. After they had walked for a while, watched nannies with their charges and riders on Rotten Row, Peter led Meg down to the water's edge. "There's only one way to see the Serpentine," he told her. "I know you're not a sailor but would you care to take to the water with me?"

Meg eyed the little boat and laughed. "I guess having

gotten this far I might as well go the bundle."

Peter paid the attendant and handed Meg down into the wobbly craft, sitting opposite her and handling the oars with practised ease. Flotillas of ducks followed in their wake, hoping for titbits of bread; willows bent low to brush the surface of the water. Children laughed at distant play and a pair of teenage lovers necked on the bank. The London traffic sounded a million miles away.

"It's hard to believe we're in the middle of a busy city. Maybe because you English don't honk your horns the way we do in the States," Meg observed.

"Tradition," Peter said, seriously. "It's just not done to display one's irritation in public."

Meg grinned. "I've read about this. But how does the Englishman burn off his hype?"

He shrugged. "Takes it out on the wife, I suppose."

"Poor Mrs Canning."

"There isn't one. I have to take it out on my cat."

"Poor cat!" Meg feigned horror. "What's her name?"

"Gladstone. He's a he . . . I think."

She laughed. "Mine's an it called ET."

Peter raised an eyebrow. "Why ET?"

"Because he just appeared from out of space, I guess. I got home one day from the Center and there he was."

"Do you live alone?" he asked.

"No. I have a girlfriend, Liza, sharing the apartment with me. She's a research pharmacist and works in the same building though in a different department, fortunately. I reckon seeing a person twenty-four hours of every day might be a bit much."

"So you don't play tennis with her?" Not that he was particularly interested in whom she played tennis with, but he wanted to keep her talking. He loved her voice, the soft New England lilt, the movement of her mouth and the way she used her eyes as she spoke.

"My regular partner is a boyfriend, Joey Martino. We

play most weekends." She trailed her hand in the water, and immediately their feathered escort paddled up to investigate. "I wish I had a bag of goodies for you folk. Oh Peter, will you just take a look at this baby, here? Isn't he cute?"

"Yes, yes. Very cute," he agreed, but he was not looking at the duckling, he was staring at the little curls of dark hair on the nape of her neck as she leaned over the gunwale.

"Are you very busy during the remainder of your visit?" Peter asked, nonchalantly, as they walked back to the road to pick up a cab.

"You could say that. Tonight we have another meeting and tomorrow morning we fly up to Edinburgh. Then on to Paris, Rome and Madrid. We get back to New York on 4 June."

He felt a surge of pleasure. 4 June! And he was due there on 5 June for a conference. "That's quite an itinerary," he said, adding, "I'll be in New York myself, then. Perhaps we could meet? If you're not dashing straight off to California?"

She hesitated, but only for a moment. She liked this English politician. He was direct, positive and self-assured yet without any of the forcefulness one might have expected, certainly in his equivalent in the US. There were times when she expected to be treated as an equal with men, but she had enjoyed being a woman in Peter's company. "Why not?"

He was glad she had not answered immediately, though he had held his breath waiting. It meant she had given a considered reply. He took out his diary while she opened her handbag to produce her own.

The taxi waited outside the Connaught while they said goodbye on the pavement. "Thank you for a splendid lunch," she said, holding out her hand. "And I loved Hyde Park."

"I never knew it could be so enjoyable," he responded,

holding the tiny fingers. He bent towards her and she stood on tiptoe to reach up and kiss his cheek.

He smiled happily to himself as the taxi took him back to his flat in Chelsea. He had not felt like this since Angela . . .

3

The Island

The icy winds did not bother Pepe Sanchez today. His nose was red and his eyes streamed but he did not care, as Salvador edged the motor vessel up to the dock. He jumped ashore with a mooring rope and looped it through an iron ring set in the stone, then ran along the jetty to catch the stern line thrown by Pablo, the crew. They had to unload the oildrums while the tide was high so they could be rolled down the gangplanks, and he worked with a will, the cheap brandy with which they had toasted their return to Isla Hoste still warming his stomach.

"You want to unload the rest, now, Salvador, or in the morning?" he called to the capitán.

"It can wait till tomorrow. I'm starving, I want my dinner."

"Me too, but I'll have to wait while Encarna cooks it."

"That's a fine bacalao you have there. Enjoy it."

"I'll bring a piece for you in the morning when I come to help you unload." He clambered back on board to collect his fish, and the plastic bag full of things Encarna had told him to get in Punta Arenas.

"'Dios, Salvador, y muchas gracias," he shouted as he made his way up the street.

"A mañana por la mañana, Pepe," the capitán shouted back.

"Encarna!" Pepe peeled off his oilskins by the back door and waited for her to come through.

"Pepe! You're early. Did you have a good trip?"

She had grown quite plump over the years, but Pepe liked a good armful, and her face was still as attractive as the day they married, the skin smooth and creamy, her eyes big and dark. He was thankful she still enjoyed a good roll in bed – not like Salvador's skinny, dried up old woman. No wonder he had to keep a fancy bit in Punta Arenas. "Very successful, mia querida. I've brought your shopping and . . . " he paused dramatically, "take a look in the sink."

She crossed the kitchen. "¡Hola! That's a beauty!" She poked a knowledgeable finger at the Antarctic cod. "Si, si, muy bonito."

Free of the outer layers of clothing, he caught her round the waist and gave her a hug. "Caught it with a stern line from Salvador's boat," he said triumphantly. "Only a couple of kilometers north of here." He would not tell her about the job he had found, yet; nor about the little apartment in the town. He would wait till they were in bed, till she was all soft and yielding. That would be the best time.

"If you want some bacalao for your supper you'd better keep that till later," she giggled, squirming in his arms.

"I'll help you fillet it," he offered.

Encarna frowned. Funny! It was not like him to take a hand at women's work. What was he after? But she said nothing. She was not going to refuse his help.

With Vicente's family and the old folk there were eleven of them around the table. Encarna made chips and opened some tinned beans and they feasted well on their fish. Pepe was pleased with himself. There was plenty left over for another meal, and for a nice big piece each for Salvador and for the crippled boy, Jesus Cardona. And perhaps even a small fillet for Father Garcia. He would take them round tomorrow.

"Leave Hoste? Go to Punta Arenas?" Encarna was incredulous. "To live?" She sat up in bed, pigtails swinging, flesh seething under her nightgown. "What would Vicente say? And Mama and Papa?"

"Vicente will understand," Pepe said. "And when we are settled, they could join us, if they wished. It is a better life, Encarna. Better for the children. There are good schools in Punta Arenas for the younger ones, and Miguel will be able to get a job. And I will earn more, much more, than I can by fishing."

"Ha!" she commented. "I suppose you discussed it with Salvador. What does he say?"

"He says that a man must wish to better himself," Pepe told her. He put his arms round her waist and brought her back down into the bed. "You will like Punta Arenas," he whispered in her ear.

"Ha," she said again, and subsided beneath his caresses. It had not been as difficult as he had feared.

But she woke him before dawn. "Punta Arenas," she grumbled. "Oh, Holy Mother, I don't feel well."

"What is the matter?" Pepe asked sleepily.

"I have one of my headaches."

Pepe sighed. He had feared this; Encarna suffered from high blood pressure. There was no hospital, and no doctor, on Isla Hoste, but, weather permitting, the District Nurse flew in every Wednesday on the amphibian and held a clinic, and she always took Encarna's blood pressure and muttered about not too much excitement. Presumably the thought of being removed to the city would be classed as too much excitement.

"Shall I fetch you a Codeine?" he asked.

"Yes," Encarna said.

Sighing some more, Pepe got out of bed, lit the candle, and fetched the pill and a glass of water. Encarna drank gratefully, and settled down again, but he could tell she was not sleeping. "Oh, my head," she groaned. "Oh, my head. I feel so bad."

By morning Pepe had a headache too, and he was not feeling all that good himself. In fact, Encarna's groans and tossings and turnings seemed to have disturbed the entire household; everyone was complaining of a pain in the head and of being generally out of sorts; as it was a Saturday the children were all at home, making their presence felt. Pepe was glad to escape into the fresh air, cold as it was, and make his way to Salvador's boat alongside the dock with some of the fish.

"You don't look too good," Salvador remarked.

"I don't feel so good," Pepe confessed. "Encarna had a bad night."

"After you told her about leaving Hoste," Salvador commented.

"I suppose so. But she accepts it. It is just her blood pressure. You know."

Salvador nodded. The community on Hoste was so small everyone knew when anyone cut their toenails. "She will get over it," he remarked pontifically. "This is a big piece of fish, Pepe. It will give us a fine lunch."

Pepe had a brandy on board with Salvador after the unloading was finished, then took the other pieces of fish to Father Garcia and to Jesus Cardona; Jesus's father, Pablo, was alcalde of Isla Hoste. Then it was time to go back to the dock and help Salvador bring the barrels up to the village. "I am returning to Punta Arenas on Monday morning," Salvador told him. "Will you be ready to leave by then?"

"I'll be there," Pepe said. "With Encarna and the kids." He walked back along the street in high spirits. He would have whistled excepting that his headache was getting worse. But he had finally achieved his ambition; at last he could take his family away. Despite her complaints Encarna had admitted that she had known the move was coming, so she was ready for it. In fact she admitted every time he went to Punta Arenas in the past couple of years that she had half-expected him to come home with the news of a new home and a job. It had given her time to get used to the idea, and he knew she would look forward to it, once she got over her excitement headache.

He got home to chaos. Pedro, his second son, had had a nose bleed. Pedro took after his mother, and Pepe suspected the little boy might have high blood pressure too. But it was really alarming to see the blood he was losing, and it would not stop, just kept pouring out. Even Encarna had got up to try to cope, and the other children were close to hysterics, while Chika the dog was barking and growling.

"What a mess," remarked Isabella, Vicente's wife. There was blood everywhere.

"Cold water," growled Abuela from her rocking chair. "Pour cold water down his back."

Pepe thought that made sense, although it added to the mess, but it was half an hour before the bleeding was brought under control. By then Encarna had returned to bed with her headache, which seemed to be worse. Pepe put Pedro to bed as well, and set the girls to cleaning up the blood. Now they were complaining of stomach aches as well as pains in the head, but Pepe supposed it was only the sight of the blood upsetting them.

Vicente returned from the police office. He was Hoste's only policeman, and was also in charge of the radio equipment, which kept them in touch with the mainland. He stared at the still obvious disaster in the living-room, and threw himself into a chair. "I need a drink," he said.

"What's the matter, honey?" Isabella poured the brandy.

"I have a terrible headache."

"Everybody has a headache," Pepe complained, drinking some brandy himself.

"I always have a headache," Abuela remarked. "It is the noise in this house. There is too much noise."

"I think it is because we are going to have a thunderstorm," Isabella said brightly. She was a pretty little thing, but like Salvador's wife, too thin, and with a pale, bloodless face; she had always been anaemic. "It is very close."

"It is close in the house," the abuelito observed. "There are too many people."

Pepe went outside, Chika at his heels. The events of the morning had not sent his headache away; rather it too seemed to have grown worse. And if he found the noise trying himself, sometimes, he found his mother-in-law even more trying all the time. While he knew that for all her complaints about overcrowding, she was going to weep and wail when she heard that he and Encarna were leaving.

The abuelito, now, was different. He was an easy-going old fellow who wore his eighty years well, even if he was bent with rheumatism and had to walk with a stick. Pepe knew where he would be: at the foot of the garden, smoking – Abuela did not allow smoking in the house.

He made his way between the rows of cabbages towards the bench which looked out over the sea, and frowned. Abuelito was not there. He quickened his pace, reached the bench, and looked at the old man, lying in a heap on the ground.

*   *   *

85

"It is a stroke," declared Father Garcia. The father was supposed to act as more than just a confessor and priest in such a remote community, and had had a brief medical training.

"But what must we do?" Vicente asked, anxiously.

"There is nothing you can do," Father Garcia said, surveying the abuelito. The old man was conscious because his eyes rolled, but it was difficult to feel he knew anything that was going on; his body was quite rigid. "He must have absolute rest, and you must pray." He left the bedroom. "Isabella tells me that Encarna is not well, Pepe. Would you like me to visit her?"

"I would be most grateful, Padre. But Padre, will Abuelito survive?"

"Who can say, Pepe? Only God."

"But . . . what could have caused it?"

"He has ruptured a blood vessel in his brain."

"He was all right yesterday."

"Of course. These things happen very suddenly, sometimes. At others they are preceded by severe headaches."

Pepe stared at him in consternation.

"A headache can be a sign of anything," Father Garcia told him reassuringly.

"But this stroke . . . it is caused by too much blood," Pepe protested.

"No one can have too much blood," Father Garcia told him severely.

"Then what is this high blood pressure that Encarna suffers from?"

Father Garcia was not going to get drawn into that; he was not too sure himself. "Strokes are caused by age," he said. "By a weakening in the arterial walls. That is all. It does not embarrass you that I should visit Encarna?"

"Embarrass me? Why should it embarrass me?" Pepe demanded.

Father Garcia did not reply, but climbed the stairs to the bedroom.

"Because you are flushing," Isabella told him.

Pepe peered into the mirror. His face was definitely redder than usual. He was not surprised, with everything that was going on.

Encarna tossed and turned all night again, complaining that her head was bursting, and now she also had sharp pains in her stomach. All the children were also complaining and crying. Pepe hardly slept and, by the next morning, his own head felt as if it was about to explode and he felt sluggish, as if he had had too much to drink. And Pedro's nose was bleeding again, as was Angelica's: their beds were a mess.

And Abuelito was dead.

Father Garcia came as soon as early Mass was finished, accompanied by almost his entire congregation. The father said the prayers over the corpse while the villagers crowded round the house with bowed heads. Everyone knew that the abuelito had been going to die some time soon, but he had still been an active member of the community.

When the prayers were finished, Carlos Morena's wife and her sister came in to wash the body and prepare it for burial; this would be the next day – in May the weather was sufficiently chilly for there to be no great hurry. The kitchen table was arranged to one side of the little living-room for the body to lie on. Father Garcia went and sat with Abuela, who had retired to bed. He held her hand and talked to her about the hereafter.

Pepe gazed at Encarna, who was lying in bed. But she had stopped her moaning. "Encarna?" he said. "Encarna?"

Her face was red, mottled with purple, and she was hardly breathing. Pepe picked up her hand; it felt a dead weight. Yet her eyes were open, staring at him, and her mouth was quivering, as if she wanted to speak, but could not.

Pepe ran into Abuela's room. "Padre!" he shouted. "Padre!"

"Hush, Pepe," Father begged. "This is a house of mourning."

"Padre! Encarna . . . she has had a stroke. Just like Abuelito."

Father Garcia frowned; his expression suggested that Pepe had had too much brandy.

"She has," Pepe insisted. "Please come to her, Padre."

Father Garcia got up – Abuela did not seem to notice him leaving – and accompanied Pepe into the adjoining bedroom. He frowned at Encarna and took her pulse. His frown deepened. "This is very strange," he said.

"Madre de Dios! What are we to do, Padre?"

"There is nothing we can do, my son."

Pepe pushed past him and ran down the stairs. He ran out of the house and along the single street to the police station, burst in to Vicente, who spent some time in the office even on Sundays; it got him away from the children.

"For God's sake make less noise," Vicente told him. "My head is splitting."

He did not look very well, Pepe thought; his face was red and his hands were trembling. But a man was entitled to be unwell when his father has just died.

"This is serious," Pepe said, his chest heaving. "Encarna is ill." His face was beetroot and his legs weak.

"Encarna? Ill with what?"

"She has had a stroke like Abuelito."

"Encarna? I can't believe it."

"She has, I tell you. And you are not well, and I am not well, and neither are my children. I don't believe Abuela is well, either. Vicente, you must call Punta Arenas. Tell them Nurse Gomez must come down now, today, we can't wait till Wednesday. Or better yet, tell them to send a doctor." Tears began to stream down his face, and he collapsed into a chair.

"Now, you know I cannot do that, Pepe," Vicente protested.

"Why not?" Pepe wailed.

"Well, it will mean starting the generator. And there are rules governing the use of the radio, you know. It is only to be used at certain times, and on particular days, certainly never on a Sunday, except in cases of emergency."

"You don't call this an emergency? Your father is dead. Your sister could be dying. That is not an emergency?"

"There is nothing anyone can do about a stroke. Padre Garcia has said so."

"I don't believe this is an ordinary stroke," Pepe declared. "I have never heard of a whole family suffering from strokes at the same time. I believe it is a sickness which is affecting all of us. I believe it must be something we have eaten."

"I cannot see how anything we have eaten can give anyone a stroke," Vicente insisted.

"Will you send for the doctor?" Pepe demanded, eyes wild.

"I would lose my position if I sent for a doctor and it was not necessary. I will come and see Encarna."

"Then hurry," Pepe told him.

They ran back along the street, entered the front garden, and stopped in consternation. Chika the dog lay outside the door, her tongue lolling. Pepe gave another wail and bent over her, then stood up again, fresh tears coursing down his cheeks. He loved that dog; she went everywhere with him, following faithfully on his heels and even coming out with him in the boat sometimes. Now she was dead.

* * *

Pepe and Vicente hurried inside, found Isabella wringing her hands. "The children," she said. "Oh, the children."

They were all in bed. Their faces glowed red and they wept; Pedro and Angelica were still bleeding from their noses, and little Pepito had bled into his potty — apparently their stomachs were hurting more than their heads.

"They are sick," Isabella said. "So sick."

"Now will you call Punta Arenas?" Pepe begged.

Vicente nodded. "I will go and start the generator."

Pepe hurried into their bedroom to see how Encarna was faring. But her flesh was cold. She was dead, too.

"This is strange," Father Garcia said. "Very strange. And very serious."

Pablo Cardona, the mayor, had come over as well. Pablo normally felt himself too important to visit the ordinary people, except before an election; he expected them to visit him. But he had never had a situation where a whole family seemed to be dying.

He took Pepe aside. "What is happening, Pepe? You do not look well, yourself."

"How do you expect me to look well?" Pepe demanded. "My wife has just died. My children are ill. We have contracted a disease."

"A disease!" A disease, Pablo thought, in Hoste! It was necessary to do something. "I must call the mainland," he decided.

"Vicente is doing that now," Pepe told him, his face deep red, eyes swollen, "as soon as he can get his generator started." The fact of Encarna's death, the end to his dreams of them settling together in Punta Arenas, had hardly sunk in; he had his sick children to worry about now.

"Ah," Pablo said, disappointed. "The matter should have been referred to me."

90

"It is an emergency."

"An emergency, yes. It is an emergency. Quarantine! I am placing your house in quarantine, Pepe."

"How can you do that? I have to go out. Encarna and I were leaving tomorrow morning, anyway."

"You cannot do that."

"Of course I cannot do that," Pepe shouted. "I am burying my wife and my father-in-law tomorrow morning. But the house cannot be put in quarantine. Vicente lives here."

"Vicente," Pablo said. "I must go and speak with him." He shook Pepe's hand. "I am sorry about Encarna, my friend. She was a good woman. I think you should go and lie down. You do not look well."

Pepe went up to Encarna's room, gazed at his wife. Father Garcia was still praying. Pepe looked in at the children; they were all in bed, being cared for by Isabella. They were crying with the pain in their heads and their stomachs, and Pedro's nose was still bleeding. "How can he have so much blood?" Isabella asked. "It is incredible."

"Are you all right?" Pepe asked.

"I am frightened," Isabella said.

"But you have no headache?"

"No."

Then it could not be something they had eaten, Pepe thought; Isabella had certainly eaten the same meals as everyone else. He felt it was very important to think about it carefully, but it was so difficult to think about it in the house, with death all around him, and his head hurting. In fact, all he wanted to think about was Encarna. They had been good for each other. He had never looked at another woman since marrying her. And they had been going to start a new life together.

Salvador! Salvador must be told what was happening. As if he did not already know. But Salvador might even have an answer.

*   *   *

He left Isabella to cope; she was the only healthy member of the household, now. He went to Salvador's house overlooking the harbour.

"It is very sad about your father-in-law," Salvador said. "Encarna must be very upset."

"Encarna is dead," Pepe told him. "So is my mother-in-law."

Salvador put his arm round his friend's shoulders, Maria hastily poured two glasses of brandy. "I have never known such ill fortune," Salvador said. "You do not look well yourself, Pepe."

"I am not well, I feel terrible," Pepe said. "I do not know what to do, Salvador."

"It takes away a man's mind when his wife dies," Salvador said, and regarded Maria speculatively. "You must pray for guidance."

"My children are ill, I am ill . . . " Pepe sighed.

"What does Padre Garcia say?"

"He says there is nothing he can do."

"Then you must send for a doctor . . . "

"We have done, but whether he will come on a Sunday I don't know." Pepe finished his brandy and got up. "Vicente will have started his generator by now. I must go and see if he has got through on the radio.

He hurried off, and Salvador watched him with sad eyes. "How can one man have so much misfortune?" he asked. He gave Maria his glass. "I will have another brandy, and then we will have lunch. What have you for lunch, woman?"

"That fish Pepe brought us yesterday morning. It has been in the cold box. You will like the bacalao, Salvador. I have prepared it with garlic, the way you like best."

Pepe stared at Vicente, slumped across his desk. He had encountered Pablo outside the Police Station, looking distraught. "I cannot understand it," Pablo complained.

"A policeman, my policeman, dying like this. It is not right." He had taken Vicente's revolver from its holster, concerned that a corpse should not be armed. Now he held the gun uncertainly, not sure what to do with it.

"For God's sake put that thing away," Pepe told him. Vicente had apparently died instantly. His face was suffused, and blood trickled from his nose, drying rapidly in the chill air. The generator clacked in the next room, but the radio was silent.

"Pablo," Pepe said. "Something terrible is happening to my family."

"Yes," Pablo agreed.

"Do you know if Vicente called Punta Arenas?"

"I do not know. I do not think so. No one is talking on the radio."

In fact, Pepe realised, the radio was not even switched on. "We must use it," he said.

"I do not know how to use the radio," Pablo told him.

Pepe chewed his lip. Nor did he. Salvador always used the radio on board the motor boat. Therefore Salvador could use this radio as well. "I will fetch Salvador," he said.

"We cannot leave Vicente like this," Pablo said. "I will call some men to help us take him home."

Pepe felt he had to go with the body, to break the news to Isabella.

Isabella stared at him uncomprehendingly, then stared at her husband as the men brought the body into the house. She had some news to tell Pepe, too: Abuela was dead. The house was starting to resemble a morgue. Suddenly the latest tragedy struck her. "Vicente!" She screamed, and threw herself on her husband's body. Vicente had always been so strong and healthy. He prided himself on his physical fitness – "A policeman must be strong and healthy," he would say – and he did fifty press-ups every morning on the bedroom floor.

To see him lying there . . . "Vicente," she sobbed, on her knees.

Father Garcia rested his hand on her head, and looked at Pepe. Pepe had never seen the priest weeping before; but then perhaps Padre Garcia had never before had to deal with four deaths in one family in a single day. "I do not know what to say, Pepe," he said. "I cannot understand it. You are such a good man. You have such a good family. Encarna was so good to me, sending me that nice piece of cod. It was such a tasty piece of cod. I will send women . . . " he sighed. "I must go home and rest. I have a headache. I will see you this evening, Pepe. I will come then and say prayers for the dead."

Father Garcia did not come to Pepe's house that evening. When Carlos Morena went to the priest's house to fetch him, because his wife had been taken ill, he found Father Garcia dead in his chair.

Carlos Morena ran through the street, shouting and wailing. "The padre is sick," he shrieked. "The padre is very ill."

Salvador was in Pepe's house. "I got through to Punta Arenas," he was telling Pepe. "It took several hours, but I got them. They say it is not possible for the doctor to come tomorrow. Or the nurse. But she will come on Tuesday."

"On Tuesday?" Pepe wailed. "My entire family will be dead by Tuesday."

"The padre is sick," Carlos Morena shouted, opening the door. "I think he is dying! Oh, God in heaven, what is happening to us?"

Salvador crossed himself. "This island is bewitched," he said. "I must go and see if Maria is all right."

He hurried home to where Maria was pressing the washed clothes with her heavy, solid flat-iron. "Stop that," Salvador said. "Pack a bag, and come with me."

"Where are we going?" Maria asked.

"To Punta Arenas."

"To Punta Arenas? But why?"

"Because there is something happening here that I do not like. It is not just Pepe Sanchez's family which is dying now. It is the priest. Soon it will be everybody. We are leaving on the boat."

"We cannot leave on a Sunday," Maria objected. She did not like the motorboat; it rolled and made her seasick.

"We will leave while we can," Salvador said, starting to lock up the house. "Hurry, woman."

It was dusk, and Pedro Sanchez had just died. Angelica was moaning and weeping, and bleeding. The rest were nearly as bad. Isabella had given up, and sat in a chair, staring at the stricken children. She could think only of Vicente. Vicente lay on the floor, because there were no tables left. She could not believe this was happening to her family.

Pepe stayed upstairs with the children, talking to them, doing what he could, although his head was so painful he wanted to scream himself. He looked out of the window and saw the motorboat leaving the little harbour. He blinked, and looked again. Where would Salvador be going at night? Pepe could not understand it. But his head hurt so much he could not think about it. He sat down beside Angelica and held her hand. His pain was getting worse, and now his stomach was hurting as well.

Isabella dozed off from sheer exhaustion, but was awakened by a great deal of noise. It came from outside the house. She opened the door, blinked into the darkness, and was struck by a flying clod of earth. She gasped and stepped back inside. "You are devils," Carlos Morena shouted. "Devils. My wife is dead. Her sister is dead. You are devils."

There were other people with him and they too were shouting. Now they began throwing things as well. Isabella gasped and closed and bolted the door. There was no light in the house so she lit a candle, and gazed at her dead husband. Then she went upstairs to find Pepe. But Pepe Sanchez was dead.

Isabella lay on the floor and wept and sobbed. She could hear no sound from any of the children, either hers or Encarna's. She was the only person awake in the house. Or perhaps alive?

She heard a banging on the door. She did not want to go to it because the people were still outside, shouting abuse and throwing things at the house. Those were her friends, and they were treating her like this when she was surrounded by death.

"Pepe!" It was Pablo Cordona. "Pepe, open up."

Because the mayor was there, the people had stopped throwing things. Isabella dragged herself downstairs and unbolted the door.

"Where is Pepe?" Pablo demanded.

Isabella could not speak. She merely pointed at the stairs. Pablo ran up them, and came back down, more slowly.

"This is very serious," he said. "This is an epidemic. It is like a plague. People are dying everywhere. And they are saying it started with this family."

"This family is dead," Isabella said.

"You cannot stay here," Pablo said.

"I cannot leave," Isabella said. "My children are dying."

"Your children are dead, Isabella. There is no one alive in this house, save you."

"Oh, God," she moaned. "My babies. My babies."

"I cannot trust those people," Pablo said. "They are desperate with fear. They are saying they must burn down this house."

"They cannot!" Isabella shrieked. "They cannot. My husband and my children are in this house."

"I know. I will speak with them. But you cannot stay here, in a house of the dead."

"How can I leave my children?" Isabella asked him.

"Isabella, your children are all dead. There is no one alive upstairs."

Isabella wailed aloud. Her babies. Her precious babies.

Pablo dragged her to her feet. "You must come with me."

He took her outside and she shivered in the cold; he had not thought to fetch her coat. The people stared at her; she felt their hostility even more than the cold.

"She is a witch," Carlos Morena shouted. "A witch."

"You are demented, Carlos," Pablo declared. "Isabella is a poor woman who has lost her entire family in two days." Carefully he locked the door of the house. "You should be ashamed of yourselves," he told the crowd.

They said nothing while he stared at them, but when he and Isabella made their way down the street they began shouting and chanting again.

Isabella could not stop herself from weeping. It was more than the loss of her husband, her children, her brother-in-law and sister-in-law, her parents-in-law, all so quickly; it was the feeling of being hated. She knew that Juanita Cardona hated her too. Juanita was afraid to touch her, and their crippled boy, Jesus Cardona, shrank away from her. They would obey Pablo and give her a bed, but they were afraid that she had brought the sickness into their house.

Isabella fell into a deep sleep. She was exhausted; she had not slept for forty-eight hours. But she awoke before dawn, disturbed by the light. She went to the window, looked out at the flickering flames. She screamed. They were burning her house, with all of the bodies in it. She wrapped herself in her blanket and ran downstairs. Pablo stopped her going out. "I can do nothing about it," he said. "They are terrified. And perhaps it is the best thing."

Isabella would not go back to bed. She huddled on a chair in the lounge of Pablo's house, listening to the chanting of the mob, watching the flickering flames rising into the sky. More than ever she could not believe it was happening. To lose her family . . . and then to have them burned, by people who had been her friends.

Eventually she dozed again, and was awakened by shrieks from Juanita. Jesus was ill.

Isabella dressed herself and left the house. Pablo did not attempt to stop her this time. He wanted to be rid of her as much as anyone.

It was very early in the morning, not yet daylight, and the mob had dispersed. But she could still hear a great deal of noise, people wailing their misery and people chanting their prayers and their Hail Marys. There was sickness everywhere. She went to her house, gazed at the blackened ruin which encompassed everything she had ever possessed, everything she had ever loved. Then she left the village and went to hide among the rocks on the hillside. She sat there, shivering and weeping. She heard a great deal of noise from the village. The wails and prayers became shrieks and shouts of anger and despair. She knew that if she went back down into the village she would be torn into pieces.

Isabella sat among the rocks all of Monday. It was Tuesday morning before the noise from the village died down. By then she was all but frozen, and very hungry. And she had a terrible headache.

A coastguard cutter saw the motorboat, clearly not commanded, steering round and round in circles. It was a miracle it had not yet hit any of the rocks which littered the Straits of Magellan.

"That is Salvador Lopez's boat," the commandant said. He called Salvador on the radio, but there was no response.

"There is someone waving," the boatswain said.

The commandant inspected the woman through his binoculars. He did not know Maria Lopez; she did not usually accompany her husband to Punta Arenas.

"We must go alongside," he said.

"It will be very difficult," the boatswain objected.

"It must be done," the commandant said.

He manoeuvred his cutter with great skill, and with a last burst of speed rattled alongside the motorboat, his crew throwing out grapples to make the two ships fast even as the boat was beginning another turn.

"My husband," Maria screamed at them. "Salvador!"

The commandant himself went on board; he and Salvador had had many a beer together. Now he gazed at his friend, lying dead on the deck beneath his wheel, his face suffused rather than pale.

"You are safe now," the commandant told Maria. "We will take your ship and your husband into Punta Arenas. But you must tell me how this happened."

"I do not know," Maria sobbed. "I do not know, and I have such a headache."

4

Quarantine

Rain hit the windscreen of the ancient Oldsmobile camper almost horizontally as it bounced and splashed down the highway. The young passengers swayed with the highsided vehicle as the wind gusted violently.

"I guess I'm gonna have to pull over if this lasts much longer. I can't see a damn thing," Rod complained. "I thought this bus was supposed to have power steering but hell, I'm having to fight to stay on the road." His vest was stained with sweat and little rivers ran out from his short-cropped hair, dribbling into the two-day stubble on his chin.

"You've been on the wheel for nearly two hours, honey. Why don't you let someone else take over?" Sally Ann Calhoun called from the rear.

"Yeah. Make way for a guy with some muscle," Dermott agreed, winking at the girls over his shoulder, raising a shout of laughter. Dermott was the weediest of them all, girls included, standing five-foot-five in his high-heeled Texas boots and peering out at life through pebble glasses. But he was definitely the brains of the outfit, with a great sense of humour.

"Okay, Big Boy, you got it." Rod pulled off on to the shoulder and edged his six-foot-four of hard, college-football-trained muscle out from the driving position. He stood in the gangway and stretched. "That was a long two hours," he agreed, "Now, you say you want a turn?"

He reached out for Dermott and, much to everyone's amusement, lifted the small man bodily and dumped him over the back of the seat behind the wheel.

"Hey! What gives? Why we stopped?" Carlie stuck his dark head over the side of the high bunk above the cab.

"Happen we've been driving up a riverbed and it just became a waterfall," Dermott explained.

"You didn't warn us you had monsoons in your country," Meryl complained. "Shall I make us a coffee while we're here?"

"Yep. Not even our Mighty Mouse can make too much progress in this." Rod swept a pile of miscellaneous clothing off a bench seat and lay down, yawning.

"Your problem is too much wine with your lunch," Meryl teased, bending her tubby frame to pick up the clothing.

Rod smacked the blue-jeaned rump, retorting, "And you had too much rice. You go on like this, my girl, and we're going to have to stick another wagon on behind and tow you home."

Meryl jumped up, sat on one of his legs and tore off his sneaker to tickle the sole of his foot. In the ensuing romp the two rolled on to the floor of the gangway.

"Watch it!" Sally Ann shouted over the uproar. "The kettle's boiling." She by-passed them by the simple expedient of crawling along the seat, not difficult for her slim shape. She was pretty, rather than beautiful, and very blonde, eyebrows and lashes pale against the suntan and her long hair drawn back, plaited and pinned up to leave her neck cool. Physically she was in the strongest contrast to her cousin Meg's family, and mentally too, she supposed. Like her parents, Meg had always been a hard worker and Sally Ann had no doubt she was appalled that her young cousin and, incidentally, goddaughter, should be bumming around South America with a bunch of what Meg probably considered dropouts. But Sally Ann had her own plans for life, her own ambitions, and one was to see as much of the world as possible before getting down to serious study and earning a living. "How far is it yet to Chillán?" she asked.

"Ten miles," Dermott told her. "It would have been further a century ago, but after the big earthquake in 1835 it was rebuilt further north. Perhaps they knew we were coming."

"I thought the big one was this century," said Carlie, lowering his legs to the floor.

"It was, in 1939. Killed over 10,000 people."

"I believe I had an aunt and some cousins who died in it."

"You mean you're not sure?" Meryl called up from her prone position on the floor at his feet, having given up the fight against superior muscle.

"Well, I've gotten one hell of a lot of cousins and aunts. It's only something I remember my Ma telling me." Carlie reached out and took his coffee mug from Sally Ann.

The weather cleared as quickly as it had begun, and soon the four young American students and their Chilean college pal were bombing south again.

"We must stay in Chillán for a day or two," Dermott said as they approached the city. "There are places I want to visit."

"The cathedral, I guess," Carlie smiled. "It's beautiful. Very modern with its rounded roof and the great cross standing beside it."

"Wasn't Bernardo O'Higgins born here?" Rod asked.

"Who's he?" Meryl chipped in.

"The great Chilean liberator," Carlie told her.

"With a name like O'Higgins!"

"Sure. I think he had an Irish great-grandfather or something."

"So when will we reach the university in Concepción?" Sally Ann wanted to know. "We're a week behind schedule already, after that blow-out in the desert."

"Next Wednesday, I reckon," Dermott said.

"I wish we had time to go on further south to the Canales region. I'd love to visit the Straits of Magellan."

"Going to be hellish cold down there at this time of year. And anyway, this camper's not amphibious. The road runs out at Puerto Montt. After that you'd have to take to the water, like the locals. Or fly. There's an airfield at Punta Arenas."

"Couldn't we do that?" she begged. "Just for a day or two. Unless it's terribly expensive. Meryl and I could find some work again for a couple of weeks to pay for it, afterwards."

"Sounds like a good idea," Rod agreed. "We'll check it out in Chillán."

In the city, they sent Carlie to a travel agent. He came back shaking his head. "No go, gang. Punta Arenas is out."

"Frozen up, eh?"

"Naw. They have some kind of epidemic down there and the whole place is quarantined."

"Well, hell," Dermott said. "That is the last place we want to be. What kind of epidemic?"

"Search me," Carlie said. "But it must be serious. People are dying."

"They need cousin Meg down there to help them," Rod quipped; the gang was always teasing Sally Ann about her godmother and her famous boss.

"If it's bad enough, she'll be in on it," Sally Ann agreed. "That's her job."

"And she can keep it," Rod said.

"Incredible," Graham Fitzroy said. He passed the newspaper across the breakfast table to Meg. "A whole village just wiped out."

Meg scanned the report; the English newspaper was a day old. "Some kind of food poisoning? Is that possible?"

Fitzroy gazed out over the Alps; they were taking a brief holiday in Salzburg before starting home – the lecture tour had ended two days before in Vienna. "Theoretically, yes. Practically, no. Food poisoning can kill some people pretty quickly. But it couldn't knock out a whole village in less than a week. I mean, why didn't they get help from the mainland? They couldn't have been that isolated. Anyway, that doesn't sound like food poisoning to me."

Meg studied the report again, and this time read it aloud:

From our correspondent in Santiago: TRAGEDY ON ISLA HOSTE

Reports from Punta Arenas on the Straits of Magellan, the southernmost Chilean town, indicate that the inhabitants of a whole village on the remote island of Hoste, south of the Straits, have been wiped out by what is called a 'mystery disease'. There has been no official statement as to what caused the catastrophe, although there are rumours that it may have been the result of some virulent form of food poisoning. The first doctors on the scene, however, seemed horrified and bewildered by what they had found, and police who flew into the area with the medical team, after discovering a motor vessel with a dead skipper drifting in the Straits, have spoken of whole families dead in their houses, unburied corpses in the streets, and a great deal of blood. "Almost like a massacre," one said, "except that none of the bodies is injured."

It appears that attempts had been made to burn some of the dead before the rest of the community was overcome. "The whole thing must have happened in forty-eight hours," an operator at the Punta Arenas radio station told this reporter by telephone. "We spoke with Isla Hoste on Sunday afternoon, when they reported some outbreaks of illness. Two days later they were all dead. It is uncanny." The only survivor of the tragedy, a woman, Mrs Maria Lopez, who was saved from the drifting boat, was unable to throw any light on the catastrophe except to say it was something they ate; sadly, Mrs Lopez died in a Punta Arenas hospital last night. Doctors say she appeared to have a stroke, caused, they suspect, by the enormous strain of the events she had witnessed.

"It *is* uncanny," Meg said.

"And frightening," Fitzroy commented. "When's our flight home?"

"Tomorrow morning we fly into London, and next day we go on to New York," Meg said.

"Could we catch a flight out today, instead?"

"I suppose so." She frowned. "You bothered?"

"When did you last hear of an entire community dropping dead in forty-eight hours?"

"Well . . . I never have. Except . . . "

"Except in your history books, eh? The Black Death."

"But . . . surely not. Anyway, the symptoms would have been recognised right off. And there is no external bleeding with bubonic plague."

"Sure. This is definitely not bubonic plague. But it is something which appears to be even more virulent. I want to get home, Meg, just as quickly as possible."

Meg finished her coffee and stood up. "I'll change those tickets."

"And could you get on the phone to San Francisco? Tell Hal that I want copies of the post mortem reports on the people on Isla Hoste, just as rapidly as he can obtain them."

Meg nodded, and hurried from the dining-room.

5

'Nothing to Worry About'

"Ladies and gentlemen, the Captain is about to commence our approach to John F. Kennedy International Airport and requests that you fasten your seat belts, extinguish all cigarettes . . . " The air hostess's voice droned through the usual routine and Peter Canning looked at his watch yet again.

It was about time! Three hours' delay at Heathrow . . . technical problems. Now there was no chance of getting to his hotel to drop off his bag and have a wash, let alone contact Meg Calhoun. To be honest, he was not too fussed about the bag or the wash, but he was cheesed off that Meg could be left thinking he had stood her up. Maybe, if they were not too hung up at this end . . . but they would be: American Immigration was the pits. Of course they had to do their job, but he had never yet arrived in the States without having to stand for ages in an endless line, watching the US citizens sailing straight through the barrier unheeded.

Doctor Margaret Kathleen Calhoun! There had been no doubt in his mind, since that afternoon they spent together in Hyde Park, that in some way she was special. Why, was difficult to pinpoint: he only knew that he had a gut feeling about her, like a schoolboy crush. Surely he was too old and experienced a hand with women, now, for anything like that? No, he just knew that she was one of those very rare females, like Angela had been, his kind of woman; unpretentious, yet totally self-possessed.

Another glance at the time had him grinding his teeth in frustration. He had to queue for a cab, too, and eventually arrived at the conference hall twenty minutes late – too late to find the people with whom he was meant to link up.

New York was hot and humid. He felt thoroughly irritable.

The xeroxed report dropped back on to Meg's lap. She was sitting in the only chair in a tiny New York hotel bedroom . . . waiting. Repeatedly, over the past two weeks she had told herself she was not really the slightest bit interested in the English MP, but the attempted con trick was not working. She was fond of Joey Martino, in an almost sisterly way, and she had really loved that fellow Mal, all those years ago, but Peter . . . She had sat here by the phone ever since lunch, waiting, willing it to ring so she could hear his voice again. He had promised to call before his health conference began at six and it was now 6.45 . . . "Don't be an idiot, girl," she told herself aloud. "It was stupid to imagine he'd even remember your name. You've got work to do. Do it, do it." She picked up the report again, found the page . . . and the phone buzzed.

"Meg? It's Gray. Thank God I got you. Have you heard the news?"

News? Oh, Lord. Don't say there's been an aircrash. "No?" She held her breath.

"This odd epidemic in South America is spreading," relieved, her breath hissed through her teeth, " . . . seriously enough to hit the headlines. I've got to get back to California immediately; the report we sent for is waiting for me there. But there are some specimens which have been dispatched to us here for some reason. I was able to get a flight this evening and I'm checking out now, but we must have those blood samples on the West Coast as soon as possible. So I'm going to ask you to stay on here another night, pick them up in the morning and follow on the first available flight. Got it?"

Yes, she had got it. And it must be very serious for Graham to change his plans so suddenly. But what about Peter? What if he turned up tomorrow and she was not here? She told him she would be eastside for some days . . . "Yes, I read you. Sounds bad. But what about tomorrow afternoon's seminar?"

"I've cancelled. This has to take priority."

"Sure. That's okay. So I'll see you just as soon as I can make it." Life was full of disappointments.

"Good girl. Say, didn't that English MP we had lunch with in London say he was coming over?"

"You mean Peter Canning?" she asked, as though uncertain.

"That sounds like the name. He was with the Ministry of Health, wasn't he?"

"Yes," Meg said.

"I was hoping we might be able to contact him. He could be a useful type to keep in touch with. If this does turn out to be a viral epidemic, and it's beginning to look like it, we may need plenty of inter-governmental co-operation to get on top of it."

"He said he would be at the World Health Organization meeting here . . . " she tried to sound vague.

"Do you think you might locate him?"

Her heart skipped a beat. "I can surely try."

"Good girl. You're a poppet," Graham said enthusiastically. "If you do see him, get his address and phone number. Be nice to the guy. Now I guess I must burn rubber if I'm to make that flight. See you soon, Meg."

"Will do, Gray. Have a good flight." And thanks for the perfect excuse to go find the man.

Some of the conference speakers were good, others indifferent. This one was abysmal. Peter stifled a yawn, arranged his papers neatly on the bench desk in front of him and let his gaze wander across the room. He was aware of someone moving up to occupy the vacant seat beside him and turned . . . to look straight into Meg's blue Irish eyes. He suppressed the urge to take her in his arms and hug her. Instead he leaned over and whispered, "Sorry I couldn't call you. The plane was three hours late and I didn't even have time to go to my hotel." Her hair tickled his nose. It smelled of fresh shampoo.

"Gray called me earlier to ask if I'd contact you here," she whispered back.

So she had not come here looking for him of her own volition. The pang of disappointment replaced any curiosity he might have felt regarding Fitzroy's reason for wanting to be in touch and he turned back into the middle of her next sentence.

". . . across South America. I've to collect specimens tomorrow and . . . "

"What happened in South America?" he asked for a re-cap.

"Sssh!" The man in front turned to frown at them.

"I'll tell you afterwards," Meg mouthed at him, and thereafter they maintained the required silence till the conference broke up an hour and a half later.

It was a good thing she did not have to write a report on the proceedings, Meg thought as they threaded their way out through the scrum: she really had not been concentrating. In the cool of the excessively air-conditioned atmosphere, the warmth of Peter's elbow on the armrest between them had been very distracting. She had been able to study his hands, surreptitiously as she did not want him to notice. They were small, in relation to his height, but strong, smoothly hairless and with nails clipped short. Generally, he could not be described as immaculate, rather as one to whom physical appearance mattered only as much as was necessary and practicable.

In the foyer Peter caught up with the people he should have met earlier. He had to repeat his excuses for his late arrival several times, politely introducing his companion to various representatives from different countries, and when she found herself face to face with a Chilean, Meg immediately took the opportunity to question him on the latest development in the epidemic.

"Epidemic?" He frowned, "Ah! I think you refer to this matter a section of the press has unearthed in the far south, down in the Canales district. It is not exactly an epidemic. Merely some unfortunate people who have succumbed to an infection. Nothing to worry about." He shook his head, smiling condescendingly at the small American woman.

"But a whole village was wiped out! And it is spreading north quite rapidly. That has to be something more serious than 'just an infection'," she persisted, "And I understand your health department is sending specimens for analysis to the Robert Koch Research Center in San Francisco because they do not know what is causing it."

The Chilean was short, stocky, and visibly irritated. "I cannot think where you obtained that information." The smile had disappeared, his head tilting back to point his chin at her, aggressively. "Probably from some sensation-seeking newspaper."

Peter had rejoined her, heard the man's offensive reply and, anticipating her annoyance, was about to lend his support . . . but she did not need it.

Meg smiled sweetly at her opponent and said softly, "I think the Chilean health department has failed to keep you up-to-date with current developments, Señor Alonzo. I have here," she tapped her shoulder bag, "the latest report. Do you know that more than a hundred of your people have succumbed to this unknown illness in less than a month?"

Alonzo flushed angrily. "How did you," he pointed at her, "come by that report? It is not intended for . . . "

Peter opened his mouth, but was again forestalled.

"I am a medical doctor at the Research Center." Meg was still smiling. "This is my field. I will be starting work on the specimens your people have sent us as soon as I get to California tomorrow. I sincerely hope we may be able to help you with this tragic problem."

"Huh? Hmm. Well . . . " the aggressive little man floundered. "Yes. Yes, I see. Well, what did you say your name was . . . "

"Calhoun. Doctor Calhoun."

"Well, Señorita Calhoun, I hope so, too. Good evening," and he stamped away without apology.

"The sod!" Peter exploded.

Meg laughed. "It's difficult enough for a woman to be taken seriously in Europe. In Chile it seems like I don't have a hope."

"Do you include Britain, when you say Europe?"

She looked up at him thoughtfully. "I guess so."

"Then I think I'd better take you out to dinner and try to dispel that idea."

"Sounds good. I'd like that, the dinner, I mean. I doubt you'll have much success with your project though!"

He took her arm. "Let's get out of here."

"Are you sure you've seen everyone you should?" She did not want him to feel obliged to leave, just because she was with him.

"On the contrary, I'm damn sure there are several more people I should be polite to on behalf of Her Majesty's Government, but there's someone else I prefer to spend that precious time with. Come on." He led her out on to the hot street, still carrying his overnight bag.

"So what's all this about flying back to California tomorrow?" Peter asked her across the table of a Japanese

111

restaurant. "You told me you would be here for some days."

Meg explained, adding, "I must get to a phone, soon. I have a god-daughter touring Chile with a bunch of college friends in a camper. I want to be sure that when one of them calls home they are warned to get out, quickly."

"I suppose outbreaks of odd diseases occur quite frequently in remote areas," he remarked, "but we just don't hear about them."

"Not true. An epidemic this virulent is quite a rarity these days." But she did not want to talk 'shop' over dinner so she asked, "How long are you in New York?"

Peter shrugged. "I don't know, now. I suppose I might as well go back tomorrow."

"Had you planned to stay on?"

"As long as you were here, yes."

"I guess you'll have to come over to California instead. Know it?" She spoke casually, but her heart was turning somersaults.

Peter gazed at her. "Are you serious?"

She frowned, wondering what he meant.

"I mean, would you have time to show me anything of the sights?"

"Sure I'll have time!" she responded eagerly. "I don't intend to stand, day and night, over a hot microscope. I could also give you some gen on this disease."

"Would Fitzroy go for that?"

"It was his idea. I can tell you that he's worried it may spread and become a world health problem. Let's say he's starting to do a little quiet lobbying well in advance."

"I'm glad he thought of me."

"But are you serious? Will you really come?"

He looked solemnly into her eyes. "Do you really want me to?"

She gulped. He was asking much more than just that. He was not looking for a 'no strings' visit . . . was she? She took a deep breath, "Yes," she said quietly. "Yes, I would like you to. I . . . I'd like the opportunity to get to know you better."

He read what was in her mind: she was not one hundred per cent sure, yet. But there was time. "Let's see if we can get seats on the same flight, shall we?"

"You mean, let fate decide?" She laughed.

"I find you can push fate around quite a bit if you try."

They gave themselves over to the dainty and decorous business of their Japanese meal, waited on by almond-eyed girls in colourful kimonos. Meg had often eaten in the many Japanese restaurants in San Francisco and explained each dish to Peter. He had never been able to face raw fish before: now he admitted it was delicious.

It was almost midnight when, having wiped their hands on hot, damp towels, they were served with scented tea.

"Where is your hotel?" Peter asked.

"Way down on Thirty-sixth. I'll get a cab."

"I'll come with you."

"And you're at the Dorset, just across this street! You will not: that would be stupid."

He hesitated, then said, "Do you want to go all that way tonight?"

She took a sip of tea, slowly replaced the fragile cup, and then reached out to place a hand over his on the table. "Shall we wait and see what fate has in store for us in California?"

Peter turned his hand to grasp her fingers. "Sorry. That was a bit premature of me, especially considering I haven't even kissed you yet."

"Oh!" She laughed softly. "You did have that in mind, did you?"

"Since before we got to Hyde Park, a million years ago."

"At least," she agreed.

They sat gazing at each other, not moving, still holding hands while the waitress refilled their teacups.

"It's been a bit sudden, hasn't it?" Meg commented in a matter-of-fact voice.

"One does become more positive as one gets older. More certain."

"Yes," she agreed. She withdrew her hand and lifted the strap of her bag from the back of her chair. "Let's find me that cab before I change my mind."

They could not leave New York until after lunch as the specimens from Chile failed to arrive until noon. Then the flight was full and the stewardess had to re-arrange some lone passengers to get them two seats together. It was six before they landed in San Francisco, and there was no question of finding Peter an hotel: Meg left him standing with the baggage while she fetched her car from the park and, as it was too late to go to the Research Center that evening, they drove together straight to her apartment.

It did not face the sea. "I spend so little time here during the day, it didn't warrant taking on double the mortgage, just to know the sea was out there," Meg explained.

The decor was an interesting blend of ancient and modern. Despite the fact that the view was limited to other buildings and TV aerials, the focal point of the lounge was the window, hung with white drapes and massed with house plants and a bronze 'Apollo'. The settees were contemporary white, against which the old maple table and sideboard were magnificent. The pictures were modern including two large, unframed surrealist canvases and a collection of four Chinese silk paintings.

"You have more view and sunlight than I have in London," Peter assured her. "Hey, this must be ET? How did he get in?" He watched in amazement as a cat emerged from the kitchenette which had definitely been empty a few moments before.

"Sweetie!" She bent to pick him up and hug him. "He has a burglar-proof cat-flap in the door on to the porch."

"Why ET? Oh, I remember, you told me . . . "

"Because he just appeared from outta space, right. I had left a window open while I was out and when I returned he was sitting on the table, watching me. I can't think how he reached the window-ledge, it's one helluva leap from the porch wall and a sheer drop below."

Peter scratched round the cat's ears. "He's jolly healthy," he said, noting the glossy black coat with white shirt front and socks.

"And your cat is named Gladstone."

"That's right. You have a good memory."

"Useful in my work." Meg deposited ET on the kitchen counter and took some Super Supper out of the fridge. "There, that should keep you quiet for a while," she said, then led the way into her bedroom. It had a king-size bed. She opened a wardrobe door. "You can hang your things in there. I must phone Gray and let him know that I've arrived and will be in tomorrow." She went off to use the phone in the lounge without waiting for his reply.

Peter felt dazed. The situation seemed quite ridiculous; apart from holding Meg's hand, briefly, in the restaurant last night, and brushing her lips even more briefly, under the impatient eye of the cab driver who waited to take her to her hotel, he had not touched her. Yet here he was in her bedroom, sharing her wardrobe, her bathroom and soon to share her bed . . . It was almost indecent. Almost as though he had hired a call girl. That was not how he wanted it to be.

She was back in a few minutes. "The news from South America is quite dramatic. I hope to God my aunt gets Sally Ann to come home immediately. And," she added, "even more alarming is the news of a possible second outbreak. In New Zealand, this time."

Peter looked startled. "The same thing?"

"It could be."

"Food poisoning, several thousand miles apart?"

"If it is food poisoning," Meg said. "We have our doubts."

"Whereabouts in New Zealand is this outbreak?"

"Somewhere down the bottom end of South Island. Gray didn't specify. Why, do you know New Zealand?"

"Not well. But I have a sister out there. I suppose I shouldn't worry. The New Zealand Government will get it licked pretty quickly. They're doubtless more efficient than the Chileans."

Meg shrugged. "We'll have to wait on an up-date. Now, food."

"Yes. I'm starving. I could eat a horse."

"Well I don't have horse in the freezer. So let's go to the little eatery down the hill; it's only two blocks away. The food is plain but good."

The cloth was red-chequered and a bottle of Californian rosé was placed on it automatically. "Hi, Meg. Good to see you back. You been far?" The short, plump, smiling Italian greeted Meg in a fatherly fashion.

"The other side of the world, Tony. Europe. But it's good to be back. How's Momma?"

"She's doing fine, but little Angelo ain't so good. Doc says he's got chicken pox."

When they had ordered antipasta, lasagna and salad, Tony disappeared into the kitchen.

Meg looked at Peter's face. "Tired?" she asked.

"No, not really. I can't get used to the time change, yet, though. It's only halfway through the evening, yet it's past midnight at least, according to my metabolism."

116

"Are you sure it's the time that's disorientating you, or is it us?"

The deep blue eyes bored into his and he realised she must be feeling the same as himself – that their relationship had got out of hand before really starting. "I didn't come to 'Frisco to bed you."

"No?" She raised an eyebrow.

He frowned. "No."

"Then why did you come?"

"Because . . . because I think you are someone special . . . "

"But you're not sure?"

He hesitated for a second. "We hardly know each other."

"True. But the chemistry's good. Correct?"

Peter laughed. "Is that the research doctor speaking?" he asked, but before she could reply he went on, "Yes. Correct. I suppose my English reserve is telling me that it's all happening too fast for a serious relationship. This speed is for one-night stands." He took one of her hands and held it between both of his. "But we are two busy people. Too busy and living too far apart to hang about, waiting on the niceties. Especially once we are certain?"

Meg's expression was solemn, the candlelight reflecting in her eyes. She took a breath, as though to speak, but no words came.

"You're not certain either?" Peter tried not to sound anxious.

"It's not that. I just hadn't realised till now how seriously you were thinking . . . "

"Does that worry you?"

"Yes, in a way." She sipped her wine, pensively. "Peter, once before, years ago, I felt like this. He and I both. I let it go too far before explaining to him that I'm a career girl, that I would never give up my work for a home and babies and playing little wifey. It wasn't deliberate, just stupid, but I was cruel to him, let him believe I was thinking the same way he was . . . until he started talking marriage." She stared at the squares on the cloth. "I hurt him, badly. And when he walked out of my life I thought I would die." Her face turned up to his, "I don't ever want to do that to anyone, or to myself, again."

Peter's mind raced. The spectre of Angela was before him. He thought of his dream home, filled with children and dogs. He thought about the Appletons and their lively youngsters. He and Grant had always shared the same ideals, the same ambitions – at least domestically. But Grant had had the sense to go for it, and had to be one of the happiest men alive, as a result. The sad thing was, he could have married Julia himself, instead of introducing her to his best friend. But he had not been interested in marriage, then. There was too much to be done, and not enough time to do it.

And perhaps it had not been a sad thing after all. Maybe even Angela had been no more than a preparation. And while these thoughts were passing through his mind he was looking at Meg. Did those dreams, those fantasies, mean anything compared with finding the perfect soulmate? Would she remain a soulmate if he began to resent being denied a family? Blamed her. He would need to take care. Could their relationship bridge the Atlantic on a permanent basis? Of course it could, if they were both determined.

She watched his expression, waiting, trying to prepare herself for the response she dreaded.

"I've been through all that, too. I've loved . . . and lost." He was still holding her hand. Now he raised it to his lips. "Now I love you, Meg. Thanks for telling me, but if things go well with you and me, that's all I'll ask."

The kisses on the back of her fingers sent electric waves shooting up her arm. "Sure?"

"Certain. What about you?"

"I'm certain. But just a little scared, too."

He leaned towards her and she towards him, for their first real kiss . . .

But Tony broke the spell with the antipasta. "There you are, the best in 'Frisco," he announced, adding, "Say, with that weirdo accent you must be from England, yeah?"

Peter smiled politely and nodded.

"I got a cousin there, maybe you've met him . . . " and he leaned over the back of an empty chair while he went into detail.

So when they arrived back at the apartment Peter had still not kissed her.

They had walked home in silence, thinking; with so much to say it was hard to know where to begin.

As the door slammed shut behind them Peter looked around. "By the way, where's Liza?"

"On a research project in Alaska for six weeks."

"Good," he said, drawing her into his arms. She went to him without hesitation, leaned her cheek against his chest, the top of her head not reaching his shoulder. When she looked up at him he bent to kiss her, and this time there was no interruption. It was a gentle kiss. A soft meeting of lips, caressing, exploring each other, but with a building excitement. Peter's tongue moved over her mouth, parting the lips. She opened to him, stroking softly on the smooth underside of his tongue.

They undressed together in the bedroom without embarrassment, slid into bed and Peter found himself thinking how different this was from being with Anna. Anna was so experienced, so accomplished a lover; her sophistication in the bedroom quite macho, the bedroom itself exotic – erotic. It was the one place she never acted, where she was totally her true self: perhaps that was what had attracted old Papagopoulos sufficiently to make him want it permanently. Not that Meg was a virgin. She made no pretence of being inexperienced but sensationalism, eroticism, obviously did not figure so largely in her life. He looked across the stretch of pillows at the pert, freckled nose, the soft, smiling mouth waiting for him to take the initiative. An old-fashioned girl, despite her lib. His forefinger traced the hairline down from her forehead to her chin; moved across to circle her lips, climbing her nose to caress the one visible eyebrow.

"You're very lovely," he told her.

His voice was so matter-of-fact that she could not resist a giggle. "Flattery will get you anywhere, at this moment," she assured him.

"I never resort to flattery unless I'm after votes."

She was in his arms again, aware of his arousal . . . and her own. Her hands were on his back, feeling the lithe muscles, tracing his spine from the nape of his neck, slowly down to the curve of his bottom. His lips were exploring her face again before taking possession of her mouth. She had dreamed of this, last night in New York – but reality was better. His mouth moved down her neck to each breast in turn, while her hips writhed with impatience. She had been drawn to this man since the first day they met and the wine at supper had removed the last doubts in her mind. The weight of his body was on her and she lifted to receive him, the sensation melting her mind and limbs.

He was slow, gentle and thoughtful, waiting for her until he could no longer contain himself. When he recovered his breath he looked down into her face. "Nothing for you?" he asked anxiously.

"Lack of practice," she smiled. "I'll improve. Don't let it bother you."

"I'm sorry, but thanks for not pretending. I'm afraid I was too quick."

"No way. Remember, we have three days. Now, I'm afraid I have to be up early, to get down to the Center so I must get some sleep."

"Can I come with you? You said Gray wanted to contact me."

"Why, of course." She kissed his nose. "I'll set the alarm."

"Peter!" Graham Fitzroy shook hands, glanced at Meg. If he noticed anything different about his assistant, or if he was surprised that Peter should have arrived in San Francisco with Meg, he did not show it. Rather he looked at once distracted and tired.

"When did you get in?" Meg asked.

"Before dawn."

"Oh, I should have come in earlier," she apologised, and flushed as Peter looked at her.

Graham shook his head. "I reckon one person looking at a slide can find as much as two at this stage," he pointed out. "I've been doing just that for four hours, and I don't like what I am seeing."

Peter was gazing around the large laboratory. It seemed to contain every known variety of microscope, as well as huge filing cabinets and others filled with specimens. "You work here all alone?"

"Not as a rule. I've given the others something else to do."

Meg was frowning. "That bad?"

"I don't know. I can't believe it. I want you to tell me I'm wrong."

Meg sat on his stool and put her eye to the microscope.

"This epidemic, eh?" Peter asked. "I gather you don't think it is food poisoning?"

"No."

"Then what is it?"

Fitzroy sighed. "If you mean what's causing it, I have no idea."

Peter raised his eyebrows. "No common or garden virus, eh?"

121

"Well . . . "

"Polycythaemia?" Meg asked in wonderment. She was still staring into the microscope.

"I was hoping you wouldn't say that," Fitzroy growled. "Yes. It is definitely polycythaemia."

"I know I'm ignorant," Peter said. "But what the devil is polycythaemia?"

"Know anything about blood?"

"Well, I know mine isn't blue."

"It's red. Because of the haemoglobin carried by your red corpuscles."

"That figures."

Meg at last raised her head. "Polycythaemia is a condition where you have too many of the little marvels."

"Is that bad?"

"Well, it can be. Too much of anything is bad, I guess."

"Okay," Fitzroy said. "Consider this, Peter. Blood is composed of four things: plasma, which is ninety per cent water; red cells, or erythrocytes; white blood cells, or leucocytes; and platelets, or thrombocytes. There are a lot of these, with red blood cells predominating. For instance, the average human being has between 150,000 and 300,000 platelets in each cubic millimetre of blood. There are seldom more than about 11,000 white cells in a cubic millimetre. But the normal red cell count, what we call the rbc, is between four million and six million per cubic millimetre."

Peter whistled. "Some difference."

"Yeah. Now all of these essential components are very carefully regulated. Blood is manufactured by our bone marrow. On the average, the marrow produces one pint of blood a week, with all its requisite cells. Now as you know, things can go wrong with white cell production."

Peter nodded. "Leukaemia."

"Right. But things can also go wrong with red cell production."

"Anaemia," Peter suggested.

"True. But there are more serious conditions even than anaemia. A red cell lives for approximately four months. Then it dies and is excreted. In a normal healthy individual the bone marrow keeps its production of red cells to the level exactly required to replace the loss. But sometimes it over-produces."

"This isn't necessarily malignant," Meg said. "Sometimes it's absolutely necessary. Then we call it relative polycythaemia. It occurs after the body has lost a lot of blood, or has suffered a draining process such as extreme diarrhoea; then there is a shortage of oxygen and the marrow produces additional corpuscles to cope with it. As soon as the condition is arrested, so is the corpuscle production."

"But polycythaemia also has an absolute as opposed to a relative variety," Fitzroy explained. "This in turn has two aspects. One, which we call erythrocytosis, occurs when there is an oxygen deficiency in any part of the body, for whatever reason. It could be an embolism or an incipient coronary. When this happens, a message is sent to the marrow calling for more haemoglobin, and more red blood cells are pumped into the system. As with relative polycythaemia, this is a benign condition, and is cured whenever the underlying disease is cured."

"But the other condition isn't benign?" Peter suggested.

"Right," Meg said. "Polycythaemia vera, or erythremia, is a real nasty. Trouble is, we don't know what causes it. It is simply a cancer of the marrow which spills red blood corpuscles into the system at an ever-increasing rate."

"Which means?"

"Well, high blood pressure, hypertension, certainly and quickly. But if it's not arrested, it can become very serious indeed. The victim goes red in the face, suffers nose bleeds or, in fact, internal bleeding, has tremendous headaches, and can die of a stroke or an embolism, depending on the state of his circulatory system."

"And you think these people have all died of this poly . . . whatever?"

"The symptoms indicated that right off. The cause of death in almost every case has been given as apoplexy. Now it's confirmed by the blood specimens. I don't know which of the victims that sample came from, and I haven't submitted it to analysis as yet, but I would say there are at least twelve million red cells to the cubic millimetre in that fellow's blood. Were, I guess."

Peter scratched his head. "Is this condition often encountered?"

"It's very rare."

"And you don't know what's causing it?" Peter snapped his fingers. "But you know what it is, and you have encountered it before. So you must know how to cure it."

"No," Meg said. "We don't know how to cure it. We can't, until we know what the cause is. What we can do is alleviate it, in normal circumstances. It's a very logical treatment. Too much blood, so we draw off a pint. That immediately restores the patient's health. But . . . "

"He continues to over-produce."

"Right. So the treatment has to be repeated every three months or so."

"There is a way of stopping it more thoroughly," Fitzroy said. "By injecting radioactive phosphorus. That acts on the marrow, and puts a stop to blood production altogether. But of course, pumping radioactive material into the human body is looking for trouble in other directions, and the side-effects can be frightening."

"And even that treatment has to be repeated fairly regularly," Meg put in. "I mean, we can't just stop blood production, or the patient would die anyway. So it has to be a carefully monitored process."

"What about busulfan?" Peter asked. "Isn't that a drug they use to combat the over-production of white cells in leukaemia? Couldn't it be used to cure polycythaemia as well?"

"It can, and is. But that too has side-effects."

"Side-effects are better than having people dying all over the place."

"Of course. But the point is, these treatments are intended for single cases of the condition. There never has been such a thing as an epidemic of polycythaemia vera in the whole history of medicine, nor has it ever been in the slightest degree contagious. Here we have an epidemic, which has to be as contagious as bubonic plague. I mean, fifty-odd people dying in a single village in a matter of days? And now it's affecting Punta Arenas. That's a big town. Meg, I've made up my mind. I'm going down there."

"To Chile? It's the middle of the winter."

"So I'll take my longjohns. I don't like what's happening one little bit. And frankly, I'm not sure they can cope. I want to talk to the health authorities, get them to institute a proper quarantining system, try to find out just how this thing is being transmitted, and how it began. I can't accept it's a form of fish poisoning. And I've got to get some more, and better, specimens for analysis. These cells were dead for several days before they sent them up here."

"I'll come with you."

"Now wait a moment . . . " Peter protested.

"You'll hold the fort here," Fitzroy said.

"Are you sure the Chileans will be glad to see you?" Peter asked.

"If I'm right about the virulence of this disease, I reckon they will be," Fitzroy said grimly. "But you'll wire their Health Ministry, Meg, and tell them I'm on my way?"

Meg nodded. "I'll get on to that right away."

There was a knock on the door.

"Yes?" Fitzroy called.

One of his assistants came in with a piece of paper. "Just arrived, Doc. Doesn't sound too good."

Fitzroy glanced at the paper. "Holy shit!" he commented. "The death count on Stewart Island is over two hundred. And some cases have been reported in Invercargill on the mainland opposite."

"New Zealand?" Peter snapped.

"Right. Meg . . . "

Meg nodded. "You go to Chile, I'll go to New Zealand."

"Today."

Another nod. "I'll organise the flights."

"Say, Peter, I'm sure sorry to have to run out on you like this, but this is a real emergency. Incidentally, though, I'd be obliged if you kept all of this under your hat. No use frightening people until we see if we can cope with it."

"Yes," Peter said absently; he would of course have to report to his minister. He followed Meg from the room and into her office. "Meg . . . "

"Get hold of Worldair," she was telling Helen, her secretary. "I'll speak to them myself."

Helen, a tall blonde whose languorous appearance concealed a good deal of energy, nodded and began punching numbers.

"I know," Meg said. "I promised you three days. I am sorry, Peter. I'll be in touch when I get back."

He sat on the other side of her desk. "I'm not thinking of that. Meg, this sounds like a highly dangerous disease."

"You aren't kidding."

"I have Worldair, Meg," Helen said.

Meg picked up her desk phone. "Hello? Worldair? Meg Calhoun. Is Margie there? Hey, Margie; Meg. Say, the Doc and I need to do a little travelling . . . Last night. Yeah, I know; here today and gone tomorrow. Okay. I want one to Chile, a place called Punta

Arenas, way down south . . . right, Santiago and then Concepción and a local flight on to Punta Arenas . . . leaving this afternoon. Great. That's for the Doc. Now for me, New Zealand. Invercargill in South Island . . . got it, Christchurch and a local to Invercargill . . . leaving tonight. Right, I'll send over for them. Thanks a million, Margie."

She replaced the phone and gazed at Peter. "I'm afraid that's it."

"We can have lunch together."

"Sure we can. And I'm not leaving until tonight. But I'm afraid, in the meantime . . . "

"You have work to do," he agreed.

They met for lunch, and he held her hands. "Meg, I was trying to say, this morning, that you are sticking your neck out. If this is a viral disease, and is as contagious as you think it is . . . "

"I've had to handle contagious diseases before, and I'm still here, Peter. Besides, it goes with the job."

"Yes, but . . . "

They gazed at each other.

"We talked about this, Peter," Meg said. "Only yesterday, remember? Meeting you, sharing with you, has been one of the big things in my life. Maybe it could become the biggest, on the personal side. But I'm also a working girl, who has to go where she's needed." She smiled at him. "Don't you want to feel that your sister is safe?"

"Hell, yes, of course. But she and her husband have a farm in North Island. That's a long way from Invercargill."

"It won't be if we don't stop this thing from spreading."

Peter frowned. "Mmm. Maybe it would be an idea to try and persuade Sarah to take her husband and kids back to the UK till it's all over." He stared into

Meg's face. "Could I ask you to telephone her when you're there?"

"Of course. What do you want me to say?"

He was still frowning. "Better not make it too positive. We don't want them phoning all their neighbours and starting a panic. That won't help."

She smiled. "Don't worry, I'll think of something."

"Meg . . . I love you."

"I love you, Peter. Please don't worry about me on this trip. I promise I'll be in touch the moment we get this problem sorted out." She squeezed his fingers. "Maybe I'll even take a holiday. I think I'll need one. How does that idea grab you?"

"I like it." He knew it was useless protesting any further. It was not as if he had any rights over her. They had slept together once, and they thought they loved each other: had even dared to admit it. "Just take great care of yourself."

"I always do that."

He went back to the Center with her to say goodbye to Fitzroy and wish him luck. The professor was just leaving to catch his plane when a short, tubby little man carrying a box hurried into the office.

"Hey, Doc! Meggy!" He looked Peter up and down.

"Peter Canning, from England," Meg explained. "Charlie Oswiecki. What brings you here, Charlie?"

Oswiecki set the box on her desk. "Present from Doc Lintell. Bits from his find down in the Antarctic. He's finished with them, but he thought you might like to take a look. Seems there's some things in there he's never seen before. He wants you to identify them for him."

"What sort of things?" Fitzroy asked.

"Oh, tinies. Microbes, germs, maybe viruses . . ."

"Sounds like fun. They'll have to wait, Charlie. Meg and I are going to be away for the next couple of days."

"Sure," Oswiecki agreed. "They're in preservative. And as they've been around for a hundred thousand years a coupla weeks more ain't gonna bug them. Say, Mr Canning, you been to the exhibition?"

"What exhibition?"

"Haven't you heard of the monster Tom Lintell dug out of the Antarctic ice?" Meg asked.

Peter snapped his fingers. "A . . . megatherium. They're calling it the find of the century."

"That's right. Gray's daughter is Tom's sidekick."

"They must be very chuffed with themselves."

"You can say that again," Oswiecki said. "That is one big creature. And it's dragging them in by the thousand!"

"No, I haven't seen it," Peter confessed. "But . . . I may stop off in New York and have a look. I have a couple of days to kill."

6

A Very Active Virus

Meg had also cabled ahead for herself, and an official from the New Zealand Ministry of Health met her at Christchurch. "I must say, we're glad you're here, Dr Calhoun," he said. "We're trying to keep a low publicity profile, of course, but the situation is, well, worrying."

"How worrying?" Meg asked.

"We've had to evacuate Stewart Island. Everything, and I mean everything, is dead there."

"Define everything."

"Well, people, animals, even birds . . . "

"But not fish?" Meg asked thoughtfully.

"No," he agreed. "Not fish." And frowned. "There's talk that this is a form of ptomaine poisoning."

"It isn't," Meg told him. "Now I have to rush. I have a flight booked to Invercargill."

"My dear Doctor," the official said. "We have cancelled that. You are now a guest of the New Zealand Government."

A government jet was waiting for them, and only a few minutes after clearing Customs Meg was airborne again, heading south.

"I'm afraid it's pretty chilly in Invercargill, in June," the official, Mr Waters, told her.

"I haven't come to sunbathe," Meg replied.

She was being brusque, she knew. But she had come to work, and during the long flight from San Francisco, via Hawaii and Fiji, she had had too much time to think. For the first time in a very long while she was resenting having to fly away for her work. Always in the past it had been not merely dedication but excitement, and not merely the excitement of new places, either. The real excitement had been the thrill of facing new challenges, new diseases, or old ones returning in a different setting, of feeling that she was important to the survival of a lot of human beings . . . perhaps of the world itself.

This time she had been dragged away from a warm bed and the most exciting man she had ever met. She could not blame him for being slightly miffed. She only hoped that it would be possible to pick up where they left off when she, or Gray, or someone, had found the answer to this disease. She would not have admitted it to anyone, save perhaps Gray himself, but she was frightened. And she knew Gray was frightened too. What was happening was outside even his vast store of knowledge and experience. Polycythaemia vera, as she had explained to Peter, was a rare and sinister blood condition, which the medical profession accepted as a maverick, to be coped with in the best way possible. If all researchers suspected that it was caused by a virus, they were happy to agree it was so rare as to be classed with being attacked by a shark while swimming in shallow water. The thought that it could develop into a viral epidemic was terrifying.

A virus spread by contaminated fish? That she could not accept. It might have originated in the gut of a fish, but it was not possible that all the population of Isla Hoste had eaten the same fish. And now it was spreading through the whole Canales Province.

"I suppose you have some definite opinions as to what is causing this sickness?" Waters asked, hopefully.

"I'd rather gather some more data first," Meg hedged.

They landed at Invercargill airport in the late afternoon. A car was waiting, and Meg was taken straight to the office of the local Medical Officer of Health.

"We certainly do have a problem," Dr Musgrove agreed. "But we don't want to create another by causing a panic. Food poisoning from fish is not an unusual misfortune, though I have never heard of it being fatal on a scale this large. Having visiting boffins flying in tends to raise the public temperature. I'd be obliged if you wouldn't give any interviews while you're here, Dr Calhoun, without prior reference to this office."

"I won't be giving any interviews at all," Meg assured him. She unlocked her briefcase. "I've come to see if I can help you, not hinder. So, what makes you think it is food poisoning?"

"What else can it be? We have definite evidence that the outbreak originated in the house of a fisherman who had recently caught a deep-sea cod. The odd thing is there were other fish in the catch, of course, including other cod, but it seems that only a few were infected, judging by the pattern of illness. However, once ashore, as it were, the disease spread rapidly. Of course we have acted very promptly, and banned all fishing in the area; the Government is discussing now a total ban on deep-sea fishing off our shores, and even a ban on imported fish. Not that we import a great deal of fish. But of course these steps would have a serious effect on our food supply situation."

"Are the symptoms those of food poisoning: diarrhoea and vomiting?"

"Well . . . they aren't," he admitted. "But you know that."

"I do, Doctor. In our opinion the symptoms are consistent with acute polycythaemia vera."

"Ah," Musgrove said. "Yes. We had observed that. Uncanny really."

"And whatever its origin, it is, as you say, also very contagious."

"Well, yes, it appears to be, Dr Calhoun. But polycythaemia vera on a large scale . . . it's unthinkable."

"It's there, Doctor."

"My God, yes. I suppose it is. Frankly, I'm scared stiff. As for what we are going to do about it . . . Stewart Island is a disaster area, and two of the men who helped bring the bodies back are showing symptoms. Then one of my mortuary attendants had a stroke this morning. We're keeping it quiet, of course."

"You don't feel the public deserves to know the facts?"

"Well, I can't see that it would help. It could only make matters worse. Everyone knows there has been a catastrophe on Stewart Island, of course. But right now they believe it was simply poison. They will have to be told in due course, naturally. But if we can contain the disease . . . "

"Can we?"

"I was hoping you would tell me that."

"Break down the symptoms for me."

"Well . . . severe headaches, nose bleeds, some internal haemorrhages, arterial failure, death either by apoplexy or internal bleeding. As you say, acute polycythaemia. But contagious."

"That is the really important thing. I'd like to see some of the victims."

Musgrove pulled his nose. "They're not a pretty sight."

"I have to see them, Doctor."

"There's also the contagion factor."

"I'm a doctor, Doctor."

Musgrove hesitated, then nodded, picked up his phone. Late as it now was, Meg was driven down to the mortuary where a Dr Hornby was awaiting her. She donned a mask and protective clothing, and then accompanied him into a chamber, where he opened several drawers for her.

"How many post mortems have you performed?" she asked.

"Six, so far," he said. "All the symptoms were the same, and we've sent samples up to Christchurch for analysis. Frankly, my staff aren't happy about the situation. Especially since one of them went sick today."

Meg gazed for a few moments at the stiff features – still showing traces of a reddish complexion hours after death – and rigid limbs. She lifted the eyelids, peered into the ears through a borrowed auriscope, probed the noses with swabs, noting the crusts of congealed blood.

Afterwards, in the anteroom, she carefully scrubbed her hands after taking off her gloves and surgical gown. "Did you say one of your people has got it, now?" she asked Hornby, as he scrubbed at the next basin.

"One of the guards, yes. Disturbing, isn't it? I mean, poor Willis only ever saw the cadavers."

"And the men who brought them across, surely?"

"Well, yes."

"Who have also now got the disease, according to Dr Musgrove. As you say, Dr Hornby: disturbing."

She had dinner with Musgrove and his wife, and after the meal she and the doctor retired to his study.

"That mortuary guard is very ill," Musgrove told her. They had kept off 'shop' during dinner, for all the gravity of the situation.

"Yes," Meg said. "Roger, you have a massive problem here."

"I know that. For God's sake, we're trying all the usual remedies: bleeding, shooting the victims with phosphorus, busulfan . . . but the disease acts so quickly. Polycythaemia vera! Do you know that in all my life as a doctor I have never actually treated a case of it?"

"You won't find many doctors who have. But there are certain facts we have to face. We are working on specimens, and I know your people are too, but right now, apart from knowing that it's some form of viral infection, we don't have any idea what it is. Until the lab boys isolate it, we are groping in the dark. What we do know is that it is highly contagious, and that it is deadly. Now, the contagion cannot be being spread by contaminated food. That might go for Stewart Island, by the longest possible stretch of the imagination, but you're not going to tell me that your mortuary guard, or the members of the rescue party, could possibly have eaten the same food as the people on the island. Therefore it is being spread by humans, and probably animals. That means mucus, or blood, or faeces, or possibly all three."

"You are speaking of a very active virus, Meg."

"I am. And it can kill in a matter of seventy-two hours. Roger, we could be facing another Black Death-type situation."

"Except that the victims turn red instead of black," Musgrove remarked in a feeble attempt at humour.

"Okay. But it's grim, and it's going to get grimmer. Roger, you have to quarantine Invercargill, until A, we find what is causing it, and B, we find an anti-dote or a cure."

He frowned at her. "Are you crazy? This is a big place. We'd need governmental sanction for something as drastic as that. Anyway, people have been coming and going from the town all the while."

"In that case," Meg said, "God help us all."

"Surely there must be some other way of handling it."

Meg considered. "You could try moving all your living victims to a high altitude."

Musgrove snapped his fingers. "Of course. People at high altitudes normally have a lower red corpuscle count. It'd be a hell of a job, mind you. And they'd probably die before we got them there."

"And they'd probably go on over-producing there as well, with the same end-result." Meg sighed. "Look, I can't keep my eyes open any longer."

"You're spending the night here. What's your plan for tomorrow?"

"I'd like to take some samples of every sort of human excreta from the victims with me, back to the States for analysis. And I want living samples this time; all we have had so far have been already dead. I would like specimens from your mortuary guard. I have the necessary cold jars with me."

Musgrove nodded. "I'll organise that."

"First thing tomorrow morning, if you will. I also want a flight to Wellington as soon as I've got them."

"Wellington?" He looked vaguely alarmed.

"That governmental action you spoke of," Meg told him.

"Hi," Meg said into the telephone. "I'm Meg Calhoun. Would you be Sarah Lawton?"

"Why, yes," said the voice on the other end. "Have we met?"

"No, we haven't. I'm a friend of your brother Peter. He knew I was paying a brief visit to New Zealand, so he asked me to call you."

"How sweet of him," Sarah Lawton said. "And where are you calling from?"

"Wellington."

"Oh, that's not too far. Are you going to be able to get up to visit us?"

"I'm afraid not," Meg said. "I have to leave tomorrow. It really has been a flying visit."

"Oh, what a shame." She sounded genuinely sorry.

"I know," Meg said. "Peter was wondering when next you were going to visit the UK."

"Oh, God knows. We were planning for this year, but I don't think we're going to make it. Tell him, maybe next year."

"I think you should go this year," Meg suggested, trying to sound casual. "I know he would love to see you. Do you have any children?"

"Why, yes. Two." Now she was sounding mystified.

"Why not take them over to see your parents? There's still a lot of summer left."

"Well," Sarah said. "I'm afraid that would be a bit sudden, Miss Calhoun."

"Meg, and I'm a doctor," Meg corrected. "Sarah, please take your children to England this summer. Soon. As soon as you possibly can. I'll tell Peter I've spoken with you."

She replaced the phone and lay back on her bed. She was utterly exhausted. This was partly the amount of travelling she had done in the past few days. But it was also partly despair, a sense of helplessness. She had told the New Zealand Ministry of Health what she had told Musgrove, and met with a blank refusal to accept the situation.

"Quarantine an entire city, because of an outbreak of food poisoning?" the Minister, a doctor, had asked in amazement.

"It is not food poisoning," Meg had told him. "It is an extremely virulent and contagious cancer of the blood. Dr Musgrove knows that. You are sitting on the edge of the biggest epidemic in New Zealand's history."

"How can you have a blood cancer that is contagious?"

"Because it's never happened before is no reason for supposing it can't happen, Minister. It is happening. Clearly there is a viral cause for this particular form of cancer. After all, polycythaemia describes a condition, not an illness. You know as well as I that we don't really understand what causes polycythaemia vera."

"And you have identified this virus?"

137

"No," she said. "Not yet. That's the trouble. I'm hurrying home to work on it. But it's there."

"I think you should know that our own people have been looking at the samples taken from some of the victims on Stewart Island, and have been unable to discover any virus."

"I know," Meg said. "I spent all day yesterday talking with them and seeing their work. I couldn't find anything either. But it's there. It has to be there. I don't know how long it'll take us to isolate it and identify it, but until we do, people are going to die, unless you do something about it."

"We are doing something about it, Dr Calhoun: we have banned all fishing off the coasts of South Island until we have found the cause of the problem. I'm afraid quarantining a whole city is not practical."

"Then God have mercy on you all," Meg had told him.

"Who was that?" Douglas Lawton asked, filling his pipe.

"Some woman who says she's a friend of Peter's," Sarah said.

"Not that dreadful Anna person?"

"Oh, good Lord, no. Someone called Meg Calhoun. Dr Meg Calhoun, she calls herself. I must say, Peter knows the oddest people."

"Meg Calhoun. Margaret Calhoun. That rings a bell." Douglas was something of a hypochondriac, and studied every medical report published in any of the newspapers or magazines that he took. "Yes, of course. She's Graham Fitzroy's assistant."

"Who is Graham Fitzroy?" Sarah asked, fiddling with the television set; she had only just put the children to bed before Meg's phone call, and was looking forward to the play of the week.

"The authority on rare diseases. Margaret Calhoun. Yes, she's written some articles on things like multiple

138

sclerosis and the bubonic plague. You say she's in New Zealand?"

"On a flying visit. Oh, bother, reception is going to be awful. I suppose it's that beastly blizzard out there."

"I wonder what Meg Calhoun is doing here?" Douglas mused. "You don't suppose it's anything to do with that epidemic down south?"

"Probably. She seemed awfully uptight. I invited her to visit, but she couldn't spare the time, apparently. Kept banging on about us taking the children home this summer. Now, in fact. Douglas, you don't suppose Mother is ill?" She gazed at her husband with a mystified expression.

"Well, hardly old dear: wouldn't Peter have written?"

"But suppose it has just happened, and he knew this girlfriend of his was coming here . . . "

"Bit far-fetched. But why don't you simply call Peter and find out before you start getting excited? I'm afraid visiting England this year as a family is most definitely out. Of course if your mother is ill you'll have to go . . . "

"As you say, it's a bit far-fetched. I'm probably imagining things. I think I will call Peter, though, and ask him if this latest girlfriend of his is mad. I mean, what a strange thing to do."

"Peter certainly picks them," Douglas agreed, and started to relight his pipe.

At Puerto Montt, Rod drove the camper on to the ferry for the Isla de Chiloé. The crossing to the tiny port of Castro on the island, a distance of some forty miles, took just on four hours and was utterly fascinating as the little steamer threaded its way between the myriad islands of the Gulf of Ancud with the peaks of the Andes rising sharply to the east, not so high here as farther north, but still topping 7,500 feet, much of which was covered in snow.

"Boy, does that look cold," Meryl remarked. They were huddled, with the other passengers, in the tiny saloon where there was heating and protection from the icy wind.

"Not half so cold as this sea," Dermott commented. "You know what I think, folks? I think we have come far enough south. My vote is for heading back up to the equator."

"Aw," Rod protested. "We said we'd go as far as we can take the bus; that's Puerto Quellon at the bottom end of Chiloé. Anyway, we're on the ferry."

"How do you feel, Sally Ann?" Dermott asked.

Sally Ann sighed, and stared into the mist beyond them. "I just wish we were going all the way down to Tierra del Fuego. I really thought that was what we were gonna do."

"Some other time, lover," Rod said. "We don't want to get caught up in any quarantine restrictions."

"So near," Sally Ann said. "And yet so far."

"It's still one hell of a distance," Dermott pointed out. He studied his map. "I make it just about seven hundred miles to Punta Arenas, and then another two hundred to Cape Horn itself. And that's as the crow flies. This here bus is no crow. Let's take a look at Quellon, and then we'll head north for the sun."

Puerto Quellon had nothing to recommend it. It faced south-east, looking across the Gulf of Corcovado to the mountains on the mainland, but even so it was bleak and windswept. Rod found a track leading farther south yet, however, and after bumping along this for a few miles they came out on an even more windswept beach, facing the Pacific. "But there are one hell of a lot of islands just down there." Rod pointed south. "The Archipiélago de Los Chonos. Well, folks, I reckon this is it."

"What a place." Meryl hugged herself. "We gotta get out of this wind."

"There'll be some shelter back there," Carlie said, pointing at some stunted trees.

There was, in fact, a hollow there, and the ground was firm. "Couldn't be better," Rod decided. "Now we can play we're Peary at the Pole."

"It could snow," Carlie agreed, looking at the lowering black clouds.

Actually, it was not all that cold; except for the wind chill factor it would have been almost mild.

"I guess it's the nearness of the sea," Rod said, as after lunch he and Sally Ann walked down to the beach.

"Um," she remarked, gazing at the water.

He put his arm round her shoulder. "Sorry to be turning for home?"

"Yes."

"Well . . . there's a long way to go yet."

"And then?"

"You'll go back to do your final year in college, I guess, while I go out and find me a job." He had been looking out across the water as he spoke; now he turned to find her eyes fixed on him. The big question lay between them, unsaid. He edged towards it. "Will you be living out for the next semester?"

"I hadn't thought about it, yet," she said.

"Sally Ann," he spoke severely, "don't give me that. We've both been thinking about it for nearly a year. Okay, so we both reckon we're in love, whatever that might mean, but remember, my folks are divorced; so's most of my family, and it plays hell with one's life." He tucked his hands under his arms to warm them. "I don't want to make that mistake if I can avoid it. Call me scared, if you like."

"Would I ever criticise you for being cautious?" She linked a hand through his arm. "We could share a place, and see how things go on. Talk about it again after I graduate."

"I hoped you'd say that, honey. I know your folks don't go much for you living in sin, but to me it seems to make sense." Half of him wanted to get married to Sally Ann just as soon as he had a job and a place they could call home, but not the other half. He hoped she was not too disappointed in him, or hurt.

"Agreed. I always knew men took longer to make up their minds about these things," she quipped, hoping to see him smile.

But Rod was staring moodily out to sea. Visibility was poor, as patches of mist swept across the landscape. "Hey," he said. "There's a ship out there."

Sally Ann squinted. "You're right. Looks like a fishing boat."

Rod was frowning. "It looks as if it's drifting. That's odd. There are a lot of rocks around here. Sally, go fetch Carlie."

She ran off, and came back with all three of the others.

"What do you reckon?" Rod asked.

"She sure don't look under control," Carlie agreed.

"She's coming closer," Dermott said.

The trawler was now clearly visible, only two hundred yards from the shore.

"There's nobody on board," Meryl said, wonderingly.

"Must've broken from her moorings," Rod said. "Heck, she's coming ashore."

The five of them watched with fascinated horror as the trawler came closer, rolling with the waves.

"Is there nothing we can do?" Sally Ann asked.

"Nope," Carlie told her. "She'll have hit long before we could get back to Quellon for the coastguard."

"I wonder if we could salvage her?" Rod muttered. "There'd be some dough in that."

"You know anything about boats?" Carlie asked.

"Some. If I could get aboard . . . "

"Forget it," Sally Ann recommended. "That water is icy."

Rod stared at the ship, but before he could make a decision, the trawler struck. They saw her tilt and then come upright again and carry on again towards the shore, but within seconds she was listing and then she struck again and tilted the other way. Now she was definitely sinking, but she did not go down very far; it was too shallow. She settled in several feet of water, listing to port, her radio aerials flopping to and fro.

"I have to get on board," Rod decided.

"I'll come with you," Carlie volunteered.

"And me," Sally Ann said.

Rod grinned at her. "The water's icy, remember?"

"I'll fetch some towels and clothes from the camper," Meryl volunteered, hurrying off.

"Now be careful," Rod told Sally Ann.

They could approach the trawler's position by crawling over a series of exposed rocks, occasionally having to jump from one perch to the next. This way they reached within twelve feet of the stranded vessel without getting wet.

"She's from Punta Arenas," Carlie said, reading the registration on her lifebelt; they could not see the stern. "Did you say seven hundred miles? That's a hell of a long way to drift."

"She didn't drift the whole way," Rod said.

There was something in his voice made Sally look at him sharply. Much taller than either of them, he could see over the gunwale of the listing vessel and look at the deck.

"Is there somebody on board?" she asked, breathlessly.

"Somebody . . . Holy Christ. I have to get over there." He sat down to slide into the water.

"Rod!" Sally Ann screamed.

"There may be someone alive," he said. The water was only five feet deep, and hardly came up to his chest.

He waded across, caught hold of the chain plates, and pulled himself up.

"You mean he saw a dead man?" Carlie asked.

"I don't know," Sally Ann said. She stared at Rod as he swung his dripping legs over the gunwale, watched him check in horror. Then he went on, and disappeared into the wheelhouse door.

"This is giving me the creeps," Carlie said. "Like the *Marie Celeste*."

Rod did not reappear for ten minutes. Then he hurried, dropped over the side, and came back to them. They reached down to help him up, gazed at his hands and windcheater; both were stained with blood.

"Rod?" Sally Ann whispered. "You're hurt."

He shook his head, shivering with the cold. But he was shivering with something else as well; she had never seen such an expression.

"That boat is full of people," he said. "At least twenty."

"On a trawler?" Carlie asked.

"Yeah. Women as well as men. And kids." He gazed at Sally Ann. "They're all dead."

"Dead?" she screamed.

"Dead," he shouted back. "Dead. All of them. I examined them all. It . . . it's horrible. They'd been bleeding . . . "

"You mean there was a fight?" Carlie asked.

"No. I don't think so. The bleeding was from inside, through the noses and mouths, and . . . the other end. Dead," he moaned. "The only thing alive on board is a cat. When I tried to pick it up the fucking thing spat in my face and scratched my hand." He showed them the torn skin.

"Let's get ashore," Carlie said. They scrambled over the rocks and told the others while they wrapped Rod in towels and blankets and hurried back to the camper. Meryl made coffee.

"What are we gonna do?" she asked.

"Get into Quellon and tell the coastguard," Dermott recommended.

Rod looked at Carlie.

"Not a good idea," Carlie said. "Once we get caught up with the coastguard and the police we could be here for the next six months. I reckon we should just sidle off and say nothing."

"But those people," Sally Ann protested. "The cat!"

"Screw the cat. And the people are dead, ain't they? We can't bring them back to life. The coastguard will find them in a day or two. They patrol along here pretty regularly. They'll get a decent burial."

"Yeah, but what did they die of?" Dermott wanted to know. "Could be some disease."

"Some disease," Rod said. "Holy Jesus! That boat is out of Punta Arenas. Where the quarantine is. Those people must have escaped and were running for their lives."

"Only they already had whatever it was . . . " Meryl's voice was trembling.

"You're damn right," Rod snapped. "Let's get the hell out of here. Next stop, Argentina."

7

The News Breaks

"Heck, Doc, I'm worried," confessed Eddie Brent, the senior laboratory technician. "Have you seen this?"

Meg wanted only to get to bed. But she had brought her samples down to be worked on before going home, and she had to get news about Graham. She also knew that between them they should get some measures started, immediately. Now she stared at the newspaper headlines:

PANIC GRIPS SOUTHERN CHILE AND
ARGENTINA
HUNDREDS FLEE HOMES AS KILLER DISEASE
STRIKES
CORDONS OF POLICE TURN BACK SCREAMING
MOBS
REPORTS OF PITCHED BATTLES BETWEEN
SOLDIERS AND REFUGEES
WORLD HEALTH ORGANISATION FLYING
OBSERVERS TO VALPARAISO
THOUSANDS OF SHEEP REPORTED DEAD

And on and on.

"And there's no word from the Doc," Eddie said dolefully.

"He's a great survivor," Meg said, grimly, and went into her office where Helen waited.

"We've had a dozen calls from the media asking for interviews, and maybe a statement, on what we feel about the situation."

"God, cheer me up. We could make this into a world-wide panic."

"Isn't that going to happen anyway?" Helen asked.

Meg sat down. "Just don't tell anyone I'm back yet. What we say has to be the Doc's decision." But she couldn't wait on his return to act. "Get me to the Health Department. I want to speak to Rensick himself." She picked up her personal phone, dotted numbers. "Hi, Auntie. Meg."

"Meggie. Where are you? Jim said he was sure you'd be involved in this funny thing down in Chile."

"I am, and it's not funny," Meg told her. "Listen, Nan . . . any news of Sally Ann?"

"Well, no. She's not a brilliant correspondent, as you know. When last we heard she was in Peru and heading south . . . my God, you don't think . . . but Sally Ann never eats seafood. She's a vegetarian."

"Nan, this has nothing to do with seafood. Not now," Meg told her. "I want you to get hold of the ambassador in Santiago, and see if he can find her, and tell her to get out of there. Tell him to have her arrested and deported if he has to. But bring her home."

"But Meg, this disease is way down in the south. She isn't anywhere near there."

"She's heading south, isn't she? Anyway, this thing isn't going to stay in the south unless something very drastic is done about it. Nan, this is terribly urgent. I'd get on to Santiago myself, but if my name gets involved it's only going to stir things up even more."

"Yes," Nan said. "Yes. I see your point. I'll start on it right away. Thanks a million, Meg, for calling. I guess this all makes for a lot of work at the Center."

"You'd better believe it," Meg agreed. "Let me know the minute Sally Ann is found, will you?"

"I have Mr Rensick," Helen said.

Meg bade Nan goodbye and waited for the call to be transferred. "Meg Calhoun," she said.

"Well, hi, Doctor. How's the microbe business?"

"Thriving, it seems. Don't you read the newspapers?"

"You mean apart from the baseball scores? I have too much to do."

"I am serious, Fred," Meg said. "How many Chilean nationals fly into San Francisco or Los Angeles every day? Or Miami or Houston?"

"God knows, honey."

"Fred, any one of those people could be carrying this disease they have down there. And that goes for Argentinians and New Zealanders as well."

"Well, hell, Meg, five'll get you ten that a quarter of them are carrying Aids. What am I supposed to do about it?"

"This isn't Aids, Fred. This doesn't take five years to kill; it takes seventy-two hours. And it is virulent. It could be the most virulent thing that has ever happened on this earth. If one contaminated person sets foot in the United States, we have it."

"Meg, you're going over the top. What the hell am I supposed to do about it? Ban all flights from South America?"

"Make everyone who comes in submit to a blood test. That's all it needs."

"Christ, the time! And the money. Let me speak to the Doc."

"He's in Chile."

"But this is his idea?"

"It will be his idea, the moment he gets back."

"Ah," Rensick commented.

Meg felt like grinding her teeth. All her life she had been bumping into the little woman syndrome, even here in the States, whenever Graham was not at her elbow to sustain her opinions.

"I'll talk with the Governor," Rensick said. "Ask Fitzroy to call me, whenever he turns up." He chuckled. "And be sure you give him a blood test."

Meg replaced the phone.

"You look kind of bothered," Helen suggested.

"I am. Get me Washington, Helen. I want to speak to Senator Winstanley."

In waiting she dialled again. This time she had to wait a little longer before she heard the voice say sleepily, "Canning".

"Peter! Meg."

"Meg? Good God . . . it's one o'clock in the morning."

"Oh, is it? It's only four in the afternoon here. And you're in tomorrow. Lucky thing."

"It seems to be raining." Then his voice smiled. "But it's great to hear from you. Where are you, New Zealand?"

"San Francisco."

"Hell, that was quick. Have you seen the papers?"

"Yes. But there was damn all I could do there. Peter, I spoke to your sister."

"Did you? That's wonderful. All well?"

"At the moment. But you should get her out of there. I suggested she take her children to England for the summer but she didn't seem to go for the idea. I didn't want to frighten her, and in fact the Government there is trying to keep it all under wraps, but . . . "

"They declared a state of emergency in the area around Invercargill last night."

"Oh? I didn't know that. Thank God they're doing something. But it's at least twenty-four hours too late."

"What do you mean?"

"This bug, or whatever it is, may have originated with some contaminated fish, but it now seems certain that once it gets into a human or animal host, it develops, and not only causes the blood cancer we were talking about, but lives in the blood, and therefore almost certainly in the faeces and mucus as well, and can be transmitted whenever anyone sneezes, or defecates, or just bleeds. And everyone, and I mean, everyone, is susceptible. You know that with most diseases, they've been around so long that most of us have built up a congenital immunity to them. This character is brand new. Or very, very old."

"Hm," Peter said. "You're painting a rather serious scenario."

"Peter, I hope I never have to paint anything as serious as this, ever again."

"So what's the end of it?"

"God knows."

He was silent for a moment. "Are you working on it?"

"I'm about to start. We've got to isolate that virus, fast. And then find out what makes it tick."

"Yes." He hesitated. "You're still being careful?"

"I'm always careful. Don't worry about me. But Peter, it is vital that your Government puts some kind of health check on all people coming from New Zealand, Chile, and Argentina, starting now."

"That's a bit of a tall order."

"Try to think of it the way you think of, say, rabies. If it gets into England you're all dead ducks."

There was another brief silence. Then he said, "Meg . . . you are quite sure of your facts about all this?"

It was her turn to hesitate. "No. I can't be sure. I am sure that we have a situation here which could make the Black Death look like a measles epidemic. In my book it's better to be safe than sorry."

"Agreed. But you are talking about a lot of disruption and a lot of angry people. And you're asking me to stick my political neck right out."

"Peter, does your political neck weigh so heavy, when thousands of human lives are involved?"

He did not reply for a moment, then he said, "I'll discuss it with my minister tomorrow morning. Meg . . . I love you."

"Red blood corpuscles and all?" she asked. "I love you too, Peter. And I will even more when I can think straight."

"I have Washington on the line, Dr Calhoun," Helen said.

The road climbed up and up, and the camper was straining. Soon Rod had to stop to refill the radiator.

"That peak over there is more than 10,000 feet," Carlie told the girls.

Sally Ann thought the Huapi National Park was utterly beautiful. The huge lakes, the steep-sided precipices, the snow-covered mountains rearing their heads in every direction, were dramatic in the extreme, while behind them was the abrupt drop to the still visible sea, and the islands. They could still see Isla de Chiloé.

But Sally Ann never wanted to see Isla de Chiloé again. She never wanted to think of it again, until she was safely back in the States. It was not just the trawler filled with dead people; that was a horrifying thought, but she had not actually seen any of them. It was the way they had turned and fled from something horrible and mysterious, and terrifying. They had behaved like criminals, trembling as they had boarded the ferry for the mainland, each feeling that at any moment they would be tapped on the shoulder and asked why they had not reported the tragedy.

Sally Ann was a very conscientious person. If she broke the law, occasionally, it was because everyone did it. Anyway, smoking a joint now and then or even sniffing a little snow was only a crime in the eyes of some old fuddy duddies. She was less sure about her godmother's feelings on the subject. Meg must know that she played with drugs, and no one was going to convince Sally Ann that Meg had not been one of the girls in her time at college. But since becoming a research doctor she had gotten hyped about some things, at least where health risks were concerned. Meg would be appalled if she ever learned that her god-daughter had walked away from a boatload of dead people without telling anyone. No, she had not walked; she had run.

But Meg lived in a different world. A world where she merely picked up a telephone and spoke, and things happened. They got done. Were Meg ever to be arrested by the Chilean police and held for questioning, the mere announcement of her name would have them kissing the carpet and taking her to the best hotel.

That was not the kind of treatment handed out to groupies in jeans and a camper! They had only themselves on whom to call for help. Thank God for Rod! She had spent last night in Rod's arms, and he had kissed her to sleep.

Rod glanced at her and gave her an encouraging smile. "Only another five miles to the border. How do you feel?"

"Okay," she said. But she meant 'rotten'. She didn't want to whinge, but she did feel rotten; she had repeated sharp pains in her stomach. Presumably nerves.

"Yeah?" he queried. "I don't feel so good myself. Well, once we're in Argentina, no one can touch us."

"Rod, maybe . . . once we're in Argentina we should telephone the coastguard in Quellon. The thought of that boat just sitting there . . . if it broke up, all those bodies, drifting about . . . "

"Relax," Rod said. "They'll have found it by now. Hell, they probably found it by last night."

"And are probably looking for us," Dermott remarked.

"Now what did you want to say that for?" Rod demanded. "The girls are upset enough as it is. Of course they're not looking for us. Hey, look there."

The road had evened out and ahead of them they could see the cluster of buildings and the evenly divided red and white flag of Chile, with the blue square and white star in the canton. While beyond was the three banded – pale blue, white and pale blue – flag of Argentina.

"Hallelujah," Meryl said.

"Passports," Dermott said, and collected them up.

"What the hell . . . " Rod braked as they saw the barrier, on the Chilean side. The camper slid to a stop, and the border guard came to the window. "You take over, Carlie."

Carlie asked a question, and the guard replied at some length. Carlie protested, and the guard shrugged.

"Oh, God," Sally Ann muttered. "They're sending us back to Quellon."

"That's not possible," Rod said. "What's the problem, Carlie?"

"This character says the border is closed," Carlie said.

"Closed?"

"On both sides. Seems he don't care if we are leaving Chile, but he is under orders to let no one in. And the same goes for the Argentinians."

"What the hell? They at war, or something?"

"It's this illness. Seems it's spreading pretty fast."

"Well we know that," Meryl muttered.

"Sssh," Sally Ann begged.

"Let me get this straight," Dermott said. "This guy says we can go through?"

"Sure. But he says they're gonna stop us over there and send us back."

"Well, we don't know that. Heck, we're American citizens. Well, four of us. This is an American registered vehicle, right? Come on. Nothing ventured . . . "

Carlie looked at Rod.

"Gotta give it a go," Rod said.

Carlie spoke to the Chilean guard, who shrugged again.

"He says we can move the barrier, as long as we put it back."

"Right. You take her, Dermott." Rod and Carlie got out and moved the barrier. Then they kept on walking towards the Argentinian post while Dermott drove behind them.

"Oh, my God!" Sally Ann cried. "What're they doing?"

Three Argentinian soldiers had emerged from their office, with automatic weapons which they presented at Rod and Carlie.

Dermott hastily braked.

Sally Ann stared in horror as Carlie started to speak with the soldiers. But the Argentinians were merely gesturing him away, obviously telling him to keep his distance.

"You'd think we were lepers," Meryl complained.

Rod was waving the American passports, but it did not seem to be doing much good. And suddenly one of the guards pointed his gun into the air and fired.

"Rod!" Sally Ann screamed.

"Okay," Rod was saying. "Okay. We get the message. Come on, Carlie." He returned to the camper. "Turn this thing, Dermott, and let's get the hell out of here. Those guys are nuts."

"Where from here?" Dermott asked.

"We'll ask." Rod and Carlie replaced the barrier a second time after the camper had driven through. The Chilean guard grinned sympathetically. "Carlie, ask this guy what we do? Tell him we have to get home?"

Carlie asked and the Chilean gave one of his shrugs.

"Well, that's it," Dermott said. "We're heading for Santiago and the embassy. They can get us out of here."

Sally Ann shivered; Santiago was six hundred miles away.

"Are you sure of your facts, Peter?" Jeremy Payne asked, peering over the top of his bi-focals.

"I was given this information by Dr Calhoun," Peter told him. "And she is one of the world's leading experts in rare diseases."

"Yes," Payne observed. "I've read of her. Rather young for the job, isn't she? Good-looking too." He studied his subordinate; he knew all about Peter's peccadillos.

"Agreed," Peter said. "She is also a dedicated career woman, who knows her job."

"Yes," Payne said, more sceptically yet. "But I must confess I think she is being somewhat hysterical at this moment. I mean, you know as well as I that after that bad patch with the ancillary workers we have at last got things pretty well under control at this ministry. The PM is very pleased with us both. To start rocking the boat now . . ."

Peter sighed. He knew that Jeremy was Minister of Health because his father was a famous surgeon and he had himself studied medicine before going into politics. He also knew that his boss believed in a quiet life at all times; had he been around in 1939 he would have advised against declaring war on Hitler, not because he was afraid, but simply to avoid disrupting the English way of life. But he simply had to be pushed into action, now . . . supposing Meg was even half right in her fears.

"Jeremy," he said, as reasonably as he could. "This thing kills people. On an unimaginable scale."

"According to your friend. Nobody else, at the moment. What are we talking about? An outbreak of some rare kind of fish poisoning at the other end of the world. Oh, I've read the papers. I'm not surprised the people are panicking. And frankly, I'm prepared to suggest some sort of a clamp on movements from South America. But in New Zealand they appear to be keeping perfectly calm."

"They've instituted martial law in the Invercargill area. However well they are suppressing what's happening there, Jeremy, that would seem to indicate they're taking it seriously."

"It is more probably so they can control movement in and out of the district," Payne pointed out. "If there is a highly infectious disease in the town, that seems to me to be an admirably sensible way of handling the situation. For us to start imposing health restrictions on New Zealand citizens arriving in this country would be going to the other extreme. And don't give me that rabies concept. We don't screen humans for rabies. With this disease, if what you have been telling me is true, there would be even less point; they die within seventy-two hours. Of course, if someone passed away on a flight over here from New Zealand we would immediately take appropriate steps . . . "

"Jeremy," Peter said, "you know as well as I that there are some people, in the case of every disease, who are carriers. They never get the disease themselves, but they can be deadly to everyone else. Didn't a woman called Molly Macguire or something cause a whole lot of deaths from typhoid in New York before she was identified as a carrier?"

"That was a long time ago, old boy. And her name was Mary Mallon."

"There will certainly be carriers for this disease as well. But in addition, presumably some people will be more susceptible than others, take longer to incubate. It needs only one person to land in this country with the disease and it's here."

"Again, according to your girlfriend. Now that is what I call a hysterical reaction. Even she admits that the disease can only be passed on by bodily excreta. In this country, nobody comes in contact with other people's excreta, thank God, or even our own."

"And suppose this character cuts himself and someone has to bind him up? What about when he kisses someone?"

"Has it been proven that the virus is carried in saliva?"

"Well, no," Peter admitted. "Not as yet."

"Quite. Nor has it been proved that it is transmitted by excreta at all. This is a theory. In fact, it hasn't even been proved that it is a virus yet. That is another theory."

"If we wait until these theories are proven we may find ourselves in deep trouble, Jeremy."

"And if we charge ahead like bulls in a china shop we may find ourselves in even deeper trouble. Just think what capital the Opposition, your friend Brereton, for example, would make out of such an over-reaction on our part. Peter, I can see that you're worried, and I respect that. I tell you what we'll do. I'll get on to my opposite number in New Zealand, and ask him for a detailed up-date of the situation and on the progress they are making in tracking down the cause. When I have that I'll arrange a talk with the PM. I can't offer you more than that. You could help matters by getting some facts from Fitzroy, whenever he turns up. Will that satisfy you?"

Peter sighed. "It will have to, won't it?" he muttered.

"And until we have reached that stage," Jeremy said, pointing his pencil, "I think it imperative that you keep your apprehensions, and Dr Calhoun's, to yourself, Peter. If the press were to get even a suspicion of what may be involved, we'd be up the creek."

Peter nodded, and went to his own office to send a cable in reply to one from Sarah which had arrived the previous night. Apparently she had been quite alarmed by Meg's telephone call, thinking that something was wrong with some other member of the family, and had tried to call him but had been unable to get through – everyone in New Zealand was calling some relative or other. He scratched his head for some seconds while deciding what to put, in view of Jeremy's instructions. Finally he wrote: "I ASKED MEG CALHOUN TO CALL YOU STOP THINK IT IMPERATIVE YOU AND KIDS AND DOUGLAS VISIT UK AS SOON AS POSSIBLE STOP WILL EXPLAIN ON YOUR ARRIVAL STOP PLEASE BELIEVE THIS IS URGENT STOP LOVE PETER."

He could do no more than that.

Before leaving the Commons Peter dialled Anna's number again. He knew she was due in from Rio and had tried earlier without success; now he was worried that she might be stuck in South America. She answered just as he was about to replace the receiver.

"Hi, handsome! When are you coming over?" She sounded as bubbly as ever.

"Er, I'm not. Well, not right now . . ."

"Why not? I've missed you like hell."

"Oh. Yes. But . . . I'm very busy at the moment." Too busy to go round and explain about Meg? That would need more time and diplomacy than he could summon up, right now. And perhaps more courage. "I just wanted to be sure you were safely home, that's all."

"Why shouldn't I be? I told you I was coming back today."

"I expected you back hours ago."

"There were delays. All so stupid. Everyone in South America seems in a total panic about some outbreak of food poisoning. Actually, I did think I was going to be stuck there, for a while."

"How did you get over the problem?" As if he could not guess.

"It was damned expensive. This slimy little official said he wasn't interested in US dollars . . . till I doubled my offer. Then he put me on a plane to Paris, would you believe? And not even Concorde."

"No problems there?"

"Of course not. The French have got more sense. Look, can't you make it over for supper? Just you and me?"

Peter looked at his watch. He wanted to say no; though he was genuinely busy he knew he could make it. He was simply evading the big issue. "Look . . . "

"Just something light, in bed," she coaxed. "Vichyssoise, smoked salmon sandwiches with brown bread, strawberries and a nice little bit of ripe brie to finish off. How does that sound? And with a sexy movie to get you started."

Oh God! He groaned inwardly. Before the advent of Meg he would have jumped at it; now . . . "Anna, I cannot stay the night. There's a big problem looming and I've got to be available, night and day. The menu sounds great, but let's have it in your little sitting-room, upstairs. I won't be able to stay more than an hour."

"Really? Oh."

He could tell by her response that she suspected something. He must not let her start questions on the phone. "Someone's just come in to see me, so I must go," he lied. "I'll be over about 9.30. 'Bye."

Anna was standing at the top of the stairs, wearing a housecoat, when he arrived. He handed his briefcase to the butler and hurried up to greet her . . . with the appropriate degree of restraint.

She led the way to her oriental den, the room Peter thought the most attractive in the house. The walls were divided into panels of Chinese silk paintings set into white-painted mouldings. The carpet was white, relieved only in the centre by a small, pale green circular rug on which stood a round, white lacquered table bearing a bowl of fresh yellow roses. Silk embroidered cushions were piled on to the soft, coral red settee and the pale green armchairs. The light fittings, exquisitely painted bowls and vases and brass ornaments, were the result of Anna's shopping expeditions in China.

"So," she said, "tell me all about her. Whisky?"

He knew she was only guessing, but he still had to feel his way with the utmost care.

"Please."

She opened a little white lacquered cabinet and half-filled two glasses, splashing each with soda. "Cheers." She settled into the armchair opposite him, eyes never leaving his face.

"Cheers," he nodded, then launched straight in. "So, who's a clever girl then? You guessed."

Anna's eyes narrowed. Sure, she had guessed, but she wanted to be told she was wrong. "Has dear Claudia finally got her way, then?"

He noted the restraint in her voice. "No. Nothing to do with Claudia . . . "

"Well then, maybe I know her." Her fine eyebrows arched above green eyes which were suddenly moist.

"No. She's American . . . "

"Oh, come on! You were only in the States three days. I don't believe it!"

"We met over here, while you were away." He could see she was about to cry. God damn it, he thought! He had expected her to be angry. He felt a perfect brute. "Anna, you and I never intended to marry; you know that as well as I . . . "

"Marry! You never asked me." Now the tears were rolling down her cheeks. "You want to marry this . . . woman?"

"Possibly. We haven't had time to think about it, yet." He, at least, had to remain calm.

"Just like that!" Anna found a lace handkerchief and blew her nose, loudly.

"She's a research doctor," Peter said, unnecessarily. But he had to keep talking. "Lives in California."

"And she's going to give it all up for love. I'd consider giving it all up, Peter. If you'd ask me."

"Anna . . . "

Now at last she was getting angry, to his relief. "Oh, I know. I'm not a suitable wife for a future prime minister. All your friends think I'm a jumped-up tart." She stood up and drained her glass. "Let's eat." She pressed the bell beside the fireplace. "Come." She smiled, held out her hand and led him across the room to a table by the window, already laid with white damask, silver and cut glass. "Aren't the roses early this year?" she commented, leaning forward to sniff two perfect blooms in the centre, revealing a great deal of cleavage.

Considering his reputation as a clever debater, he was making a total muff of this exchange. She had him beaten, hands down. Now he must either surrender or sit it out. "Yes, if those are actually outdoor. More likely out of a greenhouse. My parents only have a small garden, now, in Wimbledon, but they have a fantastic display of blooms each June. These salmon pink ones are Super Star, aren't they? And the yellow must be Doctor . . . what's the name . . . Verharg?"

"You know perfectly well that I never learnt the name of a flower in my life, darling. Now tell me what's news." She was trying to pretend he had never told her. That they would make love and it would all have been a nightmare. He did not care to imagine her reaction when he insisted he was not staying.

The butler came in with a maid wheeling a trolley. The soup was served and the other courses left for them to help themselves. They chatted amiably enough as they ate, about current social events and their mutual friends – the sort of conversation Anna always enjoyed.

It was 10.10. "Do you mind if we turn on the news?" he asked, "I'd like to know if there is an up-date on that epidemic."

"Is it that important?"

"Yes. I'm hoping you're right about it all being just a fuss." He knew she could not possibly be, but he could remain diplomatic.

Although the news was nearly half over, it was obvious that virtually the whole programme was given over to the situation in South America and New Zealand. "My God! It seems to have broken out in North Island, as well." His jaw dropped in consternation.

Even Anna seemed impressed at last. "Maybe I was luckier to get back than I thought. The whole world seems to be getting fussed."

"Unfortunately it isn't only a fuss. It's death," he murmured, eyes glued to the screen.

"Oh, really, darling. Let's go to bed."

The moment had arrived. "No, Anna. I told you . . . "

"You can't commit adultery until you're married, sweetheart. One last time . . . " She was hoping that if she could get him into bed again she could drive Meg out of his mind forever.

He could not afford to risk that. "I have to get back to my office, anyway. I still have work to do." He was dodging the issue, but he had to let her get used to the idea and take up with one of her many discarded amours again, if only as an indication that she no longer cared. She had her pride. He pushed his chair back from the table. "That was super. Thanks very much." He reached for her hand. "Do try to understand, Anna. I have always been very, very fond of you. Nothing will change that, and I do hope we will always be good friends."

Anna flushed angrily, her eyes again moist. "Oh! Go stuff your doctor, you idiot. But when you get bored to death don't be too sure I'll still be around."

He ignored the digs. Instead, he asked, "Do you mind if I keep in touch?"

"I want you to."

She waited until the door had closed, then she snatched up a couple of yellow silk cushions and hurled them at the door. Now she was crying. "I love you, you stupid bastard," she said.

He took a taxi back to the House of Commons through the usual London evening traffic. Theatres were spilling their audiences on to the pavements, chauffeurs with big, sleek cars jamming the streets as they waited for their employers. It all looked so normal. Healthy. Could there really be a sickness looming, threatening, which could destroy this city? There was a great lump of lead in his stomach. Was it the thought of the unknown virus, creeping across the world? Or was it due to the confrontation with Anna?

According to the saying, comparisons are odious. But how could he help but compare the two women? The one he had just left . . . just hurt, badly. The tall, elegant, soignée, sophisticated Anna, who in reality was just a frightened little girl. Anna of the endless energy and vitality, exciting in bed. Always bubbling with fun and laughter . . . or nearly always. Except in a situation like tonight's. Even then she had put up a damn good show, bless her.

And then there was Meg, the little brunette who cared so deeply about life, and death. Who would cross the world without a second thought for her own safety, in an attempt to discover more about a hideous virus which was wreaking death and destruction, now, at opposite sides of the world. Meg, who sincerely loved him, as he loved her, but who was prepared to forego that love, if necessary, for the cause she believed in; for medical research. Dear, darling Meg; not inexperienced, yet far from sophisticated in her love-making. She had not climaxed when they consummated their love, yet she was not worried by it, or embarrassed as some women might have been; she remained brightly confident that she would make it when they became used to each other. And he had no doubt she was right. He had been disappointed when she told him she had no intention of becoming a mother, or a 'little wifey' as she put it. It was a role Angela had rejected, too. But he did not want to marry a doormat. He needed someone who would stand as an equal with him. He had no intention of losing the woman he loved a second time. Meg he loved. Meg he wanted, come what may.

If only he knew what was coming.

The taxi drew up and he alighted, wondering what might be waiting on his desk.

Graham Fitzroy sat at his desk and rested his head on his hands. Meg stood beside him, frowning. She had never seen the boss looking so tired, or so old. Well, she was feeling pretty old and tired herself.

"It is sheer hell down there, Meg," he said. "People are going wild. We are looking at the biggest disaster in human history."

"Wouldn't the Chilean Government impose quarantine?" she asked.

"Sure. They've imposed quarantine. So have the Argentines. But it's not working. We're not talking about an isolated community any more. The whole of Megallanes Province is affected. So is Tierra del Fuego, and now it's spread across the border into Santa Cruz. People are in a state of flat panic. Both Chile and Argentina have moved troops down there to control any population movement, but it simply isn't working. People are getting out by any means they can. They're risking being shot in some instances. And the troops aren't too happy about the situation, either; in some places they've refused to bury the dead."

"What's going to happen?"

"God knows, and He isn't telling. But that disease is spreading like a bush fire. And to make matters worse, the doctors and nurses are refusing to enter infected areas to treat the victims. They say it's too dangerous."

"That's hysterical. Surely they can wear protective clothing, gloves and masks?"

"Quite. But they're still scared stiff. How were things in New Zealand?"

"People seemed fairly relaxed, too damned relaxed, when I was there. But they're getting the message now; they've imposed martial law in the Invercargill area. I don't know if they've acted in time. Certainly not to prevent it reaching North Island."

"And no joy on the virus?"

She shook her head. "I spent all last night working on the specimens I brought back from New Zealand. I know the little bastard must be there, but I haven't managed to isolate him yet. There's all the normal stuff . . . trouble is, all of our samples are either from victims who have already succumbed or are in the last stages. I thought I might have something from that mortuary guard, but he died within a couple of hours of my obtaining the specimens."

"Have you reported to anyone?"

"Yes. I spoke to Rensick, tried to convince him that we have to impose some kind of a screening process, now. He was totally unresponsive. So I called Washington and spoke with Winstanley. I don't know if he believed me when I told him how serious the situation was: you know the senator. But he did promise to speak to Howitt."

"That's not good enough. Meg, I have to get over there and speak to Howitt myself. If necessary, I'll go over his head and speak with the President. Tell Helen to get me a flight, will you?"

"Gray," she said, "you have just got to get some sleep. If you pass out on us, we're in dead trouble."

He grinned at her. "Dead could be the operative word, honey. You look pretty done in yourself. But I can sleep on the aircraft."

"I also called Peter Canning, in London," Meg said.

He raised his eyebrows.

"I felt he should know the score. Don't worry; he isn't going to go screaming to the newspapers."

"So what is he going to do?"

She shrugged. "I don't know if he was convinced either. But he promised to take it up with his minister."

"More words."

"Yes, but if the British were to take positive action it might just stir Washington."

"It might. Say, Meg . . . you and Canning got something going?"

She smiled. "We did. I think we still have. But it won't interfere with the job, Gray."

The telephone buzzed. Meg picked it up. "Calhoun."

"Hi, Meggie. Dad got back yet?"

"No calls," Fitzroy growled.

"But it's Mandy," Meg protested.

"Oh, heck." He took the phone. "Hi, doll. Where are you?"

"New York. Say, what's happening down in South America?"

"People are dying," Fitzroy said, bluntly.

"Oh, gee. I guess you're pretty busy."

"Correct."

"Tom was wondering if you'd had a chance to look at any of those specimens yet."

"What specimens?"

"Didn't Charlie Oswiecki bring you some bits of the megatherium's stomach to look at?"

Fitzroy raised his eyebrows at Meg, who could hear what was being said.

"Yes," she reminded him. "He was here last week, just before we both went off."

"He did," Fitzroy told his daughter. "But I'm afraid they'll have to wait. We have a real emergency on here."

"Oh, heck. Tom's real keen on getting your opinion."

"Why?"

"Well . . . we only got around to examining them ourselves last month, what with setting up the exhibition and all the publicity . . . "

"How's it going, anyway?"

"Oh, tremendous. They're queueing halfway down Broadway. Ira Schwartz gets a great happy grin on every time he looks at Fred."

"Fred?"

"That's what we call the beast. The thing is, well, when Tom got around to analysing Fred's blood, he came across a virus he'd never seen before, and couldn't identify."

"A virus?" Fitzroy's voice hardened.

"Yeah. Dad, he's very worried about it, in view of, well, what's happening down in South America."

"Why?" Now Fitzroy's question was like the crack of a whip.

"Well of course, we've all been reading about how the symptoms are those of extreme hypertension. In this morning's paper some idiot is even calling it the Red Death. Well . . . Fred died of hypertension."

"Fred," Fitzroy said. "A sloth?"

"A hundred thousand years ago," Amanda reminded him.

"Holy shitting cows," her father remarked.

"Tom is really bothered about it," Amanda said again. "Wondering if there is any chance there could be a connection."

"I read you, loud and clear. Get off the line, honey, I'll get back to you later," Fitzroy snapped, and replaced the receiver.

Meg was already on her way to the storage room.

8

Death in a Camper

"You look as though you've gotten a feverish chill or something," Meryl observed.

Rod was lying on the bench seat while Dermott coasted the camper back down the way they had come, hoping to save fuel. "I don't get colds," he replied. "Maybe it's the altitude; doesn't agree with everyone." He sniffed. "But maybe you're right. I do have a runny nose. Pass a Kleenex, please."

Meryl passed the box of tissues and Rod blew, vigorously. "Hey, watch it boy!" she yelled. "You've blown a fuse."

Carlie turned round in the passenger seat. "Wow! Give the man a bowl, Meryl, there's going to be blood everywhere."

"Blood!" Sally Ann peered down from the bunk over the cab. "Oh, Rod! What's up, honey?"

"Nothing, nothing at all. Just a nose bleed. The altitude must have got to me. I'll be okay in five minutes."

"Lie back," Meryl commanded.

He obediently lay back but was soon up again, choking. "I can't," he mumbled through the back of his throat, "Not without drowning in my own blood. Just don't fuss me. Anyway, I think it's doing good. It seems to have eased the headache." He sat with the bowl on his knees, ignoring his audience.

"We'll circle to the north-east of Lake Llanquihue to join the main road below Osorno," Dermott said. "Better than going back through Puerto Varas. Remember all those sheep all over the road on the way through, last time?"

The camper bumped and rolled over the bad road surface, rattling the saucepans in the cupboard under the cooker. Sally Ann put her hands over her ears; movement, every noise, made her feel worse. She knew the curse was due, but this had to be the worst pre-menstrual tension she could remember. A particularly bad pothole made her groan.

Dermott heard her. "Sorry about that, S.A.; in avoiding one I got the other. The surface'll improve when we get to the main road."

"How far is it?" Meryl asked.

"It's about 150 kilometres from that border crossing we just left, according to the map, and we're about halfway. Call it fifty miles."

"When we get to the next town I suggest we stop at a pharmacy. Rod's nose is bleeding again; he must have lost over a pint."

"Stop fussing, woman," Rod growled angrily over the plastic bowl. She was bugging him.

"Someone's got to show some sense," she snapped back. "You can't do your share of driving until it stops, and if you go on losing blood at that rate you'll be too weak anyway."

Rod did not reply. He was feeling awful, head pounding, an unfamiliar feeling of nausea washing over him every few minutes. Maybe Meryl was right; perhaps he had caught a chill. If only he could lie down . . . but the blood just went down the back nasal passage to flood his throat when he tried, and besides, it seemed to make his head worse.

Carlie took a spell at the wheel after they by-passed Osorno. Meryl made some sandwiches with crackers

170

for lunch, but Rod and Sally Ann could not face food. Within half an hour of taking over the driving, Carlie pulled off to the side of the road and leapt out of the cab. The others watched from the vehicle as he vomited into the ditch.

Rod tied a handkerchief around his face. "You get in the back, Carlie," he mumbled, "my turn to drive." They were being passed by an awful lot of fast northbound traffic. "There must be a fiesta on somewhere ahead. It'll be just our luck to get bogged down in a pile of streamers and confetti."

Dermott remained in the passenger seat beside him as they set off. His expression became grimmer by the minute as he watched blood drip from the saturated cloth under Rod's nose, down his chin and on to the front of his T-shirt.

Rod glanced sideways and caught Dermott's eye. Neither spoke, but they read each other's thoughts.

Rod's eyelids drooped and he sighed. Oh God, no. Please, please no. The petrol gauge showed perilously low. "I'll pull in at the next gas station," he told Dermott. But the next station was crammed with cars . . . and the next.

Carlie got out and spoke to a pump attendant. When he returned he was frowning. "There's no fiesta. These people are all heading away from the sickness that's spreading, down south. Bloke says we'd do better to get off the main road. There's more chance of finding gas in one of the villages. Let's see the map." He leaned through the passenger window and Dermott pointed to their position. "We can make a left on to the La Unión road and get back on this one just south of Valdivia."

There was no gas in La Unión. Dermott took over the wheel again and elected to press on in the hopes of finding gas before they ran out completely. But just as they topped a hill in a desolate-looking area the engine started to cough. His heart sank. Oh hell.

Was this it? Was this the end of the road for them all? There was a small cluster of houses near the bottom of the next incline. It was a typical farming hamlet with a communal courtyard, the farm buildings forming a linking wall between the houses.

The camper came to a sudden stop, in the middle of the road.

"Well, that's it, I guess." Dermott opened his door and climbed down.

Meryl opened the rear door and came out to join him. "Dermott, I'm worried about Rod . . . "

"Yeah, me too. He needs a medic. I wonder if anyone up in those houses might sell us a can of gas. Enough to get us to Valdivia."

"We can pray. Carlie!" she called.

Carlie appeared round the front of the van.

"Could you go up there and see . . . " Meryl paused to stare at him. "Carlie? Are you okay? Your face is scarlet."

"Tell me what you want me to do, then I'll tell you how I am." He forced a smile.

"Can you make it up to those houses and beg, borrow or steal some gas?"

"I can sure try. If I'm not back by sundown, send out a search-party." He felt in his jeans pocket and nodded. "Yep. I got some cash."

Meryl and Dermott watched him go, then turned to stare at each other in alarm.

"What's happening to us, man?" Meryl whispered, "We can't all have caught chills."

"I was kinda hoping we had," Dermott replied, and headed for the van.

"I'm starving," Sally Ann said. "What's to eat?"

Rod groaned. "Must you?"

"I don't really want to eat, but I think I've got hunger pains. I haven't eaten anything today, remember."

"Nor have I. And it'll go straight in the hedge if I try."

"But you must have something . . . "

They all turned at the sound of raised voices coming from the houses. Carlie stumbled over the ditch to rejoin them, holding his head.

Dermott rushed to meet him. "Hey! What's all the fuss?" He certainly was not carrying any gas.

"Savages!" Carlie exclaimed, panting. "They're fucking savages up there." He clambered into the camper and sat down. "The only way into the place is through dirty great solid wood doors. When I banged on them someone shouted at me to go away, so I told them we needed gas. They said they'd none to spare so I thought I'd lay it on a bit and told them that my friend was sick and I had to get him to a doctor." He looked at the blood on his hand. "That's when they appeared on the roof of an outhouse and started bunging stones at me."

Meryl stared at him in consternation. "Jesus Christ! What the hell are we going to do?"

"The guy back at the gas station said the bowzer would be refilling their tanks on Tuesday. Reckon we'll just have to hole up here till then." Carlie screwed up his face. "Hell, my gut!" He wrapped his arms round his middle and rocked to and fro.

"What's the food situation, Meryl?" Dermott asked.

"Eggs, fruit and cheese. Enough for today, I guess. And plenty cans of soup, beans, etc. And a few packets of crackers."

"Let's just have a siesta, and then get a meal together, later. Maybe we'll all be a bit friskier and be able to face food, then." Rod's nose had stopped bleeding but his voice still sounded odd.

Two hours later, far from feeling better Rod was obviously much worse. And now Meryl and Dermott were flushed and uncomfortable.

Meryl forced herself to start preparing food. She knew nobody had any appetite, that they would only eat because they reckoned they should, so she did not ask what anyone wanted: just opened cans, piled plastic bags and waxed paper packets of cheese and fruit on the table and beat up some eggs to scramble.

Nobody spoke. Nobody had the courage to voice the fear, the horror that filled all their minds.

Carlie had not told them what the villagers shouted at him. "We don't want you here, not you or anyone," they yelled angrily through the puerta and from the roofs. "You keep away with your disease. Don't bring it here." Then the stones and pieces of brick and broken tiles had followed. They were his own countrymen, and they hated him. He would remember their hatred for the rest of his life . . . which might not be very long. A leaden ball formed in his stomach, adding to the growing discomfort in that region. There was a lump in his throat, too, and he tried to blink away the tears that stung his eyes.

The five young students sat together round the table in silence. Rod switched on a tape, if only to drown out the noise in his head. He put a few forkfuls of food in his mouth, even swallowed a little, but what was the point? They were all going to die – and it was his fault. He had known while they were still up in the mountains, when his nose would not stop bleeding. That was the way those hideous corpses had been. All covered in dried blood. What the hell had induced him to go aboard that boat? To touch them, in case one might be alive? Oh God! Why? Why? He stared at the sickness suffusing the features of his lovely Sally Ann; the girl he planned to marry, if everything worked out. They would have babies together, build a life and a family. He had always wanted to have a son of his own, to act the father, the way he thought a father should be, not the way his own father had been. A deep breath shuddered through his large frame. Had he really condemned his Sally Ann, his friends and himself to death? Suddenly he stood up, knocking the table and spilling the drinks. "We can't just sit here and wait for . . . " but he couldn't say the word 'death', " . . . for, for something to happen," he groaned feebly, and sank back on to his seat, head in hands.

Dermott helped Meryl to clear the food while Sally Ann knelt beside Rod, her arms round his head, her long, blonde hair falling over his face. Her tears soaked through his hair on to his scalp. In a way she knew, too. But she could not admit it, not even to herself. They were all far too young for it to be real. People their age did not die. It was ridiculous to imagine it. It was just pre-menstrual depression.

Rod and Sally Ann lay that night in each other's arms again. But they did not sleep. Nobody did. They dozed a little, and moaned some, and wept silently into their makeshift pillows.

Meryl could not stop worrying about her little sister. She was only five and Mam had died soon after she was born. Gran had helped look after her, but Gran had had a stroke and Meryl had said she would soon be back to take care of the family, cook for Dad, nurse Gran and be a surrogate mother to little Mina. She could not let them all down, particularly Mina. The child had been all excited on the phone, saying how much she was looking forward to having her big sister back. She tried not to think, it made her headache so much worse. It felt as though someone was poking their fingers in her eyes, pressing her eyeballs into her brain . . .

Slowly, the dull, grey dawn light crept through the little curtains. The bunkbeds creaked as restless bodies sought to relieve their discomfort, turning this way and that. Birds chirruped in the hedge and a cockerel could be heard from the hamlet.

Dermott had thought of creeping away in the night. He told himself he only had altruistic motives: to get help – from as far away as Valdivia, if necessary. But that was not true. He wanted to run away from death.

Rod was dying, he knew. And Sally Ann. And he had seen blood in Carlie's vomit. He had felt okay, himself, all day yesterday, apart from a slight headache – but that had just been fear, he hoped, until he went outside for a pee at about two o'clock. Brilliant moonlight had excited the cicadas into great orchestration, lit the stream he made into the sand at the roadside . . . and the blood that was left when his bladder was empty. So instead of escaping he crawled back into his sleeping bag to wonder why he had been born in the first place. What a senseless exercise in misery his life had been, trying to impress his uninterested parents with his academic achievements, to make up for the caricature that was his face, his myopic eyes and his puny body. But Ma and Pa had only been interested in brother Eddie, the baseball star, the family hero. School life had been hell and college not much better until he had gotten friendly with this crowd. They had been good friends and this trip would have been a ball of fun . . . if he had not fallen for Sally Ann so completely. But of course, she only had eyes for Rod, understandably, and seeing them together, laughing, loving, had made hell of the fun trip. He had always told himself that one day, if he persevered, he would make a great success of his life, make Pa and Ma and Eddie proud of him. He sighed, tried to swallow the lump in his throat. To think of all those wasted hours of study. He fished a Kleenex out of his pocket to blow his nose. It was bleeding.

"Rod! Oh my God, Rod, Rod." Sally Ann's screams dwindled to a moan.

Meryl was first there. "What's up, honey?" she asked, drawing back the curtain.

"He's not moving, and there's blood oozing out of his ear."

Rod's face was scarlet and bloated, his eyeballs bloodshot and swollen. They rolled towards Meryl, and she breathed a sigh of relief. "He is moving. But he looks hellish hot." She drew back the covers, thinking he would at least be wearing shorts . . . but he was not, and that was the biggest hard-on she had ever seen in her life. "Christ Almighty!" She hastily covered it up again. "Sals! Have you been . . . "

"No I have not!" Sally gasped. "Oh, hell, Meryl. Quick, a basin, I'm going . . . " a stream of vomit shot all over the bed and she fell back, moaning and clutching her stomach.

Dermott and Meryl cleaned them both up as best they could, but the stink of bile still filled the camper.

Meryl slopped disinfectant about but it did not help much. "Do either of you want a coffee?" she asked Carlie and Dermott.

"I'll try to keep one down," Carlie nodded.

"Haven't we got something more interesting? There was some local brandy in the cupboard." Dermott got up to look and returned with a bottle and a slab of chocolate. "Let's have a feast," he said, plonking them on to the table.

"What are we celebrating?" Meryl's voice was sombre.

"Today. Today we are alive. No matter what happens tomorrow" – the corners of his mouth drooped, quivering – "today we are alive. Let's drink to that."

They drank from the neck, the three of them in turn, trying to blot out the reality of approaching death. They were forcing a bravado none of them felt. They were young. Fledglings who had only recently flown the nest, left the security of home and family, to die. They wanted to re-write the scenario, be back home again, feel the comfort of their mothers' arms, and know the maternal healing.

"Aah!" Carlie screamed, staggering to his feet holding his stomach. He half fell out of the door and lay at the roadside, rolling in agony.

Tears streamed down Meryl's swollen cheeks. "Carlie, love. What can I do? What can I do?" Her motherly instinct yearned to comfort the boy, soothe him. But there was nothing she could do.

Dermott lolled sideways. His glasses fell off but it did not matter; they were all misted up.

Next morning the camper was quiet.

9

Ten Billionths of a Meter

"The Red Death," the Prime Minister mused, looking at the newspaper. "It sometimes occurs to me that journalists have nothing better to do than dream up these catch phrases."

"The analogy is plain, of course." Jeremy Payne was leaning forward over crossed legs, snapping the cap on and off his fountain-pen. "He's comparing it with the Black Death."

"Is anyone going to take that seriously?" the Prime Minister asked.

"Well . . . " Jeremy frowned and looked sideways at Peter.

"It is certainly spreading very rapidly, Prime Minister," Peter replied, wondering at Jeremy's reluctance to join the discussion. "It only appeared three weeks ago. Chile and Argentina are both in a ferment, and it appears to be rampaging through South Island, New Zealand and has now broken out in North Island, too. There is even a report, as yet unconfirmed, that it has cropped up in Tasmania."

"What are the governments of those countries doing about it?" the Prime Minister asked.

"All that they can, now, but they were too slow in starting. They are trying to impose quarantine restrictions where possible, but the problem is the extreme speed with which incubation takes place. It is possible to say that there is no incubation period at all, in fact. The disease, once it gets into an uninfected bloodstream, acts like an intravenous injection."

"What is the medical opinion in this country?"

"Frankly, not as keyed up as I would like. The BMA attitude seems to be that something as virulent as this must burn itself out very rapidly."

The Prime Minister looked at Jeremy. "Is that likely?"

Once again he looked at his PPS, but Peter's eyes were glued to the notes in his hand. He cleared his throat. "Well, normally, that has some point to it. Diseases usually seek the weakest host, obviously, and where they cannot be combated they tend to simply exhaust their host population as it were. The trouble with this . . . er . . . Red Death, is that everyone is susceptible."

"Anaemics are less so, of course," Peter pointed out. "Although they do seem to be succumbing in the end."

The Prime Minister picked up Peter's report. "And you are afraid it may come here."

"I'm afraid it is more than likely."

"Can you imagine the problems involved in forcing every passenger, or crew member for that matter, of every aircraft and every ship landing on our shores to take a blood test? It cannot simply be a matter of planes and ships from New Zealand or South America, because passengers from those places often come in by circuitous routes. There is also the question of livestock. The disease appears to affect them as well. Has any conclusion been drawn as to how long this virus can remain alive, and whether it can survive freezing?"

"I'm afraid not, Prime Minister," Peter confessed. "The virus itself has not yet been isolated."

"Then we don't even know if it is a virus, do we?"

"That is true. But I must say," Jeremy put in, coming to the aid of his junior, "that the South African Government has already instituted emergency measures. Like Chile, Argentina and New Zealand, it has banned fishing in the Southern Ocean, and it has closed its border to the north to both humans and animals, except after taking a test."

"This Government has never yet taken the South African Government as a model," the Prime Minister pointed out in a somewhat acid tone. "Nor can I see that it is going to do them much good. If it were possible to close a land border absolutely, don't you suppose we would have done so in Northern Ireland a long time ago? In any event, South Africa does not need to import food to live. We do."

There was a brief silence, then Jeremy said, diffidently, "Brereton has tabled a question. He is going to ask for an emergency debate."

"On this Red Death?"

"Yes. I'm afraid he is going to refer back to what was said in the House on the last Friday in May."

The Prime Minister nodded. "I read what was said. Peter?"

Peter sighed. "I said what I believed to be correct at the time, Prime Minister. I had no idea something like this could boil up so rapidly."

"Things have a habit of doing that. Very well, I will handle the question myself, Jeremy, as it involves the Government, rather than one department. Now: have you been in touch with any of the governments affected by this disease?"

"Only New Zealand. Argentina . . . well, I felt they should get in touch with us, if they need us. The same goes for Chile."

"Agreed. What is the New Zealand attitude?"

"They have asked for stocks of busulfan and radioactive phosphorus, and these we are supplying. But frankly, they seem rather more concerned about the losses in sheep than humans. I suspect they're still hoping that with rigid quarantine, it may go away. Like foot and mouth."

181

"They have not asked for physical help?"

"Not yet. I'm not sure there is much physical help we can offer them."

"There is no research going on in this country into this disease at the moment?"

"Er, I'm afraid not. It has been rather sudden and as yet we have no specimens on which to work."

The Prime Minister looked at Peter. "Then where have you obtained your information?"

"From the Robert Koch Research Center in California. They are working on it."

"And are prepared to share their findings with you?"

"Well, yes," he nodded, trying to mask a smile.

"I think he's seduced one of their people," Jeremy said, attempting to lighten the atmosphere.

The Prime Minister did not look amused. "I suggest you maintain your contacts. I wish to be able to answer Brereton's question by saying that the Government has set up a task force to investigate and, if possible, find a cure for this Red Death. I am putting you in charge of the task force, Peter. You will devote yourself to it, and nothing else. It would be best if you absented yourself from the House for next Question Time. In fact, we'll arrange to pair you for the next fortnight. Parliament will be rising then for the summer so you will be able to work in total secrecy, and I will say that I am not prepared to reveal the details of your force, nor will I discuss the matter at this stage. But the force must be set up immediately. It must involve both the medical and the drug industry at the highest level. I know you have the contacts to do that."

"I'll get on to it right away, Prime Minister," Peter promised, feeling relief flooding through his system.

The Prime Minister nodded. "I want results, Peter, and fast. If your American friends come up with anything, get hold of it. You will report to Jeremy, and he can keep me informed."

Peter was on his feet. "I will. And . . . blood tests?"

"In the absence of an identified virus, what can a blood test tell us?"

"It will give us the rbc count, Prime Minister, the number of red corpuscles in the blood. If that is above normal, then the person or animal from whom the sample was obtained must be placed in quarantine at once."

The Prime Minister considered for several seconds. "You will immediately institute such tests for all animals, and all frozen meat entering the country. I wish a report from your committee within the next week as to the implications of instituting blood tests for humans. This must include costings and take into consideration loss of time and the possibility of retaliation. I will make a decision when I receive the report. I'm sure I don't have to tell you that your investigations must be carried out in absolute secrecy and not a word of any findings are to be released to the press until we are in a position to make a statement to the House. Obviously the blood tests for meat and animals will attract publicity, as will the tests for humans if we decide to proceed, but these will be described as precautionary measures. Any suggestion that we are afraid of the disease actually appearing in England must be dismissed; we do not want a panic. Also, some effort should be made to obtain sample specimens on which our own researchers may work. Thank you for calling, gentlemen."

"Duggie! Duggie, are you out there?" Sarah Lawton called across the yard from the back door. A deep frown creased her forehead as she brushed a strand of hair off her face with the back of a floury hand.

Her husband appeared at the barn door, carrying a milk pail. "Yes, what is it?"

"Jimmy Wainwright's wife, Sheila, was on the phone. They're in a terrible state. The situation down there is absolutely horrendous. Half their sheep are dead and the others look pretty sick." She sounded distraught.

"Oh, Christ! What is it, foot and mouth?" Duggie put down the pail and crossed the yard to her.

"Jimmy seems positive it's not. He says it sounds like this sickness that's spreading down in the South Island. I didn't ask Sheila to hold the line; I wasn't sure where you were. But maybe you'd better call back; Jimmy'd appreciate it and you may pick up a few more details at the same time." She saw that Duggie's face had turned a sickly shade of grey. If a disaster like that were to hit here, the farm would be finished, and the chances of ever selling it for a passable figure would be pretty remote. Like their friends, Jimmy and Sheila, who moved south two years ago, every penny they had was sunk into their smallholding and stock.

A smell of overcooked pastry reached them and Sarah dashed back to the stove while Duggie headed for the phone in the study.

He re-joined her a few minutes later, shoulders hunched. "They're finished. Absolutely finished. Half the livestock in their whole area is dead, quite apart from their own, and what's even more frightening is the rate at which the people are dying there, too."

Sarah's reaction was automatic: she filled the kettle and lit the gas under it.

Duggie switched on the radio, hoping for some update, but there was only pop music on. He lowered the volume. "I wonder if that girlfriend of Peter's knew something?" he mused, pacing the length of the kitchen.

"Maybe we should have taken more notice. She was trying to persuade us to leave for the old country. And Peter's cable suggested the same thing." She set out the mugs, stringing a teabag over the rim of each.

"How could abandoning the stock help the situation?" Duggie grumbled.

"I'm no longer thinking about the stock, darling. I'm worried sick about the human factor. Frankly, I'd rather gamble on life and poverty, than a wealthy death." Sarah's knees suddenly felt weak with fear. She turned off the gas and filled the mugs.

Duggie stopped pacing to stand and stare at her. "God! Surely it can't be that serious! There must be . . . " he paused as a voice came on the radio.

" . . . in North Island has not yet been confirmed. A Government spokesman has assured our medical correspondent that there is no need for panic. Measures are being taken to restrict movement of people between infected areas and transportation of stock anywhere is banned until further notice. The town of Invercargill and its surrounding district is now totally isolated and it is difficult to obtain accurate information from there, but it is understood that emergency services are finding it almost impossible to cope with the numbers of people already dead, or assist those who are stricken. Dead stock are being left where they lie . . . "

Sarah sipped at her tea. They had missed the first bit of that report but it sounded as though the epidemic might indeed already have spread to North Island. It was too terrifying to believe. She turned off the oven and washed her hands. Untying her apron she said, "I'm going to fetch the children from school. Whether we go or stay, the sooner we get them away from other people the better. But darling, I would much rather go, if we can. Please?"

Duggie closed his eyes and nodded. "I'll call the travel people in town while you're gone. See if we can get tickets. Maybe I can find someone to milk the cows and feed the hens. The sheep will fend for themselves."

Although it was only mid-morning, the road outside the school was jammed with cars. Everyone else had had the same thought.

Douglas was just finishing the milking when she returned with the children. She went straight to the barn door. "Well," she asked, "did you get tickets?"

"I got as far as putting our names on the waiting list," he replied, switching off the machine.

Sarah's spirits drooped lower. "Waiting list? How long is that?"

"No idea. Nor had the booking clerk. She said the computers were jammed up with flight requests and it could be days before she had an answer for us."

"We don't have to go to the UK. Anywhere, to get away from here . . . " She felt panic begin to grip her chest.

Duggie shook his head. "I told her that, but it didn't make any difference. She said that everyone was telling her the same and it was confusing the issue no end."

"Supposing we can't get away . . . "

"We have to plan with that in mind, my love. Pack bags for us to take in case we're lucky, and I'll phone around for someone to take over here while we're away . . . "

"Don't forget Rover and Rufus . . . "

"Oh, the dogs will be no problem. But at the same time I think we also ought to prepare for having to sit tight right here. Why don't you nip down to the supermarket and stock up? Get enough for a few weeks. Then we'll padlock the gate and ban visitors. Agreed?"

Sarah passed a hand over her forehead, sweeping back the straying wisps of hair. "Yes. I suppose that's all we can do."

She returned to the house, wondering how to explain what was happening to Leigh and Rupert without frightening them.

"Where the hell've you been, honey? I've tried getting you for days."

"Joey!" Meg responded, wet hair dripping down her back. "Long time since we talked. I've been away."

"You busy right now?"

"You could say that. I just got out of the shower to answer you."

"Wish I was a fly on the wall!" he said enthusiastically. Then added, "I wondered if we could fix a game, sometime?"

Tennis was the last thing on her mind at the moment, but perhaps some fresh air and exercise would be no bad thing. Besides, however exhausted, she was feeling a sense of exhilaration. After working round the clock for two days she had at last found what she was looking for. Because at last she knew what she was looking for, after investigating the blood samples taken from the dead megatherium. There was a virus in there, and it was unlike any virus she had ever seen before, so small that it was no wonder she had not been able to spot it earlier. The average virus was between 20 and 400 nanometers in size, a nanometer being one billionth of a meter: this one was only ten. But it was also present in the blood samples she had brought back from New Zealand. Dead, so far as she could make out, although she had not completed the tests there. That was puzzling, and even disturbing.

But she had made progress. If it was frightening to think that she had only reached an equivalent position to that relating to Aids, with no cure in sight, she was still pleased. And Graham was due back from Washington tomorrow to take it from there. She could afford a couple of hours' relaxation.

"Like when?" she asked, pulling the towel from round her waist to rub her hair.

"I have a court reservation for 6.30 this evening. Bob Schmitt cried off. Any good?"

"Umm." She thought of all the things she should be doing. The clothes hamper was full, she scarcely had a clean garment to put on, and ET was due to go to the vet for his next jab. And she was dead tired . . . "I'll be

187

more of a hindrance than a help; I've been on my feet most of the day . . . "

"So what's new?" Joey teased. "I read that as a positive. Great. Your wheels working or do you need a ride?"

"Judging by my last service bill the darn thing had better be working, and good. I'll see you there." She looked round the dusty, untidy apartment as she hung up and was glad she had decided to go. Washing and cleaning were not the ideal way to celebrate even a minor triumph, much less a major breakthrough. She should be opening a bottle of Cliquot with Peter . . . but Peter was not here, and she could not even call him until she had spoken with Graham.

"You haven't changed much," Joey remarked as they walked out on to the court.

"Should I have?"

"Well, it's yonks since I saw you. You gotta be older."

Meg laughed. "I warn you, it's so long since I played this game I forget which end of the racquet to hold."

Their opponents were a husband and wife team, Bill and Mary Oakes, whom they had played frequently before, and usually beaten. Meg doubted they would this evening, but surprised herself by playing quite well. After one set each, the third went to a tie-breaker which she and Joey managed to pull off.

They showered and changed in the club house and met afterwards in the bar.

"What about supper?" Bill asked, looking from Joey to Meg.

"Why not?" Joey nodded. "There's a new place down on Hopper Hill. Have you tried it?"

"No," Mary chipped in. "Have you, Meg?"

Meg was looking at her watch. "No, and I'd love to go, but I really have got too much to do at home, folks. Will you excuse me if I take a raincheck? Liza's due back tomorrow and the place is a pig-sty." She drained her beer and pushed back her chair.

Joey stood up. "Guess the girl's right. I think maybe I'll give it a miss, too. Let's leave it till next time."

"Okay. No problem. Give me a buzz at the office sometime and we'll fix a return." Bill got up to help Meg collect her gear.

"And make that soon," Mary added. "We're going to lick you fellas yet, I'm telling you."

The first thing Meg did when she got home was to fill the coffee maker; then the washing machine, with its first load including everything she was wearing.

She had stripped the bed and collected the dirty towels, heaping everything on to the kitchen floor, when the door phone buzzed.

"Oh, damn!" she swore. The last thing she wanted was visitors. She lifted the receiver off the wall. "Yes?"

"Delivery service, Ma'am!" a strange voice squeaked. Yet it sounded familiar.

"Delivering what?"

"Supper!"

"Joey? Is that you, you clown?" She sighed, and pressed the lobby door release. "Come on up," she called, and then hurried to the bedroom to get some clothes on before he reached her floor.

"Knew darned well you wouldn't give food a thought, as soon as you were out of my sight," he complained as she opened the door. "I gotta take care of you: you're the best tennis partner I have." He stepped inside, kicking the door shut behind him and dumping a large brown foodbag in her arms, together with a bunch of carnations.

Meg leaned forward over the armful to kiss his cheek. "Joey! You are a sweetie."

"I know. I keep telling you this but I didn't think you believed me." He headed straight for the kitchen, kicked the dirty washing aside and stooped to light the oven. "You put the daisies in water and I'll fix the food," he ordered.

Before she finished the flowers she heard the vacuum in the lounge. She put the vase on the table and set the plates and cutlery, by which time the bed was made up again and the bedroom vacuumed. They dusted and tidied together, and finally sat down to pizza and salad, red wine and cheese, Beethoven's Seventh . . . and the background rumble of the first load of clothes in the tumble dryer while the second lot was washing.

Meg sat back, after he had kissed her goodbye on the forehead and left, and she loaded the dishwasher and folded the first set of dry clothes, feeling pleasantly relaxed . . . No question of staying on, though she knew he was carrying a torch for her. He was a dear, good friend – kind, thoughtful and caring. She loved him dearly . . . as a friend; or maybe as the brother she never had. Dear Joey. And he was sensitive and intelligent enough to know that he could never be anything more to her, whatever he might feel. However much he loved her. Dear Joey. So totally different from Peter. To Peter, dirty clothes and dirty dishes did not exist: they were not part of his world. He was unaware of the mundane details in life, he dealt in bigger concepts. He thought in terms of what went on in cities, not kitchens; in countries and empires, rather than domestic chores, his own or anyone else's. He was a big man, in mind as well as stature, exciting and vibrant. In his company she ceased to be merely a US citizen; like him she became a citizen of the world. It was impossible to get him out of her mind. And the more she thought about him, the more she loved him.

The great miracle was that he loved her, too. It was so long since she had felt like this about any man, she had begun to think love had passed her by. She had wondered if it was an emotion only for the teens and twenties. Like Sally Ann and Rod. She smiled, remembering how the young lovers were the last time she visited Hartford: two beautiful people, clinging together, gazing adoringly into each other's eyes. Sally Ann was a sweet kid, transparently determined to break away from her staid, New England background. It was obvious that she and Rod slept together, got drunk together and occasionally sampled the current drug scene. Meg speculated on whether her parents knew; they probably did, in a way, but refused to believe or accept it.

Meg had been the one who introduced Sally Ann to camping, years ago, before Rod came on the scene. Three successive summer vacations they spent together exploring different locations: the Rockies, the Colorado Canyon and the shores of Lake Michigan. They had had fun together, a lot of laughs . . . and a lot of serious conversations. Sally Ann had been having the usual teenage traumas – difficulties with schoolwork, sport and personal relationships. She had been of an age which Meg remembered so well, when a young girl finds it impossible to talk to her mother and seeks a younger adult in whom to confide. Meg had listened to the familiar problems, knowing that the telling would surely clarify them in the girl's mind without any unnecessary advice from herself. And the fact that Meg had so clearly understood, could relate to the problems which had seemed to the younger girl so insurmountable, had bonded them together in a friendship that had survived the subsequent years when they saw so little of each other. Where was Sally Ann, now? She hoped to hell they were safely out of Chile, preferably on their way up through the middle Americas. It would be great if they came up the west coast and stopped over for a spell in 'Frisco; there were so many sights here worth visiting and maybe she could spare a day or two away from the Center to go with them. She checked the time: far too late to call Nan, now. She would try in the morning before leaving for work.

"The little bastard," Fitzroy said, eye glued to the electron microscope. "You reckon that's our boy, do you, Meg?"

"I reckon."

"Breakdown?"

Meg referred to her notes, while Fitzroy made his own. "Very small, ten nanometers in diameter. Shape: spherical. Nucleoid body composed of 1,200 B-protein molecules with a molecular weight of 2,700 Atomic Mass Units, and one A-protein molecule weighing 38,000 AMU. This is definitely the unit attaching the bacteriophage to the host. The B-protein molecules surround one single-stranded deoxyribonucleic molecule weighing 1,000,300 AMU."

"Agreed. In other words, this is a perfectly normal virus, except for its subnormal size. Which host?"

"A sample I brought back with me from New Zealand. From the mortuary guard who's since died. But here's a point. The guard had had the disease for two days before I obtained that sample. It was returned here refrigerated for me to work on. I couldn't find the virus right away, not until we had Mandy's Fred to give us a lead. But I am pretty damned sure that virus was dead when I got it here. I'll tell you why: even if I couldn't find the virus, I tried injecting some of the blood into one of our rabbits, so I could watch the symptoms from the beginning. There were none. Old Brer Rabbit is still as healthy as a . . . rabbit."

"What are you driving at?"

"That in addition to being very small, this has got to be about the most short-lived virus in medical history. It goes wild when it gets into a host, but . . . it doesn't die with the host. It dies first. Okay, it doesn't die until it does just about mortal damage to its victim, but if its progress could be arrested, for just forty-eight hours maybe, survival and then recovery could be a matter of simple medical procedure, bleeding, radioactive treatment, and what have you."

Fitzroy raised his head wearily. "Supposing we can concoct a neutralising agent, how the hell are we going to do that with nothing but dead viruses to work on? If you're right, there's none of them will survive transference from the plague area to a laboratory."

"Well, I have a pile of notes I've been making. Care to run through them?"

"You tell me." Fitzroy was disturbingly exhausted. Part of it was undoubtedly despair. He had met with no response whatsoever in Washington, although he had insisted on an interview with the President. Help for the Chilean and Argentinian Governments in their fight against the disease: fine, within existing budgets. Funds for additional research: none available at this time. Immigration barriers or blood tests on arrivals: utterly impractical – what about retaliations, panics, sheer expense? "I can't help feeling that you're over-reacting, Doctor," the President had said. "This is the end of the twentieth century. There is no way a plague like the Black Death could possibly sweep the world as it did in the fourteenth century. Hell, man, we're in an election year. You are asking me to commit political suicide. You'll find an antidote, in good time. Just keep looking. I have total confidence in you."

No wonder the boss was looking dispirited.

Meg took out her book, flicked the pages. "Okay. One: it seems certain that the virus was contained and survived in the frozen body of the megatherium for a hundred thousand years, remaining in a state of suspended animation. Now, this was really a chance in ten billion. That megatherium did not die of hypertension; it *had* hypertension. It suffered a stroke, but it must have fallen into a hole in the ice and frozen to death before the virus had completed its work. The virus was still alive and, as I say, it must have remained in a comatose state until the body was thawed out.

"Two: some quantities of it must have been released when the beast was dug up and embalmed. I've wired Amanda for a breakdown on what they did with their waste matter, but I haven't had a reply to confirm that theory.

"Three: assuming that I am right, it must have been dumped in the sea before being properly thawed, and was eaten by either fish, or krill and then fish, in the Antarctic Ocean.

"Four: infected fish, or fishes, were then caught off the coasts of Chile and New Zealand and eaten.

"Five: the fish clearly weren't obviously infected, either by appearance or smell, or they wouldn't have been marketable; I don't believe the virus affected the fish at all, merely continued in a state of suspended animation.

"Six: once taken into the mammal digestive system the virus wakes up and homes in on the bone marrow.

"Seven: once in the animal system the virus is not only sustained but replicates, and becomes highly contagious. Agreed so far?"

"Agreed," Fitzroy said.

"Okay. But as I said, the virus, despite replication, apparently cannot outlive the host; once the disease has reached a certain stage the virus dies."

Fitzroy snapped his fingers. "You mean it virtually chokes on its own spit."

"That's one way of putting it. What it does mean is that seeking an antidote or a vaccination or even an alleviation is impossible, from animal samples, because it works so fast. The hosts are dead and so is the virus before we can subject it to sufficient tests. Therefore before we are going to be able to determine whether it is lysogenous or transductive, before we can even begin to think about an interferon, we have got to obtain samples where the virus is going to continue to live long enough for our tests to be completed. Right? If we can do that, we stand a chance of developing a vaccine."

"What good will that do? People die too quickly for vaccination."

"After the disease is advanced. If my theory is right, once we find a vaccine, if it can be given to anyone who reveals a high rbc in a blood test, the disease will be arrested. But of course it would be best if everyone in a suspect area could be vaccinated beforehand."

"Do you have any idea what you're suggesting? Practically and financially?"

"Yes, Gray, I do have an idea. I know just how colossal it is. How expensive. But without it, one hell of a lot of people are going to die. We could be talking about a third of the world's population . . . or even more. And that's if it's no worse than the Black Death. I think it is going to be worse. Governments are just going to have to listen to us, and they are going to have to spend the money to vaccinate every living creature."

"That'll be the day. And that's supposing they have any money to spend. You can't collect taxes from the dead. And that's supposing they have anything to spend their money on, too. Anyway, where the hell do we find this living sample to work on?"

"Back to the notes," Meg said. "Number Five: the fish couldn't have been obviously infected, or no one would have bought them. Now we know that in humans and animals this thing takes between forty-eight and seventy-two hours to work. But in fish it obviously doesn't work that quickly, if it works at all."

Fitzroy snapped his fingers again. "Cold instead of warm blood. It's a fact there's been no report of reptiles dying, either."

"You got it," Meg jumped excitedly.

195

"But . . . we don't know for sure. It could be only one fish ate the remains; there couldn't have been that much of the beast left lying around. And we don't know what the immunisation process actually is." Gray's head nodded rhythmically in concentration, the fingers of one hand drumming on the white, plastic laminated bench.

"There has to be more than one," Meg insisted. "The same fish couldn't have infected both Isla Hoste and Stewart Island, several thousand miles apart. Anyway, if any of that beast's innards were dumped in the Antarctic Ocean, which seems most likely, my bet is that it was first of all eaten by krill. Isn't that Southern Ocean swarming with krill? That means it could have been consumed by a lot of krill-eating fish. Before we can start working on an antidote we have to get hold of one of those fishes carrying the virus. A live fish."

"The waste from the megatherium went in four months ago. They'll all have been taken by now."

"I don't think they have, for several reasons. The first incidence of the Red Death was less than a month ago. That means the virus didn't surface in *any* fish for three months. And I don't believe more than a couple of those fish were caught. The outbreak in South America began with a single community. It seems pretty obvious that it got to Punta Arenas either through the police and medics who went to the island, nearly all of whom are now dead, or through the woman, Maria Lopez, the coastguard took off that drifting boat. Once it got into an urban community it ran wild. The same thing is happening in New Zealand."

"And Tasmania?"

"It could have been carried to Tasmania by an infected person from New Zealand. Anyway, that case has still not been confirmed. So, all subsequent outbreaks of the disease have spread from the two original outbreaks; if any other infected fish had been caught we would have had other incidences in fishing communities. And in addition, as soon as the nature of the disease was discovered, and as it was still supposed to be fish poisoning, the Governments of Argentina, Chile and New Zealand put a ban on all fishing off the ice shelves. There have to be some of them still around."

"I still say the odds on landing one have got to be too long to be realistic."

"Amanda will be able to give us the exact area where the remains were dumped."

"Four months ago," he reminded her again.

"Okay, Gray, it's a chance. Maybe it's a slim one. But it's the only one we have."

He brooded for a few minutes, then nodded. "You could be right. What have you in mind?"

"I think we should charter *Ocean Secrets*."

"Dawson? That's going to cost a bomb."

"We have to have a floating laboratory. *Ocean Secrets* is that. She's equipped to go anywhere any time and do anything. And Jimmy Dawson knows more about fish habits and diseases than anyone else in the world. He'll be able to work out just where those fish are likely to be at this time."

"Hm. Where is *Ocean Secrets* now?"

"When last I heard she was in the Galapagos. That's an idea. I could pick her up in Callao, and we'd be down off Cape Horn in a week."

"Yeah? What's this 'I' business?"

"Well . . . you have to stay here and mind the shop."

"While you go gallivanting off to the Antarctic Ocean? You realise it's winter down there?"

"It's our only chance, Gray. And we don't have too much time."

10

Plans

"I'm so glad you were able to come down, Peter dear," Veronica Canning said over her Spode teacup. "Daddy does worry me, sometimes. He gets himself so worked up over things that really don't matter, or at least that he can do nothing about. I'm sure our stockbroker knows more about the market than we do."

"Pssh!" John Canning commented, knocking the doddle from the bowl of his pipe into a large, messy ashtray.

"And that's another thing," his wife continued. "The doctor has told him repeatedly that he should give up smoking, and he takes not a blind bit of notice."

Peter finished the last mouthful of rather rocky rock cake and placed his crumbly teaplate on the occasional table beside his cup and saucer. "Are the new blood-pressure pills working better than the last ones?" he asked his father.

"They probably would if he remembered to take them," his mother replied. "What Daddy really needs is a nurse, following him round all day, making sure he takes his medications and doesn't smoke and drink too much."

John looked up at her with raised eyebrows and took the empty pipe out of his mouth. "A nurse! What in heaven's name do I want with a nurse when you are doing the job so well?"

There was nothing ill-natured in their repeated exchanges. Peter laughed. "Really, you two never stop bickering, do you? Mum, I think you'd go into a decline if Dad started behaving himself and you hadn't anything to nag him about."

"Oh, Peter, how horrid you are . . . " his mother began, but was immediately interrupted.

"Have no fear, my boy, she'll always think of something! Hasn't she asked you when you're going to find a wife yet, today?" The retired brigadier pulled a decrepit tobacco pouch out of his pocket and fixed his attention on one of life's more important matters.

"Another cup of tea, Peter?" Mrs Canning held out her hand for his cup, trying to ignore her husband's teasing but unable to prevent a grin from puckering the corners of her mouth.

"Yes, please." He concentrated on handling the delicate china with care, being renowned in the family for clumsiness. He only dropped things when he had something else on his mind, like now: he had come down to introduce the subject of Meg, which he was sure would please his mother.

"Well, I've resolved not to ask you any more," she told him across the top of the silver teapot. "We've all nagged you for years about your Anna, and really, it's none of our business who you marry, so long as you love the girl." She handed the cup back. "What about another rock cake? I made them specially for you."

Peter had loved rock cakes in the old days when they had been made by Cook; they were never like these. He eyed the grey, spotty lumps with alarm, but he did not have the courage to refuse, and Veronica replaced the plate of dwindling cakes on the tea trolley beside her, continuing, "I told Claudia, when she was here last, that you are married more to your politics than you ever will be to a woman . . . "

Peter opened his mouth, to cut in with the little speech he had prepared about Meg, but his mother was in full flood.

" . . . and it seems to me, with all this generation of independent girls, it would be far more sensible for you to settle down with one of them . . . "

"I agree, Mum, and . . . "

"So do I. Absolutely." John had finished lighting his pipe and sat back, puffing happily. "But Peter, changing the subject for a moment, while you're here I wanted to ask you what you think about this awful sickness that's broken out in the Southern Hemisphere." He spoke as though the Southern Hemisphere might be on Mars. "Do you think it could spread to North Island in New Zealand? Your mother and I are concerned about Sarah."

"I don't think you need to worry about her, but I do think it would be a good idea if they came over here for a visit. We haven't seen them for ages." Sarah was much on his mind, too; she had not replied to his telegram, and he was afraid that he would be able to persuade the Prime Minister to impose some kind of a ban on visitors from infected areas – he had no doubt that the committee he was setting up would recommend it – before she actually got herself into the country. "In fact, I've told her so."

"We'd love to see them, of course," his mother said enthusiastically, "but I suppose it is a problem for them. You do realise that they haven't a bean, don't you?"

"I thought their farm was doing quite well?" Peter frowned.

"I believe they're well satisfied with the progress they're making but they've sunk every penny they had into it and borrowed from the bank, too. Finding fares for the four of them may well be beyond them at the moment," John explained.

"Can't we send them the fares, then?" Peter suggested. Both parents stared at him, saying nothing but wondering why he thought haste was so important if there was nothing to worry about. "I'll make a contribution and we can get Claudia to chip in," Peter went on, "but I think it would be best if you sent it, Dad. You can do it through your bank, can't you?"

"Of course. I'll telephone Sarah now, and tell her to book the tickets."

"Don't be silly, dear, it's early tomorrow morning, there. They won't be up yet." Veronica chided.

"At 5 am? They're farmers, my dear girl. Of course they're up, and working." The phone was beside his chair and he commenced the long dialling, frowned, replaced the receiver and tried again; and again. "Damn. The lines to New Zealand are all busy; this could take hours. That's odd, isn't it, at five in the morning?"

"Other people are probably having the same idea. I'm afraid I will have to leave you to it." Peter stood up. "It's Claudia's party tonight and she'll kill me if I'm late." He bent to kiss Veronica's cheek. "Don't worry about them, Mum. They'll be okay."

"I hope you're right. Anyway, enjoy the party."

He gave her a quick glance. There was a funny tone in her voice then. Had she and Claudia been cooking up something between them again?

He got home just on six, which gave him half an hour to bath and change and reach Claudia's, hopefully before the other guests; he wanted a word with Hartley, but had not been able to set up a proper meeting – and time was passing. Instinctively he switched on his Ansaphone as he fed Gladstone, and listened to Meg's voice.

"Sorry to have missed you. We have some developments over here which could be quite exciting. Call me some time, but not after Tuesday."

He grabbed the phone and dialled, listened to various whirrs and clicks. "This is Dr Margaret Calhoun," her voice said. "I am sorry, but I am not available right now. If you will leave your name and telephone number, and the nature of your business, I will return your call as soon as possible."

"Damnation," he muttered, looking at his watch. It wasn't yet nine in the morning in San Francisco by his reckoning. She must have left for the Center early. He called there instead, and got Helen.

"Hi, Mr Canning. No, Meg isn't in yet."

"But you are expecting her?"

"Sure, any minute."

He must have missed her at the apartment by seconds. "Would you ask her to call me the moment she gets in?"

"Sure, I'll do that, Mr Canning."

He was in the shower when the phone rang. He wrapped himself in a towel and ran to it. "Meg, darling!"

"Peter. We seem to have been playing ring-a-ring-a-roses."

"Yes," he agreed. "But it's so good to hear your voice. What's been happening your end?"

"A lot." He could hear the suppressed excitement in her voice. "We've isolated the virus."

"Tremendous. Does that mean there's an end in sight?"

"Maybe. But it's still a long way away. We're moving, though. I called to say goodbye for a couple of weeks."

"Goodbye?"

"I'm off to do a bit of fishing?"

"Now?"

She smiled into the phone. "It goes with the job. We have to obtain a live fish carrying the virus. There have to be some of them around the South Pole."

"I'm not with you." He frowned into the phone and the towel fell on the floor. "You're going to the South Pole?"

"Only in a manner of speaking. I've chartered *Ocean Secrets*. She's waiting for me in Callao. That's in Peru."

"I know where Callao is," Peter said, his brain racing. "*Ocean Secrets*? That's some ship."

"Yep. She'll be our floating lab."

"Our?"

"Well, Charlie Oswiecki is coming. You remember Charlie? He's one of Tom Lintell's people. As a matter of fact, he's the chap who actually emptied . . . it's a long story. I'll tell you when I get back. Jim Dawson is skipper, and he has his own lab boys as well as crew. What he doesn't know about fish and their movements, nobody does."

"Let me get this straight," Peter said, making himself speak slowly. "You intend to go trawling in the Southern Ocean in the middle of their winter?"

"I'll be in good hands."

"And what happens if you catch your fish . . . "

"I'm going to catch my fish, Peter. I have to."

" . . . and pick up this Red Death yourself?"

"I'm not going to eat the darn thing. I'm not even going to dissect it. I'm looking for living blood samples containing the virus. We simply have to have those before we can find out how to stop it working in humans."

"Meg, all we know about this virus is that it kills. It killed those policemen and medics who went down to Hoste. It kills without discrimination. I know you'll take every precaution. But you are still taking one hell of a risk."

"It goes with the job, Peter." There was a touch of tension in her voice.

He hesitated. He knew that if he pressed he could lose her, for ever. But the thought of her setting off on such a dangerous expedition . . . quite apart from the virus, the Southern Ocean at this time of year had to be about the most dangerous stretch of water in the world. He realised he was shivering, stooped for the towel and tried unsuccessfully to wrap it round himself with one hand. If only he could . . . but why not? He had virtually finished setting up his committee of experts to study the disease; he intended to complete that tonight. He himself had no technical knowledge to contribute to their studies, but he might persuade Meg to part with samples for him to bring back for the British medical researchers, and the Prime Minister had suggested he make himself scarce for a fortnight: he was being paired anyway until the House rose for the summer. Suddenly the adrenalin was pumping through his veins. He would have to square it with Jeremy, of course, but he had no doubt he could do that; there was no way he could do more to help quell the disease than actually help find the antidote – if it existed. Besides, another idea was germinating in his brain. If Meg was taking *Ocean Secrets* to the Southern Ocean, the odds were she would be putting in to New Zealand at some time or other . . .

"Peter?" Meg asked. "Are you still there?"

"Yes," he said. "Meg . . . how'd you like some support?"

"Support?"

"Mostly of the moral kind. But I've done a lot of sailing."

"Are you serious?"

"Never more so."

"Peter, I might be away for several weeks. I'm not coming back until I find what I'm looking for."

"That's fine with me. I can certainly come for a fortnight. I assume you'll be touching land from time to time?"

"Yes, but . . . "

"And that we'll be in radio contact while at sea?"

"Well, yes, but . . . Peter, it's going to be very cold and very uncomfortable."

"I'm looking forward to it."

There was a brief pause. Then she said. "I am going to work, Peter. All of us are."

"I'll behave," he said. "When do you plan to leave Callao?"

"Four days' time."

"I'll be there," he promised.

11

Task Force

Peter felt strangely exhilarated as he rang the bell of the apartment in Cadogan Square. He was planning on adventuring, for the first time in a long time, and with the woman he loved. There could not be anything more romantically exciting than that. So she had made it clear she was going to work; she could not do that round the clock – he would indeed be a necessary catalyst to prevent her from over-tiring herself.

"Peter!"

Hartley Briggs was of medium height, solidly built, in contrast to his slim, elegant wife. He also had a red face, which Peter had always put down to alcohol. Now he found himself wondering if Hartley already had polycythaemia: he really was getting hyped on the subject.

"You're the first. Come and have a Scotch. Claudie's just adding finishing touches."

"I'd actually like a private word," Peter said.

Hartley nodded. "I thought you might." Claudia had told him how worried the family was about Sarah. "Let's go into the study."

He led the way, and Peter smiled at the black-frocked, white-aproned waitresses waiting by the salvers laden with canapés. Hartley closed the study door and poured two whiskies. "Your father was on the phone just now. About Sarah."

"Oh, great. Did he get through?"

"No. The lines are jammed solid. There's an almighty flap going on down there."

"I'm not surprised," Peter said. "It's a nasty business."

"You obviously know more about it than the newspapers do. You must tell me the facts, some time. But what are we going to do about Sarah and Douglas? And the kids?"

"Keep trying. I want to talk about something else."

Hartley frowned, and sat behind his desk. "Go on."

Peter outlined his conversation with the Prime Minister. "I already have Witherington from the BMA, and Western, the blood man. Here's the rest of the list," he took a folded paper from his inside pocket. "I'd be grateful if you'd come in as well. When we find the antidote to this thing, we are going to need it manufactured on the biggest possible scale."

Hartley stroked his chin. "Won't it be considered unethical, giving an inside track to your brother-in-law?"

"I wouldn't care if it was. I believe this could be as big a crisis as the human race has ever faced." He ignored Hartley's sceptically raised eyebrow. "I want the best brains possible on this committee. We need you for the practical, manufacturing details. Obviously, once we know what we have to do, what has to be produced to combat the virus, then the manufacturing and marketing will be opened up to all drug companies capable of production."

Hartley was frowning. "We'd need that much? It's as bad as that?"

"Yes. Potentially. And it could explode at any moment. Try imagining what could happen if a disease as contagious, and as fatal, as this hit somewhere like Calcutta or Tokyo? Or London, for that matter?"

"I'd rather not. Are we in touch with other governments over this?"

"At the moment, only New Zealand. Everyone wants to play it down, including the PM. I can't blame them. It's a kind of doomsday situation, so they're trying to maintain a front of business as usual and maybe it'll go away."

"Everyone more frightened of over-reacting and being left with egg on their faces, than the disease itself, eh? And are there no leads at all?"

"There are some. As a matter of fact . . . " He told Hartley of his liaison with Fitzroy, and of the latest developments.

"Sounds promising," Hartley agreed. "We should wish this Calhoun woman all the luck in the world with her angling expedition."

Peter grinned at him. "Wish me some as well. I'm going with her."

Hartley spilt his whisky, got up and refilled his glass, and as an afterthought poured some more into Peter's. "Would you like to repeat that?"

"I'm going with her."

"You are going off to Antarctica in the middle of winter?"

"I'm buying my longjohns tomorrow."

"And what happens to your committee? Who is going to chair it?"

"You."

Hartley took another swallow of whisky.

"You're the obvious man for the job," Peter pointed out.

"I'm not a Member of Parliament."

"That's a very good reason for being chairman. The one thing the Prime Minister does not want is this subject aired in Parliament until we have an answer to it. You will report direct and only to Jeremy Payne."

"And our brief?"

"I'll arrange with Fitzroy to keep you up-to-date on all laboratory developments. I'll also arrange for some samples to be sent across so that our people can look at them if you think that will help, though most important will be what we bring back from the Southern Ocean. But you" – he pointed his glass at his brother-in-law – "will be responsible for the well-being of Britain, Hartley. I've already recommended that we institute blood tests for everyone coming in. The Prime Minister is a bit chary of this at the moment because of cost, disruption, and the probability of retaliation, but I can't see that that will matter. No sane person is going to want to travel abroad until this thing is licked. But if you keep banging on with it, and can present a unanimous recommendation of the committee, we may get something done. I regard it as an essential first step."

"Fortress Britain," Hartley muttered. "You know, Peter, if this Red Death does spread the way you're afraid it might, putting up the shutters isn't going to help. These islands have to be fed, and fuelled."

"I know that, Hartley. But we have to be seen to be doing something until we can find an antidote." He was speaking as a politician.

Hartley nodded. "All right, I accept. I'll need powers to co-opt whoever I require, and to demand whatever data I require – that will certainly include medical histories."

"You'll have it. Meet me at Jeremy's office at 11 am tomorrow and we'll go through the whole thing."

"He knows you're rushing off?"

Peter grinned. "Not yet. But he will. The Government is rather anxious for me to keep a low profile about now, after that exchange Brereton and I had last month."

"I remember. And Sarah?"

"Keep trying. For God's sake keep trying."

"I will. Ah . . . "

The door was thrown open. "For Heaven's sake," Claudia Briggs exploded. "Nearly all the guests have arrived and you two are hiding in here gossiping and drinking."

"Just coming, dear." Hartley hastily got up.

"I didn't even know you'd turned up, yet, Peter." Claudia tucked her arm through his and escorted him through the door. "And I have such a lovely surprise for you."

They stood on the edge of a crowded drawing-room, and Peter found himself gazing at Anna.

She had not seen him, was talking in her usual animated fashion amongst a group of masculine admirers. Peter turned to Claudia, unsmiling, his brows knotted in a deep frown. "What the hell is she doing here?" he hissed.

"No need to look so cross. I invited her, little brother. I've abandoned the effort to set you up with a more suitable mate. I capitulate. So, here is the woman of your choice." She made a sweeping gesture towards Anna. "Waiting for you."

"Oh, God! This is all I need!"

It was his sister's turn to look annoyed. "Now what? I thought you'd be thrilled!"

Peter drained his glass. So this was why Mum's voice had sounded odd this afternoon: she and Claudia had cooked this up together, especially to please him. What could he say? But there was no time to say anything – Anna had looked round and seen him, she was waving, waiting for him to go up and greet her in front of all these mutual friends and acquaintances. Ignoring his obvious discomfort, Claudia led him through the throng of guests, like a lamb to the slaughter, he thought, anxious to complete the plot hatched with his mother. She had to be seen bringing them together, publicly.

"Darling," Anna purred, eyeing him from under lowered lids. "What an amazing coincidence, meeting you here."

210

"I believe you two know each other," Claudia smiled benevolently. "So nice to have you both here, together. One of you always seems to be at the other end of the universe," she added, blithely ignoring the fact that she had never attempted to invite Anna into her home before. "I'll leave you to entertain yourselves," and she turned away to greet a clutch of late arrivals.

"I was praying you'd be here." Anna spoke softly now that Claudia had left them. She was wearing her hair loose, tonight, draped over one eye à la Veronica Lake, and falling on to the shoulders of a bright red cheong sam into which her exquisite figure had been skilfully poured. "I'm sorry about that tiff the other night, but I so expected you to call. I've waited at home every night." Her eyes became alarmingly moist. "I just don't see how you can treat me like this, my darling."

The devil, Peter thought, if she starts weeping all over Claudia's party. He could not believe she really felt as cut up as she was pretending, any more than he had believed she would have accepted a proposal of marriage. Anna just was not like that. She was simply reluctant to let go.

It was the first time he had really been angry with her. He felt her watching his reaction, waiting, as he assumed a nonchalance he did not have while he looked around for a waiter. "Excuse me, Anna, my glass is empty," he told her.

Anna saw one first, and hailed him. "A whisky and soda for Mr Canning," she ordered, taking the glass from his fingers. "But you mustn't drink too much. I want you on your best form tonight."

"Best form?"

"Well, you are coming back to my place, aren't you?" she frowned at him. "After this?"

He was puzzled for a moment. "This?" Then he realised that she must think he had asked Claudia to invite her. "Er . . . "

"And I promise to say yes to whatever proposal you make." She was smiling.

Oh Lord! We're back to square one. And if I try to tell her otherwise, right now, she is quite liable to weep and make a fearful scene and spoil Claudia's party. What the hell could he say?

"Your whisky and soda, sir." The waiter was at his elbow.

"Thank you." He took the glass from the salver and raised it in Anna's direction before taking a deep draught. "Got here early for a business chat with Hartley, which is why I'm on this stuff tonight. All hell is breaking loose, you know. Darling, I'm simply not going to be able to make it." It was a feeble attempt to evade the issue.

And Anna knew it. So, he had not changed his mind, but obviously Lady Briggs knew nothing of the American woman, supposing she existed; which was why she, Anna, had been invited here tonight. Hell! Suddenly she felt desperately hurt and angry. So he really did mean to walk out on her. No doubt his precious Prime Minister had read him the riot act. Her eyes narrowed and mouth tightened with the effort to control her reactions. Of course, she had known all along that it could not last, she tried reminding herself, and she had not exactly remained faithful to him throughout their affair. Well, the show must go on . . . she would just have to show him that he was not the only man in her world. With a smile firmly fixed on her face she asked, "Have you met Jan Geller? Come." She put a hand under his elbow and steered him towards a tall, blond man in a tan suit and cream shirt and tie. "Jan, I do want you to meet a dear friend of mine, Peter Canning," she said, interrupting his conversation with a plump, blue-rinsed matron.

Peter could guess the effort she was making and his smile was more in admiration for her than greeting for the stranger as he politely held out his hand.

"Hello, I think perhaps we have met already, your name is familiar. Mine's Geller." The voice was distinctively South African.

"Yes, Anna told me." Peter shook the hand briefly, wondering why he took an instant dislike to the man.

"Jan is visiting relatives here in London, before going home. He has a magnificent place near Cape Town."

"I've been trying to persuade Anna to come back with me for a visit." Jan looked down at the top of Anna's head with obvious interest.

"When are you returning?"

"Tomorrow night."

Peter's eyes widened in amazement. The man must be mad.

"I think it's a marvellous idea. I couldn't possibly say no, Jan." Anna tilted her head back to smile up at her prospective host.

Peter knew she was doing it in the hope of getting a reaction from him. Well she would, but not here; he would call her later, at home. "What is the temperature like in your part of the world, right now?" he asked Jan, evading the issue.

Anna's eyes followed the conversation between the two men, back and forth, white teeth still flashing between red lips wide-stretched in the stage-smile, until boredom carried her away to another group.

"Anna tells me you are in the Ministry of Health," Jan said. "What do you think of this epidemic in South America?"

"It's in New Zealand too, you know."

"Yes. I heard that. A bit of a mystery how it crossed the world like that in one leap."

"There has to be a connection. It's obviously extremely serious, virulent and fatal," Peter told him. "Aren't you worried about going back home at the moment?"

"Home? To South Africa?"

Peter nodded.

"Good God, no. There's no problem there."

"There could be, at any time."

"Don't you worry. If it ever gets to our country we'll be on top of it before it has time to spread. Our medical research is second to none," he bragged.

"I sincerely hope you're right. But knowing what I do, I'm damned if I'd visit the Southern Hemisphere at the present time."

Jan Geller stared at Peter, looked him up and down with eyebrows slightly raised. "You must visit our country, one day. You'll find we South Africans don't scare easily."

Which confirmed Peter's dislike of the man.

Anna drifted back to them. "You two still gossiping?"

"Peter is trying to tell me that I shouldn't return home till the South American epidemic is over."

Jan's tone was blatant and Anna's green eyes darted from one to the other. "Rubbish," she cooed sweetly, "Chile and Argentina are just backwoods, compared with South Africa. I don't believe there could be the slightest danger."

"You mean you'll come back with me?" Reading the situation between Peter and Anna, Jan was quick to use it to persuade her.

"Of course. Why not? I never listen to prophets of doom or to politicians." Anna smiled at Peter, enjoying the frown on his face. She slid a hand through Jan's arm. "But you will leave me time to pack, won't you?"

Peter was seething, but there was nothing he could do. It just staggered him that, after her difficulties getting back from Rio, Anna should step straight back into danger . . . just to cock a snook at him.

"Ah, there you are, Peter," Hartley boomed, clamping a hand on his shoulder, "I want you to meet Lord Swanson. I think he might prove to be a great help to us."

Anna's expression remained fixed as she watched him disappear into the crowd.

There was an enormous amount to be done in the two days remaining before Peter had to fly off to Peru. Next morning he took Gladstone to the cattery immediately after an early breakfast, did a little shopping and was in Jeremy's office at 10.30, outlining both the composition of his committee and his plans.

Jeremy considered for several minutes before agreeing. "At least no one can say you have been sitting on your ass," he commented, "but you'd better not take more than a fortnight; by then I'll need you back here. And while you're away you'll keep in touch, won't you, and be prepared to fly home the minute anything critical comes up?"

"I'll be through every day," Peter promised. "You happy with Hartley in my absence?"

"He knows about drugs and diseases, certainly. And he has the approach of a successful businessman, so it shouldn't be wildly expensive. Yes, I'll endorse that. Brereton will run amok when it comes out, of course, so before it does, you and your American friends had better come up with the answer. Then you'll be a hero. If you don't, your career could be in jeopardy. I think you should understand that very clearly."

"Jeremy," Peter said, "if my American friends don't come up with an answer, very quickly, my political career won't mean a damn thing. And neither will yours."

Jeremy stared at him blankly for a moment. "I'll brief the PM," he said, reaching for the pills in his top drawer the moment the door closed on his PPS.

Peter hurried off to sit in on the first meeting of the task force, reviewing the situation in the light of the latest news that had come in. None of it was good. The Chilean Government had fallen because of its inability to check the spread of the epidemic, and the country was apparently in a state of complete chaos; he wondered if Meg's god-daughter had managed to get out. The Argentinian Government had imposed martial law, but most observers doubted that this would make any difference. To the trauma of the disease was now being added food shortages and financial crisis; stock markets were beginning to shudder. Peru, Bolivia, Paraguay, Uruguay and Brazil had closed their southern borders, and Chilean and Argentinian appeals for additional medical help were largely being ignored, except for volunteers and drugs from the United States and Canada.

But he could not help being more concerned about the New Zealand situation. Here he had been able to organise an airlift of all the radioactive phosphorus and busulfan available in Britain – his first instruction to Hartley was to give top priority to rebuilding the stocks of busulfan. But the New Zealand Government reported that the whole of South Island was an infected area, and that people were queueing up to flee the country; obviously this involved a run on the banks, and a financial crisis was looming there too. At least the New Zealanders, acting with a proper sense of responsibility, were insisting that anyone leaving had to take a blood test first, to make sure their rbc was normal. But they had to admit they had no idea how many people might have left South Island carrying the disease before the tests were introduced; there were certainly cases now occurring in Wellington. The mood down there was apparently one of calm desperation, and prayer; Peter found himself constantly thinking of Sarah. Presumably she and Douglas were wait-listed to get out; his conscience kept telling him there was nothing he could do to help her – he could not, must not, use his position to attempt to help her and her family jump the queue.

Worst of all, cases were now confirmed in Tasmania, and the Australian Government was already imposing a total quarantine on the island.

"So it's quite a mess down there," he told his committee. "If an antidote isn't found, and fast, we could be talking in terms of megadeaths. So wish the Antarctic Expedition luck."

Which they did.

He hurried back to his flat, threw some clothes into an overnight bag, and telephoned the public house in Trebeth Cross which was his political headquarters. "Hello, Stephanie. Clive about?"

"Peter!" Stephanie Wardle shouted in delight. "Where are you?"

Tall and slender, Stephanie was an unlikely publican's wife, but her husband had always dreamed of owning a pub when he retired from the army, while, as a retired major in the Marines, he had proved an invaluable constituency agent for Peter, as well as a good friend. Stephanie supported him loyally, and her interest in mysticism and the occult had found much to feed on in Cornish folklore.

"In London. But I'm leaving now to drive down."

"Oh, super. We'll expect you."

"It's a fleeting visit, I'm afraid," Peter confessed. "All hell is breaking loose."

"This thing in New Zealand? Yes, it's frightening, isn't it? Thank God we don't have things like that over here."

"Yes," Peter said grimly. "Stephanie, could you ask Clive to convene a meeting for this evening? I know it's short notice, but I have to be on my way again tomorrow."

"Well, of course I will. What time?"

Peter looked at his watch; it was just on one. "I'll grab a sandwich before I leave . . . should be with you

217

around four or so. I'll need time for a bath and change
. . . seven o'clock?"

"We'll get on to it right away," she promised.

He always enjoyed the drive down to Trebeth Cross,
not only because it was the very heart of his constituency, but also because he had bought himself a country
cottage, not merely for residence but as a bolt hole
whenever he felt the need; he was glad he had never
ever brought Anna down here.

The village was set on moorland overlooking the sea
and close to the town of Ridding. It was a desolate
looking place of granite walls and grazing sheep, but
though the locals had been coldly remote towards
him at first, he stayed amongst them, drank with
them, visited them in their homes and sympathised
with their problems so that soon he had become very
fond of them and they appeared to feel the same way
about their young MP. He thought it politic always to
drive down in his rather ancient Ford; when he honked
as he passed through the village street several women
came out of their kitchens to wave at him, as did their
husbands from the pub, the Iron Duke, while early
tourists stared. His cottage was at the far end, looking
out at the moor over a low stone wall surrounding
the garden; the garden itself contained a few small
fir trees, masses of Spanish broom blooming red and
yellow, and a bank of tamarisk along the west wall.
In a reasonably sheltered corner a bed of hybrid tea
roses nodded regally under the weight of their petals,
surrounded with a haze of forget-me-nots, and in the
narrow borders edging the red-gravelled paths, annuals
were bedded; petunias and antirrhinums, nemesias and
lobelias providing contrast to the bleak moors with a
blaze of colour.

John Pengelley, Peter's gardener and caretaker, was
mowing the small stretch of lawn, but he hurried to
open the gate and allow the car to be driven into

the front yard. "Expected you last week," he commented, smiling.

"Things have been hectic," Peter explained. "Betty well?"

"Fine as ever. I'd better nip home and tell her you're here, so she'll get something cooking for your dinner."

The Pengelleys fussed over him as if he were the son they had never had; it was sometimes a bit smothering, but still a comforting feeling. Peter took his suitcase into the tiny sitting-room and up the open staircase to the even smaller bedroom, looking around himself as he went. Betty Pengelley always kept the cottage immaculate and ready for immediate occupancy; the double bed was made, the quilt neatly turned down, the sheets spotless. His country clothes hung in the wardrobe, his shirts pressed. He wondered what Meg would make of a place like this, and had a tremendous urge to find out. Perhaps when they got back from this expedition?

He had to be in love; he had never had the slightest desire to bring any woman down here before. He knew her natural freshness would blend perfectly into these surroundings.

He had a bath, changed into flannels and a sports jacket, and went across to the pub. It was already well filled with men and women, all of whom wanted a word and a handshake. "Sorry I haven't been down for the past few weeks," Peter said. "I've been up to my ears."

"But you'll be down for the summer?" suggested Farmer Poldarren. Big and bluff, he was reputed to be the wealthiest man in the neighbourhood, but remained totally bucolic.

"I shall indeed, as soon as I get back to England."

"You're not going to New Zealand, I hope?" inquired Mavis Tregarthen. Red-headed and plump, she was the village belle, and if the locals knew her too well to hold out much promise of marriage, she saw no reason not to dream of one day perhaps being an MP's wife.

"If I do, I'll be careful," Peter agreed. "But I'm studying the general situation down there."

"The Red Death," remarked old Mr Perry. "Whatever will they dream up next?"

Peter drank two of the offered pints and then was ushered into the back room by Clive Wardle, where other members of the local constituency party were already gathered, several having driven over from Ridding. Peter shook hands, exchanged a brief gossip, and then outlined the situation, omitting all details and of course any reference to his task force, but informing them, as he had to, that he was taking a couple of weeks off to accompany an American scientific expedition which was hoping to find the cause of the disease, and an antidote.

"It's that serious, is it?" Clive asked, stroking his military moustache.

"It could become so. And naturally the Government wishes to take all possible precautions before the situation gets out of hand."

"Let's hope someone tells old Brereton that," Mr Roberts, the newsagent, growled.

"I think the Prime Minister probably will," Peter promised, "in tomorrow's Question Time."

The meeting over, he had a quiet drink with Stephanie. She was fifty, he supposed, and had spent much of her life following Clive from station to station. Her complexion had that sallow tinge which could be dormant malaria or just a faded sun tan, but she remained a handsome woman. Her eyes held endless fascination; they were deepest blue, and seemed to stretch back for ever into her mind.

"It's so strange," she said. "Here we are, sitting in complete safety, and twelve thousand miles away people are dying. I suppose it was like that here when the Blitz was on in London."

"I'll bet you don't remember the Blitz," Peter joked.

"Because your parents were hardly born yet?" She smiled. "I've heard that one before. No, I don't remember the Blitz, but my parents certainly did. They told me about it. Peter, I'm worried about Fran, working in Japan."

"There's no sign of the disease in Asia, Stephanie. And I can't believe the Japanese Government isn't going to take every possible step to make sure it doesn't get to them. Like us, they're islands. They can keep people out if they need to."

"She's all we have, Peter. Do you think I should write and tell her to come home?"

Peter hesitated. It would be disastrous if everyone upped and ran, even schoolmistresses at the English College in Tokyo. But . . . hadn't he told Sarah to do just that?

He squeezed Stephanie's hand.

"Fran's going to be all right," he assured her. "We are going to lick this thing, and quickly." He was tempted to ask her to pray for that, but decided against it; if Stephanie Wardle prayed to any god at all, it would be some relict of a pre-Christian era.

221

12

Ocean Secrets

The flight to Peru had to be done in two stages: Heathrow to Inglewood, Inglewood to Jorge Chavez, and it was four in the afternoon, twenty-four hours after leaving London, when Peter finally landed in Peru. He hoped, as he had to wait in Los Angeles two hours for his connection, that it might be possible to link up with Meg and do the last leg in her company, but she had left the previous day.

As the jet dropped out of the skies, the Andes rising stark to its left, the Pacific Ocean sparkling to its right, Peter was conscious of a building excitement. Partly he knew it was an almost juvenile feeling of having been let off school to go adventuring, and, equally partly, it was euphoria at being able to spend a fortnight in the company of Meg. But it was also a sense of destiny, an awareness that this expedition could be the dramatic saving of the population of the world. It seemed incredible, in this age of interplanetary exploration, of scientific marvels being turned up every day, that he should be thinking in such terms. But it could very well be true. And there was no time to be lost, because if too many irresponsible people started thinking like that there could be catastrophic panic.

Jorge Chavez International Airport lay some four miles outside and below Lima proper, and only a couple of miles from the sea and the harbour of Callao. Though

Peter was flying unofficially, he did get a certain amount of diplomatic treatment; in fact his opposite number was there to meet him, together with a secretary from the Embassy. "Enrique Vita, Mr Canning." The Peruvian Health Minister shook hands and escorted Peter to the VIP Lounge. "You are joining the *Ocean Secrets*, is that correct?"

Peter nodded.

"To see if you can find the cause of this epidemic?"

Peter frowned at Collins, the embassy man. "That was supposed to be hush-hush."

Vita smiled. "It is, hush-hush. But the Koch Research Center considered it polite to inform my Government. It will be kept a secret, I promise you. But I am interested to know what an English minister is doing, taking part in such an expedition."

"I happen to have been associated with Dr Calhoun on a previous project," Peter explained; that was no lie, having in mind that unforgettable night in San Francisco. "So she invited me along . . . " which was stretching the truth a little. "My Government is naturally very concerned at the spread of this disease."

"Great Britain is a long way away," Vita observed, sombrely. "We have it on our doorstep. We have closed our borders with Chile, and there have been several unpleasant scenes, including armed clashes between Peruvian troops and Chilean soldiers trying to cross the border. This is confidential, you understand."

"Yes," Peter said. "I had no idea the Red Death had come this far north already."

"It hasn't, but it is not far away. It spreads, like rabies. The Chileans are releasing very little information . . . well, they have none to release as the country is virtually in a state of anarchy. But we know there are very few survivors where it strikes. It is the intention of my Government to raise the matter in the United Nations next month. We wish world action to be taken. The support of Great Britain in such a proposal would be valuable."

"The exact actions you propose would have to be studied, of course," Peter said cautiously. "But I may say in general that Great Britain will support any action to contain the spread of the disease that does not interfere with the sovereignty of any country."

Vita looked disappointed, and Peter wondered if he had been thinking of using the crisis to invoke some kind of invasion of Chile; Peru and Chile had a rivalry over various border regions going back a century. "Drastic action on a world scale may well be required," Vita said, somewhat stiffly. "I will tell my colleagues that Great Britain is prepared to study our proposals. And I will wish you good fortune with your expedition and your American friends."

"Thank you." Peter shook hands and Collins drove him down to the docks.

"These people really are most agitated," the secretary confided.

"With good reason. But we can't give them blanket support for some kind of takeover of Chile."

"Good Lord, no," Collins agreed. "Think of the Monroe Doctrine."

"Yes," Peter said drily.

Ocean Secrets was apparently waiting only for him; her engines were already rumbling, and no sooner was he on board than orders were given to cast off, leaving Collins waving somewhat forlornly from the dock in the midst of a gaggle of Peruvian policemen.

"The fact is, Canning, we don't want the general public to know what we're about," Jim Dawson told him. "I've only just been told myself. Even the crew don't know as yet; I'll tell them when we're out at sea. The Southern Ocean is a rather provocative term right now."

"But you're happy to go along with Meg?"

"Sure thing. I have a great respect for her. She's done some fantastic work for us in the past. Gray Fitzroy and I are old buddies, too," Dawson told him. "We've been rather out of touch with world affairs this last month, diving off the Galapagos. If Gray and Meg say this is a matter of life and death for a lot of people, that suits me."

"But you're not sure of your crew?" Peter suggested. "I think they should have been told before we left Callao."

"Meg wanted our destination kept a secret. All fishing in Chilean or Argentinian territorial waters has been banned, so we will technically be breaking the law, and to start a discussion alongside in Callao would be to let the world know what we're at. My boys will follow where I lead; they're hand-picked."

Peter nodded. He had never met the famous ocean-ographer before, but he was impressed; the Californian was a massive man, six feet four inches tall, with shoulders to match, enhanced by the heavy seaman's sweater he was wearing, and by a full red-grey beard. Peter could well believe that the wet suits and other equipment he wore on his dives had to be specially made.

"This is some ship you have here," he remarked.

Dawson grinned. "She's built to do a job. Let's hope she does this one. You know it's gonna be chilly?"

"I worked that out for myself!"

It was indeed already chilly when he left the heated confines of the bridge deck. But Meg was waiting for him. "I thought you weren't going to make it," she said.

"The Peruvian Government wanted to get into the act. Don't tell me you wouldn't have waited if I'd been delayed?"

"Um," she said, enigmatically.

They stood in the shelter of the bridge wing, watching the harbour fade into the winter afternoon's dusk, and were for the moment private. He put his arms round her and held her close, exchanging warmth even through their heavy reefer jackets, and she turned her face up for his kiss.

"You do realise we are here to work," she reminded him.

"I do. But you can't work until you have something to work with."

"Um," she said again. "I'd better show you the ship."

Ocean Secrets was, as Peter had said appreciatively to Dawson, some ship. Two hundred feet long and built of steel, her external appearance was that of any normal ocean-going trawler, with overhanging bridge windows, high bow, and recessed stern. It was in her equipment that she was unique. There was a fish hold aft, but divided into several tanks, which could be individually flooded or refrigerated as required. Forward was mounted the massive machinery, the drums and engines, for lowering equipment, and men, to the ocean floor; beneath the foredeck was a large laboratory and work-room, fitted with every instrument science could invent which might have relevance to the sea or the sand, including the electron microscopes Meg needed to find the virus. The entire crew of twelve was housed amidships, over the engine-room. Here there were six double cabins and four singles, every one as comfortable as in the most luxurious yacht, with its own bathroom; the singles were occupied by Dawson himself, his mate, Harry Grosvenor, Meg, and Peter; Charlie Oswiecki, who had also just joined the ship, had a double to himself, which Peter thought was a cack-handed arrangement, but apparently it had been Meg's decision. Although he did not doubt it could be reversed.

Also on this deck were the galley and saloon. Beneath them in the engine-room, a pair of British Polar M48M eight-cylinder diesels rumbled slowly and reassuringly at 300 revolutions per minute, delivering 3,000 brake horse-power and driving them through the sea at a steady 20 knots; in support was a General Motors 4/71. To each side, built into the hull, huge fuel tanks containing 135 tons of diesel gave *Ocean Secrets* a range of 10,000 nautical miles, and she carried food and water for a month.

"Impressed?" Meg asked.

"You bet. What's the programme?"

"Jim is going to work out our most hopeful fishing ground, relative to where Charlie dumped that gash, and then we're going to trawl."

"How can you tell which fish is diseased?"

"By taking blood samples."

"Good God! That sounds an immense task!"

"It is," Meg agreed. "You asked to come along, remember?"

Charlie Oswiecki seemed pleased to see him again; they had actually flown back from San Francisco to New York together in June, and Charlie had himself shown Peter the megatherium as well as introducing him to Amanda Fitzroy and a very worried Tom Lintell – who seemed to feel that the outbreak of the disease was entirely his fault. "You should've brought a friend," Charlie suggested.

"To share your cabin?"

"And other things," Charlie said, grinning. "We may need all the help we can get." He was worried about the reaction of the crew to being told what they were after. Especially as he had dropped the gash in the first place. Peter could guess how unhappy Charlie was about that, for all his attempted humour, but he could not believe there would be a reaction at all; as Dawson had said, his men were all hand-picked, highly trained, as much scientists as sailors. They would have taken risks before.

On the other hand, Dawson seemed to be in no hurry to inform them of the purpose of the expedition. By dawn next morning *Ocean Secrets* was hurrying due south, some 250 miles south of Callao, with the coast of Peru disappearing from sight as it bent to the east. The skies were grey and the sea lumpy, but there was not a great deal of wind, and the crew were becoming curious.

Peter spent the night in Meg's cabin, but she was too preoccupied to be responsive; a stack of reference books lay on the rug by her bunk and her mind was already lost in the fish she hoped to catch. He returned to his own bunk in time to be served fruit juice and coffee by the steward, Benetti. "Is it true you're a politician, Mr Canning?" he asked.

"In a manner of speaking," Peter agreed.

Benetti shook his head. "This is the damnedest trip I've been on."

"How long have you been with Captain Dawson?"

"Three years. It's all been pretty good. Organised. When we went to the Galapagos to study those tortoises and the underwater volcanoes, it was to be for four months. So what happens? After only a couple of weeks we suddenly go chasing off to Callao. To pick you guys up. And not a word why. Now the skipper says we're making for Juan Fernandez. Say, isn't that where that guy Robinson Crusoe spent his time?"

"That's the place," Peter agreed.

"So what are we looking for this time? Man Friday?"

"You'll have to ask the captain," Peter told him. "I'm just along for the ride." He hurried off to make his agreed call to London. But there was nothing to report, as yet, and London had nothing for him, either.

Ocean Secrets having passed close to San Felix during the second night, Juan Fernandez came up on radar just on dusk the next afternoon. The weather remained lowering but the wind stayed light, and the voyage had so far been extremely pleasant, as long as one remained within the heated superstructure. Meg and Charlie spent much of each day in the laboratory forward, preparing their equipment; Peter preferred to stay on the bridge and watch the marvellous array of instruments ticking away, pinpointing their position every second of the day.

Life on board the research vessel was remarkably civilised, with Benetti and Olsen, the cook, preparing three splendid meals a day, a good library of modern novels as well as a mass of reference books to browse through, and videos to watch after dinner each night. The crew lived very much as a happy family, with no evidence of rank – although Dawson was very obviously the boss. As several were qualified scientists as well as experienced seamen, table talk was always worth listening to.

They had been called from San Felix and asked for name and destination, and Jim had replied Juan Fernandez, asking at the same time if the island was safe. The reply had been affirmative, but the San Felix operator had warned them not to proceed further south. Now Martinsen, the watchkeeper – *Ocean Secrets* was on autopilot – looked expectantly at his captain. "You aiming to go in tonight, Skipper?"

"No," Dawson said. "We'll stand on."

"What speed?"

"Maintain our 20 knots."

The watchkeeper frowned in perplexity, but said nothing, merely gazed into the radar screen as Juan Fernandez drew abeam, some twenty miles distant, and then began to recede astern.

By now the radio was chattering in Spanish. "They want us to identify ourselves, Skipper," said Logan, the telegrapher. "They also want us to turn back."

"We're outside Chilean territorial waters," Dawson reminded him. "Make no reply."

Logan scratched his head, and obeyed.

By now it was utterly dark beyond the bridge windows, and Meg and Charlie emerged from the bowels of the ship. "Who's that guy shouting at?" Charlie wanted to know as the radio continued to chatter.

"Us, mainly," Dawson said.

Meg looked into the radar screen. "Juan Fernandez?"

"Yep. We are 1,600 miles from Cape Horn. You can start fishing in three days' time."

"We going to Cape Horn, Skipper?" asked Martinsen, still watching the radar.

"That's right."

"Ain't that prohibited?"

"That's what's exciting those characters. They must be guessing where we're heading. Harry, you'd better call the crew up for a chat."

They assembled on the bridge in a semi-circle, arms folded across their heavy jerseys, frowning at Dawson. Peter, Charlie and Meg stood behind the captain.

"I guess you guys are curious as to where we are hurrying off to," Dawson said. "Well, the time has come to tell you. This vessel is presently under charter to the Robert Koch Research Center of San Francisco. Now, you've all heard of the mystery disease that's currently sweeping Chile, Argentina and New Zealand, the Red Death. The object of this expedition is to discover the source of the infection and, if possible, a cure for it. According to Dr Calhoun here, the source is fish. She needs live ones for her experiments. So we are going to trawl, and see what we can find."

"This is a pretty lethal disease, isn't it?" asked the boatswain, McClintock.

Dawson looked at Meg.

"It is," she said. "The most lethal disease the world has known since the bubonic plague."

"And we're actually going looking for it?"

"There will be no risk of any of us catching it," Meg said. "It is carried in the blood of the fish, as far as we can make out. We are not going to eat any of our catch. We're not even going to dissect any of them. We are going to take blood samples and the operation will be carried out under maximum precautions."

"Accidents do happen," McClintock suggested.

"Not to me, they don't," Meg snapped.

"And that's a fact," Dawson agreed. "Let's have a show of support for the little lady."

"We're with you, Skipper," Grosvenor said, and gazed at the crew. "Right?"

"Right," they said unanimously. McClintock included, Peter noted with some relief.

"You know I was scared this evening?" Meg confessed as she lay in Peter's arms that night. She was more relaxed now than she had been since the voyage began, and he suspected she had been apprehensive since then, as well, about the crew's reaction.

The bunk was comfortably wide enough for one person but narrow, to say the least, for two . . . unless they were definitely in love. Meg's shoulder was pressed against the bulkhead, while the leeboard dug into Peter's hip. The heating was adequate, but not high enough to allow them to sleep without the thick flannel pyjamas Jim insisted on handing out: which in a way added to the fun.

"I suppose this sort of thing is okay for a novelty," Peter whispered as he wrestled, one-handed, with the buttons of Meg's jacket, "but I'm glad we don't live in a climate where it's a permanent feature."

"Here, let me," she got both hands to the task, "but for heaven's sake don't let the comforter slip down. I didn't come on this expedition to catch pneumonia. Mmm, that's better," she mumbled under his chin as his hand at last slid over her flesh.

"Now, aren't you glad I came along, too?" He nuzzled into her hair, enjoying the familiar scent of her shampoo, while his fingers caressed her breasts, each in turn. He loved the hard feel of her shoulder muscles, the firm, athletic flatness of her stomach, and the silky curls at her vee.

Meg wriggled, trying for the opening in his pants, then gave up. "No room for dual action in these bunks," she hissed, "I think I'll have to put in a complaint to the skipper."

"Later," Peter agreed, raising himself on elbow and knee to allow her to slide underneath his body. "I don't think he had much thought of foreplay when designing his ship. He's purely a man of direct action." Meg sighed happily as he knelt between her thighs, lifting to receive him. "You picked a good skipper," he added. "He's quite a character."

"He is one hell of a guy," Meg said enthusiastically.

Peter felt no pang of jealousy; she was simply showing appreciation of the man's outstanding abilities and as far as their own relationship was concerned she was being very sweet and attentive at the moment.

Surprisingly to both of them, despite the unfavourable conditions, Meg went into a delicious, moaning, extended orgasm that night. Peter gazed down into the strong, determined face, watched the long, dark lashes sweep her cheeks as her lids drooped in ecstasy and her body became rigid under him. He let himself go, filling her, sliding deep into her again and again until he felt her slacken and he could relax, panting, his body and limbs spread over her softness. For the first time that he could remember, he had no desire to move away, to break off the entanglement: he only wanted to lie embraced in this contentment for ever.

By morning Juan Fernandez had disappeared off the radar, and the weather was beginning to deteriorate; the wind had freshened, from the south, and whitecaps were forming, with an occasional rattle of spray across the bridge windows. Dawson gave Meg and Oswiecki seasick pills.

"Can we trawl if it's like this?" Charlie asked.

"This is just a bobble," Dawson told him. "This ship will trawl if there's a full gale blowing. If it gets up to storm force, now, well, we'll have to sit it out. But storms never last very long."

"And the ship can take those as well, I suppose," Charlie said unhappily.

"You got it," Dawson agreed. But he was pleased to discover that the Englishman was unaffected by the lurches and plunges of the ship. "You've done this sort of thing before," he remarked.

"On a much smaller scale," Peter replied, allowing his knees to bend in turn with the movement under his feet. Yacht racing had been far more lumpy than this, in fact. The radio was still sputtering. "Those Chileans still asking questions?"

Dawson watched Meg and Oswiecki descending the internal ladder, waited to be sure they were out of earshot. "That's a warship," he said. "Well, a garda costa, anyway."

"Looking for us?"

"That's right," Logan, the wireless operator, said. "She's positioned south-east of us."

"Does she know where we are?"

"Not precisely. She's out of radar range, well out, I would say. But she keeps warning the 'unknown fishing vessel' not to proceed."

"Do you think she'll be able to find us?"

"That depends on how efficient she is," Dawson told him. "If we have to put on speed, I have no doubt we're one hell of a lot faster than any warship. There is power down there." He tapped his boot on the deck. "But in fact she has no right to stop us until and unless we enter Chilean territorial waters. Right now we're 300 miles west of Isla de Chiloé; these are the high seas. On the other hand, from all we hear, these guys have become pretty high strung over the past month, so it would be better if the captain never finds us at all. Reckon you could skip your usual call to London today until we're past him, Peter?"

"Surely. They won't miss me for twenty-four hours."

The weather continued to deteriorate, and soon *Ocean Secrets* was plunging through heavy seas which broke over the bows and raced along the decks. Meg and Oswiecki definitely abandoned the struggle and retired to their bunks. Peter remained on the bridge with Dawson, listening to the constant chatter of the radio, watching the radar for any sign of the Chilean warship.

"He's moving parallel with us, keeping to the edge of their territorial claim," Dawson said. "He's gonna wait there. We'll have to see if we can wriggle past him."

By that night they were within 300 miles of the Straits of Magellan, and now definitely closing the Chilean coast. "We'll cross their sea boundary about four tomorrow morning," Grosvenor said, leaning over the chart.

"Then I'll turn in now," Dawson decided. "Wake me at three."

"What are you planning to do if he does find us and commands us to heave to?" Peter asked.

"Run for it. In these seas he won't be able to do too much about it."

Peter nodded and went down to Meg's cabin. She had dined off salt biscuits and water, and was lying curled on her bunk. "God," she said. "I thought I was doing so well."

"You'll get used to this in a day or so," Peter promised her, but decided to use his own bunk for a change. He lay in the darkness, listening to the crashing of the waves against the hull, feeling the ship drop away into the troughs and then rise again, buoyantly, to the following crests, reassured always by the growl of the diesels beneath him. He wondered what the morrow would bring, and thought it just as well he was out of radio contact with London; he did not care to think what the Prime Minister's reaction might be to discovering that one of the British Government's MPs was about to indulge in a confrontation with the Chilean navy.

He slept heavily, awoke at a quarter to four, and went up on to the bridge. Dawson was there, together with Grosvenor, watching the radar. The seas had eased a little but the night was utterly dark, with not a star to be seen.

"There," Grosvenor said, and Peter saw the white blip, on the very edge of the radar screen.

"He knows where we're heading all right," Dawson said. "But sixty miles is a lot of sea. See if you can lose him by zig-zagging. Try changes of speed as well."

"Hard right rudder," Grosvenor told the helmsman. *Ocean Secrets* turned to the west, and the blip disappeared. Immediately Grosvenor opened the throttles to increase speed.

"Steer two one zero for an hour," Dawson said. "Then come back to one seven five, and we'll take another look."

Peter went back to bed, but was up again at dawn. Dawson and Grosvenor had remained on the bridge. "He's still there," Grosvenor said. "Every time we come back to close the Horn he pops up."

"And the weather is getting better," Dawson said in disgust. "Would you believe it, in the Southern Ocean, in the dead of winter? We should be having at least a gale."

Peter peered through the spray-splattered windows at the grey sea. There was still the occasional whitecap, indicating a wind strength of about 15 knots; it had been a lot more than that yesterday. But the skies remained as grey as the sea; the wind could freshen again at any moment.

"He's closed to fifty miles on this leg, Skipper," Grosvenor said. "Do we do another zig-zag?"

"Oh, fuck him," Dawson said with sudden decision. "We are on a mission for the good of mankind. He'll have to accept that. What's the course for the Horn?"

"One five eight."

"Then steer it."

Grosvenor studied the radar. "That'll take us within five miles of him, if he stays put."

"That's the idea."

Peter went down to see how Meg was getting on, found her sitting up and having breakfast. "Boy, do I feel better," she told him.

"You look better, too." He kissed her.

"What's happening up top?" she wanted to know. "We're due to start fishing tomorrow, aren't we?"

Peter nodded. "But first we have to talk our way past the Chilean coastguard."

"Oh, Lord! He still there?"

"That's right. As we're making 20 knots, and he's holding his position rather than approaching us, I'd say the crunch will come about ten o'clock."

"I'll be there," she said. "But first I just have to have a bath."

Almost the entire crew collected on the bridge at half past nine. The warship was now only ten miles away, although she was invisible in the murk.

"He's talking to us, Skipper," Logan said.

"Reply," Dawson said. "Tell him we will speak English. I'd better handle this myself."

Logan spoke in halting Spanish, and there was a brief pause.

"Eight miles," Grosvenor said.

Peter and Meg stared through the windows to the east and south, but still could see nothing save heaving waves.

"This is the captain of the corvette *Huascar*," the radio said. "Identify yourself."

Dawson took Logan's place before the set. "This is the Research Vessel *Ocean Secrets*, United States flag," he said.

"I must inform you, *Ocean Secrets*, that you are entering a prohibited zone. I request you reverse your course, immediately."

"It is our intention to round Cape Horn," Dawson said.

"On passage?"

"We are a research vessel," Dawson said again. "It is our intention to obtain samples which may be of use in determining the cause of the Red Death. We have no intention of either selling or eating any of the fish we catch, and any waste will be properly disposed of."

"You intend to trawl," the Chilean captain said. "That is forbidden. Reverse your course."

"We are engaged upon a mission which may be of the greatest importance to mankind," Dawson told him. "To your country more than any other. I would request you to think again."

"I have my orders, Captain Dawson. It is to permit no fishing whatsoever in the area around Cape Horn."

Dawson grinned at the anxious faces watching him. "At least he knows who we are, if he knows who our skipper is." He thumbed the handset. "I intend to carry out my mission, Captain."

"And I must carry out my orders, Captain Dawson. Stop your vessel and prepare to receive a boarding party."

"Are you placing my ship under arrest?"

"Yes, until you can be escorted out of Chilean territorial waters."

"I suggest you contact Santiago and explain the situation," Dawson said. He turned to Grosvenor. "Increase speed."

"If you do not stop your vessel, I will fire into you," the Chilean captain said.

"I would think very seriously before doing that, Captain," Dawson said, speaking quietly. "This is a United States registered vessel engaged upon a mission of international importance, and I have given you my personal assurance that what we are doing can in no way assist the spread of the disease. I am now informing you officially that I intend to proceed. I am also going to call San Diego and inform them of the situation here. I have no doubt at all that the Government of the United States would regard any hostile act undertaken by you in these circumstances with extreme disfavour. Good day to you, Captain."

He got up. "Continue to zig-zag, short and sharp, for a while. But maintain an overall course south by east. Logan, call San Diego and tell them exactly what is happening and what we are doing. You want to raise London, Peter?"

"I think it would be best to leave London out of this for a while," Peter said.

Dawson nodded. "Point taken."

Meg squeezed his hand. "Sorry you came?"

"I wouldn't be anywhere else," he told her.

"I can't believe that character can be crazy enough actually to fire on us," she said.

"His problem is that he has no one to refer to, in Santiago," Peter reminded her. "If it's true that all civil authority has broken down in Chile. He's operating on the last orders given him."

"Dumb bunny," Meg commented.

"We have visual," said Schmitt, one of the seismologists, who was also the reserve radio operator.

Heads turned, and binoculars were levelled. The Chilean corvette loomed through the mist, five miles away.

"What kind of gun is that?" Oswiecki inquired.

"Something like a three-inch," Grosvenor replied.

238

"You got San Diego yet?" Dawson asked Logan.

"Not yet, Skipper. There's a lot of traffic."

"Shit!" Grosvenor said.

Meg clutched Peter's arm, as they all saw the flash of red cutting into the gloom.

"The goddamned fool," Dawson snapped. "Okay, Harry, full speed ahead. For Christ's sake, try to get through, Logan."

The noise of the explosion rumbled faintly through the morning, but the shot had been aimed well forward of the research vessel, and plunged into the sea about half a mile away.

"I've never been shot at before," Meg confessed.

"Guess what, we're in the same boat," Peter quipped.

"You reckon a ship like that will carry missiles?" Oswiecki asked, anxiously.

Dawson shook his head. "Not a coastguard. We'll shake her. Look there."

They peered into the radar; some fifteen miles to the south-west the screen was covered in white.

"That's heavy rain, or snow," Grosvenor explained. "His gun may be radar controlled, but he's still going to find it difficult to shoot accurately in those conditions, especially if it's got any sea with it. And we're definitely faster. We'll drop him for sure."

Ocean Secrets was now speeding away from the coast-guard vessel, making some 25 knots, and altering course every five minutes, slewing from left to right, sending huge spumes of water away from her bows. Already the corvette had disappeared into the mist, and she was now seven miles away on radar.

"That gun won't carry more than ten miles," Grosvenor said triumphantly.

"And there's what we're looking for," Dawson said.

Ahead of them, visually, the grey had changed into solid black, beneath which they could see the seething whitecaps.

"Heavy stuff," Dawson said with quiet satisfaction.

"The guy says if we don't stop now he'll sink us," Logan remarked from the radio set. "He's gotta be nuts."

"Keep her moving," Dawson said. "In ten minutes we'll be safe."

Peter peered astern into the gloom, saw nothing.

"Oh, my God," Meg commented.

He turned his head, and watched the plume of water, not two hundred yards away. The ship trembled, but did not lose speed.

"Those guys mean business," Oswiecki shouted.

"I have San Diego," Logan said.

"Keep zig-zagging," Dawson commanded, and sat before the mike.

"Here we go," Grosvenor remarked, as he directed *Ocean Secrets* into the storm. Almost instantly the trawler was shrouded in snowflakes, clouding to either side, bringing visibility down to a hundred yards, while the wind howled and the seas became wild. "A mini-blizzard," he shouted triumphantly.

The squall was also affecting the radio, judging by Dawson's attempts to carry on a conversation. But peering into the radar, Peter could still see the blip of the *Huascar*, on the eastern side of the bad weather – and no doubt *Huascar* could still see them, even in the clutter, he thought. But she was nine miles away, and receding . . .

Not fast enough. Even as he raised his head there was a blinding flash, and then oblivion.

For a moment. Peter found himself on his hands and knees, inhaling acrid smoke, smothered in flying snow-flakes, very cold. While the wind howled and the seas rattled against the hull. He forced himself upwards, shouting "Meg! Meg, where are you?"

"Peter!" she screamed.

He peered through a mist of smoke and twisted metal and saw her, reached for her. "Are you all right?"

"I think so." There was a cut on her left hand and she felt bruised down one side, but she felt sure nothing was broken. "What happened?"

"I would say we suffered a direct hit. Stay put."

The smoke was clearing as *Ocean Secrets* raced into the storm, her auto-pilot still engaged. But in its place came the weather, to which they were exposed because the rear of the bridge roof had been torn away by the explosion. Peter crawled across the deck and stared at Logan, who had been standing by the radio sets; he was a mess of blood and bone, clearly dead.

"Dawson!" he shouted. "Jim, are you there?"

"Jesus Christ!" It was Grosvenor, sitting up, next to the helm; the wheel itself had been shattered by a flying splinter and the mate had had a miraculous escape. "That bastard . . ."

"Where's the skipper?" Peter asked.

"Jim? Jim?" Grosvenor shouted. "Where are you?"

"Goddamn," Oswiecki grumbled, scrambling to his feet, blood pouring down his face from a cut on his scalp. "I didn't know those guys could shoot like that."

"Radar assisted," Grosvenor told him. "Jim . . ."

Peter staggered towards the radio sets. The shell had actually burst immediately above it. Here was where the roof was peeled back. Beneath it, the main radios were a blackened mess of twisted metal, across which Jim Dawson lay, blood streaming from his shattered skull.

Ocean Secrets plunged into the squall, shrouded now in falling snow and flying spray, her engines rumbling away as securely as ever, the autopilot still holding her on course. But on the bridge the four survivors of the shell burst stared at each other, unable to believe what had happened, while they shivered in the cold let in by the shattered roof and glass. That Grosvenor and

Oswiecki were bleeding from flying splinters hardly seemed relevant at the moment.

Feet stamped on the ladder and the rest of the crew arrived.

"Holy shit!" Benetti screamed, staring at the wreckage and the blood.

"The skipper!" Jonssen yelled.

McClintock knelt beside him. "God Almighty!" he muttered. "He's dead."

De Sousa made the sign of the cross.

"Meg," Peter whispered, kneeling beside her. "Are you sure you're all right?"

"Sure I'm sure," she said. "But Peter . . . "

The freezing air was redolent of crisis, and surrender. Heads were bowed, as well as shoulders.

"Those bastards," Benetti said.

"That's it," Grosvenor decided. "As we can't communicate, we'd better heave to and wait for them to come up."

Peter looked at Meg.

"What are they saying?" she asked, horrified.

"They want to surrender. Do you?"

"Hell, no! What, after all this?" She gazed around at the carnage. "What a stupid waste that would be."

Grosvenor shrugged. He was on his feet, clinging to the shattered helm. "What else can we do? Those fellows mean business. The skipper is dead . . . " He looked ready to weep.

Peter looked at Meg again as she retorted, "You have to be crazy. Don't you understand we are all at risk if we don't go on? Not just us, in this ship, but the whole human race. Your wives and children. Everyone." And seeing the disbelief in his face she went on. "So you think I'm putting it on: trying to kid you just to get my own way? Okay, don't believe me, but tell me, do you want to take the risk that I might be right?"

Peter was warmed by her courage. "The ship is still perfectly seaworthy," he reminded them. "No damage has been done apart from our communications. She's on course and steering. If we surrender, our expedition is done, our chances of finding an antidote are done . . . "

"But Jimmy . . . " Grosvenor looked dazed, bewildered.

"Jimmy Dawson is dead," Peter told him. "But he died trying to help save millions of lives. You thinking of letting him down?"

Grosvenor gazed at him. "No," he said. "I would hate to do that. But I can't risk losing the ship." The noise of the engines was dying as he reduced speed; the controls were still working, even if the radar had gone as dead as the radios. *Ocean Secrets* commenced to roll heavily in the big seas.

Peter stood up, holding on to the grab rail. "Just what are you doing?" he asked.

The others stared at him. "If we don't stop, we're gonna be blown out of the water," McClintock explained, as though talking to an idiot.

Peter lunged forward, grabbed Grosvenor by the shoulder, and threw him aside, so violently that he staggered across the bridge and into the bulkhead. Immediately Peter thrust the throttles forward again, and a reassuring surge of power rose from beneath them.

"What the hell . . . " McClintock ran forward, and Peter turned from the helm. The boatswain was a big man, but he was no match for the angry MP. Peter put up his left arm to block McClintock's blow, and swung his own right, a short but powerful jab which struck the sailor in the stomach and had him bent double and gasping.

"You're gonna kill us all," Martinsen wailed.

"How long ago were we hit?" Peter demanded.

"For Christ's sake . . . " but he looked at Grosvenor, uncertainly. At least five minutes had passed since the shell had struck; now the only sounds were the roaring of the waves and the screaming of the wind. And the gasping of McClintock, who had sunk to his knees. Harry Grosvenor had now regained his breath, but he remained hanging on to the grab rail in preference to trying to regain control. They were all too shocked to resist Peter's violence on top of the shell burst.

But they could still protest.

"The skipper is dead," Martinsen insisted. "We gotta surrender."

But Peter knew that his aggression and decisiveness had begun to sway them; he could complete the job with the right approach. "We've lost the warship," he pointed out. "Just as the skipper said we would. You going to let him die for that, and now surrender?"

"We can't go on, without the skipper," Jonssen argued. "We can't."

"We have a job to do," Peter shouted at them. "We risked our lives, we are risking our lives, to do that. Jim Dawson died for that. If you surrender now, you're making his death a mockery."

They looked at each other again.

"And if you surrender, what's going to happen?" Peter demanded. "She's a Chilean vessel. You'll be taken into a Chilean port. Where everyone is dying of the Red Death."

That gave them something else to think about, and Peter pressed home his advantage. "Harry! You can navigate this ship, even without instruments. Goddamn, if you can't, I can." He looked down at Meg. "You chartered this vessel, Dr Calhoun. Do you want to continue the voyage?"

She stared at him, eyes glowing, appreciating his determination. "You bet your damned life I do," she said. "Oh, yes."

Peter glared at them. "You heard the lady," he said. "Let's get to it."

244

13

Trawling the Southern Ocean

The crew were still hesitant, unsure of themselves. Peter knew he had to take command, get them working before they could start thinking again.

"First thing," he said. "McClintock, De Sousa and Martinsen, get the skipper and Logan down on to the well deck, and sew them into flags. Brown, I want you in the engine-room checking everything out down there. Benetti, down to the galley and help Olsen get some food going. Harry, we have to restore full controls up here. Schmitt, is there anything you can do about our communications? Even VHF will be better than nothing. Brent, you and Espinola and Harrison start repairing that roof, else we're all going to freeze."

They looked at Grosvenor, who hesitated and then nodded. They hurried about their tasks.

"What do you want me to do?" Oswiecki asked.

"And me?" Meg added.

"First thing, you can patch up Charlie's cuts. Then get some warm clothing on."

They followed the others.

It was indeed close to freezing on the bridge, with snow drifting in through the hole in the roof and settling on everything. Peter and Harry helped McClintock and Martinsen and De Sousa carry the dead bodies down the ladder, then they returned to the upper deck.

"That was quite a tour de force," Grosvenor commented. "You ever skippered a ship before?"

"A racing yacht."

"That figures. I'll bet you won your race. Sorry I panicked. But to think of Jim, cut down by some trigger-happy lunatic . . ."

"All the more reason to finish his job for him," Peter said, and hurried on; he wanted to get the mate's mind off his misery. "Let's look at this steering."

Repairing the steering was easy; the wheel had been shattered but the controls behind were intact, and the gyrocompass for the autopilot was undamaged; for full control it was simply a matter of finding a single spoke and securing it to the spindle – it would, in any event, only need to be used for sudden alterations of course. Brown reported from the engine-room that all was okay down there, and Peter increased speed again, but only to cruising level; they had definitely shaken off the corvette, and the seas were getting bigger. Without radar they had no idea what was ahead of them, and with their weatherfax also out of action they could obtain no weather synopses; even the aerial for the Navigator had been shot away, and Peter and Grosvenor had to plot their position by Dead Reckoning from the last certain fix. The idea of trawling in the Drake Passage close to Cape Horn, with its treacherous currents and outlying rocks, not to mention its weather, equipped only with a compass and a sextant, was daunting; with the skies so continually overcast even the sextant was not going to be of much use.

"What's the prospect of putting any of this stuff back together?" Peter asked Schmitt, who had at last completed his preliminary inspection of the damage.

"Not too good. The HF and MF sets are definitely out. I can repair the VHF, but that's not going to do us all that much good down here, unless that corvette gets back within talking distance; it only has a range of about fifty miles."

"What about the radar?"

He shook his head. "That's beyond repair."

"The Navigator?"

"As far as I can see, that's undamaged. All we need is an aerial. As soon as this weather improves, I'll see about rigging a jury mast and a new aerial. Unfortunately, I'm not talking about just a length of wire, Mr Canning; it's a highly sensitive piece of equipment. I'm going to have to build it from the spares I have in the workshop."

"Then you'd better get started," Peter told him. "We can't afford to wait for the weather to improve: I don't think it's going to improve."

Peter and Harry Grosvenor conducted the service for Jim Dawson and Mike Logan. Every member of the crew was there, and speed was reduced as the prayers were read, while the ship heaved beneath them and the snow clouded down. The two bodies were weighted and consigned to the deep, and then Peter returned to the bridge and pushed the throttles back to cruising speed.

Meg joined him. "You have been just marvellous," she said. "I reckon without you the whole thing would have collapsed."

"I took my lead from Dawson," he told her. "Now, you ready to start trawling at dawn tomorrow?"

"I'm ready," she said.

By dawn the bridge roof had been patched and the heating was working at full blast; the bridge was again quite habitable. This was just as well, because the temperature had dropped sharply and, although the snow had ceased, there was black ice forming on the superstructure.

"We need to keep an eye on that," Grosvenor said.

"But today we start trawling," Peter reminded him.

They had now closed to within fifty miles of the coast, by Dead Reckoning as Schmitt was still working on the Navigator aerials. The sky remained forbiddingly grey and the seas lumpy, if not rough. But the barometer was plunging, and Grosvenor and Peter did not need sophisticated instrumentation to tell them that the weather which had been threatening for the past forty-eight hours was about to break.

This made it all the more urgent to obtain early samples, and as soon as it was light, about eight o'clock, the trawls went over the stern. The catch was enormous; even the giant winches strained to bring the nets inboard, where the fish were immediately emptied into the tanks, to swim around while Meg and Oswiecki inspected them and netted out such as were thought suitable. These had blood drawn off before being labelled, numbered and returned to the tanks. Now it was Peter's turn to feel queasy as he visited the laboratory and found himself immersed in the smell of fish.

"Any luck?" he asked Meg.

She was in her element, totally obscured behind her mask and gloves and rubber apron, eyes glued to the electron microscope. "Nothing yet," she said. "But we knew it wasn't going to be easy."

He left them to it and joined Grosvenor on the bridge. *Ocean Secrets* continued to steer just east of south at a steady 15 knots; if Meg found nothing in her first batch, they would be 350 miles further on by dawn tomorrow.

"It's gonna be goddamned difficult without instruments," Grosvenor said. "But we should then be pretty close to where Dr Oswiecki dumped his gash. On the other hand, we're gonna be pretty damned close to the Horn as well. But tell me this, Mr Canning: supposing we don't find anything there, where do we go next?"

"Didn't Dawson plot it?"

Grosvenor nodded. "He reckoned, if we didn't find anything around here, we should turn west and make for south of New Zealand."

"But that's against the prevailing current," Peter argued. "Surely we should turn east, and go with the current – and the fish."

"The skipper didn't think so. For one thing, fish don't always go with the currents, not the bigger ones, anyway. And for another, it's now about a month since the first outbreak, according to Dr Calhoun. Fish travel, man, when they want to. The carriers would've gone right round and be on their way back by now. Most important of all, we're gonna need fuel, and we sure ain't gonna get any around here, without being arrested. Westabout is the shortest distance to New Zealand."

"Then that's what we'll do," Peter agreed. He was actually in a desperate hurry to get to Sarah and make sure she was all right; but he was refusing to let his anxiety interfere with Meg's work. "But we'll give the doctor a day or two here first."

He remained on watch, peering into the gloom which was oppressive even in the middle of the day, from time to time watching Schmitt and Harrison who were outside trying to erect the new aerial for the Navigator, a difficult business in their heavy jackets and gloves; their faces were blue with cold.

He thought, what an odd position to be in. In more ways than one. He was entirely cut off from communication with London, had no idea what might be happening in the rest of the world. In the circumstances, that was probably a good thing; there was no possibility of his flying back on schedule now: he could not leave the ship until they reached New Zealand. How marvellous it would be if they reached there to discover that the disease had burned itself out. But he knew that was not going to happen. Possibly the entire future of mankind depended on the efforts of that slender little woman below. His little woman. He was more than ever determined on that, now.

Schmitt was banging on the roof. "Iceberg!" he bellowed. "Dead ahead."

Peter's head jerked and he flicked the switch to take the helm off autopilot, at the same time grabbing the makeshift wheel and altering course hard to starboard. *Ocean Secrets* slewed round while the floating ice mountain drifted slowly towards them and then fell astern.

Alerted by the course change, Grosvenor hurried on to the bridge. "That's all we need," he said.

"That, and weather," Peter told him.

It arrived that afternoon, as the fitful wind commenced to blow steadily from the south-east, or dead in their teeth. By the early dusk it was gale force, and the seas were rising.

"We'll heave to under power," Grosvenor decided. "That way we shouldn't drift too far."

The ship's speed was reduced to slow ahead, and she was left steering directly into the wind; she inched her way up the twenty-foot swell, and then fell away into the trough beyond. The motion was not too uncomfortable and was preferable to the wild rolling which would result from attempting to turn away from the weather, but both men knew that without instruments they were going to be utterly lost if the storm lasted any length of time. They could only thank God that the wind direction was blowing them away from land.

By midnight the gale had reached storm force. Even in the darkness the waves were frighteningly high, rearing some forty feet above the troughs, visible only as a deeper black than the night and topped with several feet of foaming white. Now heaving to was no longer practical; *Ocean Secrets* had to be driven through the storm. Grosvenor and Peter took turns on the helm and the engine controls, their objective being to keep the decks as free of water as they could, as this was where the real danger lay. Thus the ship was directed at the waves, at slow ahead, until the crests actually broke over the bows, then speed was increased to full, to drive the hull through the water as rapidly as possible. The moment the bows were clear, however, the throttles had to be closed again, or the trawler would stand the chance of embedding herself so deeply in the following trough that she would not rise to the next wave. She thus seemed to slide down the back of the sea before gathering herself for the next assault. It was difficult to believe that she would always come up; Peter found his heart rising into his throat when the ship was still going down and already another monster was rearing above them.

But if it was frightening, it was also exhilarating to be so closely involved in the challenge of the sea, and gradually he became more and more confident that the ship could handle anything the ocean might throw at her. The noise was tremendous, the booming of the wind and the seas making it necessary to shout even in the wheelhouse, and relaxation was impossible, not merely because of the chaotic motion, but because, as they could not see beyond the next wave, they had no idea what was on the other side of it.

This thought occurred to others. Meg had by now joined them on the bridge, as it was impossible to work any longer with the ship plunging to such an extent. "What happens if we run into another iceberg?" she asked, having heard about the first.

"We disappear without trace," Peter said.

She squeezed his arm. "Don't you think we've already done that, in the eyes of the world?"

"I'm glad I'm with you. How do you feel?'

"Okay. It's too rough to be seasick. But . . . how soon will we be able to fish again?"

Peter looked at Grosvenor.

"I have no idea," the mate said. "Not for a couple of days, anyway. Peter, we're gonna have to do something about the ice; she's gotten sluggish. If we get top-heavy, in these conditions, we could go right over."

Peter nodded, and took the helm, while Grosvenor rounded up several members of the crew, and led them in playing steam hoses over the decks and super-structure to clear the black ice. It was exhausting and highly dangerous work, as although they took as much shelter as they could, they still had to use the after deck to manhandle the hose; several times one of them was swept from his feet and only saved by his safety harness.

Meg shivered at the sight of them. "To think that fishermen have to do this day in and day out, all of their lives. It's a horrifying way of earning a living."

"The average fisherman would probably say that your way is far more horrifying. Why don't you go and lie down?"

She shook her head. "I'm staying here. If we're to go, I want it to be together."

"We're not going to go," he promised her. He had never felt more confident in his life.

He had to accept relief when the ice was all cleared, however, as he had then been on the helm for several hours. His shoulders and back were a mass of mus-cular pain, but a mug of hot soup laced with brandy offered by Benetti relaxed him, and he sank into his bunk with a sigh of pleasure. Meg crawled in with him although they both remained fully dressed just in case there was an emergency, and he was asleep in seconds.

There was no emergency and they slept till dawn, aware, immediately they awoke, that the vicious storm noises were abating. They went up to the bridge, and gazed at the wildest sea imaginable. The waves were still mountainous, and stretched away interminably to either side, covered in a welter of foam and spindrift; behind them visibility was almost as limited as in front, as the great walls of water careered on their way, and now it was teeming with rain.

"God Almighty!" Meg gasped. "Was it like this last night?"

"It's eased off a good bit," Grosvenor told her. "The wind's dropped too. And guess what? The temperature's gone up; that rain isn't freezing."

"You sound almost happy," she complained.

"I am, almost," he agreed.

It was even possible to sit down to breakfast, although controlling plates and mugs was hilariously difficult. But everyone was in high spirits, confident that the worst of the storm was past. Also, the bad weather had helped to alleviate the gloom cast over the expedition by the deaths of Dawson and Logan: their grief had become secondary to the fight for their own survival. The wind continued to drop all day, and the seas became lower. Grosvenor and Peter sat down with the chart that afternoon and tried to plot a position. It was a massive problem, as current had to be balanced against drift and leeway, and some idea of distance covered over the ground worked out against the background of the sudden surges in speed as they had combated the waves of the previous night. They decided that they were probably not more than twenty miles west of the position they had plotted just before the storm struck, and laid a course from there.

Meg was by now back at work, but it seemed clear that none of the fish taken in the first catch were diseased, and they were all released. Next morning they were trawling again at dawn, the seas now no more than lumpy. The storm had indeed cleared the weather, and there was even hazy sunlight to give an impression of warmth, while best of all, Schmitt got the Navigator aerial working, and they were able to fix their position – and discovered that their Dead Reckoning had been almost a hundred per cent accurate.

"Now I feel we're in control again," Grosvenor said.

"If only we had communications as well," Peter agreed.

But they could do nothing more than stick it out. They trawled for another three days, without success, and then turned their bows west for New Zealand. This was a distance of 4,500 miles, and would take nine days even if they steered flat out, but they also had the prevailing easterly current to contend with, and they trawled for half an hour every day, and soon ran into another gale. By this time the weather seemed almost routine, but Meg was despondent at her lack of success. "Seems to me I've wasted everyone's time, and caused the death of Jim and Logan, all for nothing."

"Well, you're proving one thing," Peter suggested. "That there couldn't have been that many fish contaminated in the first place."

"But we're no nearer finding an antidote," she grumbled.

"You know that I'm going to have to leave the ship in New Zealand and fly back," he reminded her. "I'll have exceeded my fortnight as it is."

She nodded. "I may well come with you, if I haven't struck oil by then."

But she, or at least Charlie Oswiecki, did strike, the very next day. "That's the guy!" he shouted, his mask nearly blowing off his face.

Meg took over the microscope and stared at the tiny virus, noting its characteristics on her pad. "Yes," she said, quietly suppressing her excitement. "Yes. Which specimen?"

"Number 93," he told her. "An Atlantic cod, or, as it's known locally, a bacalao."

"That was the biggee," she said, adding enthusiastically, "Oh, boy. We have something here."

She was jubilant. Her theory was being proven; the virus was alive, but comatose in the fish's cold bloodstream. The unfortunate cod was again fished out of the tank and had some more blood removed, and she and Oswiecki got down to analysis. The news spread through the ship and was celebrated, although Meg warned them that there was still a long way to go. But she too had no doubts that if she could get the living blood back to the Research Center she and Fitzroy would be able to find a neutraliser. The cod was placed in an isolation tank, and the remainder of the fish examined. Meg was anxious to identify at least one more host fish as a back-up, in case the first did not survive, and not until they had found two more were the trawls at last stowed away.

That night they drank champagne, while speed was increased. New Zealand was now only two days away; they would be home in three.

Next morning they began calling on the VHF radio, but it was not until late afternoon that they attracted a response. "This is HMAS *Clarion*. Identify yourself," came the crisp command.

"Research vessel *Ocean Secrets*," Grosvenor replied.

There was a pause. "*Ocean Secrets*? Well glory be," the voice said. "You have been listed as lost with all hands."

"We had a bit of trouble," Grosvenor admitted. "And lost our main radios."

"I will report your survival and position," *Clarion* said. "Where are you bound?"

"Wellington."

"That is not possible," *Clarion* announced.

"What did you say?"

"The port of Wellington is closed."

"Ah. Well then . . . Auckland?"

"There is no port open in New Zealand. No ships are permitted to enter or leave New Zealand waters without a health certificate."

"For God's sake . . . " Grosvenor stared at Peter and Meg.

"What the hell has been happening this last fortnight?" Peter wondered.

"Look, buddy," Grosvenor said. "We're kinda low on fuel, and there's people on board with things to do. You tell us which port we can call at, and we'll do that, but it has to be within a thousand miles."

"You may proceed to Sydney," *Clarion* said. "There you will be placed in quarantine until your vessel and yourselves have been completely checked for the Red Death. You will be able to fuel. You are requested to keep in contact either with this ship or with other patrolling vessels as you approach; such contact should be made at intervals no longer than six hours and on each call you will report your position. Confirm."

"We got all of that." Grosvenor said.

Peter took the handset. "What exactly has happened in New Zealand?"

"How long have you been out of touch?"

"A fortnight."

"Ten days ago the whole of New Zealand was declared a contaminated area by the World Health Organisation. This decision has been confirmed by the United Nations. All physical communications with the rest of the world has been severed, save for medical, logistical and financial help."

"And the New Zealand Government accepts this?"

"They have had no choice."

"For God's sake . . . " he realised there would be no use asking a warship captain about the health of a single farmer and his family. "How long is our quarantine likely to last?"

"That depends on circumstances," *Clarion* said. "I would say you'll be clear in two weeks."

"Two weeks? You mean for the ship. I would like to know how soon her crew will be released."

"Two weeks for the ship and everything and everyone on board her," *Clarion* told him.

"That's impossible. My name is Peter Canning. I am a member of the British House of Commons, and it is imperative that I return to England just as soon as possible."

"I'm sorry, Mr Canning. You'll be processed as rapidly as possible, but there are other people with just as urgent reasons for getting places. Anyway, I doubt you'd get a flight, right now."

Peter stared at the handset in impotent fury, and Meg took it from him. "This is Dr Margaret Calhoun," she said, "of the Robert Koch Research Center. As we have told you, we have been out of touch for the past fortnight. Do I understand what you are saying to mean that all of New Zealand is quarantined?"

"That is correct, Doctor. So is Australia."

"Then the disease has spread?"

"Spread? It's in India."

"Oh, my God," she said. "Then listen to me, Captain. I am in possession of . . . " she hesitated, choosing her words with care, "information which I believe may help us to cope with the situation. It is absolutely imperative that I get back to San Francisco at the earliest possible moment. I need transport for myself, and a large tank."

"Well, as I told Mr Canning, the flights are jammed solid."

"Captain, people are dying, and they are going to go on dying, if we don't find an antidote, and very quickly. Our mission in the Antarctic Ocean was for this very purpose. I think I may have the basis of that antidote right here, with me."

Clarion whistled. "Very good, Dr Calhoun. I'll report the situation to my superiors and get back to you. Meanwhile, proceed to Sydney as instructed. *Clarion* over and out."

"Takes a woman," Peter said admiringly.

Meg was in no mood for even feeble humour. "Just let's hope they do something," she snapped. "India! Can you imagine what that means? It's happening, Peter, the catastrophe we talked about and couldn't really believe possible."

"Yes," he agreed absently. His mind was taken up with Sarah; he simply had to make himself believe that she had got out in time.

HMAS *Clarion* was back on the air that evening. "A helicopter will rendezvous with you at dawn tomorrow morning," he said. "It has a capacity to lift off four people, or four large boxes, whichever you prefer. It will transport you to the United States aircraft carrier *Indispensable*. I'm afraid that on board the carrier you will have to undergo tests, but these will be put through as rapidly as possible. Then you will be sent home."

"Thank you, Captain," Meg said.

"You are a genius," Peter told her.

"I'm in a hurry. You can come along for the ride, with Charlie. And my fishtank. I'm sorry, Harry, but . . . "

"Oh, we'll stay with the ship," Grosvenor said. "She has to be fuelled and there's one hell of a lot of damaged gear to be put right. Besides, there ain't nothing any of us can do to help matters now."

It was a long night. Meg was in no mood for love-making, but then neither was Peter. "If only I could find out what's happened to Sarah," he said, as they sat together in Meg's cabin.

"I know," she said. "I'm sorry, believe me. I feel the same worry for Sally Ann. We just have to pray they're all right. But . . . I'm afraid our individual relatives and friends can't be our first concern, now."

"Yes, quite," he agreed. "So what's the programme? I must confess I still don't understand what's so important about these fish of your. I would assume that you could take all the blood samples you want and dispose of the fish. And now you know what the living virus looks like surely you can identify it without too much difficulty?"

"Identifying the virus isn't curing it," she pointed out. "And using any samples we may obtain from humans isn't much good either. It's always dead. In fact, as far as we can determine, it dies before its host, although after it has set the corpuscle replication in process. In the fish, now, it remains in a state of suspended animation. By drawing off blood samples and warming them, we can subject them to tests to discover what will neutralise them."

"But . . . if the virus really came from the megatherium, which was dead, how did it survive a hundred thousand years?"

"Because Tom Lintell was wrong in diagnosing that the megatherium died of a stroke. It suffered a stroke. This must have happened when the freeze-up had already started. In that condition it fell into a pit or whatever, or more likely through a hole in the ice, and was frozen very rapidly while the virus was still alive. The megatherium actually died of the cold, not the blood condition. So the virus remained again in a state of suspended animation. Then the discarded material was still basically frozen when it was thrown into the sea. It was probably eaten by krill rather than fish, in the first instance."

"What exactly are krill?"

"A form of shrimp, really. They inhabit the Southern Ocean, and there's an enormous number of them. They have always provided the basic diet for whales, you see, and as such were kept under control. But over the past couple of hundred years the whale population has been so reduced by man's depredations that there has been no check on the krill. The result is that they have just multiplied, again and again."

"A good example of what happens when we mess about with the ecology," Peter suggested.

"But this is a rare case where it isn't all bad. Krill are perfectly edible for human beings. In fact they could be one of our principal food sources in the coming years. The Russians and the Japanese are already using them, and it is estimated that man could harvest 150 million tonnes of krill annually for the indefinite future. Do you know what the total weight of all fish taken from the sea is at present?"

"I suppose I should, but I don't."

"Not much over 75 million tonnes, so we could be tripling our food supply from the sea just like that. There are problems, of course. Krill deteriorate very rapidly once caught, so refrigeration ships would have to be up with the fishing fleet at all times. But I have no doubt they'll solve that."

"That's all very reassuring," Peter said. "Supposing we are alive to see it happen."

"Um. Anyway, I'm pretty sure the waste was nibbled away by the krill, which were then eaten by fish, and was taken into their bloodstream, perhaps before it was even properly thawed out, but certainly before the virus had a chance to die. Once in the fish's cold blood it continued to survive, inanimately. It seems likely that Charlie Oswiecki dropped the gash right into a shoal of krill for that to happen. It was a chance in a million, but it happened. Are you with me?"

"Yes," he said slowly. "Yes. So the virus survived in the fish, and only activated when the fish itself was eaten by man. And then died itself. But you said that it was passed along by excreta?"

"That's right. But the excreta has to be living, in normal circumstances. This was what was misleading us in the beginning. We thought it was being passed by any contact, because then we hadn't even identified it. But once we found it, and experimented, we discovered that by the time the host is dead, the virus is harmless."

Peter stared at her, new thoughts teeming through his brain. "Do you know what you have just said?"

She met his gaze. "Yes."

"In other words, this epidemic could have been stopped before it began."

Her eyes narrowed. "You mean by sealing off everyone who contracted it and just letting them die? That's an inhuman concept."

"Meg, we, you, are fighting a war. People are dying all around us. Wouldn't it be better to accept a certain number of casualties, amongst people who are apparently certain to die anyway, than risk it spreading throughout the world? If the virus dies with the host, then the host must die, without coming into contact with any other living creature. Without being allowed to come into contact with any other living creature."

"I'm sorry, Peter, but that is not a medical point of view."

"It's certainly a political one."

"Thank God politicians aren't responsible for our health."

"They are, you know, at the end of the day. Wouldn't you call what is now happening a political matter?"

"Finding a solution is a medical matter. You must understand that. I am certain that once I get this fish back to San Francisco we will discover a neutralising agent."

"And what will you do then? Set out to vaccinate the world?"

"It may well come to that. Peter . . . " she rested her hand on his arm. "I let you come along on this trip because I trusted you absolutely. I still do. I am sharing

261

all my secrets with you because I love you. But I love you as a man, not a politician. There are aspects of medicine in which politics can have no say. Saving life is one of them."

"I would say we politicians are aware of a dividing line. But you must accept that there are times when it is necessary to take life in order to save it." He was getting angry with her, however much he was trying to resist it, because he could see the anger in her face.

"That is wrong, wrong, wrong," she insisted. "It can never be right to condemn people to death without trying to save them." She was tired; her heart was pounding and there was a sickening lump in her stomach as she watched his intense seriousness. "Anyway, containment, even by your totalitarian methods, wouldn't work now. Not if the Red Death has got to India."

"It will work in limited areas."

"I see. You're thinking of an island like Britain. So, you'll seal yourself up and anyone who sets foot on your soil and responds to a blood test will be clapped into solitary confinement and left to die. Am I right?"

"If necessary, it could come to that. You just said the individual didn't matter in a crisis like this."

"I meant quite the reverse to what you have just said, that the individual cannot be considered separately from the mass when it comes to saving lives . . . or attempting to do so; your point of view seems to be that you deliberately sacrifice the individual, or even whole groups of individuals, no matter how many lives it may cost."

"That is my point of view, yes."

She stood up, realising her knees were trembling. "I'm sorry."

"So am I. Meg . . . " he caught her hands. "It's senseless for us to quarrel about this. We both have our points of view. I must look at the situation from a political point of view, because I am a politician. Just as you must look at it from a medical point of view, because you're a doctor. Surely we can agree to differ?"

"Not on this," she said, her face stony. "Because this is at present a medical matter, pure and simple. You are here, you are privy to our secrets, by courtesy of me. I must ask you to promise me most faithfully that you will never divulge a word of what I have told you, until I am sure it is safe to do so." She was bitterly angry and disappointed in him, but she had no doubt he would acquiesce.

He stood up as well. "I'm afraid I cannot do that."

She stared at him in disbelief. "Peter! Peter . . . if the politicians get hold of this, the knowledge I have just given you, they are going to do exactly what you just recommended: put up the shutters and wait for the Death to burn itself out. If Graham and I are allowed to get on with it, for just a few days, weeks at the most, we can save untold thousands, maybe millions of lives. You have to give us that time. But in the meanwhile, for God's sake, let the medics, properly safeguarded, care for the sick and dying. Let them have as decent and comfortable an end as is humanely possible."

In theory she was right, but the theory could not be turned into a practical possibility without endangering the rest of the world population. He was an elected Member of Parliament. He owed an immense duty not only to the constituents who had chosen him to represent them, but to his colleagues in the Government and through them to the people as a whole who had entrusted them with the management and safety of the nation. He had determined from the moment of first learning of the disease that it should be kept at bay; now he possessed the information to make even the Prime Minister realise the force of that argument. Not to use it would be a betrayal of everything he had spent his life trying to achieve.

"Meg," he said. "I will, I swear, present the medical point of view to my colleagues. But I must give them the facts. It was on that condition that I was allowed to come on this expedition."

"Rubbish! I allowed you to come," she blazed at him. "Nobody else. Against my better judgment, I allowed you to come. If you let me down now, I don't ever want to see you again, as long as I live." Her eyeballs were stinging with angry, feminine tears. It was at moments like this that a woman resented her sex. She turned her head away so that he could not see the tell-tale signs.

Peter gazed at the back of her head, hurt too, and furious that she could fail to see his sensible point of view. Releasing her hands, he slammed out of the cabin.

Douglas Lawton stood against the door of his barn, and watched as the Government veterinarian, accompanied by half a dozen helpers, took blood samples from his sheep. The buildings, the entire property, were surrounded by a cordon of armed policemen. He could not believe this was New Zealand. But then, there were a great many things he had found it difficult to believe these past few weeks.

Mr Makinson trudged towards him, boots heavy with mud. "You're a lucky man, Mr Lawton. Your flock is healthy."

"Because I've watched them like a hawk," Douglas said, wearily. "Allowed nothing to come near them. Now . . ."

Makinson gave a sour smile. "I don't think any of us has the Red Death, or we wouldn't be here. Now the important thing is to get that flock to the slaughterhouse before they do get contaminated."

"You intend to destroy my entire stock?"

"I'm afraid it is very simply a food crisis, Mr Lawton. You know the country has been put on strict rations. And I am sure you know that some supplies are being brought in from outside. But we are having reports that a large number of crews are refusing to enter our ports, because of the prevalence of the disease. We need to get hold of all the available healthy meat and freeze it, to ensure future rations." Another grim smile. "You will of course be paid compensation, as soon as the crisis is over." His expression indicated that he had no great hopes of that moment ever arising.

Douglas turned his head to watch Dr Lambert coming out of the house, followed by Sarah and the boys, followed by the dogs.

"You are a very fortunate man, Douglas," Lambert said. "Your family, your dogs, yourself, are all free of the disease."

Douglas sighed. Sarah and the boys were each carrying a suitcase; another waited by his feet. A single suitcase. "So, on that happy note, we're to be locked up," he commented.

"It's for your own good," Superintendent Martel told him. "If we can put all the healthy population together in disease-free areas, we can keep it healthy. While the doctors treat the others. And find a cure." He sounded no more optimistic than Makinson. But he ruffled Rupert's hair. "You'll like the camp," he said. "There are lots of young fellows like you there. The lucky ones."

Douglas took Sarah's suitcase in one hand, his own in the other, and walked down the path towards the waiting cars and coach. The sheep were already being herded towards the line of trucks. He stopped to look back and watch Martel carefully padlocking the front door. They had spent so many years building this farm, creating a good life here for themselves and their sons. He was born a farmer, of farming stock, but had found the agricultural scene in England very depressing. Sarah had so willingly agreed to emigrate with him, to start all over again virtually from scratch, when she was already pregnant with Leigh. The house they had designed so that they could easily add to it as money became available. It was already a lovely home, though it had been such hard work. They had beavered, outside on the land by day, indoors, painting and decorating in the evenings . . . And now? One must try not to think too much of the future. They had built once, they would build again . . .

"Will we ever come back?" Sarah whispered low, so the boys would not hear.

Douglas forced a smile. "Of course we will. As Martel said, we're healthy. We're the lucky ones. Thanks to our precautions. We'll be back, Sarah."

She squeezed his hand. "And we'll make up the flock again, Douglas."

"Of course we will." He frowned as they neared the coach which was to take them to the safety of what was called an RDFC: a Red Death Free Camp.

One of the policemen had removed his hat to mop his forehead with a grubby handkerchief. He was leaning against the tailboard . . . puce in the face.

14

Homecoming

As soon as the helicopter descended to the deck of the aircraft carrier, Meg, Peter and Oswiecki were hurried into the sickbay to have blood tests.

"Now I know what your fish went through," Peter quipped, feebly.

He met with no response. Charlie Oswiecki had become increasingly burdened with the realisation that it had been his action in dropping the gash that had triggered this now world-wide disaster. No matter that he had not known, that Tom Lintell never even suspected, that a virus could survive in a state of suspended animation for a hundred thousand years – it had still been their enthusiastic disturbance of the past that had unleashed such a terror on the world.

Peter could understand his feelings, even if, being as pragmatic as most politicians, he knew what a waste of time it was looking over one's shoulder. The disease was here. It did not matter, now, how it got here. Only checking it, and eradicating it, was important.

He was far more concerned about the rift with Meg. She had not softened towards him since their quarrel; her anger was still apparent, even now. And he knew the only chance of healing the wounds was if he gave her the promise she wanted. But he could not do that. He felt that she was being unreasonably soft-centred, for a doctor. Too feminine. And though he adored

her femininity, she simply had to separate the two
. . . or pack her career in and become a housewife.
His housewife.

But did he want that? Could she have the same positive personality without the stimulus of an intellectual
career? On the other hand, as a housewife she might
come to realise that in his position he had no option
but to lay every available alternative course of action
before the Cabinet, and if hard decisions had to be
taken, to bear his share of that burden. He considered
Meg was being irrational at the moment. She had herself
recognised the necessity to quarantine the victims right
away. What she could not bring herself to accept was
that, as the mortality rate for the Death was over ninety
per cent, nursing was no more than a palliative, while
such was the virulence of the disease that each human
being who came into contact with it became not only
a potential victim but, far more dangerous, a potential
carrier. And doctors and nurses could not be forced into
isolation with the sick . . .

"You're clean," said the surgeon commander. "Now,
the boss wants to see you."

"After I've checked out my fish," Meg said.

"I'll come with you," Oswiecki volunteered.

Peter went up to the bridge alone. The vast ship was
ploughing north-east through lumpy seas, but these
were hardly noticeable when slapping against eighty
thousand tons of steel.

"John Plant," the captain said, shaking hands.

"Peter Canning."

"There's been quite a fuss about you," Plant said.
"The Chilean navy reported that you had been lost
with your ship and all hands in a squall just north
of the Horn."

"They were stretching the truth a little," Peter commented, and told the captain of their brush with the
corvette. "I need to inform London that I'm alive."

"That was done as soon as we learned of it. They want you back."

"Well, I'm hoping you'll be able to do something about that."

Plant nodded. "I've a bomber standing by to get you up to Hawaii. From there you'll be ferried to the mainland, together with the doctors. And there'll be a flight waiting in San Francisco for London. I'm afraid you'll have to undergo medical tests at each stop. People have become mighty nervous the past couple of weeks."

"Can you fill me in on just what has been happening?"

"Well, twelve days ago at the United Nations Peru raised the matter of the Red Death in Chile. I guess up to then a lot of people had not even heard of it, or if they had, they had no idea just how serious it was and dismissed it as something on the other side of the world. The UN debate blew the lid off it. Nobody could check the Peruvian statistics, as the Chilean delegate didn't take his seat, but the figures given were something like half the population of the country dead, and the other half barricaded in towns and villages and living in a state of siege."

"Good God!" Peter gasped. "That's just like the Black Death."

"Save that the Black Death only killed about one in three, not one in two," Plant pointed out.

"Yes," Peter agreed, surprised that a US navy captain should be so steeped in pre-American history. "And is there no clue as to why some people do survive it?"

"There's really not enough evidence accumulated at the moment. A suggestion has been put forward by Dr Calhoun's boss, Graham Fitzroy, that not only the fittest, but those who take the most exercise, are best able to survive. That's not quite as obvious as it sounds. Taking exercise requires excess oxygen, and that means the body summons up an increased number of red corpuscles. But whether such people merely live

269

longer than others or can actually survive the whole epidemic no one knows. The point is that the debate stirred everybody up. Peru insisted that the Chileans could not possibly deal with the situation, because they no longer had a government. The same thing virtually obtained for Argentina, where the government and the army have retreated into Buenos Aires and turned it into some kind of a fortress, letting no one in and out. Meanwhile, if people weren't dying of the Red Death, they were starving.

"Well, the initial response was very good. Our air force was put to work, and there were volunteer groups as well, to get food and medical supplies down there. A Save Chile Fund was launched. But while all this was still being set up the disease appeared in Peru and Bolivia, as well as Paraguay."

"It was bound to," Peter sighed. "What's the response to that?"

"They're still debating. I'll tell you, though, the Panamanian Government has asked for US troops to be sent back there, to hold the line of the Canal and stop anyone, and I mean anyone, from crossing."

"Fortress North America," Peter said grimly, and wondered what Meg was going to make of that. "Now tell me about New Zealand."

"Well, of course that was easier to contain. Or it should have been. And the New Zealand Government have adopted a most responsible attitude towards the situation, even though it has meant the ruination of their country. Those sheep which didn't die of the disease are being slaughtered for food stocks before they can become contaminated. Again, supplies are being flown in, but the economy is totally wrecked, and may take decades to re-establish, while a huge number of people have died. And the tragic aspect of the situation is that for all the precautions, the disease still got out. First to Tasmania, and then to Australia."

"By contagion? Or by the original source, fish?"

"Nobody can be certain of that either. Fishing was prohibited early on, as you must know. But prohibiting something and actually making people stop doing it isn't altogether the same thing."

"And now we've heard it's in India?"

"Well, a case has been reported there, but not confirmed. As you can imagine, everyone is feeling pretty much on edge as to where the Death will strike next."

"I can imagine. I have a sister in New Zealand. I don't suppose there is any way of finding out if she's all right?"

"We can certainly try," Plant said. "Ah, Dr Calhoun. All well with your fish?"

"Yes, thank you," Meg said, closing the door of the captain's day cabin behind her. She did not look at Peter. "Now, Captain, how soon can you fly us back to the States?"

"Just give the word, Doctor. You can be airborne in half an hour."

They slept on the plane, slowly becoming aware of how exhausted they were after the continuing trauma of the Southern Ocean. Hawaii was basking in glorious warm sunshine, but there was no time to enjoy it as another air force jet was waiting to whip them across to the mainland.

Peter sat beside Meg. "How long do you estimate it will take you to find an antidote?"

"How long is a piece of string?" She gazed out of the window.

"But you will find it."

"If it can be found within the range of our present medical knowledge, we will find it," Meg said.

"So there's no guarantee?"

At last she turned her head. "No, Peter, there is no guarantee. We have to do a little praying as well."

He looked into her eyes. "But you still feel it should be business as usual until you do?"

"I still think that we must do everything we can for the sufferers, yes. I assume you still don't agree with me."

"I do, Meg. I agree with you one hundred per cent that we must do everything possible, everything we can . . . which does not endanger other life."

"Then there's nothing more to be said. I made a mistake in allowing a politician on a medical research expedition." She resumed her study of the ocean far below, dotted with puffs of cloud.

"Meg," he said. "I love you."

There was no immediate response. But after several seconds she turned her head again. "Maybe, when this is over, if it is ever over, we'll be able to think about each other again, Peter. Right now, there simply isn't time."

There was hardly time to say goodbye in San Francisco before Peter was again on his way, this time on the 6,000-mile hop to London. He was aware, for once, just how dishevelled he must look; his hair was still sticky with salt, his attempt to shave in the tiny toilet on the aircraft was not very successful and his clothes looked as though they had not been changed for weeks. At least their recovery and movements had been kept secret, and there were no reporters waiting for them, but there was a message from John Plant:

DOUGLAS LAWTON WIFE AND TWO SONS PLACED IN RED DEATH FREE CAMP NORTH OF WELLINGTON FOUR DAYS AGO STOP REGRET TO INFORM THAT THIS CAMP IS NOW REGARDED AS CONTAMINATED AND IS IN TOTAL ISOLATION STOP SO SORRY PLANT

Peter stared at the print-out while his blood seemed to coagulate. Sarah, bubbling, happy Sarah, locked up in a death camp, certainly more lethal than anything invented by the Nazis! But was that not what he had advocated should be done?

He crumpled the message into his pocket and boarded the plane. It was too late to speak to Meg again. But he did not know what he would say, even if he had the opportunity. If Sarah, Douglas and the boys were contaminated . . . Should they simply be left to die, unattended? He shuddered, felt his face go red as if he was personally guilty of abandoning them. But that was ridiculous; he had to think and work for the living.

The pilot had radioed ahead, and Peter was met the moment he touched down at Heathrow. He had had very little sleep on the aircraft. It had been impossible to rid himself of the picture of Sarah as a child, pink and dimpled in a halo of curls; as a leggy teenager, her artistic skills maturing; emerging, as from a chrysalis, into a beautiful young woman, not sophisticated like Claudia, but soft, gentle, sensitive, and falling deeply and sincerely in love with Douglas Lawton. She had blossomed so, as her body swelled with their first child and as they prepared excitedly for their adventure across the world to raise sheep and children and found their own dynasty in New Zealand. A dream which had become a nightmare. His mental picture clouded. Was Sarah now dying? Sarah, his dearly loved little sister, her face suffused with blood and misery as she watched her husband and children dwindling with her as they watched others die . . . and waited their turn? His head ached with the unsatisfied need for sleep as he left the aircraft and was taken to a medical room for a blood test; he gathered this was also being done to all the other passengers. He would dearly have loved to telephone his parents to tell them he was still alive

– though he had no idea how to break the news about Sarah – but instead he was escorted to a waiting car and driven straight to 10 Downing Street, where the Prime Minister had convened the Cabinet; it was ten in the morning in London. He was surprised, but pleased, to discover that Hartley Briggs was also present.

"I think we'll begin by asking you to tell us your adventures, Peter," the Prime Minister invited, somewhat drily.

Peter obliged as succinctly as he could while everyone listened quietly with only the occasional query for clarification.

When he had finished the Prime Minister said, "Is it therefore your opinion that an antidote may soon be available?"

"I think we have every right to hope that an antidote may soon be available, Prime Minister."

The Prime Minister gave him an old-fashioned look, then turned to the Minister of Health. "Perhaps you would bring Peter up-to-date, Jeremy."

"Ah. Yes, Prime Minister." Jeremy glanced at his notes; he looked distinctly haggard. "The matter was raised during Question Time in the House a fortnight ago, at which time it was announced that you had formed a task force to look into the disease and were presently on a fact-finding tour to investigate the situation." He looked at Peter over the tops of his glasses. "This was of course absolutely true, as it had to be. It was then announced to the House that you would make a full statement upon your return. Unfortunately, that statement was soon overtaken by events; that is, the decision of the Peruvian Government to raise the matter in the United Nations, and your own disappearance and presumed death. HM Government had no option but to take part in the UN debate, out of which the decision to quarantine countries known to be affected by the disease arose. From our point of view this particularly concerned

New Zealand, in view of our ties with that country, and everything we could do to alleviate the suffering there has been done.

"In all the circumstances, however, the Prime Minister felt it necessary to implement the suggestion put forward by Sir Hartley Briggs as chairman of your task force, and recommended unanimously by the members of that force, that everyone entering the country should undergo a blood test for signs of polycythaemia. Up to this moment there have been only six positive results. These people have all been placed in isolation wards, but two of them have already been released, as they showed no signs of developing the condition further."

"How long were they in quarantine?" Peter asked.

"For four days. That is twenty-four hours longer than any known victim has survived."

"It is perhaps still not long enough," Peter said. "There are undoubtedly some people who have resistance to the virus."

"I'm afraid the measure aroused some considerable opposition," Jeremy pointed out. "Particularly amongst travellers who could claim to have been nowhere near the infected areas."

"Just about every other country in the world has instituted such tests," Peter remarked.

"That's as may be. We have to look at the situation within our own country. I may add that it is proving a considerable burden on the Health Service. Equally I should stress that no meat imported into this country has been found to be contaminated."

"For a very good and important reason," Peter said.

"Which we are hoping you will tell us," the Prime Minister interjected. "However, the measures, inconvenient and expensive as they may be, announced in the House ten days ago, and put into immediate effect, to a large extent restored confidence. Unfortunately, during the past week the situation has deteriorated further, and over the past twenty-four hours has deteriorated further yet. I have just received the following reports. One: the entire crew of an American Air Force jet which was ferrying supplies into Chile has been found to be diseased; they were given a routine blood test two days ago when they returned from a mission and were found to have high rbc counts. The existence of the disease in the United States is now confirmed. We are informed that there has been an immediate, and understandable, reluctance on the part of other crews to continue such missions.

"Two: Congress has decided to accede to the request from the Government of Panama for assistance and is sending two divisions of troops to hold the line of the Canal. This is, in my opinion, a most unfortunate escalation of the tension and may well lead to bloodshed." The Prime Minister coughed, as if aware of a certain absurdity in that statement.

"Three: we are informed that the Russians are massing troops on their borders to resist any attempt at entering their territories by unauthorised persons. This is of course, having regard to the immensity of the Russian borders, an impossible undertaking. But it shows that the political situation is getting out of control.

"Four: there are now a number of cases confirmed in Calcutta, and there is already some evidence of a breakdown of law and order there. This could well spread throughout India."

"Five: there is a suspected outbreak in South Africa."

"South Africa?" Peter's head jerked.

"South Africa," the Prime Minister repeated. "The situation is incredibly dangerous. I accept that you warned us this could happen, Peter, and perhaps we should not have felt your warnings to be quite so exaggerated and premature as we did. However, we must face the existing facts, and in this regard I have felt it necessary to agree that the House should not recess until your return, and that the Government will make a statement in the Commons tomorrow afternoon. As Jeremy has said, we have indicated that such a statement would come from you, at least partly in rebuttal of the various criticisms made of your recent absence. I had hoped you would come back with some positive ray of hope to hold out. But I don't see that you have."

Peter took a deep breath. "We can certainly render this country free of the Red Death, or the risk of it entering," he began, a lead ball growing in his stomach as he spoke the words. "I have obtained one vital piece of information about the disease; it dies with its victims. It cannot, in normal circumstances, survive outside a living host. This is why, Prime Minister, you have found no contaminated meat. As it runs a very rapid course, this means that if all contact with a victim is ended, for a period of perhaps ninety-six hours, the virus becomes entirely harmless. I know this sounds heartless and it may well be politically difficult, but the fact is that the disease is being carried in a large number of cases by those, whether medical or lay, attempting to assist the stricken. The crew of the American transport plane are a case in point. Nor has any medical assistance been able to stem the advance of the disease when it strikes. Drawing of blood is merely a temporary measure, so is injecting with phosphorus or busulfan. In almost every case, the victim has died, after infecting the person assisting him. Were they left to themselves, placed in total isolation with sufficient food and water for four days, they would either be dead, and harmless, at the end of that time, or they would have survived." He leaned back in his chair and waited.

"You are advocating doing that with everyone found to have a high rbc count?" Jeremy demanded. "What about those poor blighters I was talking about, who were placed in isolation and found not to have the virus?"

"After four days they would have been released, as they were anyway," Peter said. "Without having had the chance to contaminate any doctors and nurses treating them." But his heart was pounding, causing a vein to jump irritatingly in his neck. He couldn't overcome the feeling he was betraying Meg as he spoke . . . and Sarah, and her family, and all those others . . .

Jeremy scratched his head. "Sounds a bit inhuman to me."

The Prime Minister looked from face to face around the table. "Gentlemen?"

"No one else has adopted such extreme measures. It would mean cutting ourselves off, morally, from the entire rest of the world," objected the Chancellor, Robert Duncan. Always urbanely confident, he, like the Prime Minister and several members of the Cabinet, was a personal friend of Claudia and Hartley – and equally a friendly critic of Peter's lifestyle and enthusiasms. "That is simply not possible."

"Nor, as Jeremy has said, is it ethical," remarked the Lord Privy Seal, looking, as always, hot and bothered.

"It could mean the survival of Britain," the Minister of Defence mumbled through his moustache.

"We'd be condemned before the world," objected the Foreign Secretary, great bald head gleaming above its white tonsure.

"Except that they would all very rapidly follow our example," the Prime Minister pointed out. "It is a measure which may have to be considered. At the moment we will adhere to our original plans. But if you will set up an immediate Summit Conference for the Common Market, Charles, I should be grateful. This has to be thrashed out at the highest level. Peter, I wish you to prepare that statement for the House tomorrow. It is possible that the Opposition may try to force a debate and a division, so I will order a three-line whip. However, I wish you to make it a very simple statement. You will just justify your two weeks' absence on the grounds that virus-carrying fish were secured and are now being subjected to the most intense analysis in California. You are entitled to say that you have every hope an antidote will soon be available. We all hope that. Do not be over-optimistic; it is far better to follow a gloomy prognostication with a cheerful up-date than vice versa. And do not mention the business of the possibility of eliminating the virus by locking the victims away. That would be counter-productive at this time. Do you agree with my suggestions?"

Peter was conscious of some suppressed humour to either side of him; the Prime Minister's 'suggestions' were famous: they carried the ultimatum of acceptance or dismissal. "I shall follow the line you have suggested, Prime Minister," he said.

"Am I glad to see you home!" Hartley confessed as they got into the back of his Rolls-Royce. "The family was quite shaken up by your disappearance. Do they know you're here yet?"

"No. I'm going down right away, as soon as I've had a bath and a shave. Hartley . . . how's it going?"

"Pretty well. You know what the British are like. All civilisation ends at Dover. Naturally there have been grumbles at the blood test business, and of course there are enough people in this country with relatives in New Zealand to make everybody very uneasy, but at first remove, as it were. The Red Death hasn't happened here, and of course we all know it can't." He glanced at Peter. "Even if we have to implement your rather Draconian solution."

"I don't think it went down very well with the Cabinet," Peter remarked.

"They're all thinking of the reaction in their constituencies, or if one of the people they have to isolate and leave to die happens to be a relative. Doesn't that bother you?"

"Of course it bothers me. But because of the relative, not because I might lose his vote. Hartley . . . Sarah is in just such a mess."

"Eh?"

Peter showed him the crumpled telegram from USS *Indispensable*.

"Oh, my God," Hartley commented. "You mean they're actually implementing your plan in New Zealand?"

"I think this is the first time. They simply don't have any choice. But if you shut people up because they're healthy, and then discover that they're not, you have a massive problem."

"Yes." Hartley's huge features creased into a frown, contorting his face. "You going to tell Dad and Mother?"

"I have to."

"Hm." He switched on the car phone beside him, "I think I'd better get through to Claudia and tell her to go down to Wimbledon as well." The car stopped in front of Peter's flat and Hartley paused before dialling. "How soon do you hope to hear from your American friends, on their progress?"

"Ah . . . " Peter wondered if he was ever going to hear from Meg again. "I should think very shortly. Certainly as soon as they've run preliminary tests. Tell Claudia I'll see her at Dad's."

He ran upstairs, unlocked his door. Everything was spic-and-span, but how empty the flat seemed without Gladstone; would he have time to get him back from the cattery this afternoon? But first . . . he sat in front of his phone and dialled International Information, got the number of Jan Geller's villa outside Cape Town, and put the call through.

The only good thing about Peter and Claudia's visit to Wimbledon was the absence of rock cakes; Veronica had not been expecting them and apologised for the substitute offering of tinned shortbread. But neither of her children could swallow even those.

They sipped their tea and Peter tried to inject a little optimism into the miserable quartet, saying, "We mustn't give up hope. Just because the illness has broken out in the camp, doesn't necessarily mean that everyone will get it. If the victims have been isolated quickly enough . . . " but his voice tailed off. They all knew, from the reports in the media, that the chances of the Red Death not spreading through the camp like wildfire were very remote. As the dreaded news sank in, Veronica's lower lip quivered ominously. Her hand shook when she lifted the teapot, spilling tea into a saucer, so Claudia took over.

They were sitting on the paved terrace outside the sitting-room French windows. The sun was shining, the little garden filled with delphiniums and larkspur and clumps of golden rod, so reminiscent of the old family home . . . when they had all been together. John's teeth ground gently on the stem of his unlit pipe. He was gazing out across the miniature lawn and flower beds, seeing nothing.

After a while Peter caught Claudia's eye and he glanced significantly at his watch. Claudia nodded, understanding. You go, she mouthed silently, I'll stay with them tonight. Peter smiled in appreciation; his older sister was certainly the most bossy of the family and had the least sense of humour for all her determination to be London's leading hostess, but she was undoubtedly the most caring and considerate of people, always to be relied upon, especially in an emergency. Leaving the three of them was painful. Mother's little lace hankie was a sodden ball; she seemed visibly to have shrunk in the past hour. The old brigadier looked at her in helpless misery and blew noisily into a big khaki handkerchief. Neither was able to answer his goodbyes.

15

Horror

Anna Papagopoulos replaced the telephone, but remained gazing at it for several seconds. Dear Peter. She had always known he had not really been dead, of course. That had just been newspaper sensationalism. He had gone off on some romantic adventure with his passing American fancy. And she obviously was just a passing fancy. Or he would not have called her the moment he returned to London. She presumed all his wild talk about the Red Death having appeared in South Africa was so much nonsense; she could not imagine this Government permitting anything like that to happen. South Africa was Anna's concept of a properly organised society, where the wealthy lived as the wealthy should, and the rest of the population worked for them. She often thought she should have been born in eighteenth-century England.

But she had no intention of staying here if there was any risk of that damned nonsense appearing; the panic in Brazil was too immediate in her memory. Besides, Jan, if a dear fellow, and very rich – far richer than Peter would ever be – was a bit of a bore. He was too macho, too concerned with playing the male animal in bed and less with being the lover. Anna did not need money . . . and she could not live without sexual love. She had a sudden tremendous urge to be back in her London house, with Peter stretched on the bed beside her.

She got up, let her cheesecloth blouse settle about her. It came to just below her thighs and was the only garment she was wearing; totally sheer, and held away from her body by her very full breasts, it really concealed nothing at all, but she considered it necessary to wear it, except when actually in the pool, when the servants were around.

She padded across the wide stretch of parquet flooring in the lounge, bare toes sinking into the carefully scattered gameskin rugs, and out through the open glass doors on to the pool patio. Jan and his friends were amusing themselves. There were four men, and four girls, without counting herself. Predictably. Jan's circle of friends believed in making the girls work harder for attention. They were all naked, very bronzed, very attractive and, in the case of the girls, very blonde, but of course all of them used a bottle to achieve the desired result. At least no one could say that about her.

She stood at the poolside drinking Buck's Fizz.

"Who was on the phone, darling?" Jan asked.

"Peter Canning."

"Canning? Not that boring politician fellow?"

"Yes. I wonder if I could have a word, Jan. In private?"

Jan looked at his friends. "These moods come over her, regularly," he explained.

The girls giggled, a shiver of breast and hair.

Jan climbed out of the pool, towelled himself. Anna retreated into the lounge doorway, and when she saw he was going to follow her, returned through the lounge and the hallway, filled with hunting trophies and crossed African spears, into the study, lined with obviously expensive but unread books.

"He's not being a nuisance, is he?" Jan asked.

"He's being a very thoughtful person," Anna said. "Jan, I would like a flight out of here tomorrow. Will you call your travel agent and book one for me?"

He frowned. "Tomorrow? Just like that? Anyway, tomorrow is Sunday."

"So? Don't tell me travel agents aren't open on Saturday mornings?"

"They'll be closing for lunch now."

"Then book the flight this afternoon, when they open."

"Anna, my dearest girl, what has brought this on? You gave me to understand that all was over between Canning and yourself. Now, at a single phone call, you wish to go scurrying back? I thought you were happy here. I have certainly been happy having you here."

"Darling," she said, "Peter tells me the Red Death has appeared in South Africa."

His frown deepened, and he sat behind his desk. "Well, I suppose he will have found out. There is always a leak somewhere."

"You mean it is true?"

"There are cases, yes."

"Cases? How many?"

"Well, half a dozen, confirmed."

"Confirmed? Confirmed where?"

"In Cape Town."

"Cape Town? My God!" she shouted. "And you didn't tell me? How on earth could the Red Death have got to Cape Town?"

Jan sighed. "It came in on a plane. From Israel. But the carrier had come from farther east. He was blood-tested, of course, found to have a high rbc count, and placed in quarantine. This is routine. But the lunatic escaped. Don't ask me how. There is an investigation going on. He was recaptured two days ago, and died a few hours later. But by then he had infected other people."

"You knew all of this, two days ago, and you didn't tell me?"

"I'm afraid I really had no idea that you were interested in what diseases the blacks suffer from. Some of them are more unpleasant than even this so-called Red Death. Anyway, there is nothing for you to worry about. All of this man's contacts are being rounded up and placed in isolation. We will stamp it out before it can possibly reach epidemic proportions."

"And you have known all this for two days," Anna said, disbelievingly.

"It has been known, privately, for the past week. We are keeping it quiet, of course, or people might become frightened. As you are doing."

"The past week! God Almighty! Jan, I want out. Tomorrow. Tonight, if there is a seat available."

"Now, Anna!" He got up, sat on the desk, held her hands. "You are being irrational. There is absolutely no risk of the disease becoming an epidemic, here in South Africa. We just will not permit that to happen. I've told you, the infected people are being locked up."

Anna shuddered. "They should be shot."

Jan grinned. "If necessary, they will be shot. We are quite prepared to take whatever measures are necessary, believe me. Now, will you stop being hysterical and come back outside and enjoy yourself?"

"Jan, I want to go home."

"Do you suppose this disease can never reach England? It is a worldwide threat, now. You will be far safer here."

"I want to go home," Anna said again, her voice hardening.

They glared at each other for several seconds, then Jan smiled. "Of course, my darling. And your wish is my command. I will arrange a flight for you tomorrow. Now, will you rejoin my party? And I would be obliged if you would not discuss this absurd fear of yours in front of my guests. The news is not generally known."

"I shan't say a word," she promised. "Just get me on a plane to England."

* * *

Anna sat on the verandah of Jan Geller's villa and looked out across the orchard and the tennis court. The guests had gone, and the house was quiet; the black servants moved noiselessly about their duties. She wore a pale coral silk dress, hand-painted with huge yellow and mauve hibiscus and green leaves. The skirt swept her ankles, the brief halter top knotted at the nape of her neck, the multi-coloured tassles on the ends swinging down her bare back.

It was a beautiful house, and however bored she might have become with Jan himself, or the succession of beautiful young people with whom he surrounded himself, Anna was keenly aware that in a very few years she would be too old to number herself in their ranks. She knew that in a way she could have been very happy living here. There was an opulent decadence about life in South Africa which appealed to her innermost instincts.

But now she hated it. She feared it. She wanted only to escape it before it caught her in its clutches. When she remembered the queuing in Rio, the nasty little officials who were playing god . . .

She looked at her gold watch, irritably. Jan should have been back by now. He'd gone out at five, and it was only a fifteen-minute drive into Cape Town . . . fifteen minutes to the Red Death. She shuddered.

"Would Mistress like a drink?"

Anna jumped. Of course it was only Thomas, the boy, but he moved so quietly for a big man. He could have been standing there for an hour, watching her. No doubt he had been. All men liked to stand and watch her, even black men.

"Yes," she said. "I would like a drink. A gin and tonic."

"A gin and tonic, Mistress."

Thomas turned to leave.

"Thomas!" Anna checked him. "Where do you live?"

"Live, Mistress? I live here."

"I mean, when you are not here. You must have a home."

"I have a house, Mistress. It is in Cape Town. In the black quarter." Thomas was surprised. This English woman with the big boobies had never before given the slightest indication of acknowledging that he actually existed.

"How often do you go there?"

"On my days off, Mistress." Thomas hesitated, but as Anna said nothing more, he went to fetch the drink.

Anna stared at the garden. She wondered when his day off was, but if she talked any more she would be telling what was on her mind. Besides, she could hear the growl of the car engine. She got up and went to the end of the verandah, looked out at the drive and the garages, watched Jan coming towards her. He appeared hot and bothered.

"Have you got my ticket?"

He kissed her cheek, took the gin and tonic from Thomas's tray and drank half of it. "Two more of those, Thomas."

"Have you got my ticket?" Anna repeated.

"There are no seats available until next Thursday."

"Next Thursday?" Her voice rose to a shout.

"Sssh," he said. "Think of the servants."

He went towards the lounge, and she ran behind him.

"Thursday is five days away."

"I know that." He finished her gin and tonic, threw himself into a chair. Thomas reappeared with two more glasses, and Anna drank a third of hers in a gulp.

"I want to leave here, now."

"Anna, you are being hysterical."

"Why are all the flights booked?"

"I suppose because a large number of people wish to leave the country."

"Because they have found out about the Red Death. You said it was confidential."

"A newspaper reporter got hold of it, yesterday. It was in this morning's papers."

"And you didn't know? You must have read this morning's paper." The newspapers that Jan took were in Afrikaans, which she could not read; up to this moment she had had no desire to.

"I didn't see any point in alarming you."

"Alarming me. My God!" She sat down, knees pressed together, glass held in both hands.

"Anna! Those people are frightened fools. Mostly visitors who are cutting short their holidays or their business trips and running for their lives. Surely you are not a frightened fool."

"I am frightened, Jan."

"There is no need to be. I have you a firm booking for next Thursday. Nothing is going to happen before then. Nothing is going to happen at all. I went to see Dr van Oppendorp. I have known him for years, and he is in charge of the situation. He is confident that they have found all the victims of the outbreak. There is no risk of it spreading. If you wish to leave on Thursday you can, but I would much prefer you to stay."

"Thursday," she said. She finished her drink and picked up the phone, dialled London.

"Who are you calling?" Jan asked.

"Peter. He will be able to help me."

"Anna! I forbid it."

Anna arched her eyebrows. "You forbid it?" she asked in amused indignation.

Jan crossed the room and took the receiver from her hand. "I will not have you using my telephone to call some British politician, who will only seek to make capital out of the situation."

"I will call who I damned well please," Anna snapped. "Give me that phone."

"I will not. Anna! Be sensible. How can Canning help you? He is only a minor MP. Do you suppose he is going to send the Royal Air Force to carry you out? You really are being unutterably childish."

They glared at each other, but she knew he could be very nasty, and very physical, when roused; he kept a sjambok in his study and would laugh as he told how he used it on the servants when the mood took him. And she was alone in the house with him, except for the servants.

She finished her drink. "I am going to bed."

"At this hour? It is not yet seven. What about dinner?"

"I don't want any dinner. I am not hungry. I don't feel very well."

He shrugged, and let her go. She locked her bedroom door, but he did not even try it. He was annoyed with her. But then, she was annoyed with him; she tried using the phone in her room, but it was dead. He was a bastard.

Anna refused to go to church the following morning. Jan went every Sunday, because he felt it was a good thing to be seen at church, and the previous week Anna had accompanied him although she was not a believer.

"Why aren't you coming?" he asked.

"I am not leaving this villa until I go to the airport," she told him.

He shrugged. "Suit yourself. You won't be able to phone out, you know. I have disconnected the system."

"Do you realise you are keeping me a prisoner?"

"I am just trying to stop you making an utter fool of yourself, and shouting hysterical tales all over the world. I really am disappointed in you, Anna. I supposed you were a sophisticated woman. Now I see that you are nothing more than a child."

"Fuck off," Anna told him.

Once he had left the house she had a swim and then tried to settle down with a book. She told herself that it was only a matter of waiting four days, that the disease could not possibly reach the villa, no matter what was happening in Cape Town. Perhaps Jan was right, and she was being hysterical. But she had never been so afraid in her life. Whatever had possessed her to come here? Simply a wish to make Peter jealous. Oh, what a fool she had been. When she got back to London, she was going to live a quieter life, settle down, and marry him. She had had enough of this gadding about, putting herself at the mercy of men who treated her like dirt. She tried all the phones, but every one was dead, as the bastard had said.

Jan did not come home for lunch, which was served on schedule by Thomas, gravely and without comment. Anna was just happy to be left alone. But she became disturbed when Jan had not returned that evening either. "Don't you think you should find out what has happened to the master?" she asked.

"He informed me that he would not be back before tomorrow, when he left this morning, Mistress."

"He did what?" Anna shouted.

"That he would be spending the night at a friend, Mistress."

Anna glared at him. The swine. The unutterable swine. Because he was annoyed with her, he had taken off with someone else. Leaving her here, with no telephones and with just the black servants for company. She went on to the verandah and stared at the drive. There was another car in the garage. But she had no idea where to go. Nor did she want to go anywhere, except the airport.

But why shouldn't she go to the airport? It was only five miles away. Her mistake had been to leave everything to Jan. She had got out of Rio by doing things for herself. She was Anna Papagopoulos. She was a woman who got things done. Why, for God's sake, she could charter a plane. It might not be practical to find one which could take her straight back to England, but at least she could start her journey – and get further away from Cape Town. "Give me the keys to the small car," she told Thomas.

"I cannot do that, without Mr Geller's permission," Thomas protested.

"Listen to me," Anna said. "I am going out. If you do not give me the keys I will walk and thumb a ride. And I will tell Mr Geller just why I had to."

"I cannot give you the keys, Mistress," Thomas said. "Mr Geller would be very angry."

Anna stared at him in impotent fury. But if Jan thought he could keep her a prisoner he was mistaken. She went upstairs, changed into trousers and a shirt, took her largest handbag, in which she placed her toilet articles, money and credit cards, and went downstairs again. She did not need her clothes. She would be in London tomorrow morning.

"Mistress is going out?" Thomas asked, politely.

"Yes. And if you try to stop me, Thomas, I will have you gaoled."

Thomas looked upset, but made no move. Anna went down the steps and stalked down the drive. The gates were open, and she marched on to the road. If need be, she would walk to the airport. But she was sure she would not have to.

The main road was half a mile away. She saw no one until she got there, but then there was a steady stream of traffic, their headlights cutting swathes through the darkness, far more than she had expected . . . but they were all going the wrong way, away from Cape Town rather than towards it. Anna stood and watched them, waiting for someone coming the other way, and smiled to herself. She had not done this since she had been a teenager, hitchhiking her way across France. She had

had some exciting times, then. Nearly twenty years ago. What memories those days brought back: before Papagopoulos. But she had no desire to turn back the clock. She had been poor then.

A car pulled right across the road to stop beside her. "Going somewhere?" a voice asked.

Anna peered into the gloom. There were three men in the car, two in the front and one in the back. It was difficult to be certain, but she decided they were all white. She still did not like the look of them.

"Nowhere you can take me," she told them.

"Now, lady, is that any way to talk to a friend? You tell us where you want to go, and we'll take you."

"I wish to go to D.F. Malan Airport," Anna said. "Not to Malmesbury."

"Lady," said the man beside the driver. "You want to go to Malan, we will take you to Malan. Turn the car, Charlie."

"After the lady gets in," Charlie said.

"Open the door, Billy," the man said to the unsavoury-looking character in the back seat.

"I don't feel so good," Billy complained. "You fellows know I don't feel so good. You said we were going up to Malmesbury tonight, and Jo'burg tomorrow."

"Just open the door, Billy," Charlie the driver said. "You're not going to leave a lady in distress standing by the roadside?"

The rear door swung open, and Anna shook her head. They must think she was an innocent. "I'll wait for another lift," she said. "You fellows are in a hurry to get to Malmesbury. Don't let me keep you."

"For a looker like you, lady," said the co-driver, "we'd go to a lot more trouble than this."

"Listen," Anna said. "Get lost."

Billy merely blinked at her, but the co-driver got out of the front seat and came round the car. "I'm Paul," he said. "You didn't tell us your name."

Anna looked from him to the steady stream of cars on the far side of the road. "If you touch me," she said, loading her voice with all the venom she could, "I will have you gaoled."

"You're all confused, lady," Paul told her. "You want to get to the airport, and we have offered to take you there. Now, you getting in the back, or am I going to put you there?"

Anna glared at him, then ran round the car and on to the road. Instantly she was bathed in light and someone honked a horn at her. It was a warm evening; nearly all the cars had their windows down. "Stop!" Anna shouted. She waved her arms. "I need help! Stop!"

Now several horns blared, but no one stopped. Paul also came on to the road and, ignoring the headlights, grasped her round the waist and began to manhandle her to the parked car. She turned and scratched his face, turned again to look at the traffic, and screamed, "Help me, you bastards. Help me!"

She might have been shouting at the moon. Charlie the driver had also got out now, and he held her arms, twisting them behind her back while Paul dragged her round the car and pushed her in beside Billy.

Anna panted. "I am going to have you locked up," she snarled. "I am going to have you castrated."

She found herself pushed against Billy so hard she fell over and lay across his lap, her head against the outer door. Someone was getting in behind her, bundling up her legs.

"Move it," Paul said.

Charlie got behind the wheel and gunned the motor.

"The next turn off," Paul commanded.

Anna got her breath back and pushed herself up, having to thrust down on Billy's thighs as she did so.

"Watch it," Billy growled. "I don't feel so good."

Paul held her waist and pulled her back against him, at the same time slipping his hands up to hold her breasts through her shirt; she never wore a bra. "Damn," he commented. "But we have a lot of woman here."

Fear began to replace anger as Anna realised what was going to happen. She wanted to hit and scratch and shout and scream, but that would only excite them. She drew long breaths while Paul slid his hands up and down, squeezing and massaging.

"I am a house guest of Jan Geller," Anna said. "You must have heard of Jan Geller."

"I've heard of him," Paul said, nuzzling her hair. His hands moved down to the waistband of her trousers.

"He'll have you gaoled," Anna said. "Listen, take me back to his house, it's just up that road, and I won't tell anyone."

"Later," Paul said. "There's a turning over there, Charlie."

"Got it," Charlie agreed, and the car slowed.

Fear and anger exploded in Anna's mind, and she attempted to turn and strike at Paul. He let her turn, and then tightened his arms and pressed down so that she fell across his lap in turn.

"Grab her legs," he told Billy. "Get those pants off."

Anna gasped and tried to free her arms, but Paul was holding them pressed against his body. Then she tried to bite his leg – her face was against his thigh – but couldn't get her teeth through the material. And now she felt Billy pulling her pants down and taking the knickers with them. She screamed and tried to kick, got one leg free and had it seized, and was struck a resounding slap on the bare buttocks.

"Ow!" she screamed. "You bloody bastards. You . . . "

"Far enough," Paul said. "Or I'll burst."

The car stopped, and Anna made another effort to push herself up. But the door was opening, and Charlie was standing there. He grasped her ankles and pulled her out. Her body and then her face banged the seat and then the doorstep, and her head began to spin. Then she struck the ground with another thud. Before she could recover she was lying on her back, her pants had been pulled right off, and someone was tearing her blouse open to expose her breasts. Someone else, Charlie, was kneeling above her head holding her arms pressed into the earth. Billy was holding her legs, and Paul was taking off his pants.

She tried to roll and twist herself free, ground her golden hair into the earth, gasped and spat. But she could not fight them. Paul knelt astride her chest and flopped himself into her face. "You bite, and I'll cut your tits off," he warned her.

Despite nearly suffocating from the sour stench of his matted pubic hair, wild thoughts roamed through Anna's mind that if she gave him what he wanted he mightn't actually rape her. But after only a few seconds he took his penis away and slid down her body to kneel between her legs. Billy had released her right leg, but was still holding her left one, pulling it to one side and pushing it up. She tried to kick the free leg, and had the thigh gripped by Paul, so tightly his fingers seemed to be forcing their way into the flesh. She screamed with pain, and he slapped her face.

"You lie still and enjoy it," he told her. "Or we're going to hurt you too bad."

Anna subsided, allowed her legs to be pushed up, allowed him to enter. She was exhausted. She could do no more until she got free. Then, oh then . . .

She realised Paul was finished and Charlie was taking his turn.

I'll have them castrated, she thought. God, I'll do it myself. I'll . . .

Charlie was mercifully quick. Both he and Paul had held themselves off her, but now it was Billy's turn, and to her disgust he actually lay down on her, searching for entry with his fingers. Anna moaned with self-horror. Love play. Her favourite pastime. But she thought that if any man, even Peter, ever touched her there again she would kill him.

"I don't feel so good," Billy explained, as he surged back and forth, his cheek grinding against hers. "God, my head hurts. God . . . " blood gushed from his nose on to her face.

"Aaagh!" she screamed. "Aaagh!".

"For God's sake," Paul commented. "What's the matter with you?"

"Christ, I don't feel good." Billy rolled sideways.

Charlie looked down at him. "He ain't going to make it," he remarked. "Let's get the hell out of here."

They left Anna lying on the verge, got into the car, turned it, and drove back towards the main road. Anna lay still for several seconds, then painfully she sat up. She ached all over; her mind was almost vacant – shell-shocked. But as she moved, awareness returned. Her thighs were sticky and there was an increasing urge to vomit. Turning on to her knees she swept a hand to and fro in the darkness, cutting the fingers on thorns and sharp dry grass stalks, until she found her trousers. She was reluctant to pull them on over the mess, but her bag was gone and there was nothing with which to clean herself . . . as though she could ever feel clean again. So she sat on the ground amongst the cruel stalks and slowly shoved each foot down a leg, not even knowing if the trousers were inside out. And when she stood to pull them up she realised her shoes were gone . . . Gathering her torn blouse together she staggered in what she hoped was the general direction of the road. She ached and she stank and she hated. And the skin on her face and hands was stiffly caked, with blood.

Billy's blood.

16

The Shortest-lived Virus

Meg Calhoun pushed hair from her eyes and rubbed them at the same time; they kept drooping shut. In the past four days she had not slept more than eight hours, and then only curled on the settee in her office outside the laboratory. She had not been back to the apartment in that time, had not bathed and hardly eaten. Now she wearily fixed her eye once more to the electron microscope.

Fitzroy, on the far side of the laboratory, was hardly in better shape. But neither would he give up the quest. Until the quest gave them up, driven as they were by several unacceptable factors, from the news that kept drifting in to the news that did not: there was still no word of Sally Ann and Rod and their friends, vanished into the catastrophe that was Chile. And they were chased by constant telephone calls from the Governor and from Washington, at last alerted to the possibility that the world might be about to fall apart without even any political decision to be taken.

They had started with high hopes, as they had gone through the initial stages. They had begun, of course, with salt solutions, because a large number of viruses are extremely susceptible to salt. When that had not worked they had had to go further afield, and begin combinations, which were endless. Their experimental animal population had taken a beating. Meg hated injecting something as fatal as the Red Death virus into the rabbits and monkeys, but there was no alternative. The moment the blood taken from one of her fishes was in the animal bloodstream, samples were drawn off continually to observe how it worked.

It worked with horrifying efficiency. The A-protein attached itself to the blood cell it intended to use, and replication began even before it reached the bone marrow. There it went wild, for perhaps forty-eight, occasionally seventy-two hours, before dying. It was as if, after being suspended in time for a hundred thousand years, it could not wait to complete its life cycle.

It was at least satisfactory to have her theory proven. The fish blood, warmed and then combined with animal tissue and kept for three days before being injected into a rabbit, was harmless. But how to arrest it for three days in its natural state?

She sighed, and tried another combination.

"Meg!" Fitzroy said.

Wearily she raised her head.

"Look at Bruno," Fitzroy said.

The animals were in cages on the far side of the room. Bruno was a sakkiwinki monkey, who had been vaccinated with contaminated blood the previous day. Now he stared back at Meg, absently chewing a peanut. His pinched face was as ever contorted but with pleasure rather than discomfort.

She frowned and punched her computer.

"How long?" Fitzroy asked.

"Twenty-seven hours."

"When last did you take an rbc?"

"At twenty-four. It was normal then."

That did not mean a thing; some animals, like some humans, resisted the virus longer than others.

"Twenty-seven," Fitzroy said. "That's the longest so far, isn't it?"

"Yes."

"Then he's the boy to watch. Solution?"

Meg was already punching the computer again. "Excess DNA."

"Holy Jumping Jesus. Not griseofulvin? As simple as that?"

"Just an idea," Meg confessed. "We'd need one hell of a lot of it."

"It's on the shelves. It can be manufactured."

"I guess. But we'll also need a retaining agent. We'll give Bruno the full seventy-two hours, though. And we don't know what damage is being done to the host. There'll have to be tests on that."

"Griseofulvin," Fitzroy muttered, scratching his head. "Puts the little bastard to sleep with indigestion. Answers are always simple, when you know them. Meg, you are a genius. This is going under your name."

She shook her head. "I should've tried it earlier, but . . ."

"It only works with viruses originating in certain fungi."

"And I didn't think this baby could possibly be a fungoid virus. But of course it makes sense. Sloths, even giant sloths, even megatheriums, live off of trees . . . and fungi."

"You got there, Meg. Congratulations."

"We're a team, Gray. You'd have tried it, sooner or later."

"I'm the boss of the team, woman. I say what goes. This credit is yours. You know something, you could just have saved mankind."

"Only if Bruno comes through. And if the side-effects are acceptable. And if we can get enough griseofulvin . . . in time."

"I'm sorry, Mr Canning," the girl said. "But it is simply not possible to raise New Zealand."

Peter sighed. "Keep trying. What about Cape Town?"

"There is no reply from Cape Town either."

That figured, going by the latest news. Poor Anna. Her wealth was not going to help her this time. She had told him on the phone she would return as soon as she could get a flight. But if she was now caught up in the middle of the explosion that was South Africa, there was absolutely nothing she could do about it. There was nothing anyone could do about it . . . except Meg and Fitzroy. Maybe.

"I have the Koch Research Center on the line," the girl said.

"Thank God for that." His heart began to pound, as it always did at the thought of hearing that quiet voice. But like everyone else he was trying to contact, Meg had been unreachable for the past couple of days. He did not know if she was going to be available now.

"Margaret Calhoun."

"Meg!"

"Peter!"

Was that warmth? he wondered.

"I've been trying to reach you for days."

"I've been kind of busy."

"Any joy?"

"Could be." There was a note of suppressed excitement in her voice.

"Serious?"

"Oh, yes. We've unearthed what could be a solution. Just this morning. But the operative word is 'could', Peter."

"When will you know for sure?"

"Forty-eight hours should do it. But there are other tests to be made. We're really talking about four days."

"Meg . . . have you been watching the news?"

"Not really. But I know it's all hell out there."

"You can say that again. Can you tell me what you've found?"

There was a brief hesitation. Then she said, "It's very simple, really. We tried adding griseofulvin to one of our phages."

"Griseofulvin?"

"It's an antibiotic which increases the rate of synthesis in deoxyribonucleic acid. That's DNA to you."

"I thought DNA was what gave us genes, and heredity?"

"It is, in a sense. DNA gives the orders to each cell, tells it what to do, and how, and when. It's also present in viruses, of course. It so happens that we are beginning to think that an excess of it keeps the virus inanimate for at least a further forty-eight hours, even in warm blood. And it won't live for more than seventy-two hours in warm blood. A monkey we contaminated with the solution has shown no ill effects for that time. Now there could be a hundred and one reasons for this which have nothing to do with DNA. But it's the first positive response we've come across."

"That's terrific."

"If true. But Peter, as I said, there's a lot of work to be done. We don't know, for instance, what side-effects this is having on the host. That has to be investigated most thoroughly before we can go any further. There's no point in saving the world from the Red Death if, just for example, we were to upset the whole genetic pattern."

"Is that possible?"

"Certainly. Any messing about with DNA could do that. There is also the point that griseofulvin is usually administered when there is a virus known to be present in the host. We can't wait for that with the Red Death. We have to find something to add to it so that it will be retained in the system until needed."

"But you're hopeful."

"Sure. I'm an optimist."

"Meg, the PM is coming back from the Paris meeting today. There's to be a full Cabinet tomorrow morning. Can I give them what you've told me?"

This time the hesitation was longer. "It has to be absolutely confidential, Peter, until we know more about it. To let the media or the public get into the act and try to push us before we've investigated this development thoroughly could be disastrous."

"It will be confidential. Cabinet meetings always are."

"Except when something is deliberately leaked."

"I'll see this isn't," he vowed then, as an afterthought, asked, "Any news of Sally Ann?"

"No."

"Meg, when will I see you again?"

"I really have no idea."

"Meg . . . I love you."

"Um," she said, and hung up.

She still had not entirely forgiven him. But she was still prepared to confide in him, which had to be something. Just speaking with her made him feel happy again. And like everyone else, he desperately needed something to give him a lift, as the news got worse and worse.

Not being members of the Cabinet, although deeply involved, he and Hartley were given chairs at the end of the table while the ministers, recalled from all over the country, took their places and the preliminaries were gone through.

"I am happy to say," the Prime Minister began, "that there is a considerable measure of agreement within the Common Market, and I have also been in touch, by phone, with the President. Before I outline the joint measures which have been concerted, I think we should have a full up-date on the situation. Charles?"

The Foreign Secretary cleared his throat and brushed the few remaining stray hairs back on his scalp. "As you know, we have colour-coded the various situations.

Condition Black indicates that there is no information emerging from a country at all; it may therefore be assumed that all communication has broken down. Condition Red indicates that the Red Death is known to be rampant in a country, but that governmental authority is being maintained. Condition Purple means that not only is the disease rampant, but that governmental authority is breaking down, or has already done so. Condition Yellow means that cases of the disease have been reported, but it has not yet reached epidemic proportions. Condition Green means disease free. Now . . . " he indicated the huge world map which was at that moment being unrolled and pinned into place against the wall by two of his secretaries. Every head turned to see the situation.

"You will observe," the Foreign Secretary continued, "that the trend really is rather disturbing, not to say alarming." He touched South America with his wand. "Chile and Argentina are both black, Uruguay, Paraguay and Bolivia are purple, Brazil and Peru are red and are estimated to be going purple at any moment, and all the rest are red. Mexico and now this small portion of the United States around Andrews Air Force Base are yellow. Remember the crew of that relief aircraft. The Americans swear that these cases have been isolated and none others reported."

"But Mexico? You mean it has by-passed the rest of Central America?" the Prime Minister asked.

"I'm afraid so. To complete the American picture, there has been shooting along the line of the Panama Canal between American troops and Colombians attempting to flee north. Obviously the business of stopping people from attempting to leave by boat or plane is an acute one. The US navy is present in strength in the Caribbean, but they have not the right, at least as yet, to bring down an aircraft which merely ignores their orders." He glanced at the Prime Minister.

"We'll come to that later. Take us through the rest of the world."

"Well, you'll see that New Zealand continues to be red, and nothing more, although conditions down there are catastrophic. Australia has now also to be classed as red, although Western Australia remains green. The biggest problem is Asia. You'll observe that the area around Calcutta is black. Reports speak of thousands of people just lying dead in the streets; it is said you can smell the city a hundred miles off. The result of all this, of course, is that those who survive the Red Death are dying of cholera and typhoid. But we suspect this is happening in all infected countries. Bangladesh is at least purple and will soon be black."

"Are we still sending them relief?"

"Well, Prime Minister, it isn't easy. A large number of doctors and nurses and just plain volunteer workers went to these areas as soon as the disease was reported, together with all the available supplies of phosphorus and busulfan, but it really has been like emptying buckets into the ocean and expecting to draw up fresh water. Additionally, a considerable number of the volunteers have died of the disease, and naturally there are less people now coming forward. I can't say I blame them."

The Prime Minister nodded. "Go on."

"Well, the rest of India, and the countries of South-East Asia, are red and expected soon to be purple. Indonesia is already purple. Pakistan remains yellow. Now, there is a difficulty about both China and Russia. Both claim to remain green, and we know they are exerting the most prodigious efforts to patrol their borders. People have been killed trying to cross without authorisation. But there is no doubt in my mind that infected sufferers have got across, and that the Russians who at least admit they have it, don't seem to have much idea of the extent. Japan is still green. Like us, they have imposed blood tests.

"Turning to Africa, South Africa is red and spreading purple. There is widespread bloodshed down there. All the states south of the Sahara are at least yellow. The pattern is therefore very clear: black, red and purple, then yellow, cover the entire Southern Hemisphere and are now moving north. Green stretches from Japan through China and Russia to Europe. I am inclined, at the present, to go along with the American claim that they have things under control there. But every day the other colours swell outwards a little more."

"Thank you, Charles," the Prime Minister said. "The situation which faces us is therefore composed of two conflicting requirements. Firstly, to keep the green areas of the world green, and secondly, to alleviate the suffering in the rest of the world until a cure for this Red Death can be found. I have to tell you that in Paris the general feeling was that preventing the spread of the disease to Europe was regarded as the first priority. Nor is this mere chauvinism. It must be recognised that our ability to save the world can only depend upon our ability to save ourselves. There is an analogy here with 1940, except that today we have a considerable portion of the world standing shoulder to shoulder with us to resist the peril we are now in.

"In the first instance, therefore, our European colleagues and ourselves have reaffirmed our commitment to closing our borders, except to those people who submit to a blood test and the necessary quarantine. The second important matter is food and fuel supplies. The Red Death has not yet reached the Middle East, but may be expected to do so almost any day; already there is talk of the various bulk carrier fleets refusing to operate in those waters. Anthony, perhaps you would be good enough to update us on the fuel situation?"

The Minister for Energy polished his rimless glasses and checked his notes. "We have oil stocks for sixty days. Coal is of course not a problem, at least in the short term. But with this looming miners' dispute I wouldn't like to forecast the situation in six months' time."

"We are, it seems, marginally better off than most other countries in Western Europe," the Prime Minister said. "For fuel. Martin?"

The Minister of Agriculture shook his head; his tie as usual had slipped an inch down from his top button and in general he looked as if he might just have come in from milking cows himself. "Food stocks are already down with the closing of South American and New Zealand sources. I'm afraid we will reach a critical position in less than two months."

"It is against this background that our European colleagues and ourselves have decided to act with as much unity as we can," the Prime Minister stated. "The measures we have agreed include a sharing of all essential supplies, from fuel to food."

The Minister for Energy was polishing his rimless glasses again. "The country won't like it."

"They will have to accept it. I may add that, as I have told you, I have spoken with the President, and will be visiting Washington next week further to concert our efforts." The Prime Minister gave a brief smile. "I am informed that I will have to take a blood test before being allowed to disembark. Now, there is also the question of finance. Bobby?"

The Chancellor of the Exchequer looked like a disgruntled bear. "You will all have seen what has been happening to the stock markets. There has been nothing like it since 1929. And this may well get worse. Gold is now fetching £1200 an ounce, and is expected to go higher. The mentality of some people is impossible to understand. How anyone can suppose that locking himself up with a fortune in gold is either going to keep out the Red Death or enable him to

306

buy food when there isn't any defeats me. But there it is.

"To compound matters, there is naturally a trade problem developing. The full impact of this cannot yet be gauged, as it has all happened so suddenly, but we know that the loss, however temporarily, of our traditional markets in Africa and southern Asia is going to have a crippling effect on British industry. Unless this thing is brought under control very shortly, I would expect massive redundancies by the end of the year. However, in this regard I am accompanying the Prime Minister to New York at the end of next week, and would hope to complete negotiations there for worldwide co-operation to relieve the financial crisis."

"All of these necessary measures are going to require the force of law," the Prime Minister said, "and it has therefore also been mutually decided that we will take all emergency powers necessary to implement our decisions. The bill is being prepared now, and will be presented on Monday. As you know, Parliament has already been recalled. We may expect some opposition, so this will be a three-line whip. The measures may seem Draconian, as regards rationing of both food and petrol, and restrictions on the right to strike, as severe as anything seen during the Second World War, but I will say again that we are in a position as serious, if not more serious, now as then. Regarding the use of maximum force to prevent unauthorised entry to this or any country, we are again, at present, in a more fortunate position than most in this island, but in the interests of unity I have agreed to place such a law upon the statute books for the duration of the emergency. I may add that the President is sending a similar package of legislation to Congress."

"Do I understand you to say, Prime Minister, that you are proposing to ask Parliament for powers enabling the armed services to shoot to kill anyone who attempts unauthorised entry into Great Britain?" asked the Home Secretary. He was a precise little man who had an irritating habit of tapping his teeth with a pencil; he had been doing so for some time this morning.

"Into the Common Market," the Prime Minister said carefully.

"That's going to go down a bomb," muttered Jeremy.

"We are, in effect, asking for the imposition of martial law for the duration of the emergency," the Prime Minister said. "The bill also authorises increased taxation where necessary to meet the costs ahead; it may be necessary for you to present an interim budget, Bobby, but we will make a decision on that when we return from Washington. I repeat, I am aware that these are extreme measures, having regard to the fact that there has been no outbreak of the Red Death in this country. However, I have been given to understand, by you, Jeremy, and your colleague, that the appearance of one case in Britain would very probably be followed by an epidemic as severe as that which has ravaged New Zealand. This Government naturally simply cannot afford to take the risk of that happening. Our measures must be ample enough, and severe enough, to prevent it happening. I therefore expect one hundred per cent support and co-operation from my colleagues." The Prime Minister looked around the faces. No one dissented, although most of the ministers were looking very grim.

"Thank you," the Prime Minister said. "Now Peter, can you bring us up-to-date on the efforts of your American friends?"

"I can, Prime Minister, and I am happy to say that progress is being made. Before I go on, however, I must say that my information is entirely confidential, and must remain so, until the results of experiments presently being carried out are completed."

It was his turn to look around their faces, and although there was no dissent, he discerned a good deal of impatience; he was the youngest person in the room and by far the most junior.

"There is no question but that your confidence will be respected, Peter," the Prime Minister said.

"Thank you." Peter then proceeded to outline his conversation with Meg.

"That does indeed sound hopeful," the Prime Minister observed when he was finished.

"Except that here we have another case of these scientists messing about," growled the Foreign Secretary. "Work should be put in hand at once. We are going to need vast stocks of the stuff."

"Sir Hartley," the Prime Minister said, "have we the capability in this country to manufacture large amounts of this, ah . . . "

"Griseofulvin," Peter murmured.

"Quite."

"There is some already available, in small quantities, under various brand names, and more can be manufactured, of course," Hartley said. "But on a large scale it will be a long process. And I may say, an expensive one. There will have to be extensive tests to establish what side-effects, if any, can be expected. These could be serious."

"If it really can act as a vaccine against the Red Death, we will have to chance the side-effects. It will also require manufacture on a worldwide scale, and will have to be made available free," the Prime Minister commented.

"Then the drug firms will require government financing of a very substantial nature," Hartley said without hesitation.

"Now wait just a moment," the Chancellor said.

"With respect, Bobby," the Prime Minister interrupted. "If we are going to end this epidemic the cost will have to be immaterial. I have said that if necessary we will not hesitate to impose additional taxes. But the burden must be equally shared."

"You intend to put that to Parliament as well?"

"When I am in possession of all the facts, yes. I would be obliged, Sir Hartley, if you would immediately mount an investigation into what is involved and let me have a detailed breakdown. I would like this by the weekend."

"I will proceed with that right away, Prime Minister."

"You will allow yourself, and any other company which may be given the mandate, a profit in keeping with the situation, but in any event not greater than ten per cent."

Sir Hartley gave a little gulp. "You might find it difficult to persuade other manufacturers to devote themselves to such a project without adequate return."

The Prime Minister's smile was cold. "That will be my concern."

"But you are prepared to do so, Hartley?" demanded the Chancellor.

Sir Hartley's hesitation was brief. "Yes," he said. "Because I understand the seriousness of the situation. Not all of my colleagues do. I would estimate that very few people in the country do."

"I intend to spell it out to the country in Parliament next week," the Prime Minister assured him. "It would be most satisfactory if I could tell the House then that measures to end the spread of the disease are in hand."

"Ahem," Peter said.

Heads turned to look at him.

"I have asked for, and have been given, by you, Prime Minister, an assurance that the information given me by Dr Calhoun will remain confidential until their tests have been completed. As Sir Hartley has said, these tests are necessary to establish what risk of side-effects may be expected if the drug is widely used."

"You assured me that the tests would be completed within four days. Parliament does not meet for five."

"The tests will be completed in four days if all goes well. I must stress, however, that it could well turn out that an attack on the virus's deoxyribonucleic acid is a false trail, or an unacceptable one. I must ask for a further assurance that the information will not be released in the event that the tests have not proved conclusive at the end of four days."

"You are being absurd," snapped the Chancellor. "People are dying out there."

"I am sorry, I have given my word," Peter said. "I must insist that my word be honoured."

There was an uneasy silence while they glared at him, then the Prime Minister gave another wintry smile. "While it is essential that one should be aware a bridge lies in front of one, it is always a waste of time attempting to cross it until it is reached. You will bring me up-to-date on the situation on Sunday, Peter; I shall be remaining in town this weekend. Meanwhile there can be no harm in Sir Hartley preparing the report I require."

"Providing it can be done in confidence," Peter said.

"I am sure Sir Hartley will be the soul of discretion," the Prime Minister said.

"I'm sorry, Mr Canning," Helen said. "But Meg isn't available right now. Things are a little fraught here."

"They are more than a little fraught here too," Peter told her. "Helen, I simply have to speak with Meg. Ask her to call me immediately she has a moment to spare. Tell her it really is most urgent."

"I'll do that, Mr Canning," Helen promised.

Peter hung up, remained staring at the phone. It was Saturday evening, four days since he had last spoken with Meg: tomorrow he had to see the Prime Minister. He simply had to have clearance from her

311

or be told that the DNA clue was negative. Was she avoiding him again?

They were four days in which the black, red, purple and yellow catastrophe had crept a little further over the map of the world, with Turkey, the Middle East and Egypt now definitely infected areas; days in which civilisation seemed to have receded a little further, in which more billions had been wiped off the stock markets. Four days in which there had still been no news of Sarah or Anna. Four days in which the world had gone just a little more mad.

The telephone jangled, and he snatched at it. "Meg?"

"I have Lady Briggs on the line, Mr Canning," the girl said.

"Oh," Peter commented.

"Peter," Claudia remarked, "you might sound a little more pleased to hear from me. Are you going to be able to visit Ma and Pa tomorrow?"

'I'm afraid it doesn't look like it. There's almost certainly a full scale debate coming up the moment Parliament reassembles on Monday, and we're all of us rushing around like chickens with our heads cut off."

"What a delightful simile," Claudia said. "Very well, I'll go down tomorrow afternoon. Will you join Hartley and me at church tomorrow?"

Peter hesitated. But he did feel like going to church. There did not seem to be anywhere else to turn.

"My text this morning is a short one," the Bishop said. "As well as a familiar one. It is taken from the Epistle of Paul to the Romans, Chapter 6, Verse 23, and says simply: 'the wages of sin is death'." He paused to look over the St Paul's congregation, which was more crowded than usual this morning.

" 'The wages of sin is death.' This is more than a biblical law. It is a law of nature, as immutable as nature itself. The wages of sin is death. And these wages now surround us, surround all mankind, with terrifying intent.

"Every day when I open my newspaper, I read of the spread of this disease we call the Red Death. In the past two months tens of thousands of people have died of it, and the number may be far greater than that. Nor is there any sign of its fury abating, of our puny human abilities being able to discover a cure or even a palliative. Truly it is, the wages of sin.

"And do we not deserve it? Have we not deserved it for many years, even many generations? We have lived our lives here on this Earth, pursuing our pleasures, and our profits, with increasing disregard of the Almighty who is the fount of all things, who placed us here, and who, we are too apt to forget, has the power to remove us whenever He chooses.

"There have been warnings enough, which we have ignored. There have been portents enough, which we have not heeded. Now the vengeance of the Lord is at hand. If it has not yet reached this green and pleasant land, no one can doubt it is on its way. No man may hold up his hand and say, thus far and no further, to the Red Death.

"Yet, my friends, it surely lies within ourselves to combat this disease. It lies within our own hearts to decide whether we choose to walk on the broad uplands, secure in God's protection. It is up to us to choose the path of righteousness, to turn our back on the materialism that is so rampant in our world. God is watching us. He is waiting. He is a forgiving God, this we know. He is a loving God, this we know. He is above all a merciful God, this too we know. He but seeks a sign, surely, that we are prepared to atone for our sins that he may raise His hand, and check the onset of this disease. Without Him, we are nothing. With Him, we are everything. My friends, will you join me in prayer, and more than prayer, that we will jointly and severally reaffirm our faith, our belief, and our determination to turn our lives once more into the pathway of God, as revealed to us by our Saviour Jesus Christ?"

"I sometimes think the old boy has gone a little gaga," Claudia remarked as they stood on the steps of the cathedral.

"Prayer has always been a pretty powerful factor when the chips are down," her brother observed. "There can be no doubt that sufficient faith does give people an extra strength."

"That's why Hartley's a millionaire," Claudia pointed out. "People have faith that the pills he sells them will cure them of whatever they have. They don't always work."

"I suspect Briggs and Company has a slightly better track record than the Almighty," Hartley protested.

"Wait for the thunderbolt," Peter quipped, and gave a sigh; he recognised the man approaching him.

"Tiller of the *Globe*, Mr Canning. Would you like to offer an opinion on the Halley theory?"

"I've never heard of it."

"Well, Professor Constant, the astonomer, blames Halley's Comet for the outbreak of the Red Death."

"Good grief. That's pushing it a bit. Halley's Comet was several years ago."

"Agreed. But the professor points out that the comet passed by Earth in 1910, and he is convinced that its appearance was responsible for the outbreak of the First World War, four years later, and for all the thirty years of catastrophe that followed."

"Ah," Peter said. "I'd prefer not to comment on that."

"Then may I take it you disagree with the professor?"

"I'd prefer not to comment on that either. Now you really must excuse me, old chap, but I have somewhere to go."

"Nuttier and nuttier," Claudia remarked, as they went towards the car. "I mean to say, a professor like Constant . . ."

"Everyone goes a bit nutty in a situation like this," Hartley observed.

"All the more reason for keeping our heads. Oh lord! This just isn't my day."

He watched Colin Brereton approaching. He had spotted the Opposition spokesman in the cathedral, but they had done no more than nod a greeting. But now Brereton was wearing that at-peace-with-the-world expression which his opponents had come to fear. He had, in fact, kept a very low profile recently, but no one could doubt he had a great deal up his sleeve – not least his ambition to replace Toby Anstruther as Leader of the Opposition. This looming crisis might well provide him with the ammunition he needed to shoot down both the Government and his own leadership for their inability to cope.

"Peter! Hartley! Claudia!" He shook hands with the men, kissed Claudia on the cheek. "Just the people I wanted to see."

"I really have to rush, Colin," Peter said. "Tomorrow's going to be a busy day."

"Oh, indeed," Brereton agreed. "I can't remember when last Parliament was recalled in the middle of the summer recess. But I agree things are serious. There's a rumour you will lead for the Government."

"Just a rumour, Colin. I'm not up there."

"But you're the actual head of this task force we've been hearing about." He glanced at Hartley.

"You could say that."

"Then could you tell me how true it is that your American friends have already found a vaccine which will immunise man against the Red Death, but are refusing to release it?"

Peter stared at him with his mouth open.

Brereton smiled. "I see that it is true."

"It is absolutely untrue," Peter told him. "The Koch Center is pursuing several lines, some of which are more hopeful than others. They are confident of achieving a breakthrough, but they have not yet done so. Now would you mind telling me where you got that information?"

Brereton tapped his nose. "I will be raising the matter in the debate."

"I thought you might," Peter grunted. He hurried home and tried calling Meg again, but got only her ansaphone at the apartment, and an 'unavailable' from the Center; this time he did not get even as far as Helen.

17

Despair

"Hi, Helen," Amanda Fitzroy said. "Think I could speak to Dad?"

"Is it urgent, Mandy? The Prof is real busy." Helen's voice sounded very weary from the other side of the country.

"Ah. Any chance of Meg?"

"She's in there with him. I've orders to let nothing interrupt them." She giggled. "I've even had to put the White House on hold."

"Um." Amanda said. "Well, if one of them could call me, just as soon as possible . . . "

"I'll make a note. I have a list here a mile long. Is it a domestic or business matter?"

"A bit of both, really. I'm worried about Tom Lintell. He really is depressed. If there is anything they could possibly give me to cheer him up . . . "

"Tell him they're both pretty optimistic," Helen suggested.

"Are they really, Helen?"

"No lie," Helen said. "They can see daylight, Mandy. Cross my heart."

"Oh, boy," Amanda said. "That is just what I wanted to hear."

She put down the phone, hurried out of the New York office and along the corridor into the main gallery of the museum. It was late afternoon and the crowds had somewhat thinned; the megatherium was still doing good business, but the initial impact had dwindled, and people had other things on their minds.

Tom Lintell sat on one of the benches facing the exhibition, just like any customer, gazing at the find which had made him world-famous. His dream, Amanda thought, gone sour.

It was a magnificent exhibit, mounted on its hind legs, eating plastic leaves from the branch of a plastic tree, towering forty feet from the floor to the specially raised ceiling. The beast to end all beasts. And it had come damn near doing just that, she thought.

She sat beside her boss. For a moment he did not appear to notice her, then he glanced at her, looked straight again. "We'll burn it," he said.

"Tom . . ." she rested her hand on his arm. A little group of people had arrived in front of the megatherium, and were peering both at it and the legend. They oohed and aahed for several minutes, then continued on their way.

"Do you realise," Lintell said, "that if those folks knew it was that beast started the Red Death, they'd lynch me?"

"Of course they wouldn't. How were you to know? Anyway, listen, I've been on the phone to San Francisco. They think they may have something."

He glanced at her, his face a mask of misery.

"Honest to God," she said. "Isn't that wonderful?"

"Will it bring back to life all the people who have already died? Or who will die before they can be immunised?"

"Well . . . " she had no answer to that.

Lintell stood up. "I hate you!" he shouted at the exhibit. "I hate you!"

Heads turned, and Amanda also got up. "Tom," she said. "Please."

"Go home," Lintell told her. "Go home and leave me alone."

"Tom . . . "

"Go home, God damn it," he snapped, and strode off towards the office. There he locked the door so that she could not get at him, stood at the window looking out at the busy street beneath him. After five minutes he closed and locked the window as well, sat at his desk, his head resting on his hands. He remained motionless for several minutes.

It had to come out eventually. The whole story. If he did not become the most loathed man in the world he would certainly become the most pitied. The man who had so carelessly opened Pandora's Box, and left not even hope behind. Of course Fitzroy and Calhoun were confident. They were always confident. But even if they were right they would not be able to avert this calamity; it was happening too fast.

All his life he had dreamed of going down in history. Well, he was going to do that now. Supposing there was anyone around to write it. Or read it. He had no desire to wait to find out. He had no desire to wait until tomorrow to discover how many more thousands had succumbed.

He emptied his pockets of everything they contained, got up, unlocked the door and went outside. He walked through the now almost empty museum, nodded goodnight to the guards. Then he went out of the front doors into the still bright July evening, mingled with the crowds as he walked towards the subway.

"Oh, you'll be well enough to travel, Mrs Papagopoulos," the doctor said. "There's no question about that. All the bruises are coming along well. I won't call again."

He looked exhausted. He was working round the clock, to no avail. And the woman on the bed was suffering more from hysteria than any actual ailment. He was in no mood to try curing that, at this moment.

Anna watched the door close, and Jan gave her a bright smile. "There. No problem."

"No problem." She shuddered. All the bruises are coming along well. What about the bruises inside her? She knew she was not at all recovered. She had a headache all the time, and a pain in her gut. She did not feel like either eating or drinking. Or making love. She thought she would never feel like making love again. But then, Jan clearly did not feel like making love either. He had not felt like making love, at least to her, since he had come home and been told by Thomas how she had stumbled back through the night, her clothes torn and bloodstained.

"And tomorrow you'll be out of the country," Jan said.

"Thank God for that. Jan . . . " A week ago she had wanted to leave him as much as his country. Now she wanted him to come. She wanted company, reliable company. She was afraid of being alone.

He shook his head. "I can't, baby. It would be letting the Government down if any prominent people started to run. We can control this thing. It got out of hand last weekend, but now we have the cities cordoned off, and are stopping movement. Now that we have the blacks herded into their villages and are keeping them there, we're getting on top of it."

Anna disliked thinking about that. The Africans were dying like flies, and no one was doing anything about it except to shoot them if they tried to get out of their allotted areas. Besides, it was not black men who had raped her.

"Have they arrested them yet?" she asked.

"No. The chances are remote."

He was not interested, the beast. He thought the whole thing was her fault, for leaving the house. He had offered not a word of sympathy. Neither had the police or the doctor. She hated them all. She hated this place.

"They could be anywhere," Jan explained, not for the first time. "The news of that fresh outbreak had everyone hysterical. They were fleeing north before the police could put a stop to it. Those fellows are probably in Zimbabwe, by now."

"I hope they caught it," Anna said. "I hope they all die."

"You just relax," Jan said. "Think of that plane tomorrow. Would you like a drink?"

She sighed. She did not really. But a drink might make her feel better. "Champagne."

"Why not?" Jan rang the bell for Thomas. "I'll join you."

Thomas brought the bottle in its ice bucket and two flutes. Jan opened it himself, poured, gave her a glass. "Wrap yourself around that."

"Aaah." She drank, reached out to place the half empty glass on her bedside table, and gazed in horror at the blood spotting her bed jacket. A moment later it had become a torrent. "Jan!" she gasped.

She heard the tinkle of a shattering glass as he leapt away from the bed.

"Jan," she wailed, spitting blood. "Help me!"

"You . . . you have it," he shouted. "You got it from those men."

"I have a nose bleed," she screamed.

"It's a symptom. Oh, my God! The Red Death, in my house!"

"Fetch a towel," she howled; her nightdress was flooded with blood. As she had always slept nude before her rape, it had only been worn twice.

Jan ran from the room. Anna gasped, and licked blood from her lips, and tried to breathe through her nostrils, but they were still blocked. She tried to get out of bed, and fell to her knees, still pouring blood which soaked the white rug beneath her. She remembered that ghastly man, Billy or something, who had had a nose bleed when he had been lying on her. Could he have given her the disease? But that was impossible. She was Anna Papagopoulos. She was not going to die of the Red Death. She could not.

Her head jerked to the sound of a car engine being gunned in the drive. Jan was leaving. He was going to fetch a doctor. But surely he could have telephoned. The stupid fool had forgotten the towel.

She pressed the bell, sat against the bed, mopping her face with the sheet. The bed would have to be stripped and re-made, anyway.

"Mistress?" Thomas stood in the doorway, staring at her.

"Where has Mr Geller gone?" Anna panted.

"I don't know, Mistress. He just left. Mistress . . . "

"I need warm water," Anna said. "And you'll have to send the maids up to change the sheets."

Thomas made no reply, and Anna raised her head, saw him backing towards the door. His expression was very similar to that of Jan's, a few minutes before.

"It's a nose bleed," she shouted. "Just a nose bleed. For God's sake . . . a nose bleed," she sobbed, as Thomas turned and ran down the stairs.

Clutching at the sheets, Anna struggled to her feet. Half blinded with tears she could hardly see what she was doing, swept the champagne bucket from the table with a resounding crash, staggered to the door.

"Thomas!" she screamed. "Don't leave me. For God's sake, don't leave me."

She staggered across the gallery, half fell down the curving staircase to the ground floor.

"Thomas!" she screamed. "Thomas! Thomas!" she reached the ground floor, on her hands and knees. "Don't leave me."

She listened to shouts and the banging of doors . . . then there was no sound. She got to her feet and staggered across the lounge on to the verandah, looked out at the drive, saw the servants bicycling towards the road. They had gone, like Jan. But Jan was surely coming back, with a doctor.

She collapsed at the top of the steps. Jan was surely coming back.

18

Majority Decision and
Unanimous Dissent

When Peter attended the Prime Minister's office that
Sunday afternoon he was surprised to find not only
Jeremy and the Chancellor already there, but also Colin
Brereton and the Leader of the Opposition.

"Ah, Peter," the Prime Minister greeted him. "What
have you got for us?"

Peter glanced at the two Opposition MPs.

"You may say whatever you wish," the Prime Minister
told him. "This thing is above party politics now."

Peter sighed. "I'm afraid I have nothing for you, Prime
Minister. I have been quite unable to raise either Dr
Fitzroy or Dr Calhoun since last we met."

"Mainly because they've been busy. In fact, they have
been in Washington, the last couple of days."

"How on earth . . .?" He checked himself.

The Prime Minister smiled. "I had a call from the
President this morning. Things are moving just a shade
too fast for our get-together to wait until the end of
the week. That's why I have convened this emergency
meeting. Firstly, I have just been informed that there is
a case of the Red Death in Naples."

"Oh, my God," remarked the Leader of the Opposition. Toby Anstruther had been chosen from the centre
of his Party in the hope that he would bring together its
divergent wings. Tall and somewhat languid, he had

indeed proved an expert reconciler, but more than once it had been observed that he disliked crises, and was a wait-and-see man rather than one to make quick decisions. All of which had encouraged more and more of the backbenchers to put their faith in Brereton, who certainly did not lack decisiveness.

These were facts of which the Prime Minister was well aware, but tonight all business was concerned with national security; if Toby had elected to bring Brereton with him, obviously in the hopes of establishing a united front, that was his affair. "Quite. Of course the authorities in Italy say the victim has been isolated and every precaution taken, but we've heard that before. We have to expect the disease to appear on the Channel coast of France within a very short time. It is against this background that the President's call becomes doubly important. It seems . . . " the Prime Minister paused and looked from face to face, "that the Robert Koch Research Center may have found an answer. A possible vaccine."

"That's marvellous," said the Home Secretary, tapping his teeth with his pencil.

"If it's true," the Chancellor growled.

The Prime Minister held up a finger. "The operative word is 'may'. Now, Doctors Fitzroy and Calhoun, understanding the gravity of the situation, have presented their findings to the President and an invited audience in the White House. I cannot go into details because I do not have them. I will return to that in a moment. I do know that it is based upon our friend griseofulvin, as outlined to us by Peter last week. Something more than this was apparently needed, and this the people from the Koch Center claim now to have discovered. The point is that this new compound, or additive, or whatever it is, has been even less tested than griseofulvin. The object appears to be to inhibit the growth of the disease itself, but again we have the problem of possible side-effects, and these I gather could be very serious. On the other hand, it is something we apparently already possess, although not in sufficient quantity.

"The crux of the matter is this: do we, against all accepted precedents, go ahead with the manufacture of this vaccine on the largest possible scale, and risk the side-effects, or do we subject it to a proper testing, which could take at least a year, and do what we can to resist the Red Death in the meantime?" Another quick look from face to face. "I realise, and I am sure you do too, that this could be one of the most fateful decisions ever to face mankind, or at least those of us entrusted with the future of mankind.

"Now, the President is looking for a consensus, at least amongst those nations capable of manufacturing the drug in sufficient quantities; effectively at this time that means the United States and Canada, the European Community, Russia and Japan. China is a possibility. The decision has to be made as rapidly as possible, of course, but naturally we wish, and the President wishes for us, to be in the fullest possible possession of the facts and the risks before taking an irrevocable step. To this end he is despatching special teams to the various capitals where co-operation may be hoped for. Dr Fitzroy, accompanied by the Secretary of State, is on his way to Moscow, Tokyo and Peking. Dr Calhoun, accompanied by the Assistant Secretary of State, is arriving in London tomorrow morning. She will present the facts to us here, and then continue to Paris, Bonn, and other European capitals.

"With this in mind, and in view of the extraordinary circumstances with which we are faced, I would like to postpone the beginning of the emergency debate until Tuesday of next week."

Anstruther nodded his agreement. Brereton grunted.

The Prime Minister continued. "I would like us all to attend the meeting with Dr Calhoun, which I have arranged will take place in 10 Downing Street. I have invited several other guests, mainly the best medical opinions we possess as well as our leading druggists, that we may obtain the widest possible informed reaction. It goes without saying that what I have told you here today, and the fact of tomorrow's meeting, must be kept absolutely confidential, at least until after Dr Calhoun has told us whatever it is she wants us to know. Gentlemen?"

When the Prime Minister got into full spate even the Leader of the Opposition was left gasping, as had happened often enough in the House. There was no dissent. Peter's brain was, in any event, whirring with the thought that Meg was going to be in London tomorrow, however briefly. But he was also aware of suddenly having been shunted from the centre of the stage to a walking-on part, and could not help but complain to Jeremy.

"I seem to have egg all over my face," he remarked, as they went down to the car park.

"In what way, old boy?" Jeremy seemed to have largely recovered from his extreme tension of a week ago, now that the Prime Minister was taking over more and more of the burden of resisting the approach of the disease.

"Well, for God's sake, Brereton had obviously been invited to this meeting before we met at church this morning."

"That seems reasonable. I believe the President actually spoke with the PM last night."

"He also knew what it was to be about," Peter snapped.

"Well, I suppose someone must have told him. I really don't see that it matters now."

Peter left it at that. What was really bothering him was that Meg had not even left a message for him to tell him what she was doing, where she was going . . . she could surely have let him know she was intending to come to

London. Could it be that she still felt he was 'dangerous' to her point of view? Or had she really decided to call it a day as regards them? He didn't want to believe that.

But he remained angry, telephoned Hartley as soon as he got home. "I am presuming that you have been invited to Downing Street tomorrow morning," he said.

"Why, yes. The whole task force has. Aren't you going?"

"Oh, I believe they are going to allow me to sit in," Peter said. "Do you know what it's about?"

"I understand we're to receive a lecture from your American girlfriend."

"Presumably about the properties of griseofulvin."

"Has to be more than that. Every druggist knows the properties of griseofulvin. I have some ideas, myself, as to what they've been trying to put together over there. And I must say the whole thing terrifies me more than the disease itself."

"Claudie with you?"

"No, she's spending the night in Wimbledon."

"Then why don't you and I have dinner together, at the Club, and you can brief me with everything you know about griseofulvin?"

"As far as I can," Hartley said cautiously.

"Ladies and gentlemen," the Prime Minister said. "I'm sure most of you know Mr Leiningen."

The Assistant Secretary of State gave a brief bow.

"But very few of you have probably encountered Dr Margaret Calhoun before. Dr Calhoun is one of the world's leading authorities on viral diseases, and she is here today to bring us up-to-date on American findings in the fight against the Red Death. Dr Calhoun."

There was a brief ripple of applause. Peter had just entered the room and was stuck at the very back, but then, he would have been placed there anyway. There were about thirty people present, the very cream of the establishment: the Archbishop of Canterbury was with the Chief of the Imperial General Staff; the Foreign Secretary sat next to the Prince; Sir Hartley Briggs was beside the Chairman of ICI; and the Prime Minister was now taking a chair between the Leader of the Opposition and Leiningen.

Facing the assembly was the diminutive figure of Meg. She did not look like a woman who had just flown the Atlantic, or had been working around the clock for more than a week. In her crisp, primrose linen skirt and short matching jacket, worn with a white linen blouse and a white silk flower with green leaves in her lapel, she looked more attractive than ever. As she glanced from face to face in her audience her gaze met his for a moment, and she gave a half smile, but was then serious again as she began her lecture.

"I don't have to tell you what the Red Death is," she said. "Or what it's doing. It is caused by a virus. A very old virus, unlike anything that exists in the world today, and twice as deadly. I'm not going to discuss how it came to surface. I'm here to tell you what we think we can do about it, and what we're up against.

"Now, the first thing we all have to be sure about is what a virus is, and what it is composed of. It is the smallest of all living organisms. It usually varies in size from 20 nanometers to 400 nanometers; the one we're dealing with is actually 10 nanometers long – that's what made him so very hard to find. Viruses, we know, are responsible for most of the diseases we suffer from, including several types of cancer. This virus, RD1 is the name we have given it, attacks the bone marrow and causes a rapid and ceaseless replication of the red blood corpuscles; it comes under the heading of a cancer-inducing agent.

"Now for the morphology, because this is what matters. A virus consists of a whole lot of B-protein molecules, and a single A-protein molecule. We can forget the A-protein for the moment. Each B-protein, like all B-protein molecules, has a core which contains one single-stranded DNA molecule. I guess we all know about the DNA molecule. It's what makes every cell tick, so it's what makes us tick. It is, if you like, the brain of every cell. Each DNA molecule also possesses unique characteristics, and the fact that these characteristics are common to every cell in one body has become of tremendous importance in recent years. The DNA also carries the genetic factors that make us what we are. We can't afford to forget that.

"So, now we drop the big boy, the virus, and concentrate on the DNA, the deoxyribonucleic acid, because that's the nub of the matter. It's another whole world of its own, inconceivably smaller than even the virus, which is inconceivably smaller than anything that can be seen with the naked eye. It consists of a whole bunch of nucleotides, adenine, guanine, cytosine, thymine, and, most important, deoxyribose for its sugar. That's where it gets its energy from. The structure of a DNA molecule consists of a double helix containing a pair of strands of polynucleotides coiled together. As the prefix implies, each strand may contain thousands of nucleotides." She smiled at the serious, attentive faces. "You with me so far?

"Now, the way a virus normally works is to get inside a bacteria, attach itself to the host, and begin what we call replicating as fast as possible. Before you can say knife, and we are really talking in terms of seconds in some instances, the whole area is infected. The rate of replication increases, and so does the infection. Combating these viruses is what modern medicine is really all about.

"Well, we have had success in some areas with vaccinations, against diseases like smallpox and polio. We have had greater success in other areas with prevention. We have, for example, no real means of combating malaria with any success once the virus is in the blood stream – but we can contain malaria by eliminating the breeding grounds of the virus-carrying mosquitoes. We can't really combat cholera, but we can prevent it appearing by proper hygiene. The virus RD1 is more difficult than any of these, because it doesn't make that preliminary attack on bacteria; once in the blood stream it goes straight for the red corpuscles. And it cannot be dealt with by ordinary methods, because it spreads so fast and so rapidly. It is the most contagious disease ever to appear. It does have a weakness, however. It doesn't really belong in this day and age. When released it burns like a sparkler for between forty-eight and seventy-two hours, then it dies. Simple as that. The trouble is that in that brief time it also kills, and spreads. What we have been working on is some interferon which will keep it dormant for at least seventy-two hours, at the end of which time it becomes harmless and non-contagious.

"Now, there is only one known antibiotic which has any effect on viruses inside the host, and even then in a most limited range. That antibiotic is griseofulvin. Those of you who know about drugs may recognise it under a variety of names: Fulvicin, Grifulvin, Grisactin, and so on. Griseofulvin only has an effect on viruses of a fungoid origin. That is to say it is used in dealing with diseases like ringworm and athlete's foot. I will admit that it did not immediately occur to us that RD1 could possibly be of fungoid origin: it didn't fit that characteristic. On the other hand, RD1 doesn't fit any known characteristics – that's the main part of the trouble. We tried griseofulvin simply because we were running out of other ideas. And it worked." She poured water into a glass from the carafe on the table, drank and recommenced.

"So, eureka! Why aren't we rushing about giving everyone doses of griseofulvin? The answer lies in the way it works. It works by altering the metabolism of nucleic acid. Specifically, it increases the rate of synthesis of deoxyribonucleic acid. You could say that it does to the DNA what the DNA is telling the virus to do to the host, flood it with the DNA's equivalent of red blood corpuscles. That's a simplistic analogy, but you get the idea. The important point is that the DNA cannot cope with the change, the messages stop going out, and the virus becomes harmless. In the case of RD1, after a maximum of seventy-two hours, it dies.

"The trouble is, griseofulvin has hitherto only been administered when a disease is diagnosed. Then it works very quickly and cleanly. It is taken through the mouth, stifles the DNA, and appears to be excreted in unchanged form in the faeces, and up to now our experience is that few serious reactions occur after treatment. But, we can't wait for a positive diagnosis of the Red Death to administer the drug. If a doctor or nurse was standing beside every patient the moment the disease could be diagnosed, with a dose of griseofulvin to pop into his or her mouth, it might just work. Unfortunately there aren't that many doctors and nurses in the world, and once RD1 has been at work for even a few hours the patient's life is in danger. What we have had to do is discover a solution which will retain the griseofulvin in the system for a period of time. We know the virus is very quick-acting and has this very short lifespan. If we can immunise people in infected areas for even a week they should survive; for a month, and the disease should just disappear.

"Now, we believe we have found such a retaining agent, which will combine with griseofulvin and maintain it in the host for at least a week, hopefully longer. It's called minaline. It's not a formula any of you will yet have heard of, but I have it with me here. What we have to understand, however, is that there has been no time to test the effects, short-term or long-term, that griseofulvin may have on the system when retained in it for any period of time. I have told you that it inhibits the synthesis of DNA in certain viruses. If we use it as a vaccine, it will be in the body whether the RD1 virus is there or not. We cannot tell as yet whether, given time, it will not attack the DNA in other cells, healthy cells, the cells upon which we depend for life. If our vaccine, griseofulmaline we are calling it, is going to be used to stem the flood of the Red Death, it is going to have to be used on the widest possible scale, and on animals as well as humans. Any tampering with DNA has got to be risky. We may get away with it. Or we may upset the whole genetic code of the human race. That is the decision which faces us now." She looked straight at the Prime Minister. "It is apparently not a decision which we of the medical profession are going to be allowed to make alone. Thank you."

There had hardly been a cough in the room while Meg had been speaking. Now there was a general murmur of appreciation and thanks and a few handclaps before the Prime Minister rose to shake her hand. "That was a masterly exposition, and I am sure we all now understand the problem and the possibilities. Are there any questions?"

"Can Dr Calhoun outline to us the possible side-effects, genetically, of using her vaccine?" Anstruther asked.

"You imagine it, and it could happen," Meg answered.

"Are you seriously suggesting it could mean the end of the human race?"

"As we know ourselves at the present time, yes. It is a possibility. But a remote possibility. As I have said, our experiences with the use of griseofulvin have so far been satisfactory."

"And on the other hand, the Red Death could mean the end of the human race, in any form, in the very near future," Peter remarked from the back.

Meg gave him another quick smile. "Quite."

"So you would be in favour of using griseofulmaline now," Brereton suggested.

Meg looked at him. "As a research scientist the very thought of using a drug which has not been adequately tested in these circumstances is very disturbing. As a doctor my concern is with the saving of life wherever possible. I am in favour of using the vaccine, yes."

The Prime Minister had signalled an aide, and cups of coffee were being handed round. Meg was naturally the centre of attention for some time, and Peter waited patiently, finding himself next to Hartley.

"What do you think?"

"I think she is absolutely barmy. The idea of using an untested drug on a worldwide scale is totally unethical. As I said last night, it is people like this Calhoun woman who scare the pants off me."

"But if the decision is taken to manufacture the drug, and use it, you'll do it?"

"Under protest. And with an indemnity from both the Government and the Opposition."

"And can you manufacture enough?"

"With a little bit of help from my friends, yes. Administering it, now . . . that's another thing."

"But not your province," Peter observed, and saw that there was some room around Meg. "I'll call you." He sidled into the gap. "Lunch?" He mouthed the word, not to be overheard.

She gazed at him, while he tried to decipher the expression in her eyes. Then, moving closer to him, she whispered, "I'd love to, Peter, but I have to get some sleep. We're flying on to Paris this afternoon, and I'm speaking at the Elysée Palace tomorrow."

"We could have a drink together, at least."

Another hesitation, then she smiled and half shrugged. "Actually, I'd love a drink. How soon can we leave here?"

"I would have said whenever you wish."

She answered a few more questions, then made her excuses to the Prime Minister, had a hasty word with Leiningen, and joined Peter outside; he had already secured one of the waiting taxis, and she sank on to the cushions with a sigh.

He sat beside her, gave the name of a discreet hotel bar. "I'm beginning to feel like the forgotten man," he said, as they drew away from the kerb.

She turned her head. "I'm sorry, Peter. I've been so terribly busy."

"Did you get any messages?"

"Yes. Yes, I did."

"But there wasn't time to reply?"

She bit her lip. "Not a lot. The main thing was, though, that as soon as we involved Washington, and we felt we had to do that right away, the President wanted no contact with anyone until he had the whole picture and been in touch with various heads of state . . . including your PM. Then, as I knew I was coming over here anyway, and you were certain to be around. . . "

"Would you have looked me up if I hadn't been?"

She gazed at him. "Yes, Peter, I would have at least telephoned you. And then, it seems, regretted it."

He was instantly contrite. To be sitting beside her, inhaling her scent, remembering so much . . . "I'm sorry. Over-reacting like this. It's been pretty fraught here too."

"I know." The taxi stopped, and Peter escorted her inside, ordered two Bloody Marys. "Any word about your sister?" she asked.

"She and her family were still alive when last we heard, but still confined in that camp where people are dying all around them. I feel like getting on a plane and stocking it with all the griseofulvin I can find, and heading south."

"They'll have griseofulvin in New Zealand."

"Yes, but not griseofulmaline. You haven't released your findings yet."

"It should be released in a day or two. But . . . it only exists in experimental quantities at the moment."

"And when it is manufactured there's no saying she'll be top of the list."

"I know," Meg agreed. "All anyone can do is pray that the politicians give the go-ahead quickly, and that it gets to her in time."

Her hand was lying on the table, and he rested his on top of it. "Any word on Sally Ann?"

She shook her head, the blue of her eyes dulled with pain. "But I must believe she's alive . . . until and unless she is officially reported dead. She is such a sweet kid, so young and vibrant." She sipped her Bloody Mary, gazing vacantly over the rim of the glass. "I have to believe she's survived."

"Of course." He smiled sympathetically and paused a moment before asking, "What's next on your agenda?"

"Well, as I said, we travel to Paris this evening, Bonn the day after. Next a whole stack of smaller countries: Stockholm, Copenhagen, Oslo, Amsterdam. Then Rome and Madrid. You could say we're on the Grand Tour of Europe."

"You're going to Rome? You know there's a case reported in Naples?"

She nodded. "Yes, Peter, I know, but we have to spell it out to all of them. Hopefully the signal will then be given for the go-ahead. But Gray and I and our team intend to go ahead anyway."

He frowned at her. "Doing what?"

"What you just suggested. Griseofulmaline is a vaccine. A preventive. But we know that griseofulvin can save lives if administered to people suffering from the Red Death, providing we can get to them early enough. We can at least hope to save some lives. Gray's arranging for a fleet of planes to be standing by, with all the griseofulvin we can raise, and we're going to see what we can do. And we have quite a team. Charlie Oswiecki is in it, and Amanda . . . she's Gray's daughter. Did you hear about Tom Lintell?"

Peter shook his head, preoccupied.

"Well, he was Charlie's and Amanda's boss. He's the guy who unearthed the megatherium. If it hadn't been him it would have been someone else, and whoever did it would have reacted in the same way. But the megatherium was carrying the virus and I guess Tom felt he had loosed the Red Death on the world. He threw himself under a subway train, last week. As he'd taken care to leave the contents of his pockets in his office, he wasn't identified for three days. A real shame. He was a brilliant man. Well, as you can imagine, Charlie and Mandy were pretty cut up. There was a moment when I thought they were going to do something stupid too. Especially Charlie. You know what they say about jolly fat men: they're really as sensitive as hell. Charlie was the one who actually emptied those remains. But the idea that we'll form a team and go out and actually fight this disease, face to face, as it were, has put the spirit back into both of them."

"And you don't think you're being almost as silly, as you put it, as Lintell?"

She raised her eyebrows.

"Where are you going with your team?"

"South America."

"My God! Is that Fitzroy's idea?"

"I chose it, Peter. It's where I want to go. It's where it all began. And Sally Ann is there."

"Meg, if you go to South America, you are going to die."

She shook her head. "Not from the Red Death. I've been vaccinated."

He stared at her. "You have done what? Are you crazy?"

"Why not? I said we had manufactured enough of the drug ourselves, for experiments. One should begin at home." She smiled at him. "So maybe I'll have children with ten toes on each foot. Or maybe I won't have any at all."

His fingers tightened. "I'd like to do something about that."

"Peter . . . "

"Will you marry me, Meg? Right now. You'll still have time to catch your flight to Paris."

It was her turn to stare. "Are *you* crazy?"

"If loving you is crazy, then the answer is yes."

"Loving me is crazy right now. Peter, I'm not going to be available for one hell of a long time."

"So I'll wait."

"Peter . . . "

"I love you, Meg."

She sipped her Bloody Mary.

"And once upon a time I was cocky enough to think you loved me too. So I know you think I let you down . . . "

"You were doing what you thought right. Maybe I over-reacted. I've run into the same point of view time and again since."

"And I've seen my theory put into practice on my own sister." He raked the fingers of both hands through his hair. "Makes one take a re-think."

"Oh, Peter!" She sipped her drink again. "I . . . if I am ever going to love anybody, it's going to be you."

"Then what's stopping you?"

"Everything. This. My work . . . "

"Meg, there is always going to be your work. You know that. You simply have to slow down some time. Or at least live a normal life. I'm not going to interefere with your work. I know how much it means to you, and I'm beginning to understand how much it means to mankind. But I want to be your husband. The question is, do you want to be my wife?"

"It'd be a crazy marriage, me in San Francisco and you in London."

"I think we'd manage to get together from time to time."

She shook her head wearily. "Peter. Of course I want to marry you. But . . . give me a couple of days to think about things."

He knew he had got as far as he possibly could, at the moment. But he was not going to let go, now. "Will you be stopping in London on the way back from your travels?"

"I guess so."

"When will that be?"

"At the end of this week."

"And when will your expedition to South America commence?"

"A week after that. Tuesday after next is D-day."

"Then surely you can take a couple of days off? You have to, Meg. You need them. You are utterly exhausted, and you know it. You keep on at this rate, and while you may be immune to the Red Death you are sure as hell going to get something else which may be just as nasty. For God's sake, Meg, you're a doctor: physician, heal thyself."

She knew he was right. She was burning herself out. And the thought of spending even a couple of days just relaxing, with Peter . . .

"What would we do with our two days?"

"Well, we could get married and honeymoon. I have a cottage down in Cornwall. It's a lovely place in a lovely village full of lovely people. You'd love them and they'll love you."

Still she hesitated. "I'll call you, from somewhere in Europe," she promised. "But Peter . . . if I say yes, I'll still be going to South America."

"I know that," he said, sadly.

The Paris plane was delayed half an hour, but it was still daylight when they finally took off. From her window seat Meg looked down through gaps in the clouds at the tiny English fields and higgledy-piggledy roads winding, apparently quite aimlessly, around the countryside; so different from the American grid system. She knew she should have her briefcase open on her lap, be catching up on her paperwork, but she could not concentrate on anything. It was impossible to get Peter and his proposal out of her mind. Marriage! The idea was really ridiculous, they were so different. Their ideals, their principles, everything . . . except sex. That had been good. Perfect. And she was still terribly attracted to him, as he obviously was to her. But sex alone did not make a marriage. If both partners were willing to talk about sex and experiment, adapt ideas and habits towards each other, sex could be good anyway, but it needed understanding and true friendship to make a good marriage. Could she and Peter really be classified as true friends?

Chalky white cliffs of the coastline appeared from under the wing and a stewardess leaned across to offer her a drink. She wanted to ask for a Bloody Mary, but changed her mind to orange juice: she was tired enough and the vodka would put her to sleep. She had been tired for so long, days, weeks, which was probably why she had let Peter ramble on about marriage. Now it would be that much more difficult to turn him down, put the idea right out of his head, and out of hers. When she closed her eyes, and her mind, she could still feel the glorious warmth of his arms around her, of him filling her . . . Her eyes snapped open again as the stewardess handed her the orange juice and she fumbled with the catch on the seat in front to lower her tray. With her eyes open some of her anger at Peter's betrayal of her trust returned. And as the plane dropped in a turn towards Charles de Gaulle Airport, her mind was still seesawing between love and anger. She was too weary to straighten out her thinking, make any decisions. Only one thing was absolutely clear: if Peter wanted to give up politics and come to live in California, well, marriage might be possible, but there was no way she would ever consider giving up her work to become a housewife.

The blood tests on Leiningen, herself, and their secretaries took ages, and the cab ride into the city seemed interminable, but her hotel room was comfortable, though small, and the bathwater hot. A light supper in her room allowed a long, deep, dreamless sleep from which she was awakened by the arrival of the breakfast table, so she was feeling comparatively relaxed and refreshed when the phone rang.

"Margaret Calhoun."

The answer was a string of spits and crackles until at last a faint voice said, "Meg?"

"Speaking. Who's that?"

There was a moment's silence followed by what sounded like a gasp. "Meggie! It's Nan here."

Meg held her breath. This could only mean news of Sally Ann. "Yes? Tell me."

"We've been contacted by the Chilean embassy. They've found the kids." There was a long pause, and Meg's heart sank as she heard sobs.

"Yes?" she prompted. And waited.

"They're all gone," Nan gasped.

Meg swallowed. "Gone?"

"Dead. Oh, Meggie. Our little girl is dead . . ." The distraught woman hung up leaving Meg gaping at the receiver in horror.

"It is then a majority decision," the Prime Minister said, "that we proceed with the manufacture of griseofulmaline with the greatest possible urgency and in the greatest possible volume."

"With respect, Prime Minister," Hartley Briggs said, "the task force, which you set up, and of which I have the honour to be chairman, wishes to be dissociated from the Government's decision."

The Prime Minister looked at Peter, as if to say, this was your idea, and then at Hartley. The Prime Minister's looks were famous, and feared, but Hartley never lowered his eyes.

"We support the decision to manufacture griseofulmaline," he added. "But we regard it as both unethical and dangerous to administer it until it has been thoroughly tested. We feel that all our efforts should be placed behind carrying out these tests as rapidly, and as completely, as possible. We should like to remind you . . ." his glance swept the people seated round the table in the Cabinet room, "that as yet there has been no case of the Red Death reported in Great Britain, and that so long as we continue our blood tests at seaports and airports, there never should be. To adopt panic measures which could do untold harm to the people of Great Britain would in our opinion be unforgivable. Our opinion is unanimous."

"I hope you do intend to go ahead and test this new drug just as thoroughly as you can, Sir Hartley," the Prime Minister said. "And your very proper dissent does you credit. It will be recorded. However, it cannot affect our decision, and I am sure I speak for all of us here when I say that I resent having the measures I have outlined described as 'panic'. It would be far more catastrophic were we to wait for the appearance of the Red Death in this country before we took steps to immunise our population. The fact that the disease has not yet reached here is, as you say, a tribute to the efficiency of the system we are using, but the events of the past two months have shown us that no system can be regarded as entirely foolproof. I will now tell this meeting, in absolute confidence, that there are increasing numbers of cases in the United States, in isolation, and that one has been reported in Japan. I believe that were I not to take the most stringent protective measures now, while we still have a breathing space, I should be unworthy of the high office I hold."

Hartley's shoulders bowed before the rebuke; he had no answers to the terrifying facts the Prime Minister had just presented.

"However," the Prime Minister continued, "there will certainly have to be a delay in administering the vaccine, for a very good reason. Since the emergency began, we have managed to keep people in this country calm by assuring them that the Red Death will never be allowed to enter this country. There have been grumbles from frustrated business people and people who have cancelled their holidays, and from the tourist industry here, which has just about collapsed, but on the whole people have accepted the situation with the fortitude and the confidence I would have expected.

"However, once vaccination starts, the mood may well change. Once, indeed, it is known that we possess a vaccine, there may well be a panic to obtain it. It is therefore absolutely necessary, firstly, that we proceed in absolute secrecy until we have sufficient vaccine to immunise the entire country; secondly, that we do not start such vaccinations until we are in that position; and thirdly, that we possess by then a comprehensive plan for dealing with the entire population as simultaneously as possible. Harry, I will leave that with the Home Office; I wish the plan on my desk when I return from Washington."

The Home Secretary nodded.

"Sir Thomas, I require the army to put cordons of maximum security around the establishments where the drug is going to be manufactured."

The Chief of the Imperial General Staff also nodded.

"Sir Hartley, your scientists will obviously have to know what they are doing, and why, but they will have to accept that they are operating under conditions of maximum security and will be unable to visit their families until the project is completed. Will you be able to get that across to them?"

"I should think so," Hartley agreed. "Am I also to be shut up?"

The Prime Minister gave a cold smile. "That is for you to decide. Now, Toby, in all the circumstances, and in view of the large measure of agreement we have reached, the emergency debate must be postponed again until we are in a position to take the entire nation into our confidence."

"They won't like it," the Leader of the Opposition said. "Neither my backbenchers nor yours. To be recalled from their holidays is bad enough, but then to be told nothing . . . "

"I will make a statement tomorrow," the Prime Minister said. "If you will promise not to challenge it or attempt to force a debate."

"Well, of course my colleagues and I will co-operate . . ." the Leader of the Opposition glanced at Brereton, who looked glum, but made no comment.

"Thank you. I am flying out to Washington, with the Chancellor, the day after tomorrow, but will be back by the weekend. I may say that the Americans are taking roughly the same measures as ourselves, and they face a much greater problem, of course, not only in having the disease already in their midst, even if at present contained, but in having to supply vaccines in the first instance for a much greater population. However, the ultimate objective, of course, is to manufacture sufficient vaccine to immunise the entire population of the world." The Prime Minister looked at Hartley. "How soon will the drug be available?"

"I would imagine within forty-eight hours. That is, first available. On the scale you ultimately wish, we could be talking of several months."

"And to immunise this country?"

Hartley hesitated. "Fifty odd million people . . . one month."

"Let us hope and pray that we are given that month."

"Have we heard from our Common Market partners?" the Chancellor asked.

"I am expecting a call from the French President today. They will have had time to assimilate the situation and make their decisions by then. Germany will be a little later, as Dr Calhoun only got there last night. I expect the other countries she is visiting will come into line with our thinking, as soon as they have been told the facts. Well, gentlemen, I am sure that we all have a great deal to do. Thank you for joining me."

"What does it feel like, to have been shot down by the Prime Minister?" Peter asked as he and Hartley drove to Cadogan Square.

"I could have done with some support," Hartley grunted.

"I don't happen to agree with you."

"You set up the task force. It is essential that we always present a unanimous recommendation. As we have done, up to now."

"You have done it all. I have bowed out."

"And you're prepared to risk the entire future of this nation. That's because you don't know enough about what's involved."

"I know enough about what's involved to be sure that there can't be a future unless we guarantee the present, Hartley. But don't you think it's rather foolish for us to quarrel about something this important?"

Hartley glanced at him, then grinned. "Coming in for a Scotch?"

"There is nothing I feel like more. There's something I want to talk to you both about."

Claudia was in the drawing-room, smoking a Balkan Sobranie, drinking a gin martini, and reading the *Tatler*. "You're home early," she commented.

"Not for very long," Hartley said. "I'm going straight down to the factory after dinner."

"Oh, Hartley," she grumbled. "What on earth for?"

"There are certain wheels I have to set in motion."

"Oh, you mean about this vaccine thing?"

Hartley and Peter stared at each other, and then at her.

"How in the name of God did you know about that?" Peter demanded.

"Oh, I don't know. Someone mentioned it at the bridge club this afternoon, I think. They said it's going to cure the Red Death. I do hope it does. Will it, Hartley?"

"I have absolutely no idea. It's supposed to be a top security matter. Who the devil's leaked the information? That's what I've got to find out. Hope to hell there's nothing in the press." Hartley picked up the *Financial Times*, ran his eye down the columns till he reached the stock-market page, slowing to read the figures. "God! Do you realise I have lost half a million pounds in the last month?"

"Lucky you," Peter remarked.

"Lucky?"

"To have half a million pounds to lose."

Hartley began pouring Scotch. "Are you trying to pretend you don't play the market?"

"On my income? I'd have probably lost half a million pence."

"I don't think it will ever recover from this one," Hartley said gloomily. "I've half a mind to convert what I have left into gold myself."

"Supposing there's any left," Peter reminded him. "How are the folks?" he asked his sister.

"Bearing up. The fact that Sarah and the kids are still apparently alive is doing wonders. They've been moved to another camp, you know. This one is absolutely guaranteed to be Red Death free."

"Oh, that's tremendous news. And now I have some news of my own." Peter took his glass from Hartley. "I think I'm about to get married."

"Think?"

"Well, she hasn't actually said yes, yet."

"You mean the Papagopoulos woman?" Claudia asked.

"No." Peter frowned. He did not want to think about Anna. The map of South Africa was now coloured purple, and even black in some places. And as Anna had not returned to London, she must still be there.

"Then who is the lucky girl?" Hartley inquired.

"Ah . . . Meg Calhoun."

"Meg who?" Claudia asked in dismay. She did like to be at least acquainted with Peter's mistresses.

"Great Scot!" Hartley exclaimed. "I always said you had something going there."

"Well . . . "

"Who is this person?" Claudia demanded.

"Dr Calhoun, darling," Hartley explained. "She's the whizzkid who's been lecturing us on the Red Death."

"You mean she's American?" Claudia was scandalised. "And a doctor? I hate women doctors."

"She also hates Americans," Hartley added with a grin to his brother-in-law.

"You'll adore Meg," Peter told his sister. "You like her, don't you, Hartley?"

"Will somebody please tell me what is going on?" Claudia insisted.

"Well . . . she is certainly a cute little number. Brains, too."

"And when is this wedding due to take place?" Claudia inquired.

347

"As I said, she hasn't said yes yet. But if she does . . . first thing next week."

"Next what? You must be out of your mind. What about the invitations? The reception? My gown? The Abbey . . . " A sudden look of horror spread over her face. "Oh Lord! Don't tell me it's a shot gun affair! Have you got her in the family way?"

Peter held his sister's hands, laughing. "Darling Claudie! You really are pricelessly old-fashioned. No, I have not got her in the family way, as you so delicately put it. Nor are we getting married at the Abbey. It will be at a Registry Office. This is simply not the time for big weddings. It is also not the time for big receptions. We would like to have a drink here afterwards, certainly, and if you can lay on a few canapés, so much the better."

"And a cake," Hartley said enthusiastically. "We'll see to the cake."

"For how many?" Claudia asked, her tone the trumpet of doom.

"Well, Meg and I, of course, Hartley and you, Mum and Dad, I suppose Jeremy and Anne should be invited . . . oh, and Grant and Julia. There we are, ten. A nice round number."

"Ten?" Claudia cried. "How can you have a wedding reception with only ten people? It's positively obscene."

"Ten," Peter said firmly. "Not a single soul more, unless you want to let the Appletons bring their children."

Claudia sighed, but she had known how determined her little brother could be for more than thirty years. She held her glass up to her husband for a refill.

"And then it's down to Cornwall for a honeymoon?" Hartley suggested.

"That's my idea," Peter said. "It'll have to be a quick one, because she's off again a couple of days later."

"Obscene," Claudia groaned.

"But I would like her to have clean sheets on her first night," he grinned. "I'll nip down to Trebeth on Saturday and get things organised there." He did not wish to consider the possibility that Meg might not accept his proposal.

"Oh, Mr Canning, best congratulations," Betty Pengelley said. "Oh, I am so happy for you. You leave it to John and me; we'll have the place looking a treat."

"I knew you would, Betty. I only wish we could stay down longer, but there's a lot going on."

"This Red Death thing," Betty said wisely. "It's not going to come here, though." She sounded quite certain about that.

He decided to agree with her. "No chance of that, Betty."

"Talking about that, Mr Canning," John said. "Dr Jones called last week, and said next time you're down he'd like a word."

Peter frowned at him. "About the Red Death?"

"Well, he didn't say."

Peter sighed. Arthur Jones was Medical Officer of Health in Ridding, and responsible for the surrounding area. He was a self-important little man who took his duties very seriously, and ran his department with a series of crisply worded directives which attempted to anticipate every possible contingency. Well, Ridding and District was renowned for the health of its inhabitants. But Peter did not relish the thought of discussing the Red Death at that level. On the other hand, it was his constituency. He dialled the Ridding number.

"Peter. Good to hear from you. Are all the rumours we hear about this disease true?"

"I'm afraid most of them probably are, Arthur, depending on what you've heard. John Pengelley said you had something on your mind."

"Yes, there is something I'd like to discuss."

"So shoot."

"It's not a matter we should discuss over the phone. I don't suppose there's any chance of your dropping in to see me while you're down?"

Peter suppressed another sigh. "Arthur, I've only just arrived here. And I am leaving again tomorrow morning at the crack of dawn. Is it very important?"

"Well, yes, old man, I regard it as very important. You say you're leaving early tomorrow morning? You have to drive through Ridding. Surely you can stop by for a chat?"

"You want to have a chat on Sunday morning at eight o'clock?"

"Whenever you can come."

"Well . . . I'll be there. But only for a few minutes, Arthur. I'm meeting a flight into Heathrow tomorrow afternoon. Expect me at eight."

Arthur Jones wore a small military moustache and obviously should have been in the services. "Peter!" He shook hands. Early as it was on Sunday morning, he wore a blue suit and a quiet tie. "Good of you to come. Sit down."

It was far more of a command than an invitation. Peter, wearing a sports shirt and slacks, obeyed, feeling rather like a delinquent fourth-former in the head-master's study.

Jones sat behind his desk. "Now. I want to know about this Red Death thing."

"Well, there's not much I can tell you," Peter confessed. "It's pretty horrendous, but we are going to beat it. Mind you, picking up the pieces is going to be even more horrendous. But we'll make it."

"I want to know the contingency plans for when it reaches Britain."

"Arthur, it is not going to reach Britain."

"You mean there are no contingency plans? I suspected as much. This nation enters every crisis in a state of total unpreparedness."

"It is not going to reach Britain," Peter told him, patiently, "because we are not going to let it. No one can enter this country without a stringent blood test. Even the PM had one on Friday after returning from the States. So you can stop worrying."

"It is my business to worry," Jones said, equably. "I have been following events in the newspapers with great care, and I have drawn up some plans of my own. Would you care to hear them?"

"Well . . . how many are there?"

"Very few. Simplicity is my motto. It is clear to me that isolation is the key to checking the spread of the disease. I have spoken with Chief Superintendent Marks, and he entirely agrees with me. The moment any outbreak is identified, the whole community affected must be placed in the strictest quarantine."

Peter opened his mouth and then closed it again. Wasn't that what he had once recommended? But he could not resist asking, "And just left to die?"

"My dear fellow, we will give them all the help possible. But the community must be sealed off, absolutely, no one allowed to leave. I would hope that you will endorse that decision."

Peter scratched his head. "You mean, if there was an outbreak here in Ridding, you would quarantine the town, immediately?"

"Of course."

Peter nodded. "Well, I'm sure it would be the right thing, Arthur." He stood up, and grinned. "Fortunately, it'll never be necessary. Now I simply have to rush."

Jones accompanied him outside. "But that isn't the only measure. As you have just been saying, prevention is surely better than cure. I also intend to institute blood tests for anyone entering the district."

Peter, his hand on the door handle of his car, gazed at him with his mouth open.

"I know it won't be easy . . . "

"It'll be damned impossible, Arthur, and you know it, unless you intend to set up road blocks on every road, lane, and cart track, and even that wouldn't work."

Jones did not take offence. "I intend to introduce identification cards. They are being printed now. Everyone will have to carry a card, and produce it on demand. It will have the date of the carrier's last blood test, and no test will be accepted if it is more than a week old."

"You intend to make every member of this community take a blood test every seven days?"

"This is a serious matter, Peter. I wish you would get that through your head."

"And what about visitors?"

"Anyone who cannot produce an up-to-date stamped card will be taken immediately to the hospital, tested, and given a card."

"And if they don't want to do this?"

"Then they'll be arrested."

"Arthur . . . "

"There's a special meeting of the Town Council tomorrow morning. I wish you could attend. But if you can't, I would certainly like to give the meeting your endorsement, as I have suggested. We will pass the necessary by-laws then, to come into effect immediately."

"If they agree with you."

"Oh, they will," Jones asserted. "I have already spoken with the mayor and the town clerk, and they entirely agree with me."

"Then you don't need my endorsement."

They gazed at each other. "We intend to be safe, rather than sorry, in Ridding, Peter," Jones said evenly. "If every community in Britain were to take the same attitude, then you could truly say that the Red Death will never take root here."

"I think you are going over the top, Arthur," Peter told him. "And let me tell you this: I am coming down here next week with my wife and if anyone tries to arrest us and force us to take a blood test I am going to raise merry hell."

"Are you getting married? Oh, best congratulations, old man." Jones held out his hand.

Peter hesitated, then grinned, and shook it. It was impossible to be angry with a personality like Jones, simply because he never got angry himself. He proceeded through life on the simple assumption that he was right and anyone who disagreed with him was wrong; he felt sorry for such people, not angry with them.

"Thanks," he said, and got behind the wheel.

"Uncle Peter! Uncle Peter!"

He turned in amazement as he recognised both the voice and the young woman who was staggering up the pavement with a heavy suitcase. "Frances? But . . . I thought you were in Japan."

"No, I'm not. I'm here. Hello, Dr Jones."

Peter got out of the car and Frances Wardle threw both arms round his neck and kissed him. As tall and slender as her mother, Frances had always called Peter 'uncle', even though she was only ten years the younger.

"Can you give me a lift to Trebeth Cross?" she asked.

"I'm afraid I'm going the other way, Fran. Where on earth have you just sprung from?"

"Oh." She brushed fair hair from her forehead; her clothes – jeans and a loose shirt – certainly looked as if they had been slept in. "From Ridding railway station, as a matter of fact. But I've been travelling for days. I left Japan . . . it must have been Thursday. I queued for fifteen hours to get a seat. Then we were all off-loaded again in Delhi. There was a terrible fuss before we were allowed to go on again. They took blood tests and heaven knows what else. Then they wouldn't let us land in Athens, so we flew on to Rome. They only let us land in Rome because we were out of fuel. There was even more fuss and delay there, because one of the hostesses was taken ill. She was rushed off to hospital, and the rest of us were given more tests." She giggled. "It was a scream, really. My blood pressure is so low they could hardly find it. They were in a tizzy until I explained it's always been like that. Then we came on to Paris and then here. There was an even bigger fuss in Paris, and I had to wait hours for a flight to Heathrow. I only landed at five this morning. And that was the biggest flap of all. Everything has gone potty. Really, everyone was so unpleasant. It really made me want to get on the plane and go straight back."

"Well, I'm afraid everyone is fairly uptight right now, about the possibility of the disease coming here."

"I know. Apparently a lot of people just didn't bother to turn up, this morning. There were no porters . . . we had to fetch our own bags from the hold, and then it took hours to get to a mainline station . . . I'm exhausted. And then, to top it all, when I got here, there were no taxis. There was no one at all, not even a porter. Really, the whole world is just falling apart. No taxis, in August!"

"Well, the tourist season has just fizzled out, you see," Peter explained. "As you say, everyone feels safer at home."

"That's where I want to be," Frances agreed. "Home. And needless to say, the telephone booth at the station is out of order. If you're not going there . . . Dr Jones, may I use your phone to call Mummy?"

"In a moment," Jones said. "You say an air hostess on your flight was taken ill in Rome? What nationality was she?"

"Well, Japanese, of course. It was an Air Japan flight."

"How long had you been flying?"

"Oh, thirty-six hours, I suppose. We stopped in Bangkok before Delhi, and then there was that long delay in Delhi . . . "

"Did this stewardess have the Red Death?"

"Well, everyone thought it was that."

"Then she must have contracted it before leaving Japan."

"I'm sure she did. There were rumours of cases in Tokyo a week ago; the Government hushed it up. That was when I decided to get out. Dr Jones, I'm very tired, and . . . "

"Did this unfortunate young woman serve you on the flight?"

"Well, yes, she did." She gazed at them, and then laughed. "Oh, you think I might have it. I've been tested. Several times."

"At Heathrow?" Peter asked.

"Oh, yes. We all were. They tested me twice, because I was the only passenger who'd been on the Japan Air flight. They even found that my blood pressure was normal. First time that's ever happened. But I was so riled up by then I'm not surprised it was higher than usual. Please, Dr Jones, may I use your phone?"

"Yes," Jones said. "After you've taken another blood test, here and now."

Frances looked at Peter with her mouth open.

Peter shrugged, and got back behind his wheel. "You'd better go along with him, Fran. He's got the bit between his teeth."

19

Easy Girl

Kitson reckoned Clarke was dead. He had stopped groaning and was lying in his bunk, blood dribbling away from his nostrils. But they were so close to home there was no point in dropping him behind Munro; he did not want to make a mistake.

Kitson knew he was thinking in very straight lines, through very long tunnels. He had always thought like that, which was why he was such a good man in a crisis. Only the light at the end of the tunnel mattered, when the chips were down. He had once stayed at the helm for forty-eight consecutive hours, living on boiled sweets, when everyone else had been out with a combination of sea-sickness and exhaustion. He had brought *Easy Girl* home. He was going to do that now, even without the skipper.

When they hurried out of Tangier the night that bint had started bleeding, Munro wanted to 'talk about things'. Munro had always been a great talker about things, and as he was the skipper and owner of the ketch they had to listen to him. Over the years that the three of them had cruised together, Plymouth to the Piraeus, Plymouth to Marstrand, they had got used to listening to Munro talking.

Not that Munro's talkativeness had stopped Clarke and Kitson joining the ketch every summer for the past five years. Munro was the ideal cruising skipper. He liked blue water, he was not afraid of a bit of weather . . . but he also liked good food and good wine, strange places and strange women . . . and he had a total contempt for all the idiots who turned yachting from the most pleasurable of pastimes into hard work by racing. Munro liked being at sea as much as he liked being in a good French restaurant. Munro had found the secret of life, and he shared it with his pals.

Now he was dead.

Perhaps he had known he was going to die, when he wiped that girl's blood off him before they sent her ashore, in tears. He had looked at his crew, and said, "Let's get the hell out of here."

It had been midnight, but they had not argued. They had dropped the mooring, set sail and started the engine at the same time. When they left Gibraltar there had been no word that the Red Death had reached North Africa. And maybe the girl had suffered a common-or-garden nose bleed from having Munro thumping up and down on her chest. Yet they had all wanted to flee.

Only one did not flee from the Red Death. Once they were safely at sea, Munro said, "We've been exposed to the Red Death. Strictly speaking we should put in to the nearest port and have a blood test."

"We've just left the nearest port," Clarke pointed out. "You mean we should put back to Tangier?"

"Well, no. We don't want to be locked up by a lot of wogs. I suppose we should return to Gibraltar."

"I thought we were going home," Clarke said. "If I have the Red Death I want to be treated by my own doctor." He had grinned. "And buried in my own cemetery."

Munro looked at Kitson, who shrugged. "Let's go home, and take a blood test there. I'd rather do that." Kitson had an important reason for getting home, if he was going to be ill: Molly was there. Molly was a treasure. After the ten years of the constant nagging, constant quarrelling, he had endured with June, to have a girl loving him like Molly did, though hardly more than half his age, was like a dream. He had nearly cancelled his sailing holiday just to be with Molly – there was no way the others would have had a woman on the trip – but she had talked him into going. "I don't want to come between you and your friends," she had said. Molly was a darling.

But how he wished he had stayed at home.

"Suppose we have the disease?" Munro had asked.

"What the hell? They can't do anything about it if we do."

Munro had nodded, and laid a course to take them well clear of Cape St Vincent and Portugal. On board the fifty-foot ketch, in which they had sailed through a lot of weather in total safety, they felt secure. A yacht at sea is a world of its own. Its crew have to obey no rules save those of the sea, and those made by themselves. For that reason it is the existence of which every man dreams, and quite a few women as well.

Until someone starts to die. They had had a fair south-westerly wind and had bombed up the coast of Portugal, some hundred miles off in the Atlantic. But thirty-six hours after leaving Tangier, when they were about abeam of Lisbon, Munro had been taken ill. He had complained of pains in the stomach, and they had supposed it was Kitson's cooking, had joked about it. Next morning, when Munro's face had turned red and he had been bleeding from the backside, they realised the truth.

They had not said anything. The course was already laid for their home port of Truro in Cornwall. So Munro was placed in the forward bunk, fed and given liquids to drink, treated like a bad case of sea-sickness. "We'll be in Truro Saturday night," Clarke had promised him.

"He'll be dead long before then, if everything they say about the Red Death is true," Kitson pointed out, when he and Clarke had sat in the cockpit in the glow of an August evening. "You don't think we should put in somewhere?"

"Back to Lisbon? To a Portuguese quarantine hospital? If he's going to die he's going to die. Nothing they can do will save him. I want to get home, Dave."

Kitson had wanted to get home too, but more than anything he had wanted to get rid of the disease. Get it off the boat . . . But Munro was still alive and one couldn't throw a live man overboard, could one? He had kept looking at Clarke, wondering if he was thinking the same thing . . .

Munro actually lived for two more days. By that time, making a steady 10 knots, the ketch had been halfway up the Bay of Biscay, on the Atlantic side, entering the Western Approaches. When they were sure Munro was dead, they hastily donned rubber gloves and slid him into the largest sailbag on board, trying all the time to touch him as little as possible. Kitson had bundled up his bedding, too, stuffing it down into the bag before attaching the kedge anchor and pushing the whole bundle over the side. They both felt guilty about not sewing him into the Red Ensign for a proper burial, but neither was prepared to take the additional risk. It was warm, and they were still nearly two days from home. "I've made the correct entry in the log," Clarke said. "You'll have to ring Jane and explain what happened."

Because by then Clarke had also had stomach ache and headache. Equally by then it had been too late to change their minds. Kitson supposed they could have put out a distress call; there was a lot of shipping around them, big stuff, one of which would have stopped and picked them up. But what then? There was no cure for the Red Death, and they both wanted to get home.

And he was still fit. Of course he had always been anaemic. He could do with a few extra blood corpuscles. But it was tempting to think that he had not caught the disease. He felt fine, better than in a long time. He intended to take the ship home.

"Listen," Clarke had said last night. "Don't hang about. Head straight up the Carrick Roads and motor up to Truro. Tell the coastguard we've just come along from Dover. You can tell them what truly happened in Truro. They know us there."

Kitson had nodded. "I'll take the ship home, pal," he promised. "With you on it."

Now it was dark. He could see the flashes of the lights on the Lizard to port and Falmouth Bay dead ahead. He shortened sail so as to reach the mouth of the inlet at dawn, about four o'clock he reckoned. There would be fewer questions asked at dawn, as long as he was behaving normally. There would be one hell of a lot of questions to be answered when he moored up in Truro, with one crew member missing and another lying dead in his bunk. But he would have done what he promised, and brought the ship home. And he would be home himself.

It was just a matter of staying awake. He was so goddamned exhausted. He had started one of his headaches, and his muscles burned with weariness. But he would be in the river in another couple of hours.

20

The Worst Thing That Could
Have Happened

Terminal 2 at Heathrow was so quiet Peter thought for a moment he was in the wrong building. The vending cabins were shuttered up, the car hire desks unattended; only a solitary Asian cleaner moved her wide mop slowly down the long hall past a group of policemen whose tunics were rucked up at the back, stretched over the bulging holsters on their hips. No travel operators or limousine drivers leaned over the rail in front of the arrivals door displaying name cards. No African dignitaries in national dress strolled by with their attendants; no Arabs, smart in Western clothes, paraded ahead of their anxious, haik-wrapped wives and dark-eyed, track-suited children.

The arrivals board was blank and he wondered if Meg's plane had been cancelled, along with so many others, but a few people started to emerge from the Customs exit.

"Excuse me, which flight were you on?" he asked a sober-looking matron.

She braked her loaded trolley and frowned at him. "What do you want to know for?"

"I'm meeting someone from Madrid," he explained, wondering at her antagonism.

"Oh." She attempted to smile and failed. "Pardon me for seeming unhelpful: I've had it up to here," she raised a weary hand to her forehead, "with third degree, blood tests and form signing. I thought you were starting another round. Er, no. Not Madrid. I've just come in from Geneva," she added, before lurching into her trolley again, desperately trying to control the direction of the self-willed wheels, and ignoring Peter's polite thanks.

There was no one in sight to ask for flight information. He looked at his watch, shrugged, and headed for the seats which were miles away at the other end of the hall. It did not matter, of course; without the usual dense crowd of travellers his view of new arrivals would be unimpaired. He sat down, drew the crushed newspaper out from under his arm and began reading.

Meg arrived half an hour later than scheduled, and dragged her wheeled suitcase along the hall to stand gazing down at him before drawing his attention from *The Times* leader. "Hello."

He leapt up, beaming, his arms extended for a welcoming hug . . . and hardly recognised her. "Darling! What's happened?" It wasn't just her crumpled suit, the same primrose suit that had looked so smart and professional the last time he saw her, nor the dishevelled hair; it was her expression. Her eyes were dull, red-rimmed, set in deep, dark hollows, her lips were pinched and drooping at the corners and her skin almost grey except for the two bright pink feverish spots in her cheeks. Her eyes closed for a second while her chest heaved with a long, shuddering breath as she leaned against him, totally unresponsive. "Let's get to the car, first," she said.

He picked up the suitcase and steered her out of the building with a hand under her elbow. Once on the M4 back to London, he turned to look at her. Even with her eyes closed her face was a mask of misery and he remained silent, unwilling to disturb her with his anxious questions. She would tell him when she was ready.

Paris? Rome? Madrid? Where was she? The pale light of dawn framed the curtains, filtering through to fill the room with grey shadows. Meg lay frowning at the ceiling, trying unsuccessfully to re-orientate . . . until a grunt from the next pillow startled her and she saw the back of Peter's head. Then she remembered arriving in London; but why had Peter stayed the night in her hotel? She raised her head to stare round the room and the increasing light showed it was not a hotel room. It had to be Peter's flat. Yes, he had brought her here from the airport, saying he had a goulash in the oven waiting for them. She remembered sitting down at the table feeling not the least bit hungry. Apart from telling him about Sally Ann and his effort to make comforting responses, they had not talked at all and she knew he had not attempted to make love to her despite sharing the bed. Peter had looked very tired, but she had been exhausted. Shattered. It had taken the last ounce of her energy to stagger through the rigorous health checks before passing Immigration and Customs. The only thing she recalled Peter saying was that there were no Red Death cases in Britain. Thank God for that.

Peter rolled on to his back in his sleep. Meg watched as his bristled cheeks puffed slightly with each breath and his chest rose and fell. So it had been kept out of England, this unspeakable horror that was devastating virtually the whole world. No doubt he had played a part in that so limited success. He had vowed he would go to any lengths to achieve that, and had he not been right? Even to the Draconian extreme of isolating sufferers? If that had been applied in Chile, right at the beginning, Sally Ann might well be alive still, as would thousands of others. She had been so angry with him on that point, and he had been so determined.

"Penny for your thoughts." His eyes were open and he was smiling at her.

"How did I get here?"

"You fell asleep in the goulash so I carried you to bed. And I resisted ravishing you," he added seriously. "Now, stop evading the question. What's on your mind?"

"Us."

"Good. At least I hope it's good. What about us?"

"Well, firstly my congratulations to you on keeping the plague out of Britain." She remained on her back, staring at the ceiling.

"Thanks. But what's that got to do with us?"

"I was thinking that maybe I went overboard getting so angry at your attitudes," she said tentatively.

"And I've been thinking that maybe those attitudes were wrong, anyway. When I think of my sister . . . and her husband and children, stuck in some isolation camp in New Zealand . . . "

Meg felt his shudder vibrate through the bed and reached out to touch his shoulder. She smiled as the night's growth of beard scraped her fingers when he turned to kiss them.

"I suppose our opinions will always differ in many respects . . . " he went on, "but I think I will always love you."

"Enough?" She held her breath. Had she meant to say that?

Peter jerked upright in the bed and stared down at her. "Are you saying what I think you're saying?"

She made a moue. "I'm not sure. Nothing is sure. We don't even know if we are going to survive, do we?"

"Life must go on. We must believe we are going to survive. We can't suspend our existence on the chance we won't."

"Mmm. There will be so many problems to iron out . . . if we . . . I mean, I'll never give up my work and

I don't suppose you'll ever give up your politics . . . "

"What the hell? As long as we love each other and we are absolutely determined, nothing can prevent us making a success of it."

He meant marriage, of course. His back was wide and strong. A tiny nest of curls lay in the nape of his neck and his hair was tousled. She had not really had time to think since last seeing him before her European trip. It had all been so rushed, so tiring. And she had been too upset by the news of Sally Ann. But did she need to think? Surely she knew that this was the one man in the world she wanted? His confidence that they could overcome all the obstacles between them, mental and geographical, was contagious.

And as for the physical aspect, there were no problems there; it could not be more perfect. She sat up beside him and scratched his chin with a fingernail. "You'd better go and shave. I don't want my face torn to ribbons during the next test run."

Peter leapt out of bed, naked, and headed for the bathroom to prepare, as he put it, for the consummation of their engagement.

Their love-making was tinged with sadness. Though they had vowed to overcome any future problems between them, and the sun now filled the room with brilliant light, it was impossible to obliterate the dark shadows of death and suffering which besieged their minds.

They shared a bath, later, and breakfasted naked in the kitchen, windows open to the close, airless atmosphere.

"There's thunder in the offing," Peter remarked.

"Yes. I can feel it. I guess that's all we need."

There was so much to discuss; the varied responses to her tour of Europe, next moves, restrictions and drug distribution and who should have the first immunisations.

"Without appearing to queue jump, I do think the people responsible for fighting the problem, doctors, nurses, pharmacists, members of the Government . . . and ourselves, should be done first," Peter said.

"Definitely. It would be stupid not to. If we succumb, what hope have the rest?"

Then there were the wedding plans, where, when and how. "Just as soon as I can get the licence," Peter said positively. "Today being Sunday, that means tomorrow. Unless you particularly want to wait until your family . . . "

"Hey! Hold on there. No, I see no point in waiting around till we can get over there or they come here; heaven alone knows when that can be, anyway. And I'm all in favour of getting on with a job once a decision has been made. We have to make it quick, if we're going to: I have to be back in the States next week. Heck, I'll have to let Gray know, I guess: he is my boss."

"Does he have to give permission?"

"I'm over twenty-one, in case you hadn't noticed. I should think he'll be delighted. But sweetheart," she tilted her head on one side, looking slightly bashful, "I've never been married before, and hell, I may never get married again. I would like a photograph, some record of the event."

Peter threw back his head and roared with laughter. "I wondered what on earth you were going to say, then. Darling," he stretched a hand out across the table to grasp her fingers. "Of course we'll have some photographs; nice, professional ones we can stand on the piano."

"Of me wearing what?" she demanded, finally coming to the point. "That dilapidated suit I've been travelling round the continent in?"

"We'll go shopping tomorrow as well," Peter promised.

Easy Girl slipped up the reach above Carrick Roads in the early dawn. When summoned by the coastguard, Kitson had carried out his plan, told them they had entered the country at Dover from a continental cruise, had undergone all necessary checks, and had been coasting home for the past three days. He had done that often before, urged on by Clarke and Munro – he was the radio buff on board – and no one had ever questioned it. That was how they always managed to return with a crate of French wine on board. As long as they never attempted to sell it or even to drink it in any company but their own, who was to know? Perhaps one day they might be found out, but one day was a long way in the future.

He dropped the sails in the Roads and continued under power. He felt too ill, his head hurting and his stomach too, to sail up to their mooring, as they normally did. He just wanted to get ashore and reach Molly.

That was wrong, of course. He definitely had the Red Death. Therefore he was going to die. Like Munro. Like Clarke, lying there still and cold in the forward berth. He should not even go ashore, he ought to get on the radio again as soon as he was moored up, call the yacht club, and have police and doctors come on board. But if he did that, he would never see Molly again. By the time he had finished explaining about Munro and Clarke, and probably being run in for not reporting the situation while still at sea, he would be near death. He would be locked away in an isolation ward and that would be that. There was no cure. Everyone knew once you had the disease, it was curtains.

The newspapers had been a bit vague about how contagious the disease was. When *Easy Girl* had left for her continental cruise at the beginning of July, the Red Death had still been only a tabloid sensation, something which was affecting 'them', never 'us'. Three men away for their annual jolly had been totally uninterested in what might be happening in South America or New Zealand or even in South Africa. Nor had they paid much attention to various radio reports or rumours discussed in continental yacht clubs; they had always preferred to stay out of yacht clubs and the radio was for weather forecasts and sending messages; they only had VHF on board.

It was in Gibraltar that they first became aware that this was a worldwide disaster. Even then it still seemed remote for them . . . until that bint in Tangier. No use looking back in self-disgust and self-pity. It had happened. So the disease was pretty contagious. She had given it to Munro, presumably by sexual contact; Kitson frowned as he remembered her nose bleed, but he had never heard of blood being contagious. Munro then had given it to them. They had been his shipmates and they nursed him when he was sick and their washing-up habits were not of the best. That would be enough to account for it.

How he longed to hold Molly in his arms, one last time. But he must not, would not, do that. He would go to her, see her, and tell her what had happened, keeping his distance. Then she would telephone the police and he would be taken away, but he would have seen her, and she would know.

There was a giant lump in his throat, thinking of all the years they should have had together: years in which to do all the things they had planned now that the mortgage was paid off. Sure he was dejected, miserable, but he was not panicking. It was amazing how clearly he was thinking, despite the headache. Tunnel vision, they accused him of. When the chips were down, it was the best vision to have.

He rounded the last bend in the now rapidly shallowing water, saw the mooring ahead of him. It was still only five o'clock, and he had passed but a single fisherman setting out; they exchanged waves, for *Easy Girl* was well known in these waters, and the fisherman called out, "Had a good trip?"

Munro's adventures with his two friends were also well known in Truro, and envied.

"Magic," Kitson replied, then the two boats were out of earshot.

Kitson reduced speed to dead slow, put the bows up
to the mooring, heading the falling tide, and stepped
forward with the boathook. As the yacht fell away he
thrust the hook through the ring on the mooring line,
and brought it inboard, looping it over the forward bitt.
It was a manoeuvre he had carried out so often he could
do it in his sleep. Yet this time he had to sit on the deck
for several minutes to regain his strength and wait for his
head to stop swinging.

Manning the davits and getting the dinghy into the
water was another long business, and again left him
weak. He took all their money with him; it went against
his instincts to leave money lying around. But nothing
else. The police could sort it all out afterwards.

Fortunately the outboard started first kick, and five minutes later he was nosing into the dock and securing the
painter. It was six o'clock on a Sunday morning, and still
there was no one about, not even in the office.

Kitson walked up the beaten earth road, stumbling
as the ground seemed to rise and fall beneath his feet,
passed the parked cars of owners who were out for the
weekend, and reached the gate. He had not driven down
and left his car in the yacht club park, because he was to
be away so long. The sensible thing to do now would be
to telephone Molly and ask her to come down and pick
him up. But he was afraid of being too close to her in the
car . . . or even becoming involved with a telephone. He
just wanted to get home, for the last time . . . his house
was only half a mile from the club, anyway.

He walked up the sloping street, gradually moving
more confidently. His strength seemed to be returning too. That had been a bad attack, while mooring
up. But now it had passed, and he felt almost well,
save for the persistent headache. Perhaps he was not
as sick as he had supposed. Perhaps he was going to
survive. But he did not care, as long as he could see
Molly again.

The street was as deserted as the waterfront, although Kitson could hear the rattle of milk churns round the corner. He reached his gate, pushed it open and made his way up the path, fumbling in his pocket. His latch key was always attached to the ring which also carried his car key and the key to the yacht cabin and ignition. He slipped it into the lock, turned it gently, and pushed the door in. Molly would certainly still be asleep. He need do nothing more than stand in the bedroom doorway and look at her and then, perhaps, go to the police himself without even waking her. It was a matter of deciding which would be the least shock for her. Dear little Molly. It was sod's law that he should have been so late in finding her, and have had so little time to enjoy her. At least she was well provided for.

He reached the landing and the bedroom door, opened it very gently. The room was dark, with the curtains drawn. It was also scented. Molly's favourite scent, of course. But also another. Kitson's nostrils twitched and he switched on the light to stare at Molly, sitting up in bed in consternation, and at the man beside her, only slowly awakening to stare at him.

Kitson stared back at him, clinging to the doorpost for support, then he turned and stumbled back down the stairs and out on to the street, his legs as numbed as his mind.

Claudia was a brick. Appalled by the idea of a Registry Office wedding, she spoke to the rector of their little local church who agreed to conduct the nuptials with a special licence, and on Tuesday morning they congregated under the old lychgate outside the church, sheltering from the summer rain, before walking up the path in a group under golf brollies. John and Veronica Canning came, both looking years older and bent with worry over Sarah and her family. The Appletons were there early, waiting with Jeremy and Anne, and they all crowded into the porch,

pinning on their buttonholes and removing their macs.
Hartley arrived in the Rolls at the very last minute looking
hot and flustered. Meg wore a dress in ivory georgette, soft
and graceful and unpretentious, which Peter had helped
her choose in New Bond Street. It had cost the earth, but
neither of them thought it mattered; the whole situation
seemed utterly unreal and, in the circumstances, what was
money worth, anyway? Her little straw hat was ivory, too,
with a tiny froth of veil over her forehead and an ivory silk
rose with green leaves pinned under the brim. Claudia had
ordered a small spray of stephanotis and cream rosebuds
for her to carry and was very annoyed to see that the
roses used were actually white. Nor was she any happier
when Meg, attempting to mollify her, said she preferred
white ones. She was disappointed with this small, hasty
wedding. The only good thing about it was the bride;
Meg was definitely the right sort for Peter, despite being
American, and a doctor.

Meg kept wondering if the situation was not a bit crazy.
She had actually said so to Peter, when they had set off on
their shopping expedition yesterday. "Your family have
never met me. Won't they think it somewhat bizarre to
be asked to witness our wedding?"

"Stop worrying," he replied, "I'll take you down to
Wimbledon this evening to see the old folk and I promise
you they'll love you."

Although Peter had a very confident and forceful personality, Meg knew he could never have persuaded her
against her will. She wanted to marry him. The only real
fear was that maybe her reasons were not good enough.
Did she want this man, this family, this ceremony, because
she adored him, wanted nothing more than to spend the
rest of her life with him? Or was he just a rock to which she
could cling in the face of the horrific tide of events which,
even if the virus was mastered today, would leave their
world changed, sickeningly and dramatically, for ever?
She watched as his sister fastened his carnation with a little

371

gold safety pin. His expression was very serious, his brows drawn tightly together, accentuating the crow's feet at the corners of his eyes, making them attractively darker, almost Asian. He had so much on his mind, as she had herself. It was impossible not to feel deeply drawn to him, pulled on invisible cords. They did not need a marriage ceremony, the knots binding them together were already tied. Long ago she had ceased to believe that fate predestined one's mate; that a man and a woman were chosen for each other out of the millions around them by a supernatural force. Now she was even wondering if she and Peter had met purely by accident. Maybe, as in the Koran, 'it was written,' after all.

Fortunately the organist was an elderly, retired gentleman, readily available and willing to play for them at such short notice, making up for the lack of a choir with a vigorous 'Trumpet Voluntary' as they all entered the church together, and accompanying Claudia's contralto render-ing of 'Love Divine, all loves excelling' heard almost as a solo above the others. The tragedies and disasters wrought by the Red Death were forgotten as they took their vows, though John put a comforting arm round Veronica's shoulders when she dabbed at her eyes with a lace handkerchief suspecting she was remembering Sarah's wedding, not so many years before.

The rector was young and positive. In his brief address he commended the happy couple's courageous determination to carry on life as normally as possible, and their fortitude under the strain of the responsibility they each bore. Claudia had apparently briefed him well.

A finger buffet and champagne awaited their return to the Briggs' home and no one suggested turning on any of the depressing, hourly news bulletins, consistently wearing joyful smiles at least until Peter and Meg piled their luggage into Peter's Ford. No confetti was thrown, nor old shoes tied to the bumper, but the shouted good wishes were sincere enough as they drove off towards Cornwall.

*   *   *

"You'll see, the rain will clear as soon as we get into the West Country," Peter promised.

"Are you sure we can be away for two days? I know Jeremy told you it would be okay, but . . . "

"There is a phone at the cottage, darling. If something vital crops up they can get us. But as far as I can see it's all over to Hartley and his crew, now, until stocks of vaccine are sufficient to commence distribution." He turned to smile at her. "Happy?"

Meg nodded. "Whatever the circumstances, my love, you have the ability to make me happy. I know research and analysis is my job, but I can't make out what it is about you . . . "

"Charisma," he answered, keeping his eyes glued to the road. They both laughed.

Sure enough, as they motored farther west, the dripping trees and hedges bordering the fields, puddles, soggy shoes and umbrellas in the towns, gave way to softly rolling hills, the cropped wheat stalks shiny rose-gold in the evening sun, and bright summer dresses swinging along the village pavements.

It was dusk when Peter switched off the engine. "This is it. Welcome to your first married home, Mrs Canning," he announced. "Come on, I've got to carry you over the threshold."

Meg jumped out, eager to see all she could of the place before dark. "Oh, Peter, isn't it just cute? I love it!"

"There's a light on at the back. The Pengelleys must still be here." He came up behind her to sweep her up into his arms like a baby.

"Oh, darling, do be careful! Don't strain yourself. Let me at least walk to the door."

"You're much lighter when you're awake, let me tell you," he teased. The front door opened before they reached it, sending a path of yellow light to greet them. "Hello, Betty. Here's my beautiful bride."

Meg was deposited on the hall rug. "Hello, Betty," she held out her hand.

Betty took the hand in solemn silence, peering into Meg's face. Then she smiled, forming dimples in the corners of her mouth and moulding her cheeks into two shiny red apples. "Welcome to Trebeth Cross, Mrs Canning. We'll be real pleased to have you here with us." She was nodding her approval of Peter's choice as she spoke. "John," she called, "come 'n help in with the bags, then."

John Pengelley obeyed the command, carried the suitcases upstairs and then joined his wife and the bride and groom in the little sitting-room, his cap still on his head and a red bandanna knotted roughly round his throat.

"What's the latest news, then?" Betty asked.

Peter knew she was referring to the Red Death. "You probably know more than I do. I haven't heard a news broadcast since this morning."

"Getting worse in India, they said," John mumbled at the floor.

"And it's confirmed in Italy," Betty added. "It's not going to come here, is it, Mr Canning?"

"No chance of that, Betty. Tell me something, did Frances Wardle get here all right on Sunday?"

"Oh, yes," Betty said. "She said she'd met you in Ridding. And she told us all about Dr Jones and his flipping identity cards. He's a right one, he is. Now then, you'll be wanting some food."

Meg was looking at Peter with raised eyebrows.

He grinned at her. "Local problems. I'll tell you about them later."

Presumably Jones had got his plan approved at yesterday's meeting; no doubt the tests were being carried out now – he just had not got around to Trebeth Cross yet. But clearly he had given Fran a clean bill of health, which was a relief.

When Meg had been shown the chicken casserole in the oven, and the saucepans of vegetables waiting for the gas to be lit under them, the Cornish couple left, throwing a few suggestive jokes over their shoulders as they disappeared into the darkness.

Peter closed and bolted the door and swung round to take Meg into his arms. "At last. I've got you all to myself in our own little love nest." He kissed her hair, her eyes, her mouth. His tongue caressed hers and as her finger combed up through the hair on the back of his neck she felt him rising against her.

She pulled away. "Not now, you randy baron! Let's eat first."

He grabbed at her. "Hey! You've got your priorities all wrong."

"No way!" She dodged into the kitchen and fiddled with the gas knobs.

He followed. "Let me show you over the place while those are cooking."

"I love it, I love it." Meg skipped from room to room, noting the laden bookshelves and deep, cretonne-covered armchairs, the flagstone floors scattered with rugs downstairs and the fitted carpet, giving way to warmth and convenience, in the bedroom.

There were loads of waiting hangers in the wardrobe so they hastily unpacked before going down to eat. Peter got a bottle of wine out of the cupboard under the stairs and they toasted each other . . . and the end of the Red Death.

"I hadn't expected to feel any different after we were married. But I do."

Meg was speaking her thoughts aloud as they walked, hand in hand, along the cliff top. Gulls drifted below them without effort on the light air currents, occasionally screaming at each other, and cottonwool balls of cloud were pulled into constantly changing shapes as they danced across the sky. Beneath their feet the ground was dry, but though very little grass had survived the drought of the past weeks, the green was replaced by short-tufted, sweet-smelling vetches, purple and yellow, and cushions of sea-pinks. The tang of sea and sea-weed reached up through the rocks and scree to blend with the aroma of vetch, creating a gloriously fresh fragrance.

Peter twirled a sea-pink under her chin. "Different in what way?"

She paused to turn her face into the breeze. Eyes closed, she sucked the delicious air deep into her lungs. "Before, it could just have been an affair; a temporary thing without depth or meaning. Ships passing in the night, in sympathy only in the roughness of their respective voyages." She pulled him against her, leaning her cheek against his sports shirt. "Now we're a unit. Now we have something beautiful and permanent. Like this." Her hand swept round in a semi-circle that encompassed sea and cliffs and moorland. "No matter what happens in the coming months, or years, there will always be this . . . and our love."

They remained standing there, her arms around his waist, his about her shoulders, nursing the precious silence, neither wanting to break the spell.

Minutes passed before Peter held her gently away so that he might smile into the Irish blue eyes. "Maybe, if medical research allows, we might even found our own dynasty that will last for a thousand years or more." It was, they both knew, more of a serious question than a figurative statement.

Meg's even white teeth flashed in a wide grin. "I'll certainly enjoy trying."

Peter gave a quizzical frown. "Honestly?"

"I didn't have much time to speak with Hartley at the reception, but I gather he regards the Briggs research department as the pulse centre of his companies. Do you think, if he gave me a job, he might allow me time off for babies?"

"You bet your sweet life!" He grabbed her round the waist and swung her round and round till they were both dizzy. "Whe! eee!" he shouted at the sea, "I'm going to be a Daddy!"

Meg collapsed on the ground, tears of laughter filling her eyes. "You darling idiot! Hold on there, I'm not pregnant yet!"

"We'll soon see about that," he said with enthusiasm as he sank down beside her and attacked the buttons on her blouse.

"No, Peter! It's too public. We can be seen for miles around," Meg protested half-heartedly, allowing him to slip the thin cotton from her shoulders.

"Rubbish. There isn't anyone for miles. Anyway, who cares? You are my wife." And he progressed to her skirt.

Lying naked on the cliff top, the heat of the sun on their white flesh tempered by cool fingers of breeze playing sensuously into their secret crevasses, immediately excited an erotic, passionate need. Feeling him hard against her thigh, knowing she was moist and hungry for him, Meg pulled his weight over her body, unaware of the sharp, dead grass stalks piercing into the flesh of her back. He needed no guidance. Her body arched to receive him and as he sank through the mound of dark curls he felt himself grasped firmly, drawn deep down into her soul. Fiercely they thrust together, her legs wrapped around him, heels pressing hard into his taut flesh. Gasping in unison they soared into a rapid, momentous climax.

Through the swaying sea-pinks by her head, Meg watched the clouds and gulls, and a pied wagtail nodding as he walked along a sandy stretch of path . . . and found herself calculating how long the swim would take up to her ovaries. She did not want to move. Considering her past reluctance to have children it was surprising, to say the least. Maybe there is some deep instinct to reproduce when humans know their numbers are severely depleted, she thought. She swatted blindly at something on her chest, heard Peter's chortle and realised he was tickling her with a grass stalk.

"Let's get back in time for a drink at the pub before lunch," he suggested. "I want to introduce my wife to my constituents."

"Great. Let's go." She jumped to her feet and began to dress. Conceiving was not the least bit tiring, she decided.

The Iron Duke was crowded: Wednesday was early closing in Trebeth Cross and the farmers all followed the example of the villagers. When Peter led Meg into the Public Bar there was a tremendous shout: the Pengelleys had told everyone that their MP was getting married, and equally that he was coming down to the cottage to honeymoon.

"You're right pretty," announced Farmer Poldarren. "I'd have you meet the wife." He spoke with some regret; Edith Poldarren might have been pretty once, but that had been a long time ago. Now she was already on her fourth gin and tonic.

"You mind what 'e says," she warned Meg. "'E's a conno . . . conna . . . 'e likes pretty legs."

"Oh, Mrs Canning," gushed Mavis Tregarthen. "It's so nice to meet you." She gazed at Peter, face crimson with thoughts of what might have been.

"You should come and live down here," said Mr Perry, "and bring 'im with you. London's no place to live."

Meg found a pint of best bitter in her hand, and after the first few mouthfuls decided she could get to like it. Peter was already halfway through his. She had a sudden sense of belonging here. This was Peter's place, far more, she suspected, than the hurly-burly of London. It was going to be her place as well.

Peter was leading her up to the bar. "Margaret Canning," he said. "Clive Wardle and Stephanie Wardle, and Fran."

"Peter, you are the luckiest chap in the world," Clive exclaimed, kissing Meg on both cheeks.

"You darling," Stephanie said, hurrying round the bar to embrace her.

"Hello, Mrs Canning," Fran said shyly, shaking hands.

"Three of my closest friends," Peter explained.

"I'm so happy to meet you," Meg said. "I'm so happy to be here. I guess . . . I'm so happy," Meg chortled.

"So are we," Clive assured her, and pushed another pint of beer across the counter towards her.

Meg was not sure she could cope with that, and looked to Peter for help, but he was talking with Frances.

"How did you get on with Arthur Jones?" he asked.

"Oh, he jabbed me with a needle. My arm is so punctured I'm starting to look like a drug addict."

"That man is a public menace," Stephanie declared. "Do you know, he telephoned last night to tell us that the day after tomorrow he is coming over here with a mobile unit to blood-test the entire village? Of all the cheek."

"Can he do that, Peter?" Clive inquired.

"Well . . . I suspect he has had a by-law passed . . . I don't suppose it can do any harm," Peter temporised.

"I still think it's cheek," Stephanie said. "What do you think, Mrs Canning? Or may I call you Meg?"

"Please do," Meg said. And decided to take her cue from Peter. "As Peter says, it probably can't do any harm. If he wants to take that much trouble . . "

"What are they doing in the States?" Clive asked.

Meg's head was beginning to spin as people pressed around her, firing questions. English beer was definitely stronger than American. "Well," she said. "I don't really know."

"Meg's maiden name is Calhoun," Peter said proudly.

"She's the doctor who's just found the vaccine which is going to put a stop to the Red Death. She's not really involved in the day-to-day business of combating it."

"Dr Calhoun!" Stephanie cried. "But that's marvellous."

The news spread through the bar, and Meg had her hand wrung all over again, while she tried politely to excuse herself from accepting yet another beer.

"You'll get the Nobel Prize, I shouldn't wonder," declared Farmer Poldarren.

Peter had not thought of that. "You should, you know," he said.

"Peter," she whispered. "If I have another of these I am going to fall over. In fact, I think I am going to fall over anyway."

"Fresh air," he decided. They made their apologies and promised to return that evening, then he got her outside and hurried her along the street.

"Do those people drink that much every day?" she gasped.

"Well, twice a day," he said. "They're a jolly lot. And they just fell in love with you."

"I'm sure I shall fall in love with them, when I can think straight," she promised.

He opened the front door and ushered her into the cottage. "I'll cook," he said. "You sit down."

"You will not," she insisted. "I'm the housewife, remember? Anyway, I'm feeling better already."

He kissed her and let her get on with it, happy that she had recovered so quickly. He switched on his Ansaphone, and clicked his tongue in annoyance as he listened to Jeremy's somewhat fruity voice, which at that moment was sounding overripe with anxiety.

"I'm afraid we must ask you to come back up to town, old man," Jeremy said. "It is most frightfully urgent. I cannot discuss it over the phone, but I'd be obliged if you would contact me, in London, just as quickly as possible."

"For God's sake," Peter said. "They can't even let me go for twenty-four hours."

"I thought something like this might happen," Meg said, breaking eggs into a frying pan. "Any idea?"

"I haven't a clue. I damn well know the situation can't have changed all that much since yesterday. Probably there's been some hitch in the production of the vaccine. Listen, Meg," he held her hands. "I have to go. I'll leave right after lunch, be there by this evening, sort out the flap, and be back with you tomorrow. All right?"

She hesitated. Instinctively she wanted to go with him . . . but she was exhausted, and the idea of driving up to London and back did not appeal to her in the slightest. Once having taken the decision to give herself a week off, her mind as well as her body was clamouring for rest.

"Okay," she said. "Do you know what I'm going to do?"

"Tell me."

"I'm going to get into bed and stay there until you return."

"Great idea. Don't forget, if you want anything, just call Betty; she'll be right over. And if you get lonely, they'll always be happy to see you at the Duke."

"I won't forget," she promised him. Not that she had the intention of contacting anyone in the village until his return. "How do you like your eggs?"

"Thank you, Hugo. That looks splendid," Claudia murmured, tilting her head from side to side to study every angle of his latest creation in the reflection from the mirror her hairdresser held up behind her chair. She smiled at him in the glass and reached for her handbag, pausing for the ritual removal of the gown and brushing of imaginary hair from the collar of her dress.

Though he was obviously one of 'those', Hugo was charming and a very good hairdresser. Besides, despite being miles away from her home, he had the great advantage of this sizeable carpark. Anyway, the distance gave her the excuse for a good run in the Mercedes 500 Sports that Hartley had given her for her last birthday. She smiled as she approached the gleaming champagne charger and tossed her handbag on to the biscuit-leather upholstery.

There were black clouds massing to the west and a fresh wind plucked at her lacquered hair: so she tied a Liberty scarf over it as the canvas car-top was down. This was like no other car she had driven. The almost silent engine gave a deep-throated rumble sending power-waves throbbing into the ground beneath as she engaged first gear and slid out on to the road. Power steering responded to her slightest touch as she sneaked past a delivery van, swayed round a pair of cyclists. On-coming traffic halted her behind a rubbish lorry and she gunned the engine impatiently until she could let the clutch out again and fly down a clear straight stretch. She swung round the corner at the end, and nearly ploughed into an accident which had apparently just happened: two cars were broadside across the road.

"For heaven's sake!" Claudia leaned on the horn.

A few people were collecting round the cars, and a man came across to her. "No good getting uptight, dear. We got a man here, hurt. But you can help."

"Me? What can I do?"

"Get this bloke to hospital. It's the third turning on your right after you hit the main road. Someone's telephoning for an ambulance but he's losing a lot of blood. Speed's the thing."

"Oh. . ." She did not want to get involved but supposed it was only Christian decency. And she certainly had the speed. "Well of course," she said. "If you're sure it's safe to move him."

"Over here, Harry!" the man called.

Two other men staggered across, half carrying the casualty between them; his clothes were soaked in blood.

Claudia gulped. "Shouldn't he be lying down?"

"I'm all right, really," the man gasped, collapsing into

the passenger seat. "It was just a bump. Must have burst a blood-vessel in my nose."

"I'll come with you," said one of the others, climbing over into the tiny, rear seat. "Let's move, lady."

Claudia put her foot down and weaved round the parked cars. "I suppose you should really have waited for the police."

"They'll know where to find him. Anyway, it wasn't a serious accident. Jim here just knocked into the rear of the other bloke. Not much damage done. It's his loss of blood that worries me. It just doesn't stop."

Claudia glanced sideways and saw what he meant. Blood still trickled down Jim's front in a steady stream . . . all over her beautiful leather upholstery. She hoped it would wash off.

On a midweek afternoon the roads were empty, even in August – Trebeth Cross had been devoid of tourists – and Peter made good time. He was in Westminster before six-thirty. The recalled House was sitting, but he preferred not to appear in the chamber, as he was officially honeymooning. Instead he went to Jeremy's office and had a message sent in.

Jeremy was with him in five minutes. "The Prime Minister is waiting for us."

"What the hell has happened?"

"What is the worst thing that could have happened, old boy?" Jeremy asked, his face a mask of desperate anxiety.

"Oh, Christ," Peter muttered. "How?"

"We're still trying to work that out."

"I'm sorry to interrupt your honeymoon, Peter," the Prime Minister said. "But we may be faced with a crisis. Before it breaks, however, I thought we should have a private word on the best way to handle it. I assume your wife came up with you?"

"No. She stayed in Cornwall. Why?"

"That is a pity," the Prime Minister commented. "I suspect she may be able to help us."

"Would someone tell me what's happening?" Peter asked.

"Jeremy?"

Jeremy had a report on the table in front of him. "Yesterday afternoon . . ." he raised his head, "while we were celebrating your wedding, old boy. Well, down in Truro police were called to a yacht moored in the harbour there, because other boat owners complained of an unpleasant smell. The yacht was called *Easy Girl*. The police boarded her, and found the decomposing body of a man in the forward cabin."

He turned a page. "The yacht was in perfect order. The police found the log book, and this too was written up-to-date or, at least, up to last Sunday. The yacht belonged to a Brian Munro. This was well known to the locals of course; he had kept his boat in Truro harbour for many years. Munro, according to the log, died at sea. The log indicates that he died of the Red Death which, it seems, he contracted from a prostitute in Tangier."

"Why wasn't his illness reported by radio?" Peter inquired.

"You may well ask. It would appear that he and his crew decided to bring the yacht home, sailing direct from Tangier to England, rather than risk being quarantined in some foreign port; obviously they had no idea how fast the disease works. But this involved them in returning a week earlier than expected and has an important bearing on what has happened. Now, the dead man on board is recorded as Tom Clarke. He was one of Munro's regular sailing companions. He apparently died on Saturday night."

Peter frowned. "Then who brought the yacht home?"

"There was a third crew member, David Kitson. It must have been him."

"Must have been? Where is he?"

"Nobody knows."

"But . . . my God! You know what you're saying?"

"Finish the report, Jeremy," the Prime Minister recommended.

"Kitson is definitely listed as the second crew member, and indeed he signed the log. A fisherman remembers seeing him bring the yacht up the river at dawn on Sunday. He then moored the boat and went ashore. Half an hour later he appeared at his house. He apparently opened the door and went up to the bedroom, where he, ah . . . found his new wife in bed with another man. As I said, he was a week early in returning."

"Good God! What did he do?"

"Turned and left."

"Did his wife report it?"

"Well, of course she didn't. She was in a state, naturally. She sent her lover home, and waited for Kitson to reappear. But he didn't."

"Didn't she realise he was ill?"

"Apparently not. Kitson is anaemic. He probably showed no signs of the disease when she saw him, which was only briefly anyway. This is assuming he had it. No, Mrs Kitson had no idea anything was wrong, other than that her husband appeared to have left her, until the police called Tuesday night and she admitted being found with her boyfriend. Even then she was still hoping he'd come back to her. The police settled down to attempt to trace Kitson's movements. It seems that he just wanted to get as far away from Truro as possible. The police have found a man who gave someone answering Kitson's description a lift in his car to Truro railway station early on Sunday morning, and the station master remembers seeing him board the 09.13 for London; it seems the two men were acquainted. After that . . . nothing."

"Jesus Christ!" Peter commented. "That's more than three days ago."

"Quite," the Prime Minister agreed. "Now, the points that need to be determined, urgently, are these. One: is it likely that David Kitson has the Red Death?"

"Almost certainly," Peter said.

"Two: if he has the disease, will he know it?"

"Yes."

"Three: if he is anaemic, how delayed would the onset be?"

"Not more than a few days, going by other anaemic victims."

"Would he still be contagious, during this longer incubation period? What about your wife's theory that the virus only survives for a few days in the human system? Would it survive longer in anaemics?"

"I have no idea. But it is certainly a possibility. We'd have to ask Meg."

"Who is, unfortunately, not here. But I'm afraid we have to accept that the Red Death may be in Britain," the Prime Minister said.

"So far it is a total secret," Jeremy said. "The police have not allowed the press access to either the yacht or the log book. They have said they are treating the case as murder, which has caused a minor local sensation, but has prevented anyone thinking about what might really have happened . . . at least as far as we know. But the story is at present only twenty-four hours old. Keeping the lid on it is going to be difficult when people stop to think."

"May I ask how the devil the yacht got back in without a proper inspection? From Tangier?" Peter demanded.

"Ah. Kitson pulled a fast one here. The coastguards admit that yachtsmen often do. Kitson called the Falmouth coastguard, as he was bound to do, and advised them that *Easy Girl* was making a landfall and was on her way to her home mooring in Truro harbour. He informed the coastguard that they had been on passage along the south coast from Dover, where they had cleared Customs and undergone the necessary health checks on their return from France."

"Which is highly illegal," the Prime Minister put in.

"Oh, quite. But as I said, apparently some yachtsmen do it. The penalties are severe, if they're caught, and can include confiscation of the yacht. However, Kitson did it, and the coastguard suspects he has done it on previous occasions too. It is a loophole that has simply got to be closed, now, even if it means some kind of central computer system for keeping track of yacht movements."

"Rather like shutting the stable door after the horse has bolted," Peter remarked.

"We are straying from the subject," the Prime Minister said. "You tell us, Peter, that Kitson would have known he had contracted the disease. From the logbook entries he certainly knew what the Red Death is. I believe you have done some yachting in your time. Can you form any opinion of what was in his mind, in evading Customs and Immigration, with a dead man on board? He must have known he would be found out very rapidly."

"Well, he wouldn't have been thinking all that clearly, in the circumstances, Prime Minister. It would seem that his sole idea was to get home to his wife . . . "

"Knowing that he was in a highly contagious state?"

"Well . . . he might just have meant to tell her, not touch her. I mean, he must have known he was dying. He may have meant to say goodbye, and then call the police. It's just catastrophic that he caught her cheating, and rushed off. But where?"

"If your theory is correct, he should then have gone to the police," Jeremy said.

"Well . . . yes. Maybe he just didn't make it. No, that's not right, because he was seen boarding the train. I just don't know what he had in mind."

"I'm afraid I have a rather unpleasant suspicion as to what was in Kitson's mind," the Prime Minister said.

"As you have said, Peter, he wouldn't have been thinking very clearly. In fact, the voyage home from Tangier, as indicated by his log book, must have been sufficiently traumatic to distort his mental balance. As you say, he was clearly governed by the homing instinct. But I fear that after discovering his wife, ah, in flagrante delicto, he may really have flipped his lid. He knows he has the disease, and he knows it is the most highly dangerous and contagious disease ever known to man. Yet he has opted to disappear, in London presumably."

"We don't know he's in London," Jeremy said. "He could merely have changed trains and gone almost anywhere."

The Prime Minister's smile was wintry. "You are a cheerful fellow, Jeremy. However, wherever he is, the point I am making is this: is it not possible that he has determined to avenge himself on the whole human race? Or at least, on as much of it as he can infect before he dies?" The Prime Minister looked at their startled faces. "I would say that we have someone who can only be described as a potential mass murderer on the loose, and what is more, a murderer who creates more potential murderers with every person he infects. Gentlemen, I am afraid that, after all our very considerable efforts, we are facing a situation as grave as anywhere in the world. The question we have to answer, now, is what we are going to do about it."

21

Emergency

Meg watched the Ford disappear, then she locked the front door. She had told Peter not to worry about the dishes, and now she returned to the kitchen and filled the plastic bowl with hot water, happy to be playing the role of housewife in her new home. The kettle was steaming by the time she finished and she made herself a cup of instant coffee, carrying it into the living-room to sit and relax in an armchair of cretonne roses.

She was aware of several very odd sensations. Partly it might be the beer, she knew. But in the main they were the result of the strangeness of her situation. She looked around her at the rough old walls of the cottage. It was a dream, the sort of place she had always wanted to own. And presumably, as Peter's wife, she did own it. Yet it was utterly strange to her, furnished so differently from anything she could have dreamed up, but harmonising perfectly. She would not want to change a thing, except maybe install a coffee-maker – and a dishwasher.

She sipped the instant brew, wrinkling her nose at it, and stretched happily. She was alone. That was another unusual feeling, in a backwards way. This was the first time she had been alone since Saturday evening: nearly four days. But those were the first consecutive days she had spent entirely in someone else's company since she had been a girl living at home. She had always been intensely private; even at medical school, once she had graduated to a bedroom of her own the door had been kept closed, more often than not with her inside.

Now she had given up all of that privacy to a man. And more than just privacy. She smiled as she recalled those fifteen minutes on the cliff top. If there was any truth in the old wives' tale that the more enjoyable it was, the more chance there was of getting pregnant, then she was pregnant.

Just like that. The end of a promising career? Of course it would not really be the end . . . but it would be a severe interruption. She understood herself well enough to know that she would throw herself into motherhood with the same total dedication as she approached her profession.

But what a time to be considering motherhood! If she was so relieved to feel that at last things were moving, that the human race was after all going to be saved, she could not disguise from herself the enormous amount of work that lay ahead, work which might take years, and in which she was going to be totally involved. She was being absolutely crazy.

Just as she was being absolutely crazy in contemplating a child before the possible genetic effects of griseofulmaline had been determined. But that might take years.

She finished her coffee, washed the cup and saucer, went upstairs, and undressed. It was a close afternoon, and she thew open one of the windows, looked out at the moor and, in the distance, the sea, made more dramatic by the huge black clouds rolling in from the Atlantic. The rain they had driven through yesterday had been just the harbinger of a storm. But she looked forward to it. This was a part of England a foreigner normally only read about, in books by people like Daphne du Maurier. Now she was a part of it.

She got into bed, stretched luxuriously. The great thing was, that with everything that was looming above her and above everyone, she was simply happy. She felt at peace, surrounded by friends. She thought she might after all go down to the pub this evening and have a drink with the Wardles, Peter's friends . . . such nice people. Meg fell asleep.

She awoke to the sound of a bell. Drowsily she supposed it was the telephone, and reached out to pick it up. But then she realised there must be a doorbell. She muttered a few curses, pulled on her dressing-gown, and went downstairs. She unlocked the door, and gazed at Stephanie Wardle. But the laughing, happy woman of that morning had changed to a rather distraught looking caricature.

"Oh, Mrs Canning . . . Meg . . . I'm so sorry to disturb you, but . . . is Peter about?"

"Well, no. He had to go up to London. He'll be back tomorrow. Is anything wrong?"

Obviously something was.

"Oh, Meg . . . " Without warning Stephanie burst into tears.

"Stephanie!" Meg cried. "You'd better come inside." She virtually dragged Stephanie into the house. "What on earth's the matter?"

Stephanie collapsed on to the settee. "It's Fran. She's not well."

Meg wondered if she should give her a drink, sat beside her instead. "Not well?"

"She has this headache, and stomach pains."

Meg frowned at her, while an icy hand seemed to close on her heart. But it was impossible for the disease to occur spontaneously in the heart of England.

Stephanie blinked through her tears. "Didn't Peter tell you about her?"

"No, he didn't." Her frown deepened. "He was going to, but he didn't. I think you had better."

Stephanie told her about Fran's return from Japan, and Meg began to feel physically sick.

"She was given blood tests, everywhere," Stephanie sobbed. "Arthur Jones gave her one just Sunday."

"If Fran normally has really low blood pressure, the tests wouldn't have shown anything," Meg said.

"Do . . . so you think she has it? The Red Death?"

"Yes."

"Oh, my God. What are we going to do? She's going to die, Meg. My little girl is going to die."

"No, she isn't," Meg said. "We can save her."

"We can? But . . . "

"Wait here." Meg ran upstairs, threw her housecoat across the bed, dragged on jeans and a shirt, ran a comb through her hair. Then she opened her handbag, and took out the little box. In it were four griseofulvin tablets, and one phial of griseofulmaline vaccine. The griseofulmaline she had brought along for Peter, just in case the unthinkable happened and the Red Death did get to Britain.

Now it had done so, but Peter was not here. Thank God! She wanted to scream.

She ran back down the stairs. Stephanie was standing staring out of the window.

"Let's hurry," Meg said.

"But . . . "

"I have some griseofulvin tablets here," Meg said. "If they're administered in time, at this stage, she should be all right."

"Oh, thank God!" Stephanie said, and began to cry again.

They hurried along the street. There were only a few people about, but these stared and called out to ask what was wrong.

"Don't reply," Meg said. She did not want the news to get about.

They entered the now closed pub and ran up the stairs. Fran was in bed, her face flushed. She was groaning and holding her stomach.

392

"Get some water," Meg said, and held the girl up to take the pill.

"I can't," Fran moaned. "I can't. God, my head hurts. Just leave me alone. For God's sake, leave me alone," she screamed.

"We will, once you've taken this pill," Meg said. "You'll have to force her mouth open, Clive."

Cautiously Clive gripped his daughter's jaw. She attempted to strike at him and Stephanie held her arms. Meg put the pill at the base of the girl's throat and poured some water in. "Just swallow," she said. "Please, Fran. Just swallow."

Fran swallowed involuntarily, and the pill went down.

"Now, drink some more water," Meg said.

Fran, exhausted from her brief struggle, obeyed.

"That's a good girl," Meg said. She stood up.

"How soon will we know, if . . ." Clive bit his lip.

"If there's no bleeding, in another twelve hours there should be some sign of a return to normal."

"She's going to be all right," Stephanie told him. "Meg says so."

"Thank God!"

Meg carefully laid Fran down again. "Now we should do a little praying."

Clive licked his lips. "What . . . what about . . . "

"I have only three more tablets here," Meg said. "I know you're at risk, but at the first sign of anything wrong with either of you, you'll have a tablet. What we have to decide is how many other people could possibly have been contaminated."

"How is it passed?" Clive asked.

"Any bodily contact. I don't mean just touching. But sneezing . . . "

"She didn't have a cold," Stephanie said, gazing at the now comatose girl.

"But if it can be passed by sneezing . . . " Clive gulped.

"Oh, indeed, it is passed even more easily by kissing," Meg agreed. "Which is why we're going to watch you two very carefully over the next forty-eight hours."

"But . . . " Wardle's face was ashen. "Fran kissed just about everyone in the village, when she got home."

"Oh, heck," Meg said. "I think I had better call this Dr Jones of yours."

"The first and most important decision we have to take is how we handle this," the Prime Minister said.

"With respect, Prime Minister," Peter said. "Our first priority is surely to find David Kitson. Even if he is already dead."

"The two are connected, Peter. Now, as Jeremy has said, the police in Truro have been superb. Immediately the inspector who handled the initial investigation read the log book and realised that Clarke and Munro had died of the Red Death, he contacted his station superior, and he in turn went straight to the Chief Constable of the county. The Chief Constable, while putting every available man on to tracing Kitson's movements, did two things of vital importance: he telephoned Scotland Yard and gave them Kitson's description, but said no more than that the man was wanted in connection with a murder investigation. The second thing he did was to telephone my office and ask for further instructions. That was when I asked Jeremy to bring you back."

"May I ask what instructions you gave the Chief Constable, Prime Minister?"

"I told him absolute secrecy had to be maintained until I got back to him. I promised to do so tonight. Now the point is that Scotland Yard, still assuming they are looking for a possible murder suspect, have not found Kitson. As you remarked just now, Peter, he has therefore been on the loose for more than seventy-two hours, and he has evaded the police carrying out a fairly routine duty. The question we must decide is whether we now release the true reason we must find this man. This may well have the effect not only of redoubling the police effort, but also of retracing his movements and bringing forward anyone who is aware of having come into contact with him during these last three days. We may even unearth the person who has been giving him shelter, because someone certainly has. On the other hand, we risk starting a panic before the vaccine is coming off the production line in any quantity."

"I don't think we have any choice," Peter said. "The disease is here, and it is going to spread like a bushfire after a drought, unless it is checked, and in a hurry."

The Prime Minister looked at Jeremy, who nodded, unhappily.

"Very good. I will have a word with Toby immediately we are finished here, and there will be a full Cabinet meeting tonight. Once we are all agreed, I will make a statement to the nation." The Prime Minister considered for a moment. "There is no hope of getting it out tonight after the Cabinet meeting, and we can't wait until tomorrow night. We'll have to break with precedent. Put it out early tomorrow morning."

"On breakfast television?" Jeremy was aghast. "Nobody watches breakfast TV."

"Yes, they do, Jeremy. And there's radio as well. The broadcast will be repeated every hour until we can be sure the message has reached the whole nation. Now, the second vital question is our attitude to vaccination. I have the Home Secretary's plan here," the Prime Minister tapped a folder. "But that of course was compiled on the assumption that we would be taking no action until we had sufficient vaccine for a nationwide programme. We do not, at this minute. Have you been in touch with Sir Hartley, Jeremy?"

"Yes. Obviously I couldn't tell him why, but I asked him how the production was coming along. I'm afraid he was rather brusque. He is of course doing his best.

I gather there is sufficient vaccine for perhaps ten thousand innoculations at the moment, and the supply is building up all the time. I told him a vastly increased output was essential, and he made a rather rude remark. But I am sure he will do his best."

"Ten thousand," mused the Prime Minister. "Well, gentlemen?"

"You, of course," Peter said. There was nothing else to be said, in the circumstances.

"Am I indispensable? If I am, surely the whole Cabinet is. But what about the Opposition? What about the Royal Family? What about the reaction of the country if it is learned that the establishment is being safeguarded but not the man in the street? What about the police who are looking for this man? The doctors and nurses who will have to treat the people he has infected? I gather that in other countries they have been most at risk. And then, faced with this situation, what do we do with the stocks of vaccine as they become available? Is it to be a case of women and children first?"

"That would be pointless," Jeremy said. "They couldn't possibly cope if all the men were wiped out."

"What an incredible conversation to be having," the Prime Minister remarked.

It occurred to Peter that the Prime Minister was genuinely unable to make a decision, for the first time that he could remember. It was a measure of the gravity of the situation.

"Is there no possibility of obtaining stocks of the vaccine from other countries which are now in full production?" he asked.

"Which other country would you suggest? Only America and Japan have managed to move into full production already, and both of them have the Red Death themselves, even though they are still claiming to have it under control in the States. The matter will be discussed in Cabinet tonight. Meanwhile, Peter, I would be obliged if you would ask your wife to join you in London. I am sure her advice will be invaluable, and it might be reassuring, when I give my talk tomorrow morning, to have such an expert at my elbow, as it were, to tell people what to do, and what to avoid."

"I'll call her right away," Peter agreed. "Do you wish me at the Cabinet tonight?"

"Of course." The Prime Minister gave a wintry smile. "This is very much your baby, Peter."

A thousand and one thoughts raced through Peter's mind as he drove home. The Red Death was loose, in London. Whether or not it was being spread around malignantly, as the Prime Minister feared, or whether Kitson was just a terrified man, running from pillar to post, it was here. And the evidence of what had happened in the rest of the world suggested that the results were going to be catastrophic. He wanted to telephone his mother and father, and Claudia, or at least Hartley, and tell him, warn him, perhaps ask him to smuggle some early vaccines out and at least make his family safe. But to do that would be a breach of his governmental responsibility, indeed, his duty to the country. After the Prime Minister's broadcast he could call them and warn them to avoid any contact with strangers.

Thank God, Meg was safe. Not only was Trebeth Cross on the other side of Cornwall from Truro – but she had already been vaccinated. Thus he could, without fear, obey the Prime Minister's command and ask her to come up to town, where they would be working side by side. That at least was a heart-warming thought.

He unlocked the flat; poor Gladstone was still in the cattery and, as usual in his absence, the place seemed horribly empty. He dialled his Trebeth Cross number, and waited; there was no ringing tone, in fact, there was absolutely no sound. That was ridiculous. He dialled again, to the same silence.

He dialled Enquiries.

"I'll come back to you, Mr Canning," the woman said, and did so ten minutes later. "I'm afraid that line is out of order at the moment, sir."

"Out of order? How on earth can it be out of order? It was all right earlier today. Listen, get Ridding Enquiries."

"Yes, Mr Canning. I'll have a supervisor check into it. But the weather is very bad down there at the moment, and there could have been a lightning strike on a transformer or something like that. They'll have the line back again in a couple of hours, I'm sure."

"Put my call through as soon as it is," Peter said, and hung up feeling thoroughly disgruntled. And disturbed, as well: he was running out of time. It was already past eight, and the last train from Ridding was the 10.30. It would be bad enough anyway to have to ask Meg to travel half the night, but if she missed that one and had to catch the early morning milk train it would mean getting up at an unearthly hour. And even then he doubted if she could make it by seven.

He boiled himself a couple of eggs, had a bath and a change of clothing. The Cabinet meeting was scheduled for 10 pm, and it was now 9 pm. He turned on the television, watched the news, which reported various outbreaks of the Red Death in Europe, carefully downplaying the incidences; there was no mention of any appearance of the disease in Britain. In that regard they were still ahead.

9.30. He had to leave. He dialled Trebeth Cross again, without result, then Enquiries again.

"One of our supervisors has been on to Ridding, Mr Canning. I'm afraid all lines to Trebeth Cross have been temporarily disconnected."

"Temporarily disconnected?" Peter shouted. "What the hell does that mean?"

"It can mean any number of things, Mr Canning," the woman said, somewhat stiffly. "The Ridding operators were unable to give a reason. But as I said, there is this storm . . . "

"Are they doing something about it?"

"It is nearly ten o'clock at night, Mr Canning. I am sure they will do something about it first thing tomorrow morning."

"Tomorrow morning is no good to me at all."

"Is it an emergency?"

"Yes," he said. "Yes, it is an emergency."

He hung up, chewed his lip. How the devil was he going to get Meg to London if he could not reach her?

"Very good, gentlemen." The Prime Minister looked around the weary and anxious faces at the Cabinet table. Tonight they included the Chief of the Imperial General Staff and the Commissioner of the Metropolitan Police. They had been going over the situation for more than two hours.

"We are agreed on the following measures. One: immediately this meeting ends, the Ministry of Health will mobilise every medical unit in the country; these units will be divided into emergency stations, and each will be equipped as far as possible to deal with anyone revealing symptoms of the disease. You will have to organise the telephone service as well, Jeremy; we don't want people queueing up and terrifying each other. They must all wait at home to be attended."

Jeremy nodded, and wiped his forehead with a silk handkerchief. He had sweated profusely throughout the meeting, and Peter, sitting beside him, had become aware also that his boss must have had several stiff whiskies earlier in the evening. He could never have anticipated a crisis of this immensity being dumped in his lap when he accepted the ministry.

"Two: the armed services are to be put on the alert, immediately, and troops moved to cover certain strategic localities. In line with our agreement on the prevention of panic evacuations, as has happened in so many other countries, they will also immediately establish road blocks around London and all important towns, as well as all the main railway stations."

The CIGS nodded.

"It being clearly understood that discretion will be used as far as possible and that there will be no interference with ordinary commuter traffic. Equally, essential travel must be permitted; our objective must be to maintain normality, at least until we are forced to do otherwise, which contingency hopefully will not arise.

"Three: the Metropolitan Police to be turned out in force, and to commence a house-to-house search for Kitson. I assume you will see that your men take proper precautions."

The Commissioner nodded.

"Additionally, every police force throughout the country is to be informed of the emergency and told to stand by."

The Home Secretary nodded.

"Four: I will make a broadcast at seven o'clock tomorrow morning, informing the country of the facts, of the measures we are taking, and of the imposition of Martial Law to enable the army and the police to carry out their duties. You will be with me, Toby."

The Leader of the Opposition nodded.

"And you will support my statement. You will also support my announcement of the imposition of Martial Law, and you will promise the support of your party in the House tomorrow."

This time the nod was more hesitant.

The Prime Minister smiled. "We will undoubtedly be accused of dictatorship, and ruling by decree, in that the measure should have been put to Parliament first. It is up to us to convince our supporters that there is simply no time for that. Martial Law must come into effect the moment the announcement is made, or we could have unstoppable panic on our hands and be unable to do anything about it. We will also have with us Dr Calhoun . . . " The Prime Minister looked at Peter. "Or should I now say Dr Canning?"

"Ah . . . I'm afraid I have been unable to get through to Trebeth Cross, Prime Minister," Peter said, and wished he had had the foresight to drink a couple of whiskies himself: the Prime Minister had never been one to accept failure, at any level.

"Why not?"

"Well, the lines seem to be out of order."

"Have them put right. Or send someone down. Go yourself, if you have to. Use a helicopter. I wish Dr Calhoun with me when I make my broadcast. I require her to reinforce my statement. We will remind people that there is no cause for panic as long as ordinary precautions are met. We will advise anyone who develops any of the symptoms to report immediately by phone to one of the emergency numbers given, and under no circumstances to leave where they happen to be at that time. A medical team will be with them as soon as possible to test them and give them griseofulvin if necessary. Harry will follow me with the details of his nationwide vaccination plan, as soon as sufficient vaccine becomes available."

The Home Secretary nodded again.

"Now, as to the other matters," the Prime Minister continued. "We have agreed that the vaccine already available shall be distributed to the various medical centres for immediate use upon the medical teams; whatever other stocks of either vaccine or antidote are available or become available will also be distributed amongst the Emergency Centres for use on possible victims of the disease. A small amount of griseofulvin will

be retained as a kind of central reserve in case anyone
of supreme importance may be exposed to the virus,
but . . . " again the Prime Minister looked from face to
face, "we have decided that none of us will, as it were,
pre-empt the nation by being vaccinated at this time."

There was a general nodding around the table.

"Very good. The other questions raised here tonight
we have agreed to postpone for twenty-four hours,
until we see how things develop. I have to say that
I feel that the concept of a national day of prayer,
while very appealing in the abstract, does not make
much sense to me in the concrete. There seems little
doubt that we are going to have to accept quite a few
deaths, no matter how hard people pray. It would be
best to wait until we have this crisis under control and
then have a national day of thanksgiving rather than
risk undermining people's faith. Yes, I shall be seeing
Her Majesty later on tomorrow morning, this morning I
suppose, and will bring her up-to-date on the situation;
she has, in any event, been kept fully informed. Yes, I
shall immediately offer all members of the Royal Family
vaccination, but I should be very surprised if she accepts
it, except as part of the nationwide plan. Yes, I agree that
food and fuel rationing be made more stringent as of this
moment; I will announce that in my speech. Yes, I think
it is a good idea that I should not face the House until
the day after tomorrow, when we will have a clearer idea
of what is happening, and that when we have had our
debate Parliament should again be recessed until this
crisis is over, always providing that Members remain
available for contact by telephone. They will doubtless
be fully occupied with the needs of their respective constituencies. I trust you will support that, Toby? Thank
you. I may say it seems most likely that we will either
re-assemble to pick up the pieces in a month's time
. . . or we will never re-assemble at all. Very good,
gentlemen. It is half past midnight, and we all have

a great deal to do. Peter, I shall be speaking from this room. The technicians are standing by to move the equipment in as soon as we leave now. I would like you to bring Mrs Canning, or Dr Calhoun, here at half past six, if you will."

Peter and Jeremy went immediately to the Ministry of Health.

"How do you feel?" Peter asked.

"God! It's all very well for the PM to make plans and issue pronunciamentos, but nothing we can say or do is going to prevent the most almighty panic when this news breaks. How the hell did I ever get myself into a mess like this? What are you going to do about Meg?"

"Get her here, as the PM wants. By hook or by crook."

He went to his office, telephoned his secretary, getting her out of bed. Sleepily she agreed to dress and come down. She was only the beginning. But Meg came first.

He telephoned the RAF station at Culdrose and spoke with the duty officer.

"I'm afraid we simply cannot make a helicopter available in the middle of the night, Mr Canning," the Flight-Lieutenant protested. "Not without some authority. Unless of course there is an emergency."

Obviously he could not be told what the emergency was at that moment. "You will have your authority," Peter said, and called the Air Ministry. They agreed to co-operate when he explained who he was and suggested that if they had any qualms they should try the Prime Minister's office.

By now Joanne, his secretary, had appeared. While waiting on the phone he had scribbled out a list of key personnel to be alerted, and she got down to it right away, more often than not having to wake them up in turn. There was a good deal of grumbling, but once the staff understood they co-operated willingly enough; gradually a team was assembled and the work of setting up the Emergency Centres began. This involved waking even more people up, calling on off-duty doctors and nurses, and explaining the situation to them as well, while insisting on secrecy; here again full co-operation was obtained once the words 'Red Death' were mentioned.

Peter meanwhile tried Trebeth Cross again, to tell Meg to prepare herself for the arrival of the helicopter. The lines were still out of order, so he called Ridding himself.

"I'm sorry, Mr Canning," said the operator, "but we are not allowed to say why the lines have been disconnected."

"Not allowed to say?" he shouted. "What in the name of God is going on down there? Who says you're not allowed to say?"

"We are acting on the instructions of the mayor, Mr Canning."

"Then connect me with the mayor."

"I'm sorry, Mr Canning, but the mayor is taking no calls tonight."

Peter gazed at the phone in impotent fury, then snapped his fingers. "Put me through to Dr Jones."

"I'm sorry, Mr Canning, but I have instructions not to put any calls through to the Health Department, either."

"For God's sake . . ." No calls to the Health Department. Then Jones was involved. "Total isolation," the pompous little twit had declared. Total? But why?

"This is the Ministry of Health," he said. "I'm afraid I must insist on being put through to Dr Jones, immediately."

"Dr Jones has instructed us that there are to be no exceptions whatsoever."

"No . . ." Peter slammed the phone down and went into Jeremy's office. Here too a collection of secretaries were all telephoning and correlating, while Jeremy wiped his face with a handkerchief.

"Look," Peter said, "I am going to have to ask for a couple of hours off and the use of a helicopter."

Jeremy stared at him.

"Something has happened down at Trebeth Cross. Something which sounds like . . ." he snapped his fingers again. "Oh God, Fran Wardle."

"Look, old man, you'd better have a drink," Jeremy said. "I'll join you. It's in that cupboard."

Peter leaned over the desk. "I don't need a drink. Look, Kitson isn't the only person in this country with the Red Death. There's a girl down in Cornwall with the disease, and the local MOH is doing things off his own bat. I must get down there."

"God, God, God," Jeremy moaned, while his staff looked at him in consternation. "We can't do anything about that. You can't, anyway. And I need you here."

"Meg is down there. Right in the middle of it. And that damned fool Jones has cut off all communication. I am going down there, Jeremy. PM's orders, remember. Besides, everything's running smoothly here now. The centres are being set up. Anyway, I should be back by dawn."

He went back to his office, called Culdrose again, still hoping that he might be wrong.

"Ah, Mr Canning," the Flight-Lieutenant said. "I was just about to call you. We sent a helicopter over to Trebeth Cross as instructed, but it was sent back."

"By whom?"

"Well, sir, it seems that the whole of the village has been isolated, and is surrounded by a police cordon. No one is allowed in or out, unless authorised by the Ridding Medical Officer of Health, Dr Jones. It seems there's something wrong down there."

"So your pilot returned," Peter said grimly.

"Well, sir, it is not our business to oppose the civil authorities. The police who spoke to our pilot by radio told him that they were acting under a local by-law which gave them total authority in the area. I must say, our people aren't very happy about being called out at night on a wild goose chase."

"I'm not very happy either, but thank you," Peter said. "You have done all you could."

He replaced the phone, gazed at the wall while he got his emotions under control. If it was terrifying to think that a man like Arthur Jones could have virtually assumed dictatorial powers in Ridding, it was even more horrifying to realise that all over Great Britain there were local councils at the mercy of the strongest personality, regardless of how misguided and eccentric he or she might be. So Jones might have done the right thing in isolating Trebeth Cross the moment he learned there was Red Death in the village, but he certainly had not done the right thing in failing to contact the Ministry of Health to inform them of the situation, nor was he doing the right thing in trying to deal with it entirely on his own.

As for locking Meg up with everyone else . . . of course Meg had her vaccination, but griseofulmaline had not yet been exposed to the disease. It might not work. And anyway, when he thought of what might be happening down there . . .

All manner of actions to be taken flitted through his mind. But they all had to be rejected. He could not pre-empt the PM's broadcast and cause a panic before the measures to prevent one had been taken. He could only get down there himself and use his personal authority to get Meg out of there.

Besides, that was what he wanted to do.

He called the Air Ministry again.

"Bit of a flap on, Mr Canning," agreed the duty officer. "And now you want to go down there yourself? You know our people from Culdrose were turned back?"

"I do know that," Peter said. "That is why I must get down there myself. This is a matter of national importance."

Well, the PM had insisted that Meg be present for the broadcast, and that was . . . he looked at his watch; the time was 3.15 am . . . less than four hours off.

"Very well, Mr Canning." The duty officer was beginning to sound rather tired. "I will arrange for a machine to pick you up at . . . where are you?"

"I'm at the Ministry of Health."

"Well, we'll come down on Horse Guards Parade. Can you arrange to have as many lights on as possible, sir?"

"I hope you know what you're doing," Jeremy said. He had clearly had that whisky he so desperately wanted and was feeling better.

"I am doing what the PM told me to do," Peter reminded him. "And I'll be back in four hours. Just hold the fort."

It was drizzling, with distant flickers of lightning serrating the western sky. "It's a fact there's a storm down there," the pilot confirmed. "But we should manage." He made no comment at being dragged, at the very least, from a comfortable mess, to take some lunatic MP on a mysterious mission. But he did ask, "Will you be coming back, sir?"

"Yes," Peter told him. "With a passenger."

They flew into darkness, and increasingly bad weather. The wind gusted quite strongly, and the lightning cut the sky to ribbons. One fork came very close to the shuddering machine.

"With respect, Mr Canning," the pilot said. "Just how urgent is this mission of yours?"

"Well . . . " Peter said.

"Because if it isn't, we're chancing our arm. We're . . . " the darkness was lit up by another brilliant flash, and the helicopter seemed to sizzle. "I'm sorry, sir, we're going down."

"Under control, I hope," Peter said.

"Oh, yes, sir. But we'll have to wait a while for this storm to clear." He began chattering into his radio.

Peter looked at the crewman. "Is there an airfield near here?"

"Oh, yes, sir. We'll put down at Eastleigh."

"Eastleigh?" Peter shouted. "What the devil are we doing down by Eastleigh?" Eastleigh was just outside Southampton.

"Well, sir, there are head winds blowing us all over the place. That's why we have to stop. We could wind up over the Channel."

They landed safely, despite the fact that the airport was closed. The rain poured down as they ran for the terminal building, where they were not welcomed by the night staff.

"What were you doing up there, anyway?" the duty officer wanted to know.

"Emergency," the pilot said, and they all looked at a bedraggled Peter, who was now becoming quite anxious. "I have to get down to Cornwall, in a hurry," he said.

"Cornwall? You'll be lucky. There's a real storm blowing down there. Fifty-mile-an-hour winds, electricity, low cloud, you name it."

"When do you expect it to clear?" Peter asked.

"Could be some time. Not before dawn, anyway."

Peter looked at the pilot.

Who shrugged. "I'm sorry, Mr Canning. I'll go if it's a matter of life and death . . . "

Peter hesitated. But he could not ask these men to take such a risk. Yet he had to get on; he was beginning to feel as uptight as Jeremy. "No," he said. "You stay here until it clears. But come down the moment it does to fly me back, understood? Trebeth Cross."

"Yes, sir, Mr Canning. But . . . how are you going to get there?"

"There has to be a car hire firm someplace around here," Peter told him.

It took an hour to get a hire car organised, as it again necessitated waking people up, and not everyone was in a co-operative mood.

"You be careful," the helicopter pilot warned. "There's a lot of weather out there. It would make much more sense to wait for it to clear; instead of a three-hour drive through this muck, we can get you there in an hour."

"I'm relying on you being there," Peter reminded him, "to bring me back. But I simply have to get down and organise it, otherwise you're just going to be turned away, too."

The thought of sitting around an abandoned airport for three or more hours while the whole country was falling apart was not acceptable. Equally, neither was the thought of abandoning Meg and returning to the ministry.

Of course there was no way now that she could possibly get up to London to support the Prime Minister's seven o'clock broadcast – that was only a couple of hours off. He would have to phone and warn the PM's office before leaving the airport, saying she could be there to comment on later repeats which, as word spread and people began to tune in, would be the more important ones.

He used the A31 and A35, heading for Exeter, where he would pick up the A30 to Okehampton, and thence over the moors to Ridding and Trebeth Cross. But even on the dual carriageways and although the darkness was beginning to turn to grey, progress was very slow in the teeming rain, and he was still some miles short of Exeter when the radio announced that the Prime Minister would now address the nation.

The Prime Minister spoke, as usual, in a careful, well-modulated and totally calm tone, but with slightly more emphasis than usual; there was no indication of annoyance at the non-appearance of Meg. "You must be wondering why I should address you at this hour in the morning. What emergency can have made it necessary. I have to tell you that we are indeed faced with a grave emergency, but one which, with courage and determination and faith, we shall overcome.

"Despite all our very considerable efforts, the disease we know of as the Red Death has appeared in our country. It was brought in by a man who deliberately avoided all our checks, and who is still at large. His name is David Kitson. Let me give you his description. He is five feet ten inches tall, with brown hair and a sallow complexion. When last seen he was wearing a pea-jacket over blue pullover and jeans. Now, this man is being sought by every policeman in the country at this minute, but it is certain that his whereabouts are known to more than one person, who hopefully is listening to or watching this broadcast. This person must know that Kitson is ill. If he is still alive, he will be suffering from pains in the head and the stomach, from a very high colour, and perhaps from some external bleeding. Anyone sheltering him must understand that their life is in grave danger. Indeed, anyone who has been in contact with this man is in danger. Worse, any such person is a possible carrier, and may be the cause of spreading the disease. I appeal to anyone who has been near Kitson, or has developed any of the symptoms I have just listed, to telephone the nearest police station. There they will be put in touch with immediate help.

"Because help is available I can now tell you that a treatment which checks the disease has been discovered, and preventative vaccine is now being manufactured on the widest possible scale. It is my intention that within the next two months every man, woman and child in this country, and every warm-blooded animal, will be vaccinated, free of charge. This is not yet possible. But there is sufficient of the vaccine available to take care of all medical teams, police, and anyone who has had contact with the disease. Providing they act promptly, and providing, too, that Kitson, and everyone who may have associated with him during the past three days, reports immediately to one of the emergency telephone numbers which will be given at the end of this broadcast, they will receive the life-saving treatment. Not to do this is to place the entire nation at risk. Once these people act with good sense and responsibility, there is nothing to fear.

"However, my Government considers it necessary to put into force certain measures we have long prepared in anticipation of a situation such as this arising. Now, I am sure there are many people watching me today who can remember the war against Nazism, the dark days when we stood alone and awaited invasion. The Government of that day was forced to take some crucial, and even harsh, measures to ensure our survival as a people. I have to tell you that the danger we face today is even greater than that of guns and tanks, and our response to it must be in that higher key. As I have said, we are hopeful that if everyone plays his or her part, the outbreak of this disease can be stifled at birth, as it were, in our country. The measures I would urge upon you are these: one, do not panic. Two, go about your daily routine as normal. Three, do not have any intimate relations or even touch anyone you do not know very well, or you are certain is disease-free. Four, report any suspected cases immediately. Five, and this is most important, do not attempt to escape your usual surroundings for fear of contracting the disease. This will only cause panic and disruption, and may even spread the disease. I am hoping everyone will co-operate in this vital matter, but I must tell you that I have already given instructions that the police and the army are to stop people travelling beyond municipal boundaries unless they have an essential purpose. Please obey the instructions that may be given you by those in authority. In this regard I must also tell you that a decree imposing Martial Law on the country has been drawn up and is at this moment being published. This means that there will be a curfew imposed on movement after dark, beginning tonight, and that the police and the army have the power to override existing laws, if need be. Again, I would ask you to co-operate with them in every possible way.

"Tomorrow I will be presenting to Parliament a series of additional measures necessary to cope with this emergency, and I shall be asking for immediate permission to have these become law. The moment the emergency is over, these special measures will be discarded. I repeat, I have no doubt at all that if we all do our duty, this disease will be stamped out before it can take hold, and we will all be able to resume our normal lives and move forward once again with confidence and prosperity. Thank you."

"The Prime Minister's broadcast will be repeated at eight o'clock, and on every hour throughout the morning," the announcer said. "And now, the Leader of the Opposition would also like to address you."

To keep his part of the bargain, Peter thought, and switched off the set. Well, that was it, now. One could only hope that the nation reacted sensibly. But it had never been faced with such a situation before. Perhaps, as the Prime Minister had said, in the grim days of 1940, when a German invasion had been hourly expected . . . but then the enemy would have been visible, something tangible with which to grapple, heroically . . . and no enemy soldier had actually landed. Now the enemy was already in their midst, perhaps carried by someone they knew very well, and who must be shunned and locked away.

He pressed his foot harder to the floor and continued on his way to Exeter, which he reached at 7.30. It was broad daylight by now although the rain limited visibility.

Here there was already a road block in the process of being set up, manned by both police and soldiers. Peter explained who he was, and was let through. In Exeter, however, there were crowds of people running into the streets to chatter about the implications of the broadcast. He was glad to be out the other side, heading for Okehampton. But now he was low on petrol. He saw a filling station, and pulled into a deserted forecourt. It was not a self-service, so he hooted several times, then got out of the car and began to serve himself; the pumps were unlocked.

"What do you think you're doing?" asked a voice.

Peter turned left and right, decided it came from the small office building.

"I'm sorry," he said. "There was no one here."

"Just leave the money," the man said.

"I'm afraid I don't have the money," Peter said, waving his card wallet and walking towards the building.

"Then clear off," the man said.

"Don't you take cards?"

"Not today," the man said. "Clear off."

Peter hesitated, shrugged, got back behind the wheel and drove out of the station. Presumably it would be possible to send the money when this whole thing settled down.

There was another road block outside Okehampton, but again he got through by explaining that he was on a vital mission for the Government. Then he swung on to the small roads leading over the spine of Cornwall towards Ridding. And heard a peculiar noise as the steering became sluggish and lop-sided.

"For God's sake," he groaned.

He pulled the car into the side of the road, got out, looked at the flat tyre in disgust. He opened the boot, found a spanner, unfastened the spare and pulled it out, dumped it on the road, and gazed at it in consternation: if anything, it was as flat as the flat.

"Oh, shit!" he commented. A hire car?

He sighed, shaded his eyes against the rain, and looked over the countryside. There was a farmhouse about a mile away, down a cart track. It was certainly his only hope. He ran down it, panting, saw cows waiting to be milked, and, more importantly, a car sitting beside the tractors in the lean-to garage.

He pushed open the gate.

"Stop right there," said a voice.

Peter obeyed, looked towards the house, and saw a man, carrying a shotgun, standing in the doorway.

Peter raised his hat. "Good morning to you. I'm afraid my car has two flat tyres."

The man stared at him. "You're from London," he said, pinpointing the accent.

"Well . . . yes. But . . . "

"You're running from the Red Death," the man accused.

Peter frowned at him. "Of course I'm not. But I am on a mission connected with it. My name is Peter Canning. I'm sure you've heard it. I'm the MP for Ridding, and Parliamentary Private Secretary at the Ministry of Health."

Magic with the police and armed services, but meaningless to a Cornwall farmer. "You admit it then," the man said. "You're running away."

"I am not running away," Peter said. "I am trying to reach Trebeth Cross, on a very important mission. If I could use your phone . . . "

"Clear off," the farmer said.

"Now look here," Peter protested.

The man levelled the shotgun and fired. Peter saw the movement coming, and however unbelievable it was that the man would actually fire at him, his reaction was instantaneous: he hurled himself to one side, and then regained his feet, covered in mud but still moving – he had noted that it was a single-barrelled gun. Even so he felt a sting in one leg.

The farmer had already broken the gun, and was reaching into his pocket for a second cartridge. But Peter got to him first, spurred on by the blood soaking his trousers. He tore the gun from the man's grasp, and holding it in both hands, swung it in military fashion; the butt struck the farmer on the jaw and he collapsed into the doorway.

Peter looked past him at several well-built females coming out of the kitchen in various stages of déshabillé, brandishing pokers and even a carving knife. He decided against taking them on, or even trying to explain. The farmer had a bunch of keys hanging from his belt. Peter stooped, tore these free, and ran for the vehicle, still carrying the shotgun. A quick inspection told him one of the keys was for the car and he got behind the wheel, then dropped the shotgun, started the engine and drove out of the yard. The women shouted at him and waved their various weapons, but he was already at the road and turning west. Explanations, and settlements, would have to come later.

"I'm afraid I cannot agree," Colin Brereton said into the telephone. "I understand that this is a national emergency and all that guff, but it is our biggest chance in some time to bring the Government down. The PM is simply insufferable with these pontifications. The fact is, the Government is faced with a situation it really has no plans to deal with. It is clutching at straws. As for instituting Martial Law by decree and then referring the matter to Parliament forty-eight hours later, what are we, a bunch of schoolchildren? I quite accept that that is how the PM would like to think of us, but are we going to put up with it?" He listened. "Yes, I know you have agreed to support the Government line, Toby, but quite honestly I feel you were pressured into it, and I suspect a lot of the rank and file will agree with me. You know there is a groundswell which is suggesting that you are too anxious to be all things to all men rather than truly representing the Party's interest . . . "

Again he listened. "I refuse to believe things are as bad as the PM is making out, Toby," he said. "What are the facts? Some seaman has come ashore with the disease. Three days ago! He has penetrated our so-called impenetrable vetting system, and has now remained at large for three days despite, apparently, a nationwide police hunt. If that is not an indictment of the Government's efficiency I don't know what is."

Again he listened, his shoulders hunching. "I'm sorry, Toby," he said. "You have given your word, and you have committed yourself to the nation on television. But you cannot commit me, or the members of the Party who think like me . . . Yes, I will be asking for a division . . . Oh, quite, I realise that if the Government is solid for the PM we shall lose the vote . . . No, I do not think we shall achieve nothing but discord. I believe now is our chance to discredit this mob. I honestly believe they have mishandled the entire situation and that we can and will do better . . . My dear fellow, if you feel that, there is nothing more to be said." He slammed the phone into its rest.

"That was a bit abrupt," Janet said, emerging from the kitchen fully dressed despite the early hour.

"The bastard had the nerve to suggest that I am only making a fuss about this because I'd like to set myself up as the next leader of the Party," Brereton said.

"Well . . . " Janet paused, pregnantly.

Brereton grinned. "Well . . . of course I should be leader of the Party. Toby is revealing himself to be nothing more than a yes man for the Government. He's got no guts, no statesmanship: all he's really concerned about is the next opinion poll. Yes: if he can't cope, then there has to be somebody else."

"I think you'd make a great Party leader. I think you'd make a great Prime Minister," Janet said.

"That's my girl. I intend to get there yet," Brereton agreed.

"But you won't get there if you continually allow yourself to get so het up. Calm down, dear." She pecked his cheek. "Now I must rush."

He frowned at her. "Where?"

"The Berwick Street market. We are having a lunch party tomorrow, and I can only get the spices I want in Berwick Street. And then there's dinner at the Briggs' tonight. I simply must have my hair done."

"Hold on. The PM did say to stay away from crowds."

Janet chucked him under the chin. "But you think the PM is just building this thing up to boost the Government, don't you, Colin? So do I." She vanished down the stairs.

Claudia awoke at 7.30, as usual, and switched on the television while she was having her breakfast. Her first reaction to the broadcast was sheer irritation. She hated things cropping up to disturb the even tenor of her existence. There had been enough of that recently, but this was simply the end. She felt irritated with Peter for not telling her what was happening, and doubly so with Hartley, both for that and for not being here at such a moment.

Then she thought of her parents. The poor dears would be scared stiff. She simply had to reassure them. She considered, then decided against phoning, which would probably only alarm them more. She dressed, went down to the garage and drove down to Wimbledon herself in the old shooting brake; she would not be using the Merc again until it had been properly valeted.

By the time she got there she had decided to forgive Hartley. The poor man was working round the clock and, going by what the Prime Minister had said, doing a very good job too. He would be in touch with her once he had produced enough of the vaccine. To think of it, Hartley Briggs, saviour of the nation. Because there could be no doubt that he was. Or one of them. That peerage was coming closer every day. Lord and Lady Briggs of . . . of . . . she wondered which of the names they had discussed he would choose. But surely he would leave the final choice to her. Countess of . . . she would have to give it some thought.

"Now, there is absolutely nothing to worry about," she said, over a cup of milky, instant coffee. "The Prime Minister has said so. It may be that there are some carriers of the disease in London, but really they are not the sort of people that you or I are likely to come into contact with. Just remember not to admit any strangers, and to remain indoors until this dreadful Kitson person has been found and . . . ah . . . "

"Eliminated," suggested her father.

"Well, taken care of," Claudia preferred.

"Has Peter tried again to get news of Sarah?" Veronica asked. "It is so ghastly, just waiting, not knowing."

"Yes, he has, Mummy. But he hasn't been able to find out anything more yet. Poor darlings! I wish I could stay with you but I must be getting back because I'm having a dinner party tonight. Fearful bore that Hartley can't come. He's working awfully hard, manufacturing this vaccine. And there is absolutely no money in it. We'll certainly be out of pocket at the end of it all."

"I'm sure he will be adequately rewarded," her father said drily. He knew the ambitions of both his daughter and her husband.

"Well," Claudia said, "one certainly hopes so. Now remember, don't open the door to any strangers."

Obviously, she thought as she climbed into the old estate car, there was no risk of that; the old folk never let anybody in without virtually a birth certificate as identity.

She coaxed the engine into life and moved on to the road, clicking her tongue in annoyance.

On top of everything else, she had suddenly developed a gonging headache.

22

Desperate Remedies

"Where is he?" the policeman asked. His tone was harsh. Like all his colleagues, he was exhausted. And perhaps a little frightened. For the past twelve hours every man in the Metropolitan Police had been on the streets searching, and not finding. It seemed as if David Kitson might have disappeared off the face of the earth, leaving only his dread disease behind.

Until this telephone call.

The girl who had opened the door shivered and pointed over her shoulder. "I think he's dead," she said.

The policemen pulled on their gloves and face masks, with which they had been issued before leaving the station, and entered the little flat.

"Why didn't you call us sooner?" one mumbled through the plastic.

"I didn't know it was serious. It was only when I saw the broadcast . . . I couldn't get rid of him," the girl explained. "He said he wasn't well and just had to rest for a day or two."

"And he paid you," the other policeman suggested.

"He had money, yes," she said.

The policemen went towards the bedroom.

"Not in there," the girl said. "I have another room. I put him in there." She led them to a second door. "Well . . ." she shrugged. "A girl has to live."

The first policeman opened the door and stared at the crumpled figure on the bed, the bloodstained sheets.

"All that blood didn't bother you?"

"It was a nose bleed."

"Don't you ever read the newspapers, watch telly?"

"I watch *Dallas*. And videos."

The second policeman was going through Kitson's pockets. "It's him, all right."

"When did he turn up?" asked his mate.

"Oh . . . Monday. Just after lunch." The girl remained in the doorway.

"And you let him stay for four days? When did he die?"

"Well . . . must've been a couple of hours ago. He said he wanted to rest. And he had money. Then he started to feel ill, like I said . . . "

The policeman took his walkie-talkie out of his breast pocket. "It's him," he said, trying to make himself understood through the mask. "We need an ambulance. Oh, yes, we'll keep it quiet." He replaced the radio. "You tell anyone about this?"

"Well . . . no," she said.

"Come on."

"Well, I was scared. I told my girlfriend. She has the flat upstairs. We work together, sometimes. You know, parties."

The policeman was struck with a sudden, horrifying thought. "You worked since he got here?"

"Well, like I said, it was Monday afternoon. A girl has to live."

"Oh, shit," the policeman said. "How many?"

"How should I know?"

"You know your customers, don't you, Jennie? You wouldn't claim to be a tart, would you? You're a call girl. Men have to have your phone number, right?"

"Well," she said sulkily. "They get given it."

"Jennie," he said. "How many?"

"Well, maybe twenty."

"Twenty?" he gasped.

"Then there was the party . . . "

"What party?" he shouted.

"The convention on Tuesday night."

"Whose convention?"

"I don't know. Sally organised it."

"And you went off and left Kitson here?"

"Why not? There's nothing to steal. And he had money."

"Yes," the policeman said, wearily. "Tell me about the convention." The mask was stifling and he had an urge to scrap it.

"Well, Sally and I were the girls. We came out of a cake, and did a few shimmies. I used to be a dancer, you know."

"And then?"

"You know what these characters are like. North country men, all brass and hard-ons. Blow-jobs mostly. We'd have been too tired otherwise."

He grabbed her arm with his gloved hand, pushing her towards the table. "You just sit down and you start writing, the name of every man you've serviced since Monday."

"Well," she protested. "Every one I can remember."

"Sid," the policeman said. "There's another one in this building. Sally. Get her down here. Maybe she can remember who the party was for."

"Right away," Sid agreed, and hurried up the stairs outside the flat.

"Come on," the policeman said. "Start writing."

"I can't think," Jennie said. "I have such a headache."

It was after eight when Peter drove the 'borrowed' car into Ridding. There had been road blocks outside every village and policemen asking awkward questions, but the magic phrase 'Member of Parliament on Government business' had got him through, and now he was in his home territory, as it were.

There was naturally a road block on the main road into Ridding manned by ponchoed and very wet policemen; the rain had slackened into a drizzle, but the clouds were still very low and there were still rumbles of thunder. They peered at him, not recognising the car. "Oh, it's you, Mr Canning," the sergeant said. "Bit of a flap going on, eh?"

"Yes," Peter said. He wondered if he should attempt to explain the car, if the farmer would have been on to the police, but decided that even if he had they would be far too busy to worry about a stolen car; anyway, if he started to explain they might want him to go to the station, and then there would have to be explanations about the pellet in his leg – it was quite painful and he knew his trouser leg was soaked in blood. He drove down the High Street, which was unusually empty – several of the shops were shut; no doubt the initial reaction of most people to the Prime Minister's broadcast had been to take a day off work.

He had no doubts about where he should go first, pulled up outside Jones' house and hurried to the front door.

"Peter!" Alice Jones said, and frowned at him. "Are you all right?"

Peter remembered he had not shaved. "Just a little pushed for time. Arthur in?"

"Well, yes, you just caught him. He's shaving. He's hurrying off again right away, you know. Only two hours' sleep. He's been working round the clock."

"So I gather," Peter said grimly.

"He'll be here in a moment. Peter, you're dripping wet, and covered in mud." Alice Jones – a large, homely woman, twice the size of her husband – believed in dealing with essentials.

"It's raining, Alice. And I took a bit of a fall."

"Have you had breakfast?"

"As a matter of fact, no."

"I'll get you something."

"I really am in a hurry, Alice."

"It'll take no time at all. Arthur," she called. "Peter's here."

Jones came down the stairs. "Good heavens," he remarked. "You look like something the cat dragged in."

"Arthur, I want you to tell me just what the hell is going on."

Jones gazed at him for a few seconds, then sat down. Peter did likewise. "We have it. So has London, according to the television just now. It's probably everywhere. People are very upset, I can tell you."

"Where do we have it. Down here?"

"Well, in Trebeth Cross. That Wardle girl. How she slipped through . . . low blood pressure."

"So you have sealed off the entire village. On whose authority?"

"On the authority of the Ridding and District Council," Jones snapped. "I told you what I intended to do if anything like this happened."

"The matter should have been reported to the ministry. You could have condemned an entire village to death."

"Well . . . my job is to keep it from spreading. I did what I thought best. And the council is entirely behind me."

"Arthur . . ." Peter kept his temper with difficulty. "Tell me exactly what happened."

"Well . . . yesterday afternoon I received a call from Dr Calhoun . . . "

"Dr Calhoun happens to be my wife." Peter spoke between gritted teeth.

"Is she? Good heavens, she never told me."

"She's not like that. Go on."

"My dear fellow, I had no idea your wife was in Trebeth Cross. I am most terribly sorry. I can't imagine why she didn't tell me. Good heavens, her life is in danger."

"I don't think it is," Peter said. "I am praying that it is not, and you had better start praying too. Because if anything happens to Meg I am going to break your neck." Peter looked up as Alice appeared with a tray, gratefully drank some black coffee and sank his teeth into a slice of toast: he had discovered he was starving.

She inspected him with a frown. "You're bleeding."

"Just a scratch," he assured her.

"I must put something on it." She bustled off.

"Will you for God's sake tell me what happened?" Peter begged.

"Well, Dr Calhoun . . . your wife . . . told me on the phone that there was a suspected case of the Red Death in Trebeth. She also told me that she thought she had caught it in time; it appears that she had some griseofulvin with her. But she was afraid for the rest of the village, and asked me if I had any supplies of the drug available myself."

"How did she sound?"

"Oh, perfectly calm. I am sure she is. But of course, I had to take immediate action."

"Such as sending over all the griseofulvin you could find."

"Well, I did that of course. At least, as much of it as I could risk sparing. What with our having sent supplies all over the world there isn't a lot of it about at the moment. But I also had to isolate the village. The police had been briefed, of course. I called the mayor immediately I had spoken with Dr Calhoun, and he gave the go-ahead. A cordon was thrown around Trebeth in half an hour."

"And did you also find it necessary to cut off the telephone?"

"Well . . . I encountered some resistance. I mean people like Farmer Poldarren were quite aggressive. Frightened, of course. I understand that. But when I told him he couldn't leave or return to his farm he wanted to start telephoning all over the place. So did others. Well, I couldn't allow that. It would have started a panic. Of course I had no idea you already had the Death in London. I did what I thought best, Peter, and now that I've heard the Prime Minister I am sure I acted correctly."

Jones looked at his wife who had heard most of the conversation; the study door had not been closed. Now she knelt beside Peter, pushed up his trouser leg, and peered at the little wound, which was steadily oozing blood. "Oh, my word, that's a shotgun pellet."

"Well, grab a pair of tweezers and yank it out," Peter suggested.

"You really should go to hospital."

"Alice, I am not going to hospital. If you don't want to take it out just forget about it. I have to rush."

"Men!" Alice commented as she went into the kitchen to sterilise the tweezers, calling over her shoulder, "Does this new wife of yours know what she's taking on?" She returned almost immediately. "This is going to hurt, I hope."

It did, but the pellet had not penetrated very far and she made a clean job of it, smothering the puncture with antiseptic cream and then bandaging it. "I still think you should go to a hospital and have it properly dressed as soon as possible."

"It'll have to wait," he told her. "Right now I'm on my way to Trebeth Cross."

"Now look here, old man," Jones said. "I understand your concern. But you can't go there. If you do, I won't be able to allow you back out."

"Arthur," Peter said evenly. "My wife is in Trebeth. She happens to be vaccinated against the disease, but I still intend to get her out of there."

"I'm afraid I cannot permit that," Jones declared. "She may have been vaccinated, but that doesn't mean she can't be a carrier. She understands that. I explained it to her."

"You have spoken to her?"

"Well . . . by loudspeaker. It wouldn't do anyone any good if I caught the Death, now would it?"

"It would be the best bloody thing that could happen," Peter shouted, entirely losing his temper.

"Oh, dear," Alice said.

Peter turned to her. "You had better talk some sense into him, Alice. Meg is required in London, and I intend to take her there. And if you try to stop me, Arthur, I am going to have you out of here and walking to some hospital in the East End of London."

"You can't do that. I did what I thought was best."

"Then just keep out of my way. Who is the doctor in charge in Trebeth?"

"Well, Dr Calhoun."

"Then you will have to arrange for somebody else. I suggest you take over yourself."

"My dear fellow . . . "

"I am sure you kept some griseofulvin for yourself," Peter said. "Just make sure it's handy. I am going over there now. I wish you to accompany me."

"Me?" Jones' voice was high with a mixture of apprehension and outrage.

"This is your baby, Arthur. In this kind of warfare, generals lead from the front. Come along."

Jones looked at his wife again.

"You can't ask anyone else," she said. "And if you have griseofulvin . . . "

"I wish your instructions given to me in writing," Jones said.

"Just get in the car," Peter told him. "You can drive. I'll write them out on the way over."

Claudia reclined on her chaise-longue and picked up the telephone. "Oh, Julia, my dear, how good it is to hear a civilised voice."

"Claudie! Do you think we should come tonight?"

"Well, of course you should come tonight. Why on earth shouldn't you?"

"Well, after what the PM said . . . "

"I'm sure that the PM, above all, would like the upper classes to continue living their normal lives, Julia," Claudia said severely. "We are supposed to set an example. Anyway, it's only a small party. Just five of us: Colin and Janet Brereton and yourselves."

"But . . . where's Hartley?"

"Hartley, my dear, is unable to come. He is manufacturing this wonder drug which is going to save the world."

"Oh! Well, are you sure you can cope?"

"Of course I can cope. Mind you, I have had the most harrowing couple of days. There was this accident yesterday . . . "

"You've been in an accident?"

"Well, not exactly. I went down to my hairdresser's in the afternoon and I was coming home when there was this accident. I was the only other car around, and some people commandeered me to drive this man to hospital. Well, it was all rather fun, really, except for this poor fellow. He had bumped his head and there was blood everywhere. It just didn't seem to stop. The car is a total mess and I've had to leave it at a garage for cleaning."

"But . . . what had happened?"

"Only a minor boot-bump. I took him and his friend to hospital and left them there. I really didn't want to get involved, so I just drove away. Then," she paused to draw breath, "after the PM's broadcast this morning

I felt I had to go down to Wimbledon to my parents . . .
you know what old people are like in a crisis, and on
the way back I had a fit of conscience and pulled into
the hospital to ask how the man was . . . "

"Has he recovered?"

"I have no idea. Since the broadcast the hospital has
been besieged with what one hopes are imaginary cases
of the beastly Red Death and as I didn't remember the
man's name they said they couldn't possibly help me.
Well, at least I tried."

"Claudie, you really are a brick. All of that and people
to dinner. Are you sure . . . "

"Yes, of course," Claudia said. "See you at 7.30."

She replaced the telephone. She did wish Julia would
not carry on about things. In fact, it had been a great
temptation to cancel the dinner party when Hartley had
said he could not make it. But Colin Brereton was such
a touchy fellow. Now he would hold forth all evening,
with no one to contradict him.

But it was still a temptation. Which was growing all
the time. She had such a headache, and she really felt
she could not eat a thing, much less cook it.

While Jones got his gear together, which seemed to
take a very long time, Peter tried to get his thinking
under control. So far he had merely been obsessed
with regaining Meg, had told himself he was doing
what the Prime Minister had wanted. On the other
hand, his business now was to get back to London to
support Jeremy. He had to get there just as quickly as
possible. But he had no intention of going without Meg.
If civilisation was about to dissolve he wanted her with
him at the end.

He called Eastleigh and spoke with his helicopter pilot.
There was little joy there; the weather remained thick
and stormy, and was now spreading east. "Even if I
got down to you, Mr Canning," the pilot said, "I don't

429

know that I'd get you into London. Mind you, I'll have a go if you wish."

Peter made an instant decision. There was no point endangering the helicopter crew, and with the roads deserted he could be back up in London in a few hours. "You stay where you are," he said. "I'll call you if I need you."

He finally got Jones moving. They raced along the lonely road over the moor, and soon came in sight of the rooftops of the village; in the dip before the main street was reached there was a road block, manned by four policemen.

Jones screamed to a halt. "Any trouble?"

"No, Doctor," said the sergeant. "Just those lads."

Peter gazed at four boys of between five and eight, standing perhaps fifty yards away, staring at the policemen.

"We've warned them to keep their distance," the sergeant said. He, and his men, were clearly on edge.

Peter knew all the boys. He got out of the car, vaulted the barrier, and walked towards them. "Hello, Jimmy," he said. "How are you?"

"I'm fine, Mr Canning. But the copper says we're going to die. All of us."

"You don't want to believe everything a copper tells you," Peter told him, and looked over his shoulder. "You coming, Arthur?"

The doctor got out of the car, opened his valise, and began to equip himself: green gown and cap, rubber mask and gloves.

"Has he got it, then?" Jimmy asked.

"You'd think so, wouldn't you? Come along. You shouldn't be out here in the rain, or you'll catch cold."

Jimmy held his hand, reassured by his presence. The other three boys followed at his heels. Peter wondered if he was afraid. He was aware only of anxiety to see

Meg again, of the pressures that were clustering about him, to get back up to London. He was also very aware of his physical discomfort, the pain in his leg and the various bruises on his body. Not surprisingly, after his sleepless night and all his exertions, he had a splitting headache.

He was also deeply concerned that this village, his village, should be in such a catastrophic situation.

But he did not think he was afraid.

They passed his cottage. The door was ajar, despite the steady drizzle.

"Is anyone in there?" Peter asked.

"I don't think so, Mr Canning."

"Then where's Dr Calhoun?"

"Oh, she's at the pub. That's where it's happening."

Peter looked over his shoulder to make sure Arthur was following, then hurried up the street.

Outside the pub several people were gathered, muttering at each other; apart from them the street was deserted.

"Mr Canning!" John Pengelley hurried towards him. "Thank God you're here! But . . . you'll catch the disease."

"Have you?"

"Well, not yet. But we're all in danger, they say."

"Who says?"

"Well . . . Dr Jones." He stared past Peter at Jones, who was approaching more slowly. "Glory be. Is that really him? He's not been here before."

"Well, he's here now." Peter hurried inside.

Clive Wardle stood behind the bar, forlornly: the room was otherwise empty. "Peter?" he asked incredulously. "You shouldn't come in here. This building is quarantined."

"Where's Meg?"

"Upstairs. But . . . "

431

Peter took the steps three at a time, burst into the living quarters. These had been converted into a make-shift hospital. There were four beds in each room, and all were occupied. In the first room Peter saw Fran Wardle and two other women, with one man; one of the women was Mavis Tregarthen. But they all looked quite cheerful.

"Oh, Mr Canning!" Mavis shrieked, dragging her sheet to her neck.

"Uncle Peter!" Fran called.

Stephanie Wardle appeared in the doorway of the next room. She had her hair tied up in a bandanna and there were bloodstains on her dress. She also looked exhausted. But quite well.

"Peter?" she asked, as incredulous as her husband.

"Where's Meg?"

"In there." She gestured at the third room, the door of which was shut. "But you can't go in there."

Peter stepped past her, looked into the second room. Here there were two men and two women; one of the men was Mr Perry. They did not look too good, and there was some blood.

"They're going to be all right," Stephanie said. "We think."

Betty Pengelley was giving them food.

Peter opened the third door, and Meg straightened from the bed she had been bending over. "Who . . . Peter? Oh, my God!"

He stared at her. Her clothes and hands were bloody, and there was blood on the sheets and even on the floor. "Meg!"

"Oh, Peter!" She came towards him, checked.

He pushed the door shut, still staring at her, and past her at the four people. One, Farmer Poldarren, lay absolutely still, blood coagulating round his nostrils.

"Yes," Meg said. "He just died."

"But . . . "

"I've run out of griseofulvin. I've been bleeding them, trying . . . Peter, I must have griseofulvin."

"You will have it. But you . . . "

"I'm all right. I've been vaccinated. But . . . oh, my God! You!"

"I'll survive."

"You won't, you know. Did you kiss Frances Wardle when she came home?"

"Ah . . . yes, I did. Way back on Saturday."

"Then you're overdue." She peered at him. "How do you feel?"

"Well . . . I've had a long night."

"Your face is redder than usual. Do you have a headache?"

"Well . . . yes. But I've been rushing around like mad." He decided not to tell her all of his adventures.

"That's something. You must have been using corpuscles like mad as well. God, let's pray we're in time. Push your sleeve up." She dived into her bloodstained bag.

"I thought you'd run out."

"Of griseofulvin. But I have one vaccine left. I've been saving it for you." She broke the seal on her one remaining needle, filled it.

Peter pushed up his sleeve. "Will it work if I already have it?"

"I see no reason why not. It's got griseofulvin in it."

"Could you have saved the life of Poldarren by using it?"

Meg injected him. "I don't know."

She raised her head to look at him. "I knew you were coming back." Her expression was defiant. "I love you." Her shoulders drooped. "Anyway, I think he was too far gone. He had high blood pressure."

"Oh, Meg . . . " she looked so tired, ready to drop at his feet. "And these others?"

"I can't do anything for them, Peter, except bleed them every couple of hours. I have nothing left to give them."

433

"Tell me what happened?"

She drew a long breath. "That girl, Fran Wardle, was really ill yesterday afternoon. She obviously brought the virus into the country with her. Well, I had four tablets with me. I gave her one immediately, and it worked. I also gave griseofulvin to Mr and Mrs Wardle, and to Betty Pengelley, all people who were known to have kissed Fran when she returned. But there were many more. So I telephoned Ridding, spoke with the MOH there, and explained the situation. He seemed to understand, said he would send over all the available griseofulvin, and asked me if I could cope until help arrived.

"Well, of course I said I could. Stephanie and Betty were prepared to help; they've been a tower of strength. Then suddenly all hell broke loose. The town was surrounded by police and no one was allowed to leave or even approach within fifty feet of them. One of them threw a packet of griseofulvin on to the road and shouted that we could pick it up. It was medieval. You'd think we had leprosy. I got on the phone to protest, and was cut off. But not until I'd been told that these were the procedures decided by the Ridding and District Council and that the village would have to remain in total isolation until the outbreak was over. Or everyone was dead, I suppose. I tried to call you but all the lines had been disconnected. Then that man Jones started shouting orders at us by megaphone from the other side of the road block . . . "

"He's here," Peter said, hearing Arthur's feet on the stairs.

"My God!" Jones stared at the charnel chamber.

"You haven't met my wife, Arthur," Peter said. "Meg Canning, Arthur Jones."

"Thank you for coming, Dr Jones," Meg said, her tone icy. "At last."

"I had no idea. I . . ." Jones gulped behind his mask.

"Farmer Poldarren has just died," Peter told him. "You'll have to arrange for him to be carried out. How much griseofulvin have you still got in Ridding?"

"Well . . . an emergency supply."

"Arthur," Peter's voice was menacing, "this is an order from the Ministry of Health. Every last tablet of griseofulvin you possess is to be brought to Trebeth Cross immediately."

"I cannot leave Ridding unprotected."

"I will obtain some more supplies for Ridding. But the medicine must be applied here, and now. Otherwise all these people are going to die."

"If you can guarantee that my supplies will be replaced . . . "

"I will guarantee that," Peter told him. "I am also putting you in personal charge of Trebeth Cross. Get yourself together a team of doctors and nurses and move in."

"I can't do that," Jones protested. "I can't tell my people to take such a risk."

"You can and you will, because you must. For God's sake, you have your griseofulvin. At the first sign of any symptoms in yourself, take one. In any event, I'll get some griseofulmaline down to you just as soon as I can."

"But . . ." Jones looked at Meg. "Can't she . . . Dr Calhoun, I mean Mrs Canning . . . "

"Mrs Canning is exhausted, Doctor."

"Well, aren't we all? I mean . . . "

"I can manage, Peter. If we're going to get some more griseofulvin . . . "

"You're needed in London."

"London?"

"It's there, too, Meg. Brought in by some crazy yachtsman. It's spreading like wildfire."

"Oh, heck." Meg frowned, looking at her ward of patients. "But, these people. Our friends . . . "

" . . . will understand, sweetheart. The Prime Minister wants you in London."

23

Crisis

"I am certainly not leaving here until I have an adequate replacement," Meg declared. From the expression on her face as she looked at Arthur Jones, she did not consider him a possibility. "Nor am I leaving here until additional supplies of griseofulvin are made available. These people are dying."

Peter knew better than to argue with her on matters as fundamental to her principles. "Then let's get to it. Arthur, you organise a relief for Meg, immediately, and get all the griseofulvin you have over here. And get those telephones reconnected."

"I'll have to explain to the mayor," Jones said.

"Do that. After you've done the others."

Jones hurried off.

"Now don't you think you should have something to eat and a sleep?" Peter asked Meg. "You can't do anything until the griseofulvin gets here."

"If I stop now I am going to pass out," she said. "I'll sleep later."

Again, he decided not to argue; she could sleep in the car on the drive up to London. Instead he waited, with all the patience he could, while the minutes and the morning ticked away, until the telephones were restored. Then he returned to the cottage and called the Ministry of Health.

It took some time to get through, and then Jeremy

exploded. "Where the hell have you been?" he shouted. "We expected you back here at seven. And now . . . it's fucking well eleven o'clock."

"Calm down," Peter suggested. "My helicopter was grounded by the weather. What's it like up there now?"

"The weather? How the hell should I know what the weather is like?"

"Why don't you look out of the window?"

"For God's sake . . . it's pouring with rain. It's as dark as night out there."

"That was the impression I got earlier."

"Look here, where the hell are you?"

"I am in Trebeth Cross."

"Still?" Jeremy's voice was getting higher with every word.

"I told you; I'm afraid we have the Death here too."

"What?" He was screaming now, having apparently forgotten. "What did you say? How in the name of God could it have got there?"

"I'll explain later. Suffice to say someone slipped through the blood tests at Heathrow. Inadvertently, but there it is."

"My God, my God, my God!" Jeremy appeared to be sobbing. "Then we're done. I'm not sure we can contain it here in town. But if it's all over the country . . ."

"Jeremy, it is not all over the country. This is an isolated case, and it is being contained here. Arthur Jones, he's the local MOH, acted rather beyond his jurisdiction, but it is being contained. I give you my word on that. However, people are dying, and we are using our very last stocks of griseofulvin now. You must arrange for a fresh supply to be sent down to Ridding, immediately. To Dr Jones."

"A fresh supply?" Jeremy wailed. "Where am I to obtain a fresh supply? Every drop of the stuff is committed. You have no idea what it's like up here. It is sheer hell. And I'm having to cope on my own, while you are gallivanting around bloody Cornwall. Peter, I want you here. Now."

"All right. I'm on my way."

"How, if you can't fly?"

"I'll drive, dammit. Expect me this afternoon."

He put the phone down and wiped his brow. He simply had to get back up now: Jeremy was falling apart.

But getting out of Trebeth Cross was easier said than done. It took a good deal of time for Arthur to get hold of the necessary medical staff and persuade them to risk entering the village. Meanwhile, Peter himself, John Pengelley and Clive Wardle lifted Farmer Poldarren's body downstairs.

"I've called Reverend Ellis," Clive said. "And he said he'd come over when he could for the service. He didn't seem too keen."

"Well, you can't altogether blame him," Peter said, and looked at his watch. It was twelve. But at least he was not feeling any worse than earlier; he could hope that the vaccine had taken.

It was 12.30 when Jones finally appeared with a very nervous doctor and four equally apprehensive nurses, as well as some supplementary staff. By then Mrs Poldarren had also died.

But by then too the reserve griseofulvin from Ridding had arrived, and Meg felt that, by keeping everyone who had had no contact with Fran or the Wardles in general at a distance, they could contain the disease.

Peter had arranged with Clive to borrow his car and now at last Meg was persuaded to return to the cottage, strip off her bloodstained clothing, and have a hot bath. Betty Pengelley accompanied them. "You can't possibly drive all the way up to London on an empty stomach," she said, and frowned at her employer. "Your leg is all bloody."

Peter had entirely forgotten about his leg; its pain had

merged into his general feeling of discomfort. Now he explained what had happened while Meg redressed the wound and Betty fried eggs.

Stephanie Wardle arrived to say goodbye.

"I feel so dreadful about the Poldarrens," Meg said.

"My dear girl, you did everything you could. When I think what might have happened if you hadn't been here . . . my poor Fran!" She bit her lip. "Is she going to be all right, Meg?"

"I think she is," Meg said. "In fact, I'm sure of it. Just as long as there is sufficient griseofulvin." She looked at Peter.

"There will be," he promised.

It was nearly two when they finally left. "You must be absolutely exhausted," Meg said. "Why don't you let me drive?"

"Because I know the way," he reminded her, peering at the road from behind whirring windscreen wipers. "And you are far more exhausted than I am. Besides, I have a notion you are going to be put to work the moment we get to town. So grab some sleep while you can. I think that seat reclines."

Meg groped for the lever and pushed the seat-back right down. "Mm," was her only reply as she closed her eyes.

Peter had a lot on his mind. The radio now consisted entirely of reports, up-dates, and advice; all normal services had been cancelled. And the news on the whole was not good. Kitson had been found, dead, but there were fears that he might have infected a much larger number of people than had been anticipated; several minutes in every hour were devoted to calling on anyone who had been in contact with two young women who went under the names of Sally Minter and Jennifer O'Connell to report immediately to their nearest emergency centre.

But the news from the emergency centres was not good either; nearly all the ones in London had run out of the vaccine as well as griseofulvin. "I'll bet that's because almost everyone with a headache has been calling for pills," Meg murmured drowsily. "Whether they've been exposed to the disease or not."

New stocks were apparently being produced as rapidly as possible, but whether enough could be made available soon enough was arguable, and it was now reported that a van carrying drug supplies, and with the name of the Briggs Drug Company painted on its body, had been attacked by a mob on the King's Road, despite having an escort of armed soldiers; several people were reported to have been injured as the troops had been forced to open fire to protect their precious cargo.

"A complete breakdown of society," Peter growled. "And they said it couldn't happen here."

"When you think of the stoicism of the people down in Trebeth," Meg said.

"Yes. I wonder what colour the Foreign Secretary has the London area coloured now?"

"Your people still have control," Meg reminded him. "As long as they keep that, you'll be all right."

He did not reply. He was thinking that he had to drive through West London to get to either the flat or Westminster. He certainly wanted to go to the flat first; he needed a bath and a change as well as a shave. But getting there was what mattered, and it was not going to be easy. There was the usual halt at every village to talk his way through the road blocks, which consumed an enormous amount of time, though that eased after he joined the A303 which by-passed many of the villages and towns. Then when the fuel gauge hovered on the quarter full mark, still west of Stonehenge, he pulled into a garage. But this was locked tight, and so were the pumps.

"Hell," he said. "We'll have to go into Deptford.

There'll be something open there."

That meant negotiating a road block manned by policemen.

"No point going in there, sir," the sergeant said. "Everything's shut up tight."

"Look," Peter said, "I have got to get up to London, urgently. I have got to have petrol."

The sergeant considered, while large drips of rain fell from the brim of his cap. "We might be able to let you have a little, sir," he said. "It'll carry you as far as the M3 and Basingstoke. You might get some there."

"I doubt that. Look, just let me through and I'll catch a train at Salisbury."

"That won't do you much good, Mr Canning. All train services have been cancelled until further notice."

"For God's sake," Peter muttered. The Prime Minister's proud boast that it would be business as usual seemed to have been overtaken by events. "And don't tell me . . . there are no taxis available either."

"I'm afraid not, sir. In fact, all intercity and intercounty travel has been banned."

"When did this happen?"

"Instructions came through an hour ago. From the Ministry of Health, but supported by the Home Office."

Jeremy, Peter thought. Growing more and more hysterical.

"Of course," the sergeant went on, magnanimously, "as you're from the Ministry, why, you're welcome to continue. Would you like that petrol, sir? I can let you have two gallons."

Peter sighed, and accepted. They got up as far as Basingstoke, where the whole rigmarole had to be repeated. By now the afternoon was getting away from them, and they had to wait an hour while a gallon of petrol was found for them. The motorway stations were definitely closed, so he stayed with the A30, and the same thing happened again when he got to Sunningdale.

"We'd do better to walk," Meg suggested. "Or steal a couple of bicycles."

"We may wind up doing just that," Peter said savagely. He had promised Jeremy to be at the Ministry by mid-afternoon; it was now nearly eight, while as they approached London the road blocks grew in number, and when they reached the Staines area the colonel in command was uncertain whether to let even Peter Canning through.

"The fact is, Mr Canning, there have been considerable disturbances in various parts of the city, and I simply cannot spare the men to give you an adequate escort."

"We'll manage," Peter promised. "Just let me have some petrol."

"Well, Mr Canning, if you're prepared to take the risk."

The barricade was lifted but there was only one gallon available. Peter did not think it would get them to the flat, but it should take them fairly close.

"You happy about this?" he asked Meg. "Or have you had enough?"

"We can't stop now," she said. "Just let's get somewhere we can do some good."

He drove up the Chertsey Road, crossed the river at Richmond, again at Kew and on into Chiswick. It was just after nine, and thus far the roads had been empty save for the occasional police cars and one or two ambulances. Beyond Hammersmith, however, there was a growl of noise, and they could hear the sound of shots: Chelsea was in eruption.

"We'd better give that a miss," Peter decided, and swung right into Fulham, thinking of crossing the Fulham Road and approaching Westminster more from the south; the petrol gauge was hovering on empty and they were definitely going to have to walk the last mile or so.

When they emerged on to the Fulham Road itself, it was into the midst of a horde of people, mainly youngsters, who were smashing shop windows and taking everything they could find. Peter put his foot down to get across as rapidly as possible, but had to brake violently as several teenagers ran in front of the car, yelling and waving their arms.

He blared the horn, and they shouted some more. They had now surrounded the car, and began shaking it to and fro, as if intending to roll it over. Ominously, there was a car turned on its side only a few yards further down the street.

"Peter," Meg muttered, for the first time sounding afraid.

Faces appeared at the windows. "You're going to die!" they shouted. "Haven't you heard? We're all going to die! Come and join the fun. Dying can be fun."

They pulled on the doors, and someone shattered one of the rear windows.

"My God!" Meg gasped. "How sick can you get?"

Peter opened his door and got out.

"Peter, be careful," Meg begged.

Peter grinned at the people who surged at him. "Of course we're all going to die," he shouted. "I'm dying now," he confided. "I have the Red Death. Who's coming to hell with me? You, darling?"

He reached for the nearest mini-skirted girl, and she gave a shriek and hurled herself back into the arms of her friends, who all turned and ran down the street. Peter hastily got back behind the wheel and gunned the car down another comparatively empty side street. Behind them they heard the wail of a siren.

"Golly," Meg said. "I thought we were in big trouble."

"Just let's hope they weren't right," Peter said, as the car engine coughed and died.

*   *   *

"That was a delicious meal, Claudie," Colin Brereton said, sipping his brandy. "Such a pity Hartley couldn't be with us, but you coped splendidly even without his support."

"It was always more moral than physical," Grant Appleton suggested with a grin.

"He's working awfully hard," Claudia said loyally.

"I know," Brereton agreed. "He has my total admiration. Where's young Peter tonight? Shouldn't he be here?"

"Oh, he's gone rushing off into the country on some hush-hush Government business."

"Ah," Brereton said.

Claudia pointed in mock severity. "Now, Colin, just forget I said that."

"Oh, I shall. I was merely wondering if he'd be in the House tomorrow. It's to be this so long delayed debate on the emergency, you know. Should be quite a show."

"Sounds more like a damp squib to me," Julia Appleton commented. "Seeing that Toby gave the PM unqualified support this morning."

"Well . . ." Brereton coughed gently.

"Anyway, the crisis is just about over," Claudia said. "It said on the six o'clock news that that dreadful man Kitson had been found, dead, in some prostitute's flat." They had carefully stayed off the subject throughout the meal. "Now it's simply a matter of rounding up all his associates. They should all be locked up."

"Well . . ." Brereton began again, bristling. "The way the whole thing has been handled is a fairly typical example of the incompetence of this Government."

His wife understood the danger signals. "I think we all need an early night," she said. "Especially with a big debate tomorrow. Besides, there is a state of emergency on; I supose we'll be stopped by policemen and road blocks on the way home for being out after dark."

"It's hardly dark," her husband protested. "It's not yet ten."

"It will be by the time we get home, if we don't hurry. Must set an example. And Claudie, I think you should go straight to bed. You are not looking well. You've been overdoing it."

"I do have a headache," Claudia admitted. Her head had been splitting throughout dinner, and she had hardly eaten a thing, because she had a stomach ache as well – but she hoped it had not been noticed.

"Then you'll excuse us early," Janet said firmly. "And you go to bed."

She and Brereton each gave Claudia a big hug and a kiss, and took their leave. The Appletons lingered behind. "We can't possibly leave you with all the clearing up," Julia insisted.

"Oh, my Mrs Lilburne will be in at eight tomorrow. I'll leave everything," Claudia said.

"You don't know she's going to come in at all, with all this going on," Julia said. "Come on, we'll clear the table at least. It'll only take a minute. Grant, you do the glasses."

They fussed back and forth. Claudia got up to help them, and then sat down again. She felt quite dizzy. And her head was simply pounding.

"Oh, Claudie," Julia said. "I think I'd better help you to bed. I think . . . oh, my God!" she shrieked. "Grant! Quick!"

Grant Appleton ran in from the kitchen, gazed in consternation at the drops of blood trickling down Claudia's upper lip. Then he ran into the office and picked up the phone. "Emergency Station Seven? I'm calling from Sir Hartley Briggs' flat. Cadogan Square. There's a case of the Red Death . . . yes, Lady Briggs. Yes . . . what did you say? What? For God's sake, man, that can't be true. . . . Yes . . . Yes . . . Very well." He hung up.

"I can't think what's happening to me," Claudia was sobbing. "I've always been such a healthy person. Oh, Julia, what a mess . . . " she was holding Julia's hand between both of hers, and Julia was looking like a rabbit seized by a snake.

She gazed at her husband with her mouth open.

"They've run out of griseofulvin," Grant said. "They're trying to get some more from another station. But they don't know how long it'll be."

"What about the vaccine?" Julia's voice was sharp.

"They've used all of that too. Again, they're expecting some more, but . . . there's apparently quite a list in front of Claudie, awaiting treatment . . ." his voice tailed away.

Claudia's fingers relaxed, and Julia stepped away from the table, then checked herself. She still stared at her husband.

Claudie inhaled, a ghastly sound as she was spitting blood at the same time. "You must leave," she said. "Quickly."

"We can't just abandon you," Grant protested. "Alone in the flat, with . . ." he bit his lip.

"You must leave." Claudia shouted. "What about the children?"

"Oh, my God!" Julia said. "The children. Grant . . . "

"We can't go home," Appleton said with sudden decision. "We've been exposed to the disease. We dare not go home."

"Grant . . ." Julia's voice was shaking.

"When a new supply of the vaccine arrives, we'll be given some too," he said, as reassuringly as he could. "It'll only be a matter of hours."

"Grant!" his wife shrieked. "We're going to die."

"No, we are not going to die. Don't be silly. Listen, put Claudie to bed. I . . ." he snapped his fingers. "I'll telephone Hartley. He'll know what to do. He'll get the vaccine to us."

He ran back into the study, picked up the phone again.

"I'm afraid Sir Hartley Briggs is not available at this time," said what sounded suspiciously like military tones at the drug manufacturing centre.

"Listen," Appleton said. "This is a matter of life and death, and it concerns his wife. I have got to speak to him."

The WAAC on the other end of the line hesitated, then said, "I'll see if he's available."

There were various clicks, and then another voice said, "Sir Hartley is sleeping. He is not to be disturbed. He will awake in an hour's time."

"I can't wait an hour," Grant snapped. "You wake him and tell him his wife is dying."

That brought reaction. Only a few moments later Hartley was sleepily on the line. "What the devil is happening? Who is this?"

"Grant, Hartley. Grant Appleton."

"What do you want?" Hartley asked irritably.

Grant told him.

"For God's sake," Hartley shouted. "Right. I'll be right down with some griseofulvin. Who else was at dinner?"

"The Breretons."

"Well, you had better telephone them and warn them that they may have contracted the disease. How in the name of God did Claudie get it?"

"I don't really know. Something to do with an accident yesterday, and a man who wouldn't stop bleeding . . . "

"I'm on my way," Hartley said. "Tell her I'm on my way."

"I will." Grant hung up, looked at Julia, who was standing in the doorway, covered in blood. "Where is she?"

"In bed. God, I'm scared, Grant."

"Well, relax. Hartley's coming with enough stuff to do

us all. But I must call Colin." He punched the numbers, while his wife, with a shaking hand, poured them each a glass of brandy.

Janet answered. "Grant? We were just switching off the light."

"There's something you have to know, Janet: we think Claudie has the Red Death."

There was a moment of appalled silence. "How do you know?" Janet asked at last, her voice barely audible.

Grant brought her up-to-date, and found himself talking to Brereton.

"You say the Emergency Station has run out of vaccine? My God, the incompetence . . . "

"Colin, they're doing the best they can. Anyway, look, Hartley is on his way with enough for us all. As soon as he gets here I'll bring some over."

"Yes," Brereton said, seething with anger, his voice ominous with things he clearly intended to do, and say. "We look forward to seeing you."

Grant replaced the phone and drank some brandy. "He has his priorities all wrong," he said, and jumped as the phone bleeped again. "Yes?"

"Look!" Hartley was obviously labouring under an immense strain. "You won't believe this, but I am to all intents and purposes a prisoner here. Seems the blithering brigadier who is in charge has orders to let no one in or out, except with shipments of the vaccine, and the vaccine is to go only to the Emergency Centres as listed in some fucking sheet of paper he has been given. Certainly he is not allowing any to be taken out by individuals. 'Where would we be if everyone started taking the law into his own hands?' he asks. I can tell you I goddamn well nearly took the law into my own hands and throttled the bastard." He paused for breath.

"What are we going to do?" Grant asked, refusing to accept the panic which was clawing at his mind.

"Pull strings. I have tried to get hold of Peter, but he's not at his flat . . . "

"I believe he's down in Cornwall."

"Trust him to be out of action when he's wanted," Hartley grumbled. "I've also tried to get hold of Jeremy, but he's not taking any calls, apparently. Now I have to get on with it here. I want you to keep trying, either Peter or Jeremy, until you raise one of them. Explain the situation."

Grant nodded, slowly. "I'll do that."

"Good man. How's Claudie?"

"We've given her some Panadol and she seems to be in less pain. But she's bleeding."

"Oh, shit!" Hartley said. "Keep trying, for God's sake!"

The phone went dead.

"Oh, Grant . . . " Julia whimpered.

"Just keep calm. We're going to get help. We are." He picked up the phone again.

"Who're you going to try first?"

"I'm going to call Shirley and tell her she'll have to spend the night with the kids. Then I suppose I'll have to call Colin back and put him in the picture. He's going to go straight through the roof. And then I'd better keep trying Jeremy. God, how I wish Peter were here."

Julia refilled their brandy goblets. There did not seem to be anything else to do.

It took Peter and Meg almost another hour to reach the flat as they dodged down side streets to avoid groups of rampaging young people as well as patrolling soldiers and policemen – it was dark now and they were breaking the curfew. When the door was finally securely locked behind them, Meg collapsed in a chair while Peter poured them both a drink and switched on his Ansaphone.

"Peter! For God's sake, where are you? You should

449

have been back yonks ago. Call me the minute you get in." That was Jeremy.

"Peter! For God's sake, where are you? Something terrible has happened and you must call Claudie's number as soon as you get in." Grant Appleton?

"Peter! . . ." Hartley's voice.

"Bugger that," Peter said. "Two are enough to go on with." He looked at his watch. It was half past ten. But surely nobody in London was sleeping.

He punched out Claudia's number first, got an exhausted Grant, listened in appalled silence to what his friend had to say.

"How is she now?" he asked when Grant had finished.

"She really is very sick."

"And yourselves?"

"Well . . . I don't know. We both feel kind of woozy, but that could be nerves . . . or brandy."

"And exhaustion. Look, keep trying the Emergency Station. I'm going to see what can be done. I'll get back to you." He looked at Meg. "Did you hear all of that?"

She nodded. "I must get over there."

"And do what?"

"Simple. Back to square one. I'll bleed her. If necessary I'll keep bleeding her until the vaccine arrives."

"Meg, you're exhausted. And those streets . . . "

She grinned at him. "And I'm not licensed to practise over here. You going to run me in?"

They reached Cadogan Square without incident, and Meg got to work, using a willing but frightened Julia as a nurse, sterilising her instruments in the kitchen. They had to boil everything as the only antiseptic was of the household variety, her own small supply having been finished long ago in Trebeth Cross.

Peter got on to Jeremy.

"Where in the name of God have you been?" Jeremy

shouted. He sounded even more hysterical than that morning.

"Busy. We had a spot of bother getting up from the West Country. Some idiot had closed down the railways."

"A spot of bother? Hells bells, have you any idea what's going on here in London?" He seemed to have forgotten who cancelled the trains.

"Some," Peter said, "but never mind about that; what the hell's happening with all the griseofulvin supplies? The Emergency Stations in this area say they've run out."

"Well then, that's your answer."

"Don't tell me they've been allowed to hand it out to anyone who asked for it? That would be crazy. The situation is going to be very grim unless we can get more vaccine in a hurry."

"We couldn't possibly ask the Emergency Services to test everyone," Jeremy exploded. "You'd better get on to your brother-in-law. He's not in a very co-operative mood."

"Because you wouldn't co-operate with him. Why the hell has he been imprisoned in his factory by the army? There has got to be a radical re-think, Jeremy, starting now. We've got to stop the mindless handing out of vaccine to people who don't need it. Okay, don't say it. I know it's going to slow things up, but people who claim to be ill have simply got to have a blood test first. For Christ's sake, it shouldn't be that difficult."

"Well . . . you handle it. I have enough problems. Do you realise that through his two girlfriends that crazy man Kitson infected an entire North Country business-man's club in town for a jolly? I'm having to cope with that. And I've had Colin Brereton on the phone, raising merry hell. He thinks he's contracted the disease from your sister, and he can't get hold of any vaccine either. The Emergency Stations are just being swamped. I just can't cope any more. You sort it out, Peter." To Peter's consternation, he was sobbing.

"Are you giving me carte blanche?" Peter asked, somewhat dazed.

"Yes. Just sort it out," Jeremy begged.

"Then I would like you to telephone the Prime Minister to put that on record," Peter said. "And have an armed escort, either police or soldiers, sent to my sister's flat."

"An armed escort? I don't understand. At Claudie's flat?"

"That is where I happen to be at this moment, Jeremy. If I am going to get round to Emergency Stations I need protection. There are some very odd people out there right this minute. I've met some of them."

"Oh. All right. I'll do that. And I'll call the PM. Just get on with it."

"I'll start just as soon as my escort turns up." It was terrifying to believe Jeremy had cracked so under the strain. But the signs had been there long enough. He wondered if the Prime Minister had spotted them.

He put down the phone, went into the bedroom. Meg and Julia were both soaked in blood, but Claudia was lying peacefully, her eyes closed. "How is she?"

"She should be all right for another couple of hours, anyway, but there's a limit to how much I can draw off," Meg said. "Hopefully by then vaccine will have arrived. As to whether we can actually save her . . . " she looked at him.

Peter closed his eyes, trying to blot out the unthinkable. "What about Grant and Julia?"

They both looked grim.

"How do you feel?" Meg asked, gently taking Julia's wrist.

"Well . . . a bit sick. But really, all that blood . . . "

"It would be best to see how it goes and keep our fingers crossed," Meg said. "If you show the slightest sign of the disease I'll bleed you too. Unless the griseofulvin gets here in time."

Julia's pulse was a bit erratic but she was otherwise normal.

"We'll be back in a few hours," Peter told them. He could hear the wail of an approaching siren.

Meg raised her eyebrows. "Are we going some-place?"

"If you can stand it. Jeremy seems to have cracked up so I have to take over. You could be an enor-mous help."

"I had actually thought of at last going to bed," Meg confessed. Every bone in her body ached. "But let's go." She squeezed Julia's hands, kissed Grant on the cheek. "You have both been just marvellous, truly marvellous. Now why don't you take turns trying to get some sleep? And don't worry. You're going to be all right. And your kids."

"You should have been a GP," Peter told her as they went down the stairs. "Do you really believe all of that?"

"It costs nothing to be optimistic." She held his hand. "Peter . . . I'm so terribly sorry about Claudia."

"Yes," he sighed. "A little close to home."

"When you think that I left all that griseofulvin down in Trebeth . . . it just never occurred to me I might need more of it up here."

"You did what you thought best," he said. "And I love you."

The front door opened as they reached it, and they gazed at a Metropolitan Police Sergeant who wore a revolver on his hip. "Mr Canning?" he asked.

"My God! What have you done," Meg looked at Peter in alarm.

"These natives are friendly," Peter promised her, and led her to the waiting police car with its escort of motor cyclists. "Let's get moving, Sergeant. We have a lot to do."

453

*   *   *

"Where first, sir?" the sergeant asked from the front passenger seat as the cavalcade started to move off.

"I want to see what's happening at the Emergency Stations. Where is the nearest?"

The officer consulted lists on his clipboard. "Quite near; at the hospital in Sydney Street."

"Good. We'll begin there."

The driver obviously knew the district and by a devious course turned on to Sydney Street from Ixworth Place, having avoided the Fulham Road. But they were all shaken by the long queue down the footpath outside the hospital.

"There must be hundreds waiting there!" Meg exlaimed. "And they say they have no vaccine? This is crazy. Anyone in that crowd who has the virus will be infecting the others."

Peter tried to suppress the exasperation he was feeling. "Let's just get in there. How near can you get to the door, driver?"

"This is it, I reckon, sir." He could not get the car near the footpath as people were spilling out on to the road.

"Will they let us through, do you think?" Meg asked.

"Don't worry, ma'am; we'll see you safely inside," the sergeant assured her.

In fact nobody seemed at all aggressive. With typical British stoicism, they stood patiently waiting, the brighter characters even cracking the odd joke and raising ripples of laughter. Peter and Meg had no difficulty getting through, but inside the foyer was another matter.

"'Ere! No bloody queue jumpin', mister. First come first served. Get to the back." A fat, brassy blonde was barring the way.

"Yeah. That's right, mate. Out the way you come in," her companion agreed. He was tall, with a barrel stomach, and stood with arms akimbo, glaring at Peter, eyeball to eyeball.

"No need to get excited, pal," the sergeant said sooth-ingly. "This man is from the Ministry of Health and is here to help speed things up."

The man's eyes narrowed suspiciously. "Oh yeah? Try pulling the other one."

"Saw a pig flying yesterday, dinya Bert?" the blonde shouted, then squealed with laughter as her audience tittered.

But they fell back in silence as the police escort moved up, truncheons in hand.

Further down the hospital corridor people were shouting.

" . . . children should be first," someone asserted.

"What good's a country full of kids if the grown-ups are all dead?" another argued.

"People most at risk should be done first. The wife's pregnant . . . " A woman with a grey face and huge stomach clung to the speaker's arm.

At last Peter and Meg were ushered past them into an office and the door behind them closed on the arguments.

"Sorry about that," the doctor in charge cleared a pile of papers from a chair for Meg. "The name's Ashwari." His tie was loosened and the top button of his shirt undone; there was dark stubble on his chin and he looked exhausted.

"Please don't apologise, Dr Ashwari. You seem to be coping very well, under the circumstances," Peter assured him. "Tell me, when did you last receive sup-plies of vaccine?"

"None since the first delivery yesterday morning. That's the problem. There was only enough for about 700 people."

"And those people out there have been queueing ever since?" Meg's eyes widened, "No wonder some of them are getting agitated."

"What guidelines were you given as to who should

be vaccinated?" Peter hitched his weary frame onto a corner of the littered desk.

"None. But I didn't want to waste time and vaccine on people who weren't at immediate risk so I tried to get the staff to question everyone first." He swept thick, black hair away from his forehead. "Unfortunately the people who were turned away told the others who were waiting what to expect and when their turns came most of them had plausible stories. It was impossible to know who to believe. It's a pity we weren't equipped to run tests."

"Exactly," Meg stood up. "Where is your pathology department? I can set that up for you right now."

"Didn't you tell me there's a simple standard test that any hospital can do?" Peter asked her.

"Depends on the equipment the English hospitals have. Is your path department fairly average regarding facilities, Doctor?"

"Yes, I would say so. Will you excuse us, Mr Canning, while I show Dr Calhoun what we have to offer?"

"Of course. And may I use your telephone while you're gone?"

"Naturally. Feel free."

Before Peter finished dialling the first number a police motorcyclist arrived with a large buff envelope addressed to The Assistant Minister of Health. He replaced the receiver. It was from 10 Downing Street. First was a hand-written note from the Prime Minister:

". . . like you to take over full responsibility for the Ministry until further notice. Please make any changes you feel necessary for the distribution and use of the vaccine . . . I rely on you to refer back to me before making any wide, sweeping decisions of national importance . . . Enclosed is a document giving you full powers on the authority of the Cabinet, signed by myself and two other Ministers.".

Peter handed the papers to the sergeant to read while he returned to the telephone, desperate to get supplies moving and especially to Claudia.

Meg and Dr Ashwari hurried back ten minutes later.

"Any joy?" Peter asked.

"No problem. I've written out a detailed method of procedure which the doctor will xerox for the police to distribute to all Emergency Centres."

"Marvellous. I will do a covering letter ordering implementation of the tests immediately." Peter turned to Ashwari. "Can you have photocopies made of that, too? Sergeant, get through to your chief and ask him to organise police couriers, will you?"

"Yes, sir." The officer, fed up with standing around doing nothing, went straight into action.

Ten minutes later Peter gathered up his notes. "Right. That's that sorted out. Now let's get down to distribution. Can you get us to Westminster, Sergeant?"

"Or die in the attempt, sir," the man grinned.

"We'll hope that won't be necessary. Ready, darling?" he said to Meg.

She saw Ashwari's left eyebrow twitch.

"I am his wife, incidentally," she explained.

The Indian doctor smiled. "Makes for excellent team work. I wish you both good luck."

Three hours later, still with the escort of screaming police sirens, they arrived back at Cadogan Square. They had lost all track of time and moved like automatons, forcing themselves on, having passed the ultimate in exhaustion long ago. The phone calls and discussions both at Westminster and Downing Street had seemed endless, and often frustrating. It was incredible that, in a situation such as this – of impending national disaster – one still had to fight through so much red tape and blockheaded thinking.

"Do you think there may be some milky beverage in

the house we could have?" Meg asked as they ran up the steps to the door. "There is a limit to the amount of foul coffee a person can take."

"There's sure to be something. I seem to remember Claudia extolling the virtues of Horlicks when one was tired. We'll take a look in a minute." Peter's face was tense with the added worry of Claudia's condition. He had managed to organise Hartley's release from the factory but, when he called the flat later, his brother-in-law reported that Claudia was very ill indeed. Apparently, although she had always appeared to be very fit, she had been treated for high blood pressure for over a year.

She looked terrible. The pills had arrived an hour before but Meg needed only a quick glance at the beetroot complexion and features distorted with pain, to know that they were not working . . . yet? Perhaps there was still a chance they might. But only a chance.

Claudia opened her eyes. "Hello," she whispered, trying to smile. "Isn't this damned ridiculous?" Then her eyes screwed up with agony as her hands clutched at her abdomen. "I'd like to know what the hell's going on down there. I'm sure I'm not preggie but it certainly feels like labour pains."

Meg wanted to weep at the brave attempt at humour. There was no way she could tell her sister-in-law that all her vital organs were rupturing and bleeding; that even if the griseofulvin did work at the eleventh hour, the chances of her surviving the terrible internal damage were remote. Instead she spread her mouth in a wide grin. "Well I sure hope it's not a baby. Hartley doesn't look in the mood for commencing fatherhood, right now."

"You can say that again!" Hartley took his wife's hand, not quite disguising the wince of horror as he felt its heat. "However, that's not to say that when you're better we can't . . . I mean, it's never too late . . . " He turned away as the full implication of his words dawned on him.

Claudia opened her eyes again, wide. "I've just had the most awful thought. I went down to Wimbledon yesterday morning to tell the old folks . . ." She winced with pain, but whether it was mental or physical was hard to tell. "Dear Lord, don't say I've infected them." A tear squeezed out between her lids.

"Don't worry, old girl. The supplies of griseofulvin are available now. I'll keep in touch and dose them if necessary," Peter promised. Then he asked Hartley, "How are Grant and Julia?"

"They looked all right when I sent them off to lie down a couple of hours ago. Very weary, of course, and Julia was scared as hell."

"I'd better go check them out." Meg moved to the door.

Hartley left the room with her and when the door was closed asked, "For God's sake, Meg, can't you do anything for her?" The heavy jowl quivered, his eyes were swimming.

Meg shook her head helplessly. "Oh, Hartley, how I wish I could. But . . . I think any further medication would only lessen her chances."

"To think that I have put my entire workforce to making the stuff to save thousands, millions of people from this Red Death and yet I couldn't get any here in time to save my wife. She knows the score, you know. And she's being so brave . . ." he turned away from Meg to lean his head against the wall, shoulders heaving.

There was nothing she could say. She squeezed his arm sympathetically, then moved away to look to the Appletons.

Grant emerged from a doorway at the far end of the hallway but Meg hardly recognised him, he looked so flushed and dishevelled. "Hello, Meg. Thank God you've arrived. I hate to say this but I think Julia and I may be in trouble. She has an unstoppable nose bleed and I'm feeling absolutely terrible."

Meg swayed on her feet. "Okay. Let's take a look at you both," and followed him into the spare bedroom. There was little doubt he was right. She did what she could to stem Julia's blood loss, then said, "Go back to bed, Grant, and I'll be back in a few minutes."

She returned to Claudia's bedroom where Hartley was sitting on his wife's bed. "Where is your griseofulvin? I need it for the Appletons," she whispered to him.

He frowned. "I don't have any more. They only allowed me enough for Claudia."

Meg's heart sank. "Where's Peter?"

"Said he was going downstairs for some Horlicks."

She nodded wearily and hurried out.

Peter was in the kitchen. "Found it! Now for some mugs."

Meg took the receiver off the wall set. "I'll do that while you get some more griseofulvin over here. Grant and Julia . . . "

"Both?"

"Seems so."

"Christ!" He handed her the Horlicks jar and took the phone. "I'll have to call my parents and check whether they have any symptoms, yet. And tell them about Claudia, too. They should be prepared, I suppose, for the worst."

"Awful, having to tell them by phone."

"Terrible. But I cannot possibly risk trying to get down to Wimbledon, now."

"Of course not, darling. In fact, I think you should try to get some sleep. They have your number, here, and I promise to wake you . . . "

"Rubbish . . . Yes, yes I'll hold," he told the voice at the other end of the line and held his hand over the receiver. "Yes, rubbish. You are the one nearly dead with fatigue. You go and find a bed. I'll keep an eye on the others till the griseofulvin arrives."

"You can't bleed them if the stuff is late," Meg argued.

"What do you call late? A couple of hours?"

"Maybe more – maybe less. Depends on the individual patient." She stirred hot water into the powder in the mugs. "Anyway, I should stay with Claudia."

"Is there honestly anything you think you can do at this stage to help her?"

Meg sighed and shook her head.

"Darling. If my sister is going to die, I want to be with her. Understand?" She nodded. "Then for God's sake just take that mug and go. While you've got the chance. I'm not just thinking of you, my dearest. I'm thinking how much more use you'll be after some sleep, when we have to tackle the next operation."

Meg shrugged. "You win. But promise me you will take a turn later. And you will call me if I can be of any use to anyone?"

Peter nodded, but before he could say any more a voice hailed him from the phone.

Meg wrapped her hands round the hot mug and crept out of the room.

Hartley had fallen into a restless sleep on Claudia's pretty little bedroom chair – which was not designed for his bulk – and was snoring softly.

Peter felt sick. Sick with frustration and misery as he sat watching his sister becoming weaker by the minute; sick at the inadequate words he would have to use when he broke the news to his parents. Sick that there had been no word of Sarah and her family, that he had been unable to get them out of New Zealand in time . . . But would it have helped? Were any of them going to survive here in England? In the world? Over the centuries there had been many prophets of doom forecasting the end of the world, but had any of them visualised it being like this? He had never before given the subject much thought. Somehow, in the back of his mind, he had imagined the world would end with some mighty explosion from the Earth's centre shattering the globe into a million pieces and sending them spinning into eternity. Had anyone foretold that it would merely be the end of mankind and that the Earth itself would remain intact to be repopulated, in some dramatic evolution spanning millions of years, by a new form of creature, unrelated to homo sapiens?

Damn it! This was rubbish. The wretched meanderings of an exhausted mind. Claudia was quite peaceful at the moment; perhaps he should take the opportunity of looking in on Grant and Julia. Where the hell was that griseofulvin? Why was it taking so long; they said they had some in stock? He looked at his watch but could not remember what time he had ordered it.

Grant was leaning over Julia – who was choking. His own nose was bleeding but he did not have a hand spare to mop up, so it just dripped on her sheet to mingle with her blood. He looked up at Peter in misery. Speechless. He knew there was little anyone could do without the medication.

Peter ran for the nearest phone in desperation, misdialled. Dialled again. "Canning here," he shouted. "What the hell's happening? You told me hours ago that a supply of . . . " He paused, listening. "Surely it doesn't take more than three hours. . . " He frowned as the voice spoke again. "Murdered? You're telling me they're committing murder out there to get hold of the stuff?" He felt his hand begin to tremble. "Well send the couriers out in mufti, so they can't be identified . . . Oh, you have. When?"

He slammed the receiver down and hurried back to Grant. "The first lot they sent was waylaid. Another lot left half an hour ago. It should be here any minute." He hoped he sounded more confident than he felt.

"Peter! Peter, come quickly!" It was Hartley shouting from Claudia's room.

He could hear the breath rattling in her throat before he reached her door. "I'll get Meg," he said, wondering where she was.

Opening the drawing-room door, he saw her curled on the sofa, dead to the world. He hated to wake her . . . but he had to. He bent to kiss her. "Meg, darling. Wake up, please."

"Uh? What? What is it? What's the time?" She started to turn over, burying her face in a pink silk cushion. Then suddenly she was awake. "Oh darling. What is it?" She looked at her watch. "Heavens! You've let me sleep for three hours."

"It's Claudia. Can you come?"

Peter's face was grey and haggard, not helped by the twenty-four hours' growth of beard. Meg swung her feet on to the floor and led the way back to Claudia's room.

Hartley was trying to prop his wife up with pillows, his face ashen. "She can't breathe. Do something, Meg," he pleaded. Between them they piled the pillows behind her, but they had seen the trickle of blood starting from her mouth. Her eyes were open, but she did not appear to recognise anyone.

Lacking a stethoscope, Meg laid an ear on Claudia's chest and heard the labouring of stricken lungs. She straightened and gently shook her head at the men.

"Her breathing is a bit easier, I think," Hartley said. But he knew she could not last much longer.

"You both stay here with her. I'll go and see if I can do anything for the others." Meg left the husband and brother standing on either side of the bed.

Grant was lying beside Julia on her single bed. Though deeply flushed and in great discomfort himself, he was trying to comfort her. Her nose had stopped bleeding, but tears dribbled over her scarlet cheeks.

"Sorry about the delay in delivering the griseofulvin. Peter's phoned again and they say it should be here any minute." Meg tried to sound more cheerful than she felt.

"Will it be in time, for us?" Julia gasped. "It's the children . . . What will happen . . . ?"

"Yes, it will arrive in plenty of time for you both. So there's no need to worry about the children." Meg took her pulse as she spoke. "But you really must try not to cry. You are inflaming the nasal membranes and you'll start your nose bleeding again." She replaced Julia's hand on to the coverlet and grasped Grant's. "Splendid. You are both coping very well. I know you feel ghastly but . . . "

" . . . you've seen a lot of people a great deal worse." Grant anticipated her words.

"You'd better believe it!" She laughed brightly. "Unfortunately Claudia is very bad indeed. I must get back to her but I'll pop in again every ten minutes, or as soon as the griseo turns up."

Julia had stopped crying and both of them looked somewhat better for Meg's visit.

It was fortunate that the Appletons could not see the young research doctor moments after she left their room. She, too, wanted to weep. She had never been more thankful that she was not in general practice. The thought of having to lie like that repeatedly, in the attempt to keep one's patients' spirits up, horrified her.

Leaning against the wall, forcing down lungfuls of air, she tried to calm the turmoil in her mind. This scene, and others similar, was being re-enacted thousands, millions of times, right now, all over the world; ordinary, innocent people, like Sally Ann and Rod, were dying. Lovers watching each other in death throes: mothers cradling their dying babies, old and young seeing their families decimated. She had realised months ago that life on Earth could never be the same again. But the past forty-eight hours had brought the fact home to her in far greater emotional depth. Was there any hope for Grant and Julia, even if the griseo did arrive in the next hour? Who could tell? And if they did not survive, what would happen to their children? And all the other orphans?

Suddenly she was aware that she was weeping, too.

Fifteen minutes later the griseofulvin arrived.

When Grant and Julia had been dosed, Meg washed their faces and tidied their beds. Assuring them that sleep was their next priority, she closed the curtains and withdrew, leaving the door ajar so that she might look in on them every so often.

In the other bedroom, Claudia was still holding on to a thin thread of life. Peter and Hartley sat beside her, mopping her forehead with a damp facecloth, brushing strands of hair away from her cheeks; watching, waiting.

The waiting was mercifully brief. Gradually, over the next hour, Claudia's breathing slowed dramatically. Meg, Peter and Hartley found they were hardly daring to breathe themselves, watching and listening for her next laboured gasp for oxygen. Her eyes were dulled and only half open when all at once her lids raised and, as she took a deep breath, she smiled at them.

The smile remained – long after her heart had stopped.

Five hours later, Peter was driven to Westminster in a police car. After telephoning Trebeth Cross to assure himself that additional stocks of griseofulvin had arrived and that everything was under control there, with no more deaths, Peter had taken Meg's place on the sofa, his long legs dangling over one arm most uncomfortably: but he had slept. When he woke up he borrowed Hartley's razor and having had a shower he felt, and looked, much better. Meanwhile, realising it would be impossible to find anyone to lay out Claudia's body, Meg had undertaken the task herself.

Grey-faced with grief, Hartley had returned to the

factory, uncertain how or when arrangements could possibly be made for Claudia's funeral.

Meg remained in Cadogan Square to take care of the Appletons who were both responding well to the griseofulvin, and now Peter was bracing himself to the immense task ahead.

"This Government cannot, and will not, accept responsibility for acts of madness such as that committed by David Kitson," the Prime Minister said, facing a crowded House of Commons with indomitable aplomb. "We did everything that could humanly be done to keep the Red Death out of this country. Now that it is here, we are doing everything that is humanly possible to bring it under control. And we are winning. Make no mistake about that. There were errors yesterday and last night. There were riots by that brainless element which unfortunately plays so large a part in our modern civilisation; they have been brought under control. I regret to say that this was not done without bloodshed. There will be a full enquiry into each incident. But I may say that this Government stands four-square behind the forces of law and order in this terrible situation. Our policemen and our soldiers were given a job to do, and they have done it magnificently.

"More important, there were errors in the distribution of what stocks of the vaccine and the antidote were immediately available. The doctors and nurses manning the Emergency Centres, not unnaturally, tried to be safe rather than sorry, and distributed their vaccines to anyone who felt at all unwell or was suspected of having the disease. I repeat, this was a natural reaction to a situation unimaginable only a week ago; no one can be blamed.

"However, the crisis had to be met, and conquered, with great rapidity. I can now tell you that the Parliamentary Private Secretary to the Ministry of Health,

Peter Canning . . ." the Prime Minister paused to smile down at Peter, who despite the fact that the House was packed, and certainly every minister was present, had been given a seat on the Front Bench, "was given charge of correcting the situation. He worked all night, aided, I may say, by his wife, whom you know better as Dr Margaret Calhoun, of the Robert Koch Research Center in San Francisco, and he has now brought the situation under control." The Prime Minister paused while the Government cheers rang out, and after a moment these were joined by the Opposition; the only man who might have opposed such a spontaneous outburst of relief and congratulation, Colin Brereton, was not in his place.

"I might add that while working so hard, he has had to cope with personal grief in the death of his sister, Lady Briggs, from the Red Death, for which we all offer him, and Sir Hartley Briggs, who has done so much to help on the production side, our sincere condolences. I will not say, I cannot say," the Prime Minister went on, when the sympathetic murmurings had dwindled, "how many more people are going to die of this disease. What I can say is this: we have got matters back under control. Stocks of both the vaccine and the antidote are now coming out of the drug companies at an ever-increasing rate. My original estimate that it would take a month to have sufficient vaccine for the entire population of this country can now be halved, and in addition most, if not all, of the people known to have contracted the disease have been located and are under treatment.

"I want to make it very plain to this House that we have a long and terrible road ahead of us. Not merely in this country. God knows our plight is severe. Our finances are stricken, our businesses have ground to a halt. But we will recover and rise again. How much worse must it be for those countries which have almost entirely succumbed to this dread pestilence. It is to them that our thoughts must turn, to them that all the aid in our power must be given. We shall not fail them, as we have not failed ourselves."

The Prime Minister sat down, amidst more tumultuous cheers, and the Leader of the Opposition rose to speak in reply. Peter felt a tap on the shoulder and looked down at the message being put in his hand, then hurried out to the phone.

When he returned the Prime Minister raised a questioning eyebrow.

"It was the doctor I sent round to the Breretons' home," he whispered.

"Yes? How are they?"

"Brereton has had a stroke, I'm afraid."

"My God! But . . ."

"It's not polycythaemia. It's a common or garden stroke, brought on by stress, excitement and sheer bad temper. Fright, if you like, at being unable to get hold of the vaccine immediately."

"Will he survive?"

"The doctor seems to think so. Though it was a fairly severe stroke, but at this stage he suggests Colin's days in politics may well be over." Peter coughed softly. "Er . . . on a personal note, I wonder if I could be excused from the House as soon as possible? My parents haven't been told yet of Claudia's death. I just couldn't tell them over the phone: I must see them in person, but felt that in this instance it was more important for me to come here first."

"My dear Peter! Of course, you must go immediately . . . But do return as soon as you can."

They knew as soon as they saw him at the front door. "Claudia?" Veronica gasped.

Peter nodded and took her in his arms. He had always thought of his mother as a tough little body, even if she was a bit scatty. Now she seemed so frail. He could feel her shoulderblades through her summer dress and every

468

bone in her spine: she had lost so much weight through worry. Standing in the hallway, Peter reached out for his father and the three clung together, weeping.

Today it was John who put on the kettle for tea. The storm had cleared leaving a perfect, cloudless sky, so they took their cups out on to the terrace where Peter explained what had happened. "It's a miracle poor Claudia didn't infect you," he said, thankfully.

"She never was a very demonstrative girl," Veronica remarked. "She seldom actually kissed us. And she was in such a hurry, the day of the Prime Minister's speech, because she had people coming to dinner that night." Then she looked up in consternation. "Oh dear. Those nice friends of yours, the Appletons, were going to be there. I do hope she didn't infect them!"

"I'm afraid she did, but fortunately the griseofulvin arrived just in time for them. But it was touch and go at one stage."

"How is Hartley?" John asked.

"Shattered, of course. He's gone back to the laboratories; work is probably the best thing for him at the moment." He looked down the garden at the profusion of flowers, which so reminded him of their childhood, his and Sarah's and Claudie's. Was it possible that he was the only survivor of the three? No! It was ridiculous to think so negatively. Claudie would be appalled.

He took his mother's hand. "Claudie was so incredibly brave, still cracking jokes even when she knew she was going. We must all try to be brave, too."

"If only we could hear something of Sarah." His mother looked so forlorn, sitting hunched in her deck-chair.

"I telephoned the Red Cross people who are trying to open lines of communication with other countries. They said they were in contact with some of their people in Australia and New Zealand and would try to get information for me if they could. I'll use your phone now to see if they have anything yet." He doubted if there would be any news; it was too soon. But it gave him something positive to do.

The telephone was on a desk in the sitting-room, through the French windows behind them. He waited for his call to be transferred from one secretary to another, the person he had asked for being unavailable. His fingers drummed impatiently on the tooled leather and he was about to tell them to forget it, he would call later, when a new voice came on the line.

"Is that you, Mr Canning? Ah, good. I've been trying to get you at the House of Commons."

"Yes, yes. You've heard something?" The room was suddenly very hot . . . and he was almost afraid to listen. Chance of the news being good was so remote.

"Douglas and Sarah Lawton and two sons, correct?" The woman's voice was calm and gentle.

"Yes."

"You'll be happy to know that all four are safe and well."

Peter's thighs became weak and he collapsed on to the chair in front of the desk. "Thank you. Oh, thank you so much." In fact he felt weak all over. "Er . . . Are they still in the same camp?"

"No. They have been transferred to a certified F.F.I. location . . ."

"What's F.F.I.?"

"Free from infection. An old army term. Have you a pen handy? I'll give you their address," she added. "You understand there are no normal postal services and letters may take a very long time . . . "

What the hell did that matter? They were alive! Sarah and her family were safe and well! As soon as he had taken down the address he rushed out on to the terrace.

Once again the three of them clung together and wept. If only they dared to believe it.

Epilogue

"I suppose one of the most terrifying aspects of this disease is the way it strikes so indiscriminately," the Prime Minister said. "Do you feel up to talking?"

"Yes," Peter said.

"Good. There are two things I wish to speak with you about. The first is your constituency. I have received a report from Trebeth Cross. I'm afraid another two people died before the disease was brought under control there. It appears that many people are pointing their fingers at the local MOH, Dr Jones, and saying that it was largely his mismanagement that is responsible."

"I think he did the best he could, according to his ideas, Prime Minister. And he actually did contain the disease. Where he was wrong was in not releasing all the griseofulvin he possessed, immediately. But I think he knows, and he will have to live with that decision for the rest of his life."

"It is good of you to defend him. Even so, you must have some very unpleasant memories of the place. If you would like to change constituencies before the next election, we'll find you a safe seat."

Being the Prime Minister's blue-eyed boy was a dazzling experience. "I'll stick with Ridding and Trebeth Cross, Prime Minister. They were frightened, but so were we all. And they actually behaved magnificently."

"Well, if you're sure. The other matter is where you go from here. As soon as the domestic crisis is over, which hopefully will be in a couple of months, I intend to have a Cabinet reshuffle. Jeremy has indicated that he would like to return to the back benches . . . " the Prime Minister's lips twisted to indicate total acceptance of the offer. "Therefore you could very well move up to the Ministry of Health. With Cabinet rank of course. However, I would prefer you to go to Energy." The Prime Minister frowned as Peter made no reply. "I know it is not exactly one of the glamour posts, but frankly, you would be very young for the Foreign Office or the Exchequer or even Trade and Industry, and anyway," the words were relieved by a smile, "a possible future prime minister should have experience in every office before the final one. In any event Energy will involve getting Britain's industrial effectiveness back on its feet and so will be one of the most important of governmental departments over the next year or two. I would like you to think about that."

Peter held the Prime Minister's gaze for a long moment before nodding, slowly and positively. "Yes, Prime Minister. I am thinking . . . and I will accept. Gratefully."

"Oh, good."

"But I would like a brief leave of absence, commencing now." Peter held his breath.

The Prime Minister frowned. "Now is surely not the time for a holiday."

"I do not intend to take a holiday, as such. There is something I need to do. It is, incidentally, connected with medicine," he added, grinning. "But I know Jeremy can hold the fort till my return."

"Ah," the Prime Minister's face broke into an answering smile. "I think I understand. Very well, Peter. The publicity value will be enormous. You have my blessing."

*   *   *

Throughout the country there was a continuous stream of funerals every day, keeping clergy, gravediggers and crematoria constantly busy. The funeral of Claudia Briggs was the sixth service held at the Knightsbridge Crematorium Chapel that day, the mourning party being limited to family and immediate friends. Peter held Veronica's elbow, Meg on her other side, and Hartley stayed close to John Canning.

Hartley appeared to have aged ten years in the past week.

Peter wished he could think of something to say to him. Dear Claudie. Just over a fortnight ago, on the occasion of the last family get-together, she had done all the organising. He shook hands with Grant and Julia Appleton, neither looking well enough, yet, to be out of bed, and with Jeremy, Ann and the Prime Minister. Janet Brereton had sent flowers.

There were messages of condolence from all over the country. When they had assembled at Cadogan Square for a drink afterwards, Peter opened them and read them out.

It was the sixth, with a Red Cross logo on the envelope, which he read without anticipating: "SO TERRIBLY SAD STOP SO MUCH LOVE FROM US ALL STOP WISH WE COULD BE THERE STOP RETURNING AS SOON AS POSSIBLE STOP ALL LOVE SARAH".

"Oh, Peter!" Veronica's thin voice wavered, eyes filled with tears.

John Canning stopped filling his pipe to reach for her hand.

Peter closed his eyes for a private prayer of thanks. For the first time since being given news of them on the phone by the person from the Red Cross, he really could believe they were safe. He thought of Anna. Only yesterday he had found out she was dead; so was Jan Geller.

"Darling," Meg said as they drove back to the Chelsea flat, "I am so very happy that Sarah and her family are

473

coming home. It'll be so good for your parents."

"Yes," he agreed, "but I am even more happy to be assured that they have survived. Meg, I just wish you could have had a message like that about Sally Ann."

"Mm." She stared along the street ahead of them, unseeing. After a few moments she turned to look at him. "You realise that tonight is our last night together, for some time. I'm on tomorrow morning's flight to San Francisco and then Chile."

"Snap," Peter said, not taking his eyes off the road.

She frowned at him.

"True. I've been given leave of absence by the PM."

"Oh, Peter!" She hugged his arm, causing the car to swerve. Then added, "But we're going to work, you know," her expression becoming serious. "All the medical services are exhausted, in manpower, equipment and organisation, and they need total restructuring . . . quite apart from the treating of the millions who are still suffering."

"Of course. I do realise that."

"And I am going to be away for a lot longer than you can be spared by your Government."

"I realise that, too. But you know I'll be waiting for you when you get back." Slowing at a traffic light he turned to stare at her. "You are coming back?"

"Of course," she replied, casually. "Hartley *has* offered me that job, remember?"

He knew she was teasing him: knew that neither of them could ever bear to be parted for long. "Tremendous."

"Whenever I can take it up, that is."

"Oh, quite. But . . . do you intend staying long in South America, jabbing people, even though you're pregnant?"

"Well . . . I don't think that would be very practical. Certainly not in the later stages." She was looking out of the passenger window so that he could not see she was grinning.

"Oh good," he said. "Then you won't be away so long after all." Ignoring the fact that the lights had changed he leaned over to kiss her on the nose.

The driver behind hooted.

Peter released the handbrake and the car moved forward. "We must buy a house as soon as you get back . . . and a pair of puppies. And don't forget to bring ET, if he can stand the quarantine. Gladstone will need help coping with the dogs."

LAWRENCE SANDERS

STOLEN BLESSINGS

Marilyn Taylor is The Most Beautiful Woman in the World. Golden and tanned, hers is the face and figure that has launched a million headlines and teased the imagination from ten million posters and billboards.

And mostly she's the meanest woman in the world. After fighting, calculating and back-stabbing her way from casting couch to stardom, she's not about to let go. She eats directors for breakfast, snacks on the soft and tender parts of PR persons, bites the heads off anxious underlings . . .

Now, just to prove she has a heart of gold, she's decided to do an old friend a favour. Marilyn Taylor is donating her egg or eggs of the month for *in vitro* fertilisation and embryo transfer to a childless woman.

Except that this is where a bunch of low-lives decide to get into the action, steal the Most Beautiful Eggs in the World and hold them, very carefully, to ransom . . .

A Royal Mail service in association with the Book Marketing Council & The Booksellers Association.

Post-A-Book is a Post Office trademark.

LAWRENCE SANDERS

CAPITAL CRIMES

Brother Kristos, he called himself. Barefoot, dirty, coarse-woven robe, greasy, shoulder-length hair and unkempt, food-stained beard. But his eyes, staring and intense, looked deep into you, held you.

He spoke: 'We are all created in God's image. It is written. And since God is without sin, so are we. Men and women are divine. The only hell is to resist your will.'

His poor, Southern-country audience listened, believed and gave as the two young women passed amongst them. Afterwards, backstage, as he drank straight from the bottle, the two women shucked off their white cotton robes . . .

In the White House, the President and his wife are sick with worry over their nine-year-old haemophiliac son. A woman friend of the First Lady has just discovered a remarkable new faith-healer.

Brother Kristos is about to be invited into the very heart of the nation. About to lay his rough, grasping hands on the arteries of power.

HODDER AND STOUGHTON PAPERBACKS

LAWRENCE SANDERS

THE TIMOTHY FILES

Meet Timothy Cone, Vietnam vet turned private eye.

Working for a Wall Street operation, he checks out the people and companies the clients are dealing with. It's a discreet, sober-suited world of high finance — at least on the surface.

Underneath? Now that's different. Very, very different. For instance: there's the real estate clan whose private pastimes include drugs, incest and maybe murder. There's the fertility clinic that specialises in creating life and, Timothy suspects, violent death as well. There's the Middle Eastern enterprise that invests in some strange places indeed . . .

Meet Timothy Cone, Lawrence Sanders' latest and most street-wise creation.

'Suspenseful, well wrought and stamped with Sanders' special insight into the baser aspects of human nature.'

Publishers Weekly

HODDER AND STOUGHTON PAPERBACKS

LAWRENCE SANDERS

TIMOTHY'S GAME

Timothy Cone is not a smooth man.

In fact he's a scrawny, scruffy, chain-smoking, junk-food-stained disgrace. In his barely furnished, hardly ever cleaned, lower Broadway loft, he and Cleo, his live-in, neutered tomcat, exist on take-aways and left-overs.

Yet many of the people he deals with are very smooth indeed.

For Timothy Cone is also the smartest, toughest, most persistent private investigator around, working for an off-Wall Street outfit that provides financial intelligence for corporate and individual clients. He moves in a world of stock market scams, insurance fraud, commercial espionage and legit business fronts for laundered Mob money.

So beneath the smooth manners and the expense-account veneer are some very rough customers indeed. People who will kill to win in a world where greed rules.

Timothy Cone, like his cat, is a street-fighting, life-scarred veteran. A survivor.

HODDER AND STOUGHTON PAPERBACKS

MORE FICTION TITLES AVAILABLE FROM HODDER AND STOUGHTON PAPERBACKS

LAWRENCE SANDERS

☐ 40481 1	The Eighth Commandment	£2.95
☐ 42404 9	The First Deadly Sin	£3.99
☐ 05903 0	The Fourth Deadly Sin	£2.95
☐ 43107 X	The Tangent Factor	£3.50
☐ 43108 8	The Tangent Objective	£3.50
☐ 05597 3	The Case of Lucy B.	£2.95
☐ 05835 2	The Passion of Molly T.	£2.95
☐ 05744 5	The Seduction of Peter S.	£2.95
☐ 40939 2	The Marlow Chronicles	£2.50
☐ 51511 7	Stolen Blessings	£3.50
☐ 42246 1	The Timothy Files	£3.50
☐ 49176 5	Timothy's Game	£3.50

All these books are available at your local bookshop or newsagent, or can be ordered direct from the publisher. Just tick the titles you want and fill in the form below.

Prices and availability subject to change without notice.

HODDER AND STOUGHTON PAPERBACKS, P. O. Box 11, Falmouth, Cornwall.

Please send cheque or postal order, and allow the following for postage and packing:

U.K. – 80p for one book, plus 20p for each additional book ordered up to a £2.00 maximum.

B.F.P.O. – 80p for the first book, plus 20p for each additional book.

OVERSEAS INCLUDING EIRE – £1.50 for the first book, plus £1.00 for the second book, and 30p for each additional book ordered.

Name ....

Address ....

....